PRAISE FOR
CHANGELING

"A powerful, supernatural urban fantasy with a touch of a whodunit that works because the cast, especially the sisterly trio, and the Were world seem genuine. The action never slows down as the witch, the vampiress, and the 'kitten' battle evil knowing the risks they must take. Subgenre fans will want to join the siblings on their daring escapades to keep the Earth realm safe from demonic possession."
—TheBestReviews.com

"Captivates the reader with unique and fascinating connections to the world we know, and a creative fantasy world that opens your mind to endless possibilities. I absolutely loved it!"
—FreshFiction.com

"With sex, danger, unique characters, great storytelling, and fantastic world building, Yasmine Galenorn has created another winner in her Sisters of the Moon series. *Changeling* is a can't miss read destined to hold a special place on your keeper shelf."
—*Romance Reviews Today*

"Galenorn's thrilling supernatural series is gritty and dangerous, but it's the tumultuous relationships between all the various characters that give it depth and heart. Vivid, sexy, and mesmerizing, Galenorn's novel hits the paranormal sweet spot."
—*Romantic Times*

continued . . .

The Otherworld Series

WITCHLING
CHANGELING
DARKLING

DARKLING

YASMINE GALENORN

BERKLEY BOOKS, NEW YORK

THE BERKLEY PUBLISHING GROUP
Published by the Penguin Group
Penguin Group (USA) Inc.
375 Hudson Street, New York, New York 10014, USA
Penguin Group (Canada), 90 Eglinton Avenue East, Suite 700, Toronto, Ontario M4P 2Y3, Canada
(a division of Pearson Penguin Canada Inc.)
Penguin Books Ltd., 80 Strand, London WC2R 0RL, England
Penguin Group Ireland, 25 St. Stephen's Green, Dublin 2, Ireland (a division of Penguin Books Ltd.)
Penguin Group (Australia), 250 Camberwell Road, Camberwell, Victoria 3124, Australia
(a division of Pearson Australia Group Pty. Ltd.)
Penguin Books India Pvt. Ltd., 11 Community Centre, Panchsheel Park, New Delhi—110 017, India
Penguin Group (NZ), 67 Apollo Drive, Rosedale, North Shore 0632, New Zealand
(a division of Pearson New Zealand Ltd.)
Penguin Books (South Africa) (Pty.) Ltd., 24 Sturdee Avenue, Rosebank, Johannesburg 2196,
South Africa

Penguin Books Ltd., Registered Offices: 80 Strand, London WC2R 0RL, England

This is a work of fiction. Names, characters, places, and incidents either are the product of the author's imagination or are used fictitiously, and any resemblance to actual persons, living or dead, business establishments, events, or locales is entirely coincidental. The publisher does not have any control over and does not assume any responsibility for author or third-party websites or their content.

DARKLING

A Berkley Book / published by arrangement with the author

PRINTING HISTORY
Berkley edition / January 2008

Copyright © 2008 by Yasmine Galenorn.
Excerpt from *Dragon Wytch* by Yasmine Galenorn copyright © 2008 by Yasmine Galenorn.
Cover illustration by Tony Mauro.
Cover design by Rita Frangie.
Interior text design by Stacy Irwin.

ISBN: 978-0-425-21893-8

BERKLEY®
Berkley Books are published by The Berkley Publishing Group,
a division of Penguin Group (USA) Inc.,
375 Hudson Street, New York, New York 10014.
BERKLEY® is a registered trademark of Penguin Group (USA) Inc.
The "B" design is a trademark belonging to Penguin Group (USA) Inc.

PRINTED IN THE UNITED STATES OF AMERICA

10 9 8 7 6 5 4 3 2 1

To all the scary bad-ass chicks out there
who refuse to put up with injustice
and who have suffered through their own nightmares.
Keep up the good fight.

ACKNOWLEDGMENTS

Thank you to: Meredith Bernstein, my agent. With you behind me, I am achieving my goals and dreams. To Kate Seaver, my editor, for her enthusiasm and trust. Thank you to my husband, Samwise, an endless source of support and love. Thanks to so many friends for professional and personal encouragement: Brad and Tif, Thera and Jeremy, Margie, Siduri, Katy and Don, Fran and Lillian, my sister Wanda. Big hugs to my Witchy Chicks blogging group: Lisa, Linda, Kate, Terey, Maddy, Candy, Annette, and Maura. More thanks to Cathy C., Mary Jo P., and so many more for their encouragement, support, and input.

To my cats, my little "Galenorn Gurlz." To Ukko, Rauni, Mielikki, and Tapio, my spiritual guardians.

Thank you to my readers—both old and new. Your support helps keep us in ink and fuels our love of storytelling.

You can find me on the net at Galenorn En/Visions, www .galenorn.com, on MySpace, and you can contact me via e-mail on my site. If you write to me via snail mail (see my Web site for the address or write via my publisher), please enclose a stamped, self-addressed envelope with your letter if you would like a reply.

The hardest thing in this world is to live in it.

—BUFFY

He who fights with monsters should look to it that he
   himself does not become a monster.
And when you gaze long into an abyss,
   the abyss also gazes into you.

—FRIEDRICH NIETZSCHE, *BEYOND GOOD AND EVIL*

CHAPTER 1

"Magregor, if you think you're going to toss your cookies all over my clean counter, think again. Get to the bathroom now, or I'm going to kick your butt into the middle of the street and teach you the meaning of roadkill."

I wiped my hands on one of the crisp white rags that we used to clean the counters of the Wayfarer and carefully draped it over the railing behind the bar while keeping a close eye on the goblin. I didn't like goblins.

Not only were they conniving little sneaks, but they posed a potential threat for my sisters and me. The goblin bands were in league with our bitch-queen back in Otherworld who had effectively exiled us by means of a death threat. Until the civil war was over and she was vanquished, we either had to stay Earthside, or head for cities other than Y'Elestrial if we decided to go home to OW. One loose tongue—and goblins were squealers—and Queen Lethesanar might find out where we were.

The elves had helped us rig the portal leading from the basement of the Wayfarer so it pointed into the shadowed forests of Darkynwyrd, but that only eliminated the immediate threat of the Queen's guards coming through. Now we had to cope with all sorts of skulking creatures wandering into the portal. But we didn't dare close the portal permanently. We needed quick access to Otherworld.

I wouldn't have minded the occasional goon poking his head through my doorway, but the elfin guards watching on the other side were lazy. This week alone I'd been in four fistfights with miscreant Fae, taken out three kobolds, put the kibosh on a touchy feely gnome, and barely corralled a butt-ugly baby troll who'd somehow managed to sneak through.

"Try an' make me leave, dolly . . . I'll show you jus' what women are good for." The goblin thrust his pelvis toward me with a lewd grin and grabbed his crotch. He was plastered all right. He had to be sloshed, or he would have slunk out of there, shaking in his boots. By the look on his face, I figured that I had about five minutes before his supper paid him a return visit.

"No, let *me* show *you* what women are good for," I said softly as I leapt over the bar. His eyes went wide as I landed silently beside him. I could smell his pulse, and the beat of his heart echoed in the back of my mind. Even though you couldn't pay me to touch goblin blood unless I was starving, my fangs extended and I gave him a slow smile.

"Holy shit." He tried to scramble away but only succeeded in wedging himself between his stool and the next one. I yanked him up by the scruff of his collar and strode over to the stairs leading into the basement, dragging him behind me. He struggled, but there was no way he could squirm out of my grasp.

"Chrysandra, keep watch on the bar for a minute."

"Sure thing, boss." Chrysandra was my best waitress. She'd been a bouncer over at Jonny Dingo's for awhile, but got tired of being harassed by sleazeballs for minimum wage. I paid her more and *my* patrons knew better than to harass the help. Or at least most of them did, I thought, looking down at the goblin as I hauled him toward the basement and tossed him over my shoulder in order to carry him down the steps. The goblin squealed, kicking the hell out of my stomach.

"Can it, dork. You can ram your size fours into my midsection from now until doomsday without making a dent," I said, then hissed at him.

He blanched. "Oh, shit."

"Yeah, that about sums it up," I said. Being a vampire had its perks.

As I entered the basement, Tavah looked up from her post near the portal, which shimmered like a nebula between two large standing stones. She glanced at the goblin, then at me. "I didn't think he was supposed to be here . . ." She let her words drift off as I tossed Mr. Unlucky on the floor.

"No way can we allow him to go back through the portal. I suggest you take an early lunch," I said.

Tavah blinked, then broke into a toothy grin. She wasn't as picky about her meals as I was. "Thanks, boss," she said as I turned to go back upstairs.

The goblin let out a startled cry behind me, cut off in midshriek. I stopped for the briefest of moments. The basement was silent except for the faint sound of Tavah, lapping gently. I quietly shut the door and returned to the bar. There was no sense in taking a chance the goblin might run back to Otherworld or Y'Elestrial and spread tales. Neither the Queen nor the tattered remnants of the OIA knew we were still here. And we wanted to keep it that way.

The Wayfarer was rocking. When I'd first been assigned to work the bar, I resigned myself to serving a bunch of drunken sots and sad-assed streetwalkers. But to my relief and surprise, most of the Fae who came to the Wayfarer drank enough to have fun, but not enough to cause problems.

The full-blooded humans who came in were pretty good sorts, too. They spent good money to fritter away the evening in the presence of various Fae and Earthside Supes. All except for the Faerie Maids, that is, and they only irritated me because they were cheap. Cheap as in, buy one drink and nurse it half the night while taking up valuable booth space. They were there for one reason and one reason only: to be taken advantage of by some pussy-hungry denizen of Otherworld.

To be honest, I felt more pity for them than irritation. It wasn't their fault they were vulnerable to Sidhe pheromones. And if anybody should have exercised restraint, it was my father's people. We all knew what could happen when sex worked its way into the mix, but a number of humans didn't understand. Over the months, however, I'd learned to keep my mouth shut. On the rare occasions when I tried to dissuade a love-struck Faerie Maid from her quest, I'd been met by disbelief. And a few times, by outright anger.

With the goblin taken care of, I returned to the counter just in time to see Camille and Trillian wander through the door. My oldest sister, Camille, was gorgeous, with long raven hair and violet eyes. She was curvy and buxom, and dressed á la designer BDSM, decked out in a leather bustier and flowing chiffon skirt. Trillian looked like an escapee from the *Matrix* with his black suede duster, black jeans, and black turtleneck. A Svartan—one of the darker-natured cousins to the elves—his clothing and skin blended together in one long jet silhouette while his silver hair hung free to his waist. Wavy and coiling, it had taken on a life of its own, that hair. As a couple, they sure turned heads.

I waited until they chose a booth and then wiped my hands on the bar rag and tossed it to Chrysandra. "I'm taking a break," I said, heading over to join them, carrying a goblet of Blossom wine for Camille and a Scotch on the rocks for Trillian. I could do without the Svartan, but I needed to talk to Camille. She glanced up as I slid in beside her and gave her a quick squeeze.

Trillian flashed me a brief smile. As usual, I ignored him. "What did you find out?" I asked her.

She leaned back, shaking her head. "They've disappeared. Trillian looked all over but couldn't find any sign of either Father or Aunt Rythwar. There houses were deserted, everything gone."

"Shit." I stared at my nails. They were perfect, and they always would be. "Anybody have any idea where they went?"

Trillian spoke up then. "No. I checked with all my usual sources without any luck. Then I managed to scare up a few who weren't happy to see me—they owe me big and were hoping to stay hidden a little big longer. But nobody seems to have any idea where your father and aunt went."

"You don't think that Lethesanar found them and killed them, do you?" Camille asked.

I grimaced. "Ugh, that's not the question I really want to hear." But even as I said it, I knew she was right to ask.

"No. Their soul statues are still intact. I checked your family's ancestral shrine. For another, you know that she wouldn't be able to resist parading them around the court and we'd hear about it for sure. Lethesanar loves to flaunt her victories over her enemies. She'd schedule public executions with full fanfare. No, I think your father and aunt just found a damned good place to hide and are waiting it out."

Trillian leaned back, draping his arm around Camille in an easy way. Someday I'd have to come to terms with the fact that they were back together and likely to stay that way. Svartans by their very nature are trouble, and I didn't like that my sister was hooked up with one. I might not be happy about it, but there wasn't much I could do. And he *was* helping us, I had to give him that much credit.

I thought about this for a moment, then decided to ask another question I really didn't want to ask. "What about our *other* problem?"

"No word yet," Trillian said.

Camille let out a long sigh, the violet of her irises flecked with silver. She'd been running magic and running it heavy. "Queen Asteria's guards can't pick up any sign of Wisteria, and the Elwing Blood Clan seems to have disappeared from the radar. They aren't anywhere near their usual haunts, and nobody's heard anything about what's going on. But they're up to no good. We can guess that much." Wisteria, a floraed gone bad, had teamed up with a Degath Squad of demons—Hell Scouts—to kill us. She'd gotten a little surprise when we'd deposited her in the Elfin Queen's dungeons. Unfortunately, she'd escaped. Rumor had it, she was now teamed up with somebody I really didn't want to remember.

"I know what the Elwing Clan is capable of." I closed my eyes for a moment, pushing away the memories that haunted me if I let myself dwell on them for more than a moment. At least during the night, when I was awake, I could shake them off. "So," I said, meeting her eyes. "What do we do next?"

Camille shrugged. "I don't know what we *can* do. I suppose we watch the portal, watch the news, and hope to hell the elves finally get some luck scouting for them."

"Asteria told us to visit Aladril, the City of Seers, and look for a man named Jareth." I wanted to do something. Sitting around, waiting for something to happen, made me fidgety. The best defense was a good offense, was my motto. Surprise the opposition before they had a chance to surprise you and you didn't have to worry about getting stabbed in the back. Or staked in the heart.

"I know, but what do we say to him? How can we expect him to give us answers when we don't even know what questions to ask?" Camille tapped her foot on the floor. I could feel the vibration of her leg.

"I don't know," I said after a long moment. "But we'd better think of something soon. With a clan of rogue vampires on her side, Wisteria could do a lot of damage if she makes it back Earthside."

"You really think they'll listen to her and not just drain her?" Camille frowned, tracing a spiral with her finger in the condensation that dripped to the table from her glass of wine.

"Maybe. At least long enough to get here. Psychos tend to stick together, and the Elwing Blood Clan is run by Dredge, the biggest psycho of them all. Aren't we the lucky ones?" I glanced over to the bar where a sudden rush of customers appeared. "We're headed into a rush here so I'd better get back to work. I'll meet you at home. Just be careful. Something's going on—I can feel it."

Camille lifted her face, letting the overhead light bathe her in a golden glow. "You're right, I can smell it on the wind. We're in for a bad jolt. I just don't know what *it* is." She motioned to Trillian. "Come on. Delilah and Iris are probably waiting dinner."

As they bustled out of the booth and headed toward the door, Trillian lingered behind. "Eyes open," he said. "The Elwing Clan will take to Wisteria like a duck to water. Keep a tight watch on who comes through the portal."

I nodded as he turned to go. I might not like him, but he had a good head on his shoulders. I turned back to the bar and surveyed the room as the crowd thickened. Within five minutes, the joint was packed. Over the past month or so, the Earthside Supes had discovered the Wayfarer and were making their way out of the closet in droves.

In addition to several run-of-the-mill Fae from Otherworld, I spotted two lycanthropes whispering in a corner booth, a gorgeous werepuma woman who was reading a copy of Daphne du Maurier's *Rebecca*, a half-dozen house sprites engaged in some sort of drinking game, and a couple of FBH neo-pagans who were taking divination lessons from one of the Elfin seers who'd taken up residence Earthside. There were also four Faerie Maids, all looking for a good, hard fuck. They'd been here two hours and had bought two rounds of drinks.

I was headed over to shake them down when the front door burst open and Chase Johnson strode through, a nasty ketchup stain covering the front of his shirt. About to make a snarky remark, I stopped cold when my nose picked up the fact that it wasn't ketchup after all. Chase was covered with blood. Swept under a sudden wave of dizziness, I forced myself to close my eyes and count to ten.

One . . . two . . . Don't even think of attacking. Three . . . four . . . Remember that I ate before I came to work. Five . . . six . . . Chase is Delilah's boyfriend, hurt him and you piss her off. Seven . . . eight . . . Push the temptation to the side. Chase is a nice guy, don't even go there. Nine . . . The blood isn't coming from Chase, it's merely on his suit. Ten . . . Take a deep breath even though I don't need to breathe, let it out slowly, loudly, send the tension and thirst with it to be cleansed and negated.

As the last of the air left my body, I opened my eyes. Each time, it got a little easier. Each time, I felt a little more control returning to my life. During my hunts, if I wasn't out scouting for pervs but instead had to drink from someone who was just an innocent bystander, I made use of the technique. It kept me from doing permanent damage, although I'd given up retraining my psyche to view the process as nutrition rather than pleasure. It always felt good, and it always would.

"Chase, what's going on? Are you hurt?"

His eyes widened as he met my gaze, but then he shook his head and nodded toward the door. "Across the street, at the theater. We got a report about some sort of fight going on. By the time we got there we found four dead. Two men, two women."

"What went down?" Whatever it was must have been bad. Chase knew better than to come around my bar all bloodied up. With Earthside Supes and denizens of Faerie hanging out here, it was an unwritten rule: If you were sporting a nasty laceration or a woman in the middle of a heavy menstrual flow, stay away from the Wayfarer. Blood scent risked setting somebody off because blood was an aphrodisiac to a number of Supes.

Yeah, something had happened to make Chase break with convention.

"Vampires," he said. "The victims were drained of blood but no obvious cuts or wounds. Sharah examined their necks and sure enough—twin punctures on every one of them. They were up in the balcony, near the back, where nobody else was sitting. So nobody saw what happened."

Vampires? Of course there were vamps in Seattle, but ones who would resort to attacking humans in a theater? That didn't track right. Vampires Anonymous (V.A.) had been working hard to combat feeding on the innocent.

I shook my head. "Did you catch them?"

Chase frowned. "We couldn't find any sign of them. We thought you might be able to help. The wounds are fresh; the vamps are probably close by. If anybody can find them, you can."

I groaned. "You want me to play Buffy? Give me one good reason why I should go staking my own kind."

Chase gave a rough laugh. "Because you're part of the OIA. Because you're on the right side. Because you know what they did was *wrong*. Hell, you can dress up in drag and call yourself Angel, for all I care. Just help us."

Great, just great. This was the price I paid for being nice

to my sister's boyfriend. But as he stared at me, pleading for my help, how could I say no? I untied my apron and tossed it on the counter.

"Chrysandra, I'll be back in awhile. Watch the bar for me." I hurried to follow Chase out the door, into the dark January night.

My name is Menolly D'Artigo and I used to be an acrobat. In other words, I was damned good at getting into places and spying on people. Or rather, most of the time I was damned good. I happen to be half-human on my mother's side, half-Fae on my father's. The genetic mix leads to trouble, and whatever powers a half-Fae, half-human child is born with tend to get swallowed up in a mix of uncertainty. My sisters—Camille, a witch, and Delilah, a werecat—learned that lesson only too well.

During a routine spying mission, thanks to faulty wiring and a random roll of the dice, I slipped up. It was the last mistake I ever made. The Elwing Blood Clan took me down, and they play to win. The torture seemed to last for an eternity, and now—so will I. After Dredge killed me, he raised me into the world of the undead, turning me into a vamp just like him. But I refused to let the bastard win. *Nobody* ever gets the last word with me, especially a sadist like Dredge.

My sisters and I work for the Otherworld Intelligence Agency, which went bust a couple months ago. Civil war broke out back in Y'Elestrial, our home city-state in Otherworld. Queen Lethesanar recalled all operatives and filtered them into the military. We opted to stay Earthside, especially since she'd stamped a death threat on our heads at home.

Now we're in a race against time against a powerful demon lord named Shadow Wing. He's big and he's bad, and he's currently ruling over the Subterranean Realms. Together with his hordes of Demonkin, Shadow Wing intends to raze both Earth and Otherworld to the ground and take over. We do have a few allies back home in Otherworld. The Elfin Queen, Asteria, is giving us all the help she can, but it isn't much. Together my sisters and our ragtag group of friends are the only ones standing in Shadow Wing's way. And that's a scary proposition, at best.

The Delmonico Cinema Complex is the oldest theater in the Belles-Faire district of town, where the Wayfarer is located. Still outfitted with the original décor complete with squeaky chairs and a balcony right out of the fifties where lovers used to grope and fondle their way to celluloid ecstasy, the Delmonico had seen better days. But it still held nostalgic charm for the Seattle suburb, and hearkened back to a time of ushers who actually did their jobs and real butter on popcorn and monster movies on Saturday afternoons.

The theater was empty. The moviegoers hadn't even been aware of what happened. I doubted there had been many patrons to begin with. There wasn't much call during the week for late shows unless it was a cult classic, like *The Rocky Horror Picture Show* or *Plan 9 from Outer Space*. A young woman, the ticket taker by the looks of her uniform, and two food-stand attendants were sitting on a bench waiting for Chase's team to give them the go-ahead to leave.

"They don't know why we're here, so don't say a word in front of them," Chase said to me in low tones. "Depending on what happens, we'll tell them that a fight broke out and somebody ended up with a nasty broken nose."

He led the way up the threadbare carpet-covered stairs and I followed. Luckily I had enough control to keep my instincts reined in. I shook the smell of fresh blood out of my thoughts and focused on what he was saying.

"We received an anonymous tip about an hour ago. The call came directly to me, so somebody knew this was a case for the FH-CSI," he said.

The Faerie-Human Crime Scene Investigations unit was Chase's baby. He'd created it when he was first accepted into service by the Otherworld Intelligence Agency, Earthside Division, and it became the standard for all nationwide divisions that followed in its wake. The team responded to all law enforcement matters dealing with the Fae or Earthside Supes.

"Direct to your *office*, you mean? Your number isn't public, is it?" For some reason, the situation seemed odd to me.

Chase shook his head. "No, but it wouldn't be hard to trace if somebody really wanted to know. Thing is, caller ID was blocked and whoever was on the line sounded pretty damned sure that the FH-CSI was necessary. But when we got here it took a little while to ascertain that the victims had been attacked by vampires. A cursory glance wouldn't have shown anything out of the ordinary. If you can call any murder ordinary. So whoever called me had to know they were killed by somebody other than an FBH."

It was odd to hear the term FBH come from Chase's lips, especially since he was one, but it made sense. The acronym was easier than constantly saying "full-blooded human, Earthside born."

"Were the bodies moved? Could someone have checked to see if they were alive and, in doing so, noticed the punctures?" I stared at the victims. The OIA medical team was still looking them over. Well, they'd been an *official* OIA medical team until a few months ago—now the Otherworld Intelligence Agency was our baby and we were calling the shots.

"Nope. Don't think so. Sharah said that while there's a lot of blood, the patterns indicate they're right where they were when they died."

"Speaking of blood," I said slowly, gazing at the four bodies that, until earlier this evening, had been alive and—probably—happy people. I was no angel, that was for certain, but I chose my victims from the lowest of the low, which kept me in the clear as far as my own conscience was concerned.

"Yes?" Chase tapped me on the shoulder. He looked a little worried. "Menolly, are you okay?"

"Yeah," I said, shaking off my thoughts. "I'm fine. I was just going to say that there's something else odd about this massacre. There shouldn't be this much blood. There shouldn't be much blood at all unless we're dealing with one incredibly sloppy vamp, and even the grimiest bloodsuckers I know are usually fairly neat and tidy. That's why vamp attacks have generally gone unnoticed over the years. Unless . . ."

A thought ran through my head but I didn't want to entertain it. There had been a lot of blood when I was turned, and I had the scars to prove it.

"Unless what?" Chase sounded impatient and I didn't blame him. He still had to think of something to tell their next of kin. We weren't passing on information about the demons, nor were we in the habit of telling people that their loved ones had been killed by vampires and Earthside Supernaturals. There were enough locos in the world who would gladly go hunting anybody or anything who even remotely resembled a Supe if they got word that one of us had been responsible for somebody's death.

"Unless they either wanted to hurt these people, or leave a calling card. Are there any scars? Any signs of torture . . ." As I glanced up, Chase returned my look and I tore my gaze away when I saw the pity in his eyes. I quickly turned and strode over to the bodies, searching their expressions for some sign of pain, of anger.

Sharah was finishing up her notes. She and her assistant, an elf who barely looked old enough to shave, were getting ready to bag the bodies and take them back to the morgue for closer examination. Sharah's gaze flickered up to catch mine, and she softly nodded.

"I don't know yet," Chase said. "There doesn't appear to be extensive damage but we'll know more when we autopsy them."

I examined their faces, but couldn't tell whether they'd been in pain at the end. Mainly they looked surprised, as if they'd been simultaneously attacked. One last surprise for the night. For life.

With a sigh, I stepped out of the way and let the medics get on with their work. Over the past few months, I'd worked closely with Wade Stevens, the brains behind Vampires Anonymous, and we'd managed to enlist promises from at least fifteen vamps who lived in the city to avoid taking blood from the innocent. Or, at least, they took an oath to avoid killing anybody during the process, or leaving them damaged.

We'd developed quite a following, and we were contemplating our next goal, which would be to take control of vampire activity in Seattle and run it like an underground police force. Those who didn't cooperate would be asked to leave or face being staked. Essentially we were aiming to become the Mafia of the undead set. We hoped to inspire other groups in other cities, until vampires could walk among the living without fear of being skewered.

"Wade needs to know about this," I said. "I'll contact him and we'll see if we can find out anything on our end."

Chase nodded. "I appreciate it, Menolly. I really don't know how to go after vampires, except with a butt-load of garlic and a wooden stake. You said crosses don't work . . ."

"No, they don't. Neither do pentacles, ankhs, or any other religious symbol. All claptrap contrived to give hope to the country dwellers who lived in fear of vampire activity. Of course, sunlight's a sure cure. Fire's pretty freaky, too, but not nearly so dangerous. There are a few spells to ward off vampires. Camille knows a couple, but no way in hell will I let her practice on me, so only the gods know if she can work them right."

He snorted. "It's a crapshoot every time she gets it into her head to cast a spell."

I couldn't help but grin along with him. "Not necessarily. She's getting better at offensive magic, though her defensive and household magical skills leave a lot to be desired. Don't write her off, Chase. She can do a lot of damage if she wants."

Chase relaxed then, and gave me a full blown smile. "Yeah, I know. And so can Delilah. And I already know what you could do to me. But I trust you girls. *All* of you," he added.

Recognizing the significance of what he said, I accepted the compliment graciously. A month or so ago Chase still jumped whenever I entered the room, and I used his fear to play him to the hilt. We still weren't fond of each other. Much. But I'd developed a sense of respect for the tall, handsome detective who had wooed Delilah's heart. She may not know it, and I was pretty sure Chase was blind as a bat, but the two of them were falling in love. I wasn't about to be the one to tell them. They'd figure it out soon enough on their own.

I silently made my way to the steps leading down to the main entrance of the Delmonico. "I'll get back to you when I've talked to Wade. Meanwhile I suggest you think up a good excuse for why these four died. We can't possibly let out the truth. Too much chance for mayhem. Call me when you know more."

"Right," he said, sighing and turning back to the crime scene. "As if we don't already have enough to deal with."

Silently agreeing, I left the theater and returned to my bar. The night was a frozen wonderland, but all I could smell was blood.

CHAPTER 2

Back at the bar I was in for another surprise, this one welcome. Iris was sitting at the counter, nursing a glass of Granover wine from the vast swath of vineyards that skirted Y'Elestrial, back in Otherworld. Her face lit up when I came through the door and she waved.

"I wondered where you'd gotten to," she said, polishing off the wine and holding out her glass. "Another, please. It's my night off and I don't feel like sitting at home."

Iris was a Talon-haltija, a Finnish house sprite who lived with my sisters and me. She helped by taking care of the house, watching out for Maggie—our little calico gargoyle—and by occasionally whopping a bad guy on the head with her five-pound stainless steel skillet. As pretty as a Norwegian maiden, she was older than all of us, and easily as dangerous. She was also one of my best friends.

"I'm glad you're here," I said, refilling her glass. "We may have a problem."

Her expression soured. "Oh great. What's going on now? Another Degath Squad in town? A skinwalker come to avenge his brother? Drunken trolls making an appearance?"

I shook my head and leaned on the bar so nobody else could hear what I had to say. "None of the above. I think we have rogue vampires on the loose—possibly new to the life and unaware of the V.A.'s attempts to corral bad behavior."

She blinked and took a sip, her eyes sparkling like a dazzling spring morning. I had blue eyes, too, but they were almost frosty gray by now, growing more so with each year I'd been a vampire. That is, when they weren't glowing red, which usually happened when I was hungry, hunting, or in a bad mood.

"Not good news," she said. "You told Camille and Delilah yet?"

"No. I'm going to take off early. I need to fill them in before Chase finds any more victims. This isn't really our department—well, not theirs—but they should know. And I better call Wade and ask him to meet me out at the house. You want a ride home when I'm done?" I picked up the phone and started to punch in Wade's number.

Iris nodded. "Might as well." She looked around. "I was hoping . . . oh never mind," she added, her gaze glued to the house sprites in the corner booth who by now were so intoxicated that one of them had keeled over face-first on the table. He was going to have a nasty backache in the morning, considering he was kneeling on the seat of the booth.

I stared at her for a moment. "You were hoping to find a date, weren't you?" I smiled as she blushed and ducked her head.

"No—yes—I mean—"

Relenting, I reached out and patted her hand. "That's nothing to be embarrassed about. Why don't you go over and talk to that group of louts while I'm on the phone. Maybe sober, they'll wash up better than they look now." As I picked up the receiver, Iris took a deep breath and slid off her bar stool. She cautiously approached the group of sprites and I kept one eye on her to make sure she was okay while I waited for Wade to pick up.

Wade was the first vampire I met Earthside, and he ran the local V.A. group. Vampires Anonymous was a support group for vamps who were having trouble adjusting to life as one of the undead. It sounded silly in theory, but it helped to have a social life that didn't depend on cruising the blood bars and Supe clubs all night long. *Breathers* just didn't understand some of the dilemmas and problems we faced. Sometimes, we needed a safe place to vent.

When I'd joined, Wade enlisted me in his pet cause: turning vampires away from preying on innocents and teaching them how to feed without killing. At first, I wasn't sure what I thought about his idea, but the more I examined my own reactions, the better I liked it. Of course, the self-control went against our innate natures—there were certain urges that came with the life . . . or afterlife . . . that I hadn't ever confided to Delilah or Camille. But they could be corralled with the right amount of caution and care.

But I made it clear to Wade that I wasn't about to extend my newfound enthusiasm to the nutjobs of the world. Once somebody crossed the line between antisocial geek boy and active harmful sociopath, they forfeited their rights and became fair game. And, quite often, dinner.

When Wade answered the phone I ran down the situation and asked him to meet me at home in an hour. "I just have one request," I said, staring at the counter. "Please leave your mother at home."

Wade and I'd dated for a bit, if you could call it that, but I hadn't been comfortable with his advances. And his mother had been the deciding factor in my ending our budding romance. Now we were just buddies.

"No problem. I set her up on a date with Count Creakula," he said, referring to an old-school vampire we knew who mainly kept to his loft, puttering among his collection of moldy old books.

Relieved, I signed off. Somebody had turned Belinda Stevens into a vampire out of spite, leaving Wade stuck with an overbearing albatross who wasn't about to let go of her little boy. Stuck *forever*, unless somebody got busy with a stake. I'd considered it more than once but had managed to restrain myself. Sooner or later, though, somebody, somewhere, was going to get fed up with the woman and dust her.

As I hung up, I noticed that Iris had reeled somebody in.

The sprite walking her back to the bar was close to sober. On second look, he was also pretty damned cute with curly black hair that kissed his shoulders, a sparkle in his eye that warned he might be full of piss and vinegar, and biceps that glistened even under the dim bar lights. Take away the smell of booze and the spilled mustard on his muscle tank and he'd wash up mighty fine.

Iris glanced up at me and I pointed toward the clock. "I've got to run, Bruce," she told him. "I'll give you a call tomorrow."

He nodded, an eager look on his face. "Right then. But not before noon. If I don't get my tea in the morning, I'll be speaking in one-syllable words." A clipped British accent echoed in his voice. He'd probably spent some time among high society, even if he was slumming with the boys now. He waved as we headed out the door.

The night was atypical for January—far colder than usual with a blustery wind picking up. We were due for a major storm. Camille had confirmed the forecast with her magic. The wind elementals were working their way down from the Arctic, bringing with them a snowstorm that would be pounding the area by tomorrow night. She and Delilah spent the entire day making certain that everything was tied down or put away. Morio had helped, along with Chase. I'd been asleep during the actual work but when I came up from my den around sunset, I noticed that the storm windows had been hung and the porch cleared of all the clutter that had accumulated over the holidays.

As Iris and I set a good pace along the sidewalk, she zipped up her jacket and stuck her hands in her pockets. I wasn't cold—I'd never be cold again—but it was obvious that the wind chill was playing havoc. On the way to my car, which was parked in an all-night parking garage three blocks west of the Wayfarer, she chatted away.

"This winter's been odd," she was saying. "When Camille first thought it was unnatural, I figured it was her imagination, but now I think she's right. I can feel it, too—there's something in the air. We're due for another snowstorm. We never have more than one or two snows during the winter, but this year, it's been off and on for over a month."

I nodded, unsure of what to say. I was neither a weather mage, nor a meteorologist. But when I paused to examine the energy of the city, there was something that didn't quite click.

Iris changed the subject. "Maggie is near to taking her first steps, I think."

I beamed, a ray of pride burning through my chest. I'd been working with her, trying to help her learn how to balance and stand. "I hope I'm awake to see it. What makes you think she's getting close?"

"She's been using the coffee table to brace herself. That tail of hers gives her the most problem—and the wings. I don't think she's quite got hold of the notion to compensate for their bulk by leaning forward a little. She tried once, but she leaned so far that she toppled over." Iris giggled. "I didn't dare laugh. Her feelings turn on a dime and I've seen her go from smiling to crying if you so much as give her a sour look."

"I noticed that, too," I said. Hmmm, the bulk of the wings and tail. I hadn't thought of that. "I'll work on teaching her how to offset the extra weight."

"Good thing, but be careful—she's very sensitive lately."

"I've noticed that." Maggie was finely attuned to nuances in demeanor and I was cautious to avoid teasing her too much. "She'll get the hang of it pretty soon and then, watch out. We're going to have to . . . well . . . gargoyle-proof the house. She's too young to understand what trouble she could get into and we don't want any accidents."

Iris gave a vigorous nod. "That's for certain. Look at what happened when Delilah got hold of the Yule tree. If that had been Maggie, she could have been killed. I'll go shopping and pick up some baby-proofing supplies. They should work the same."

We were a block away from the parking garage when we passed an alley. A noise caught my attention, and I froze, motioning for Iris to stop talking. Muted cries drifted out, along with the sound of rough laughter. Something was going on between the two brick buildings that loomed over Wilshire Avenue, and whatever it was, wasn't good. The noises were muffled by the sound of the rain hitting the pavement, but I could still catch a girl crying out, "No, please don't!"

I glanced down at Iris and she gave a slight nod. We flattened against the damp bricks and slowly inched our way down the gloom-filled alley. It was dark enough that we were able to blend into the shadows. I made no noise at all as long as I didn't shake my head vigorously and rattle the beads that were braided into my hair. Iris was almost as quiet as I, and we shuffled along until we were far enough down the back street to see what was going on.

In the dim light coming from an apartment halfway up one of the towering buildings, we could see two men accosting a girl who looked to be in her early teens. One of the men had an arm wrapped around her waist and he was struggling to keep his hand over her mouth. The other man had ripped open her blouse and her pale young breasts gleamed in the dark night. He reached out to finger her budding nipples and I tensed.

Iris sucked in a deep breath. I touched her arm, motioning for her to stop where she was. Slipping through the shadows, silent as a knife, when I gauged that I was about two yards away from them, I closed the distance with one leap to land right beside the man who had hold of the girl. My fangs extended as a rush of adrenaline washed through me.

The man was tall and pale, wearing a short trench over what looked to be a pair of khaki trousers. He had a Panama hat on, the brim pulled low over one eye. His buddy was wearing a pair of jeans and a thick sweater.

"Didn't count on company, did you, boys?" I said, grabbing Mr. Smooth by his jacket collar. He let go of the girl and I gently pushed her out of the way.

"What the fuck—" he started to say as I lifted him up, slamming him against the side of the building with one arm. His buddy turned to run but Iris muttered something and there was a flash of light in front of his eyes.

"Shit, I can't see, man!" he said, stumbling past me. I

stuck my left foot out, looping the toe of my boot around his ankle and yanked. His feet slid out from under him and he hit the ground, hard.

"What the—" he started to say, but then Iris was on him and I'm not sure what she did, but he slumped to the ground. She hurried over to the girl, who was cowering against the opposite wall, clutching her blouse closed across her breasts.

I turned my attention to my captive and knocked his hat off so I could see his face. He struggled but there was no way in hell he could get away from me. A look of shock washed over his face when he realized that he was powerless, caught in the grip of a woman barely skimming five one, with glowing red eyes.

"What's your name, jerk wad?"

He struggled and I shoved him harder against the wall. "I asked you for your name, boy!"

"Okay, okay! Robert. I'm Robert. Jesus, what the crap are you on?" He squirmed but I gave a little squeeze to his windpipe and he immediately froze.

"Get this straight. Nothing about *me* is of any concern to you. The only thing that matters is what you were doing with that girl. Tell me, freak, what were you going to do to her? And don't say you were giving her a tour of the city. I'm in no mood for idiots." I flashed a sideways glance at Iris. She was comforting the girl.

He let out a strangled gulp and said, "None of your business, bitch."

"Ten, nine, eight . . ." I gave another squeeze, careful to avoid crushing his trachea. "You know, it's cold out, and I've had a bad day. Maybe you'd better talk faster."

"Jesus, let go! Let go!" He seemed to get the message that I held all the cards because he slumped in my grip. "Okay, okay! We were taking her to a party."

My boy was starting to turn blue. I eased up just a tad on his larynx.

"They were trying to rape me," the girl said, sniffling. She stepped out of the shadows and I could see that she was dressed in skintight jeans, a blouse, and a leather jacket over the top of that. Poor kid looked tired and cold. "They told me they'd take me to a party where I could get some sleep and something to eat, but instead, they brought me here . . ."

"Where did you meet them?" I asked her, while motioning to Iris. "Search him, would you?"

"At . . . at the bus station," the girl whispered. "I just got into town. I don't have any place to stay. I was trying to find a spot at the station where I could hide out and take a nap when these guys found me. They had a girl with them, and they all asked me if I wanted to go with them to a party. They said there would be food there and a place I could sleep. When we got outside, the girl disappeared and these guys . . . they brought me here."

An old story, even back in Otherworld. I pointed to a step leading into one of the businesses on the bottom floor of the Whitmore Building and said, "Sit down for a minute. You're safe for now."

Iris finished patting Robert down and held up a nasty-looking gun. I knew that iron didn't affect her but it would burn my hands. Not all of the Fae were affected by the metal, but some of us—even half-breeds—definitely held no love for it, cast iron, especially. I let go and watched as Robert tumbled to the ground.

"Stay put or you're dead," I said, taking the gun from Iris. My hand sparked on contact, but the fact that I was a vampire helped rather than hindered me. I couldn't feel the pain as the iron burned my skin. And ever since I'd made the transformation to vamp, I tended to heal from most wounds within minutes or hours. Too bad the wounds that Dredge had inflicted on me hadn't been able to heal up before I died, but he'd killed me too quickly afterward.

Pointing the gun at Robert, I said, "Nice, huh? You like to play with guns, do you?"

His eyes grew wide and I gave him a slow smile. Oh yes, this could be quite the fun little game. He scrambled away, pressing his back against the wall. "Don't shoot me, don't hurt me, lady! I'm sorry. Just let us go and—"

"Shut up and sit still." I opened the chamber and shook the bullets out into my hand. Then I put my hand around the long barrel of the gun and held it up where Robert could see nice and clear. Slowly I bent the barrel back on itself. "There, that's much better. Now this can go back to doing what iron does best—rusting."

Robert trembled as I showed him the bullets before squeezing them into crumpled bits of slag. I tossed them down the sewer grate next to where he was sitting. The gun followed as I bent the bars on the grating just enough to slip it through, then bent them back.

I leaned over him. "You shouldn't play with toys that go boom," I said, trailing one finger down his cheek, my nail scratching the skin ever so slightly. "You might hurt somebody. You might even kill someone."

The terror in his eyes mirrored the scent of fear on his skin and I let out a little gasp as a wave of desire raced through me.

"Tell me, Robert, what were you going to do to the girl? Just what kind of *party* did you have planned for her?" As I felt the pounding tattoo of his heart, my hunger began to grow, deep and coiling out from the dark swirl of bloodlust that had been part of my nature since Dredge forced my mouth to his wrist as I was breathing my last.

I yanked Robert to his feet and slammed him against the wall. "And don't even think of lying to me. I'll know if you do. Let one false word slip through those lips and it's good night, my friend." I was stretching the truth there a bit—I wasn't really a magical lie detector—but he wouldn't know that. He was so nervous already that he was ready to piss his pants. His pheromones were hopping like jumping beans.

He cleared his throat. "All right, all right! You know what we were going to do—"

"No. I want you to say it. I want you to *admit* it."

"Fine, bitch," he said. "You want to know? You want to watch, maybe? We were going to fuck her brains out, then put her to work."

"You're a two-bit pimp, aren't you?" I had nothing against hookers, but I hated pimps with a passion. They were nothing but extortionists. "So you were going to rape her, then sell her on the streets. And that would put a stop to any hope she ever had for a normal life."

"He's also a drug dealer," Iris said, holding up a bag full of tablets that were half black, half white. "Z-fen. The newest drug in town. Used by ravers, date rape gurus, and sex addicts. Reduces inhibitions, causes blackouts. A lot more dangerous than Ecstasy ever was. Addictive and an overdose disaster waiting to happen."

I narrowed my eyes. "How on earth did you find out about *that*?"

She shrugged. "Saw a program about them on *Night Talk with Carly Ivers* not long ago. Apparently they're chewable and taste like mint. Makes it easier for the dealers to get kids hooked that way."

I let out a harsh laugh. "Robert, Robert . . . what am I going to do with you and your friend? I'll bet you make a habit of convincing runaways that you'll protect them, don't you? After you con your marks into going to your *parties*, you get them high and let your buddies play fuck-and-suck?"

His eyes told me everything I didn't want to know.

"The kids won't fight because they're drugged," I continued. "Then it's easy for you put them on the streets, sit back, and collect their money, providing enough drugs to keep them addicted. They keep working. You beat them if they try to run away. You use them when you're horny." I'd seen his kind all too often during the night, when I prowled looking for dinner. The seamy underside to a beautiful city.

He squeezed his eyes closed, his Adam's apple bobbing as he swallowed a wad of fear. "What are you going to do to me? You a cop?"

I glanced at Iris who leaned against the wall, her arms folded to keep herself warm. She shrugged. "Whatever you like," she said. "We need to get home pretty soon but . . ."

As I turned back to Robert, I thought over what I should do with him. My guess was that he'd done a lot more with that gun than just point it at people. "How many kids you got turning tricks? How many people have you shot?"

Robert was starting to fade. "Jesus, lady, just arrest me or something."

Suddenly tired of the grime and the gloom, I tossed him against the bricks again. "How many in your stable?"

Rubbing his throat, he deflated like a pricked balloon. "Four boys and fifteen girls. What else do you want to know? And if you're not a cop, what the fuck are you doing? Playing superhero?"

The self-righteous tone in his voice gnawed at me. I motioned to Iris. "Give me those pills, then take the girl out to the street. The two of you wait there for me." After they were gone, I turned back to my new buddy. "Superhero? I prefer to think of myself as a blade of justice," I said, opening the bag.

His gaze darted nervously toward the end of the alley but I held up one finger. *"Look at me,"* I said, freeing the glamour that I usually held in check. Between my half-Fae blood and my magnetism that came with being a vamp, I could charm just about anybody. And they always obeyed, willing or not. Unable to resist, Robert gave up the fight and gazed into my eyes.

"Hush," I whispered, and he fell silent. As I searched for any sign of remorse, a shroud of energy flared around him. Like tendrils of a sickly vine, it crept out from his body, searching for fresh meat.

"You know," I said softly. "I'm a vampire." I opened my mouth to show him my fangs and he tried to pull away but the thrall wouldn't allow him to move. "The thing is, you see," I continued, "you're a vampire, too. You don't feed on blood, but you suck young girls and boys dry, feeding on their bodies by selling them to others. Don't you?"

He nodded like a good boy.

"Yes, that's right, it's always best to tell the truth. But you know there's an important difference between us. Unlike me, it doesn't take much to kill you."

Robert began to shake, shivering as the lust swirled thick between us, but I didn't want him enjoying himself. I could make the experience incredibly sensuous, or I could make it exquisitely painful. For Robert, there would be no sweet kiss of death.

I wasn't thirsty, but his street prowling days were done. I wanted him to know fear, to know what it felt like to be a victim before I kicked him off the wheel of life. If I handed him over to the cops, he'd be out in no time because no one in his stable would dare rat on him. Robert struggled but I pressed him back against the wall.

"Hold still," I whispered, and he froze. A bead of sweat dripped from his brow to land on my forehead but I ignored it as I pressed my lips to his neck. I slowly licked the skin. He trembled and I could feel his erection pressing against me, but then his arousal faded as I sank my teeth into his neck and began to lap as the blood spurted in my mouth.

It ran down my throat like liquid fire. Sweet honey and wine, I thought, my mind buzzing as I drank to soothe my frayed nerves. A wave of relaxation and desire rippled through my body. It was always rough on me after feeding—I wanted to fuck, and fuck hard, but it would be a cold day in hell before I screwed any of the perverts I fed on, and I refused to turn on my friends and use them to satisfy myself. And there was always the memory of Dredge's hands that held me back, that made me shy away from intimate encounters.

This was what the FBH vamp-wannabes were looking for—this sensual communion. But most of them couldn't handle it, most weren't strong enough to withstand the madness that came with losing yourself to the bloodlust. So I kept myself in check, waiting for the day when I could find a partner to match my passion and strength, and with whom I could feel safe.

As Robert weakened, I gave one last lick to his neck and stood back. I held out the bag of pills.

"Eat," I said. He whimpered, but I gave him a smoldering look. "If you don't, I'll make you beg me for death," I said. "Do you really want to go out screaming on your belly?"

Without a word, he began popping the pills. I waited until he'd eaten about thirty and then turned my attention to his buddy. I yanked the man off the ground and jammed a handful of pills in his mouth. He was barely conscious, but began to chew when I pressed my hand over his mouth and refused to let him spit them out. I kept on until the pills were gone.

My task done, I stepped back. Robert was struggling, his

hand around his throat. His friend wasn't faring any better. *So much for a couple more wack jobs*. I wiped my mouth, took a moment to calm down. When my fangs had retracted, I joined Iris and the girl, who were waiting around the corner.

"You don't have to worry. They won't ever bother you again," I said. "Now, how about a name?"

She blinked, looking bewildered. "Anna-Linda. Anna-Linda Thomas. I'm from Oregon."

The girl probably thought life up here would be better. I tried to gauge her age. She looked sixteen, but my guess was closer to twelve. "How old are you? And tell me the truth."

She ducked her head and stared at her sneakers. "Thirteen."

Iris stepped in. "Why don't we take her home for the night? She can eat dinner and sleep, and then tomorrow we'll sort everything out."

I glanced at the girl's face. No guile, just pure stupid naivety. "Come on," I said. "You'll be safe for the night. I give you my word of honor."

Iris's presence seemed to calm her down and she followed us docilely. Iris whispered in a voice that I could hear but the girl couldn't, "You okay?"

I nodded.

"Robert and his friend?"

"Forever asleep," I said, heading for the parking garage.

With Anna-Linda a few paces behind her, Iris swung in step with me. "Tell me something."

"What is it?"

We stopped at the light, waiting for the signal to cross. When we were on the other side of the street, the parking garage in sight, Iris softly said, "Camille once mentioned something about being worried about you drinking demon's blood. That it might change you or hurt you. What about the blood of murderers, rapists, wife beaters? Does it taste different—or have any bad effects—on you?"

I frowned. Now that she mentioned it, I could see how they might think that way. "The demons' blood I'm still concerned about. They're a breed apart and things are very different with their genetics. I have no idea what drinking from them has done to me. But with humans? Blood is blood. If they're diseased in body, it won't affect me. Viruses can't live in me. And as far as anything else . . . well, the taint is in the soul, not the blood. Blood is pure. It sings, but not with their sins."

Iris nodded and we entered the garage. As we bundled Anna-Linda in the back of my sleek, black XJ Jag, the girl immediately leaned her head against the side window. Within less than a minute, she'd fallen asleep.

I slid into the driver's seat.

Iris gave me a sideways glance. "Thanks."

"For what?" I started the ignition and eased out onto the road, heading north to our house on the northwest corner of the Belles-Faire district. We had about twenty minutes till we got there.

"For being you. For caring. For doing something." She grinned then and threw back her head, laughing.

"Well, thank *you*," I said, feeling suddenly lighthearted. Sometimes Iris understood me better than my sisters did. "You're pretty handy in a pinch, too, you know that?"

"Indeed I do." She snickered, and we changed the subject as I popped in a CD of Holst's *The Planets*.

As we neared the turnoff leading to the road that led to our house, I wondered what Delilah and Camille would have to say about Anna-Linda. And what would Anna-Linda say about them? It was going to be interesting to find out.

CHAPTER 3

By the time we arrived home it was almost two-thirty, but
the house was blazing with light. Our home, a three-story
Victorian, had a full basement where I lived. The house was
a wondrous old white elephant, as Mother used to say. Our
mother had taught us a lot about customs and expressions
Earthside, and we'd taken every scrap of information to
heart. Unlike my sisters, who were content to live at home in
Otherworld, I'd always secretly longed to visit Earthside,
with all its exotic technology and customs. Now that I'd
been here about a year, I wasn't sure what I thought.

Our acreage was bordered on three sides by a thick copse
of woodland. One side led into the wild wood, with a trail
meandering down to Birchwater Pond. The other two ended
at boundary lines midforest dividing our land from the land
of other homeowners. Everybody in this area had at least
three to five acres, most of which had wisely been left unde-
veloped.

The house itself was old enough to be affordable, yet still
new enough not to need major repairs. Delilah's suite of
rooms was on the third floor, Camille took the second, we

shared the main story, and I, of course, had the basement. Iris lived with us and had a cozy nook off the kitchen where she comfortably made her home.

Maggie usually slept in Iris's room, although if everybody was off gallivanting around, Iris would sneak her down to my lair where the gargoyle would curl up in a special bed we'd prepared for her, safe and sound and protected from the world. Though I usually woke with a snarl, I never turned on Maggie. The very aspects that led others to fear me worked in reverse when it came to her. I'd taken her under my protection.

Iris and I hopped out of the car. Iris woke Anna-Linda and bundled her toward the porch behind me. Before I could unlock the door, Camille opened it and hustled us in.

"Chase wants to talk to you. Chrysandra said you were on your way home so we've been keeping a watch—" She stopped suddenly. "Who's that?"

"A guest," I said. "Is Chase here?"

"He's in the living room," she said, trying to peek behind me.

"I'll tell you about the girl in a bit," I murmured.

As we entered the living room, I saw that Delilah was watching Jerry Springer as usual—this time Jerry was ambushing unwary women with their grooms-to-be who were about to reveal that they'd been sleeping with their future mothers-in-law. *Delightful.* I had no idea what Delilah got out of this crap, but she liked it and so I humored her. I halfway suspected she had a case of the hots for Springer himself, but that thought was so unappetizing that I tried to avoid it as much as possible.

Chase was curled up on the sofa next to her, snoring softly. Trillian and Morio were nowhere to be seen. Morio was Camille's other lover—the other member of the little harem she had going. Morio was a youkai-kitsune, a fox demon. Japanese and as gorgeous as all the other men anxious to be in her entourage, Morio had been teaching her death magic, a skill which she was picking up all too easily. I glanced at the clock. Wade should be along before long.

Delilah woke Chase and he yawned, rubbing his eyes as

he sat up. They made for a striking couple. They shared the same height of six-foot-one, but Delilah was as golden as Chase was swarthy. Her felinelike features sparkled with energy, while his Mediterranean good looks could make the cover of any *GQ* magazine. He wasn't my type though. Neither were Camille's lovers. Most men didn't appeal to me and with good reason.

I pulled Iris aside. "Would you take Anna-Linda into the kitchen and get her something to eat, then tuck her into bed? If you have any sort of 'don't run away' spell, now would be a good time to use it."

She nodded and gently led the girl away, asking in soothing tones what she'd like to eat. As far as I could tell, Anna-Linda still hadn't pegged me for a vampire, and I wanted her feeling refreshed and safe before she realized what I was. No sense in having her so terrified she'd run again.

When they were out of earshot, I settled down on the ottoman and motioned for the others to lean in. "I don't want the girl overhearing what I'm about to tell you," I said. "She's been traumatized enough for one night."

Chase frowned. "I have news for you, too—"

I shook my head. "Slow down there, bronco. Chase, you're going to find the bodies of two drug dealers in one of the alleys off of Wilshire Avenue, near the parking garage. They *accidentally* ingested every tablet of Z-fen that they happened to have on them. I stopped them from raping that little girl. They were going to drug her and put her to work turning tricks. Her name is Anna-Linda Thomas and she's a runaway from Oregon. I smell a bad home life, but you should check it out before saying anything. She's skittish."

"Whoa. That's some evening you had." Delilah blinked, turning her winsome face toward me. She had grown up a lot over the past few months, that naive spark missing from her eyes. But it wasn't just the demons who'd vanquished it. No, a black scar in the shape of a scythe adorned the center of her forehead. She was a marked woman, and it had changed her in ways I could only begin to fathom.

I turned my attention back to Chase. He yawned and flipped open his notebook.

"Can I get some coffee?" he said. "Meanwhile, give all that to me again. Slowly this time."

Delilah unfolded herself from the sofa and headed toward the kitchen in search of caffeine. Camille caught my eye and gave me the thumbs-up. She was a lot like me, although I could out-ruthless her any day of the week.

I went over the incident again, step by step, not bothering to hide my impatience when Chase let out a loud sigh.

"Look, I don't give a flying fuck that you're squeamish about my methods, but you'd better get one thing through your head," I said. "Not only are we at war with the demons, but with a world full of perverts out there. If Iris and I hadn't shown up at the precise moment we did, that little girl would be on her knees sucking cocks, pumped up on Z-fen. Or maybe she'd be taking it up the ass for some businessman looking for a game of rub-and-tickle. You want that to happen? Fine. But I can't stomach the thought of waiting for the cops to answer a nine-one-one call. And I don't like the odds of those bottom-feeders buying their way out of jail."

Chase stared at his notes. I'd either made him furious or hit a nerve, because he closed the notebook and returned it to his pocket. His eyes cool and glittering, he said, "Before you three came along, I played by the book. I was a good cop. Or so I thought. I obeyed the rules. Now . . . I don't know what I am."

I repressed my urge to shake him by the shoulders. "Listen to me. You've learned to adapt. We all have to. And because you have, you'll have a better chance of surviving the chaos that's coming. Go ahead and return to playing good cop and bury your head in the sand. We'll go home, and leave the portal to Shadow Wing. Where will all your rules and regulations get you then?"

He paled and I felt a flicker of guilt, then squashed it. Of all of us, I was the most pragmatic. Trillian was right up there behind me, and Camille and Morio next in line, but Chase and Delilah tended to hesitate when facing difficult choices. I didn't blame them. It simply wasn't in their natures to play rough. But if we were to stop the evil filtering in from the Sub Realms, we couldn't afford to be picky when it came to breaking a few rules.

"Yeah, I know," he said after a moment. "I hear you loud and clear, even if I don't like the message."

Delilah returned from the kitchen carrying a tray with the coffeepot and mugs. She'd added a glass of milk for herself and an empty goblet for me, which she held up. "Drink?"

I shook my head. "No thanks, I'm not thirsty."

"Okay, truce on the pimp issue," Chase said, accepting the coffee. "Now, tell me, where do you get that blood you keep on ice, anyway? Or do I really want to know?"

I grinned. "I wondered if you'd ever get up the guts to ask. Every few weeks, Camille visits one of the smaller farms around here."

Chase turned an inquisitive eye her way. "Yes?"

Camille laughed. "One kiss and the manager gives me anything I want. They keep some of the blood they drain from their livestock for us. Since it's an organic farm, the blood's untainted by chemicals."

"So animal blood works?" Chase asked, looking less freaked out than I'd expected, though that might be because the answer was a lot less frightening than he'd probably been imagining.

"Oh sure. It's not my favorite, but it serves a purpose, at least for awhile. It won't stave off the hunger for too long, but it's enough to get me by for awhile. Our freezer's packed with it—enough to last me four or five months if I have to hole up." I paused for a moment. "Okay, what's *your* news, Johnson?"

He stared into his cup and then looked up to meet my eyes. "The four bodies we took in tonight? The ones killed by vamps?"

The tone of his voice told me I wasn't going to like what was coming next. Camille and Delilah stared at the ground. Apparently they already knew.

"They're gone."

"What do you mean, they're gone?" I stared at him. "Corpses just don't walk away. Well, not all that often."

"Use your head, girl," Chase said, looking exhausted. "We have four newborn hungry vamps on the loose. One of the laboratory techs saw them rise. He managed to hide until they left. He's an elf who works with Sharah." Chase lifted his cup to his lips. The coffee was scalding, but he didn't even flinch.

Freakin' bloody hell. "Do you think they were wannabes, then? Groupies who found a willing vamp to sire them?"

He shook his head. "I checked into their background. None of them hung with that crowd. They didn't cruise the clubs, they had good jobs, apartments, pets, families. Now I have to decide whether to notify their families or not. What can I say? *Your daughter's dead, but she got up and walked away?* Or do I just wait until they're reported missing? This is a sticky wicket, and I'm so damned glad that so far, only the FH-CSI is involved. But what I really need is for somebody to get out there and catch these new vamps before they start preying on the people of Seattle. That's on top of catching the joker who sired them."

Great. This night was just getting better and better. "Got any clues?"

"I don't know. You know the vamp community better than I ever could. My men and I'd be sitting ducks if we went into some of the sub-cult clubs that have sprung up over the past few years. And don't think I don't know about what goes on in there. I've heard about the parties at Dominick's." He set down his mug and gave me a tired shrug. "I know it's a lot to ask on top of finding whoever killed them in the first place but . . ."

I looked from Delilah to Camille. "I assume you two will go along for the ride?"

Camille nodded. "What else can we do?" She looked like she was going to say something, but then shook her head.

"Okay, you've got something on your mind. Give it up."

She stared at the floor for a moment. "As far as you know, how often do vamps leave their kills out for others to find? Wouldn't they normally take someone back to their nest if they were intending to sire them?"

What she said made sense, but I didn't see how it related. "Go on."

"I just think . . . it seems like this might be a message. That we were meant to take notice of those bodies, especially since Chase received that anonymous tip. Whoever it was didn't try to hide the bite marks, did he?" She frowned, pursing her lips in a gesture that reminded me so much of Father it was hard to look away.

"What she's trying to say is: Do you think this might be the Elwing Blood Clan's way of letting us know they made it through the portals?" Delilah rattled out her thoughts like staccato bullet play. She shivered and I realized that she was waiting for me to explode.

Both my sisters knew that I hated discussing the Elwing Blood Clan. My blow up shortly after Yule when they told me that the Clan might be headed this way proved that I wasn't ready to talk about them yet

Trouble was, Delilah might just be right, and if she was, I was in for a world of hurt. I crossed to the fireplace, gazing into the flames that crackled and popped. The winter was cold all right, and suddenly it seemed bleak and dark. Spring was a long ways off, and for me, the returning light would never again cross my face. After a moment, I turned.

Chase looked mildly confused, as usual, but Camille, Delilah, and Iris eyed me cautiously. Once, I'd lived like them. Once, I'd taken deep breaths, felt my pulse race, enjoyed the cold and heat and the sun on my face. The Elwing Blood Clan had taken all of that away. *Dredge* had taken it away.

Stronger, older than any of them, he was their leader, dark wine on a hot summer's night. Dredge had shredded my skin. He'd taught me how closely pleasure is tied to intense and exquisite pain. He'd used every weapon he could think of that wouldn't kill me outright, including his own body. He'd ripped open my soul and nobody bothered to put Menolly back together again. And then at the end . . . he forced my lips to his wrist where he'd opened a vein. His blood trickled down my throat. I had no choice. It was swallow or choke. And so I swallowed. And then, the end came that was only the beginning to torment . . .

Shaking my head, I quickly barricaded my thoughts. Some roads were too dangerous to walk down. The OIA brought me back to sanity, but they couldn't take away the scars that were left on my body and heart. Sometimes wounds never heal. Sometimes memories never fade.

"Then I suppose we'd better find out if they're behind this," I said. "Wade should be here any minute. If anybody knows about anything new going down in the vamp community, he will. He keeps close ties with most of the nests and clubs."

Wade made it his business to know what was happening in the underground. There were three layers within the Supe community—those who were out of the closet and lived open lives; those who hadn't mainstreamed, but who could still pass for humans; and then there were the Supes who hid themselves away and steered clear of the human side of life. At least the average FBH's life.

"If it is them . . ." Camille said, her words drifting off.

"If it is Dredge, then Wisteria's going to be with him and my guess is they'll be trying to find their way into the Subterranean Realms to meet up with Shadow Wing." I paused, wiping my hand across my eyes. I usually didn't tire but right now I felt a thousand years old. "I want you to promise me one thing."

"What's that?" Chase asked, staring at me.

As I dropped my hand, I realized it was wet—slick with bloody tears. I'd been crying and didn't even know it. I didn't bother wiping the blood off my face but looked him straight in the eye. "If the Elwing Blood Clan's involved, Dredge is mine. And nobody says a word about what I do to him, no matter what I do. Understand? He's *mine*."

Delilah let out a small mew. Camille blinked but didn't say a word. She gave me a look that told me she understood. Chase nodded once. I turned back to the fire as Iris came up, carrying a towel over her shoulder.

"Menolly? Maggie's awake and looking for you. Would you like to come hold her for me while I make up her cream and sage? I think she's hungry." Her flaxen hair shimmered under the incandescent lighting, her gaze showing no pity, only clear, pure support. Grateful, I forced my lungs to take a long, deep breath. I didn't need to breathe, but it helped me focus when I was stressed out.

"Thanks," I said. "I'm right behind you."

We headed into the kitchen, where Maggie was sitting in her playpen, blinking. I glanced at Iris. "You woke her up, didn't you?"

Iris shrugged. "Hard to say. I went in my room to get a notebook and must have made too much noise. She started whimpering so I brought her out." She turned away, avoiding my stare, but I knew her too well. Maggie hadn't woken up on her own.

"Thank you," I said, shaking off my gloom. "How's the girl?"

"Anna-Linda is sleeping. I slipped her a potion. She needs the rest and I don't want her waking up during the night." Iris pointed to her room. "I put her in my bed. I can sleep in the rocking chair or on the sofa if need be." She set a pan on the burner and added cream, sage, sugar, and cinnamon. Maggie's special drink would help her grow up big and strong. And smart, we hoped.

"You want tea?" I asked, reaching for the orange blossom tea in the cupboard, Iris's favorite. Just then, Maggie spotted me and held up her arms. She was tiny still, the size of a small dog, and her fur was a swirl of orange and black and white. She was a woodland gargoyle, and Camille had rescued her from a demon's lunch bag. Over the past few months, I'd grown close to the little twerp, even though I'd never had much leaning toward animals or babies before.

I picked her up, careful not to bend her wings, which were still pliable. In time they'd grow leathery and wide, able to hold her aloft. Until then we had to make sure that they weren't damaged. She hadn't spoken yet—just let out her little *moophs,* and we weren't sure if she'd ever develop to normal intelligence. She'd been bred by demons, and most likely she hadn't received her mother's milk long enough to jumpstart the quickening process. Whatever the case, we'd love her and take care of her and protect her. She had a long, long time to live, and we'd be there.

She threw her arms around my neck and clung tightly as I moved to the rocking chair and sat down, rocking her gently back to sleep. I nuzzled her neck, breathing in the musky scent. Her little heart slowly pounded out the rhythm of her life, but I felt no urge, no temptation, no draw.

"Hush, little baby, don't you cry; Mama's gonna bake you a sugar-plum pie," I whispered, singing the song our mother had sung to us when we were little. "And if that sugar-plum pie's too sour, Mama's going to buy you a golden tower . . ." Smiling, Maggie closed her eyes and drifted off. I rocked her gently, trying not to think about the Elwing Blood Clan. After a few moments, there was a knock on the door.

"That should be Wade," I told Iris, reluctantly handing her Maggie. "But let me get it just in case."

I peered out the peephole and sure enough, Wade was standing there. He gave me a little wave and I opened the door. Other than me, he was the only vampire allowed past our threshold. It just wasn't a good idea to give bloodsuckers free access to a house. True to form, we couldn't enter any private residence where we hadn't been invited. I opened the door and invited him in.

Wade was an odd fellow. With spiky blond hair and pale eyes, he could easily be mistaken for a geek, if you didn't look too close. He was wearing a pair of blue jeans, a thick flannel shirt, and his ever-present glasses. The lenses were fake, but he'd worn them all his life and couldn't get used to going without them now that he was dead.

"What's shaking, beautiful?" He winked.

That's one thing I liked about him—he'd accepted his place as a vampire and was using it to help others new to the life. And yet he hadn't lost his humanity. He enjoyed a good joke, a good book, a good cigar.

"Bad juju, Wade. Bad news." I reached out and gently pressed my fingertips against his—our usual greeting—then led him into the living room.

Wade bowed to my sisters and tossed a wave at Chase. The two had met once or twice, but had never really had a chance to sit down and talk. Chase started to hold out his hand but I gave him a warning shake of the head. Delilah touched his arm lightly and he pulled back.

"Oops, that's right. Sorry," Chase said.

Wade shrugged. "I'm not hungry, but even if I was, I

make it a point to not eat the other guests." He looked around and I motioned to one of the side chairs. When he'd settled himself, we filled him in on what had happened.

"We need to know if there's anything stirring in the underground." I flipped the desk chair around and straddled it. "Seriously, Wade. There could be some deep shit going on here, and we have to know what we're up against."

He didn't know everything about Shadow Wing, but he knew enough to keep him on our side. Wade thought we might be able to raise a small army of Earthside Supes should the demons break through in any great number. They'd be our best fighters, far more effective than guns and soldiers.

Wade leaned back, lacing his fingers behind his head. "Well, crap. And we've made such good progress with the V.A. group so far. Listen, what makes you think it's your sire rather than some rogue Earthside vamp, somebody who went over the edge or someone new to the area? I don't want to limit my search."

Chase looked at me. I shrugged at him.

"We *don't* know for sure," he said, staring at Wade. I had the distinct impression that facing an Earthside vamp unnerved Chase more than facing me did. I was from a different land, different world in fact. He could tie me up neatly in a box. *"Menolly's from Otherworld; of course she's a freak."* But Wade . . . Wade had sprung up right in the middle of Seattle. A homeboy of the distinctly dangerous type.

The pause became noticeable and I reached out to tap Chase on the knee. He jerked his head up and I snorted. "Calm down, I was just going to suggest you finish your thought. You seemed a little lost in the ozone."

"Oh, right. Thanks . . . I think." Blinking, Chase continued. "The girls think the Elwing Blood Clan might be involved. But you're right. We should run on the assumption that it could be any vampire. Let's not close any doors."

"So what's our first step?" Wade looked at me, a faint grin on his face. He was used to jumpy mortals. He saw them often enough at friends and family night down at our V.A. meetings.

I glanced around. Camille and Delilah had curled up together and were eating Cheetos. Chase was fiddling with his notebook. Iris was filing her nails. I waited for a moment, but it was obvious that we'd reached a painful lull in conversation.

"Don't everybody talk at once," I said, shaking my head. "I'm not the only one with a brain around here, am I?"

Camille shrugged, wiping the corners of her mouth, somehow managing to keep her lipstick perfect. "Well—"

"How'd you do that?" I interrupted.

"Do what?"

"Your lipstick. It didn't smear."

She grinned. "It's long-lasting lip lacquer. Won't budge unless I take a Brillo pad to it. Makes it easier to eat out in public. Now, may I continue?"

"Sure," I said, wondering how the chemicals in the lip gloss would react with my skin now that I was a vampire. Sometimes things didn't wash off that were supposed to be temporary. I'd seen a horrible example of rouge-gone-bad on a vamp who had been passing through town last month. Think great balls of fire on the cheeks and you get the picture. What made it worse was that it was a pudgy geek boy who's so-called friends—all of whom were still alive—had played a joke on him when he was sleeping. And breathers wondered why we didn't always let them know where we made our lairs.

"Anyway, we thought you'd have some ideas. After all, you know vampire habits better than we do." Camille glanced at Delilah, who gave her a nod. "In other words, tag, you're it."

With a burp, during which she barely covered her mouth, Delilah vigorously nodded. "That's right! You're the leader."

"And how did you decide to bestow this dubious honor on me?" I had the feeling I wasn't going to get out of this.

"Hey, you guys made me deal with things when Zach's tribe was getting slaughtered," Delilah said. "And Camille had to take the reins with Bad Ass Luke. It's your turn now, Menolly."

I glanced at Chase. "Have anything to add to this, Johnson?"

He tugged on his collar, frowning as Delilah dropped a

couple of the crunchy orange puffs on his impeccably black suit. But he didn't say a word, merely quietly moved them off and tossed them onto the coffee table. I caught his eye and smiled. If he was pissed that she'd dusted his Armani with cheese powder, he didn't say anything about it.

"No," he said after a moment. "No, because they're right. I haven't the faintest idea of what to look for. Given that you're . . . well . . ."

"Just say it." I scowled, wishing people wouldn't tiptoe around me so much. "I'm dead. Undead. A vampire. I'm scary as hell, I drink blood, and if you pay me enough I might consider running around yelling *bleh bleh bleh!* while pulling a Bela Lugosi with my long black cape!"

They all stared at me like I'd grown another head. Wade snorted so loudly that if he'd been alive, he would have blown snot all over his face.

I shook my head. "I know what I am. You aren't going to offend me by stating the obvious, so can everybody just relax and get on with life? I'm not going to rip out your throats for being blunt."

After a moment, Camille let out a delicate cough. "A bit high strung tonight, are we?" In a falsetto, she added, "Can't blame the hormones anymore, that's for sure."

I stared at her for a moment, repressing a smile. Chase darted a glance at her like she was crazy. Delilah was having an all-out affair with the junk food and ignoring everything else. Iris stared at the ceiling, pretending to examine the corners for cobwebs. And Wade . . . well . . . Wade just sat there, waiting for us to get it out of our systems.

"You know," I said softly, "you could keep that gorgeous figure forever if you'd let me take a bite out of your neck."

Camille's hand fluttered to her throat, but then she laughed. "Ask me again in two hundred years, okay?"

"Deal." I dropped the Big Bad act and laughed with her. "Can we finish this conversation? I'd like to have a little free time before I have to go to bed and there aren't many hours left until sunrise."

Chase rolled his eyes. "Then it's settled. You're the designated brains for this situation because you know what it's like to be a vampire. Both you and Wade have been down this road. So what do we do? Where do we look?"

I walked over to the window, staring out into the icy night. The winter was taking its toll on all of us, I thought. We were all jumpy and tired and worried about what was coming next, and yet . . . we had no choice. We did what we had to do and that was pretty much all she wrote.

"If I were a newborn vamp, where would I go? It depends on whether my sire called me to come to him—or her. Wade," I said without turning. "What's the procedure over here? Do most newborn vamps train with their sires like they do in Otherworld?"

He frowned. "I don't know, actually. We're so used to hiding that I don't think there's any real protocol for newborns. When I was turned, I found myself alone in my office. Apparently, even though I'd been missing for a couple of days, nobody thought to check there because it was a holiday and they thought I'd taken off for the beach. When I woke up, it took me a while to figure out what had happened. Well, after the hunger hit it was pretty self-evident."

"Hmm . . . living Earthside sure makes it hard on Supes, doesn't it? No guidelines, nobody to keep a watch over you. Even in the darker Blood Clans back in OW, they keep a watch on those they choose to turn, unless—as in my case— it was a spiteful act, meant to hurt others."

I pushed aside the memories that threatened to swarm up again. We didn't have time for me to give in to my anger. "If they're prowling the streets, they could be anywhere. But they'll be clumsy at first; they'll leave a trail because they won't really know what's happening to them. It takes a while to figure out what's going on."

Chase gazed at me, his eyes unreadable. "I won't even pretend to understand what happens during the transformation, but it can't be pleasant, even if you're a willing participant."

"It isn't," I said abruptly.

Wade gave a short nod and I could tell he was thinking about his own death and rebirth. "I suppose our first step is to figure out who sired them. I'll put out feelers in the community. Meanwhile, Menolly, keep your eyes open at the Wayfarer. The scariest part, really, is that whoever sired them, sired four at once. That's almost unheard of. I've never known any vamp to raise more than one newborn at a time, have you?"

"I don't know . . ." I thought back to Otherworld, to the Elwing Blood Clan and what they were capable of. "Dredge was picky about his kills. I knew that even before he caught me, from spying on them. Surely he wouldn't grab victims off the street? Especially humans? Most vampires looking to build a new nest are just as choosy. After all, you're going to be tied to these people for a long, long time."

Wade frowned. "Maybe something's changed? Or maybe it isn't connected to Dredge at all. Either way, we have to work fast because newborn vamps need to feed, and feed they will. If we don't get to them first, they'll go on a killing spree."

I motioned to Chase. "Get out your notebook."

He obeyed. "Okay, give it to me."

"First, you should monitor the hospitals and morgues for an increase in violent attacks. Four newborns can drink a lot of blood, and quite frankly, with as little as we've got to go on right now, we're probably in for a one-sided battle until we can get our shit together."

Delilah broke in. "You know, maybe it's time we acted on that idea about having a Supe community roll call. I know it's dangerous to keep information of that kind on record, but the way things are going we need all the help we can get. We can't make it mandatory, but let's at least start building the database. With Shadow Wing on the move and Degath Squad creeping in on scouting missions, we can't go it alone anymore."

Camille let out a long sigh. "She's right. We have to organize. The reins of the OIA are unofficially in our lap and we've got nobody left for us to turn to. Delilah, you get to work on the format for the database. Maybe we should have a summit meeting of the Supe community leaders at the Wayfarer? Ask the leaders of the various nests, clans, and packs to join us? Would that be okay, Menolly?"

"Oh yeah, that sounds like a butt load of fun." I made a face. "Just keeping peace between the Were groups will take an army, let alone when you add in vamps and Earthside Fae and visitors from Otherworld and everybody else who fits in the not-quite-human category into the mix. I think we should find another place to host it, though. The Wayfarer isn't set up for that kind of crowd, for one thing. And the gathering's guaranteed to be a little tense—we really don't want liquor involved. Our audience members just might take to breaking glasses and bottles over each other's heads."

"At least it's a place to start," Camille said.

"And now, I need to decompress. I'll be in my lair if anybody needs me. Wade, you'd better get back home before dawn breaks." As I escorted him out the door before stalking toward the kitchen, I suddenly felt alone. Everybody else could stay up talking, they could lose sleep and not worry about it. They didn't have to be concerned with the sun rising in the morning. For me, it was just another one of life's inequities I had to deal with. I lived during the dark hours, in the shadows of life. Sometimes I felt like throwing a tantrum but in the end, I never did. Wasting energy just wasn't my style.

I slipped through the secret entrance to my basement apartment and headed down the stairs, wondering for the umpteenth time just what my life would have been like had I not fallen off the ceiling and the Elwing Blood Clan caught hold of me.

Trying to shake off my gloom, I turned my attention to the stack of books sitting on the nightstand next to my bed, which was clad in a green toile spread and sheets. As I picked up the first, a story about a group of men scaling Mount Everest, I settled back on the bed and lost myself to a world of ice and snow, where the days were brilliantly white and blinding, where the snow sparkled—pristine and pure—and where the sun was friend rather than foe.

CHAPTER 4

❦

Do vampires dream when they sleep?

Camille asked me that question once, when she came to wake me up. How could I explain? She walked in three worlds: in Otherworld, Earthside, and within the Moon Mother's realm. But hers was a far different path than my own.

Yes, I wanted to tell her. We dreamed of blood and sex and passion. But that wasn't entirely the truth, even though my drifting thoughts were often filled with frightening images that warned me when I slipped a little too far into the predator, away from my essential self.

Or perhaps I should have told her that vampires walked the halls of the dead when we slept. Walked through meadow and forest, wandered city streets and glided over the sea. We walked on the winds, we walked on the water. *We* were the true Windwalkers. But again, that would only be part of the answer.

The fact was that mostly, when the pull of the sun dragged me down into the dark slumber of the undead, I dreamed about home—about Otherworld and my childhood. I dreamed about the first time I kissed a man—my neighbor

Keris. I dreamed about the first time I kissed a woman—Elyas, a fellow operative in the OIA. I dreamed about becoming a priestess in the Sisterhood of the Ancients, a hope that died when I got my first moon blood and became a woman. I dreamed about movement and patterns and fractals, about dance and music and poetry.

And after particularly stressful nights, I dreamed about Dredge. Unfortunately I no longer had the luxury other people have of waking from their nightmares. Once I was asleep, if the memories came to visit, there was no other option than to ride them out, to relive the torture and rape and—eventually—my own blessed death. Over and over again I dreamed about my transformation. Sisyphus reborn, only instead of trickery against the gods, I was guilty of stealing secrets from a very nasty tempered vampire and his crew. For that, I earned my eternal punishment, damned to walk among the undead until the day I'm ready to let go and die the final death.

I never told Camille and Delilah about the nightmares. There was no need. Why should we all carry such dark memories? There's nothing they could do to change my destiny, and I refused to weigh them down with the knowledge of just how vicious people, whether living or dead, can be. Though they'd rapidly been discovering that savage truth for themselves, with our battle against the demons.

I put away my book and slowly removed my jeans and turtleneck. Thinking about Dredge had brought up too many memories. I glanced down at my body. No use looking in a mirror, not anymore. My reflection was never there to look back at me. And yet every time I undressed and saw the scars, how could I help but remember?

Their meeting was almost over . . .

A few more minutes and I could creep out, free and clear and with the information we needed. I took a long, slow breath as I held myself steady, clinging to the precarious handholds that kept me aloft in the higher reaches of the cave. At this distance, the Elwing Blood Clan couldn't sense the heat my body gave off, but my ultrasensitive hearing would catch what they were saying. Another perk of my mixed blood. I could hear the soft fall of a footstep in the next room.

Satisfied, I merely had to wait them out a little longer. As of five minutes ago, I'd collected enough information to take them down. Dredge was brilliant, but he didn't seem to comprehend that someone, somewhere, might be plotting against him. Nobody else but the OIA would be daring—or foolhardy—enough to spy on the Elwing Blood Clan. That's where I came in.

Now all I had to do was wait until they left the cave. They always dispersed for feeding after they'd had their meeting. I'd been here three times before, and each time, I had easily slipped away. This was my last assignment on the mission. I had what we needed. I'd found out for sure what the OIA had suspected: Dredge and his cronies were plotting to start up their own Court with Dredge as their king. Vampire courts were outlawed in Otherworld by an agreement among all of the Fae governments. They were allowed to form nests with a maximum of thirteen members before hiving off a new enclave.

Dredge had already broken that rule—I'd counted twenty-three members of the Elwing Clan. And he was out to rule far more than his turf here. He wanted to set himself up to be a vampiric lord—and we suspected he planned on trying to muscle in on the money flowing through the thieves' and assassins' guilds. And if he had his way, he'd be in a position to slake his sadistic thirsts without worrying about reprisals. People would be too afraid to fight back if he ruled a Court instead of a nest.

With the knowledge I'd discovered, by tomorrow morning the OIA would be able to send a team in to stake every last bloodsucker in the rogue clan of vamps. Threatening to exile them to the Sub Realms hadn't proved all that effective when they escaped capture every time.

Just hang on, keep quiet as they filed out, and I'd be home free. I might even get a promotion for my work—a first for the D'Artigo girls. In fact, the way things were looking with our track records, it would take a promotion to prevent the OIA from assigning us to some lowlife town down south to watch over the riffraff. We weren't lazy . . . just a little unlucky at times.

I shivered as a cold draft blew by, even though I was in a spider-silk body suit. My hair was pulled tightly into a bun, to keep it out of my face. I'd made sure to stretch out before coming on duty, but now every muscle in my body hurt and all I could think about was going home and taking a long hot bath. Camille and I had plans to head out for a party at midnight. There was an opium bash at the Collequia, and Camille wanted me to meet someone there, some guy she'd hooked up with a few weeks back. His name was Trillian or something like that. The fact that she wouldn't tell us anything about him made me know right off that there had to be something wrong with him. Camille had a taste for bad boys.

A ripple of pain washed down my left arm. Damn it, what was taking the vamps so long to clear out? I squinted, trying to make out what was going on below. From where I was sequestered, I couldn't see them very well. On the plus side, they couldn't see me, either.

Ten more minutes, I thought. Just ten minutes. I forced myself to ignore my burning muscles and tried to focus on something else. Father had promised we'd take a vacation before the next full moon to go visit relatives in the Windwillow Valley, or maybe spend a few days in Aladril, the City of Seers. Either way, we all needed a holiday. All four of us had been working hard lately. I was so tired I fell asleep the minute my head hit the pillow each night.

Damn it. An itch on the back of my neck was driving me nuts. As I shifted, trying to shake it off, the rock on which my right hand rested crumbled without warning, shearing off at surface level.

Holy shit! I scrambled for the nearest outcropping, frantically hoping to snag hold of some niche, crack, or crevice to keep myself from falling, but there was nothing under my fingers but smooth rock. My feet slipped as my fingers slid along the granite. I lost my grip and went tumbling to the floor below.

They say your life flashes before your eyes when you're ready to die, but the only thing that ran through my mind was a prayer that I'd be lucky enough to break my neck in the fall, considering just who I knew was prowling around in the caverns. And then I hit the floor with a bone-shaking thud.

Hell. I was still alive, and my landing had made a lot of noise. That meant one thing: to have any chance of escaping unscathed, I'd better run like hell. As I scrambled to my feet and headed toward the nearest entrance, I heard a commotion behind me. They'd heard me and were coming to investigate. Fuck. Was this the end?

As I raced through the corridor, I had no delusions about what would happen if they caught me. The Elwing Blood Clan vamps were rogues, arrogant predators led by a vampire who bathed in the blood of his victims. The clan ignored the Vampire code of ethics, which was why I'd been spying on them in the first place.

I skidded around a bend in the corridor, a searing cramp running through my calf as the sudden burst of movement stirred up lactic acid. The faint glow of starlight ahead told me I was almost out. Maybe I could lose them in the forest—I was good at camouflage. Sucking in my breath, I pushed my protesting body faster, my gaze fastened on the opening to the cave.

Ten yards away, and I could taste freedom. Nine yards and I fumbled at my belt for an emergency stake. I managed to yank it free and pumped my arms, covering the distance that would give me a fighting chance for survival. Just a few more steps—a few more yards.

And then, the silhouette of a man stepped in front of the cave opening. Tall and swarthy, with long curling hair, he was wearing black leather and a smile that would shatter stone. I knew who he was. Dredge. Leader of the Elwing Blood Clan. He glorified torture, reveled in pain.

I put on the brakes, forcing a hard right toward the passage out of which he'd just emerged. Dredge didn't move to follow me, but I could hear his voice from behind as he said, "When you tire of the chase, bring her to me. Don't mark her. This one's in for a *special* treat."

A chill of dread washed over me as I realized that the passage was taking me back into the central cavern. Shortly before the corridor ended, I noticed a beam of moonlight shining down through a crack in the ceiling. A quick look up showed me that I was just small enough to fit through the fracture in the rock. As I pulled myself up the wall, I scrambled for handholds. By now every joint in my body was on fire and I'd torn at least five different muscles. Repressing the pain, I forced myself to focus on the ceiling. Just get to the fissure. Get out of the cave.

Two feet from the exit, a hand grasped my ankle. I tried to kick off my assailant, but his grip was iron-strong and with a single jerk he yanked me away from the wall. As he let go, I fell to the floor, landing on my back.

The sound of my ribs snapping echoed through the air seconds before the pain hit. Moaning, I blinked away the tears only to find myself looking up into the face of an elf. Or what had at one time been an elf. Ageless, pale, and wan, he bent over to pick me up and I remembered the stake. Where was it? I'd stuck it back in my belt when I started to climb. As I fumbled for it, the vampire gazed into my eyes.

"Relax . . . just relax." His voice was soothing, gentle as a spring breeze, and I felt an overwhelming desire to close my eyes, to surrender to those three little words. But he smiled, and in that moment, I saw the extended fangs, glistening needles that would end my life.

"No," I whispered, trying to keep control of my senses. I forced my hand down to my belt where the wooden stake lay pressed against my body.

"It will be so much easier if you let me help you," the vamp said. "My name's Velan. What's your name?"

I licked my lips, blinking. He wasn't my friend and he wasn't going to help me. His voice promised a gentle embrace but I forced myself to remember what he was and where I was. Shaking my head, I managed to get my fingers

around the stake, my chest burning with the pain of the fractured bones.

Velan hadn't noticed what I was doing, he was so intent
on capturing me with his gaze.

"Come closer," I whispered. "Help me . . ."

As I waited, he leaned in. Timing my movement because
one shot was all I'd have, I flipped the stake point-side up
and shoved toward his chest as hard as I could, biting my
lips as pain shot through my ribs, my chest, my lungs.

Contact! I hit him square on and the shocked look on his
face was the most beautiful sight I'd ever seen. He opened
his mouth but before he could say a word, he shattered into a
cloud of ash and bone, showering me with all that remained.

Coughing, I pushed myself up, biting my lip to keep from
screaming. Every fiber of my being hurt—every muscle,
every bone . . . like my nerves were raw, scraped with a knife.
I managed to stagger to my feet. The passage was empty but
it wouldn't stay that way for long. The only direction in
which I could head would lead me back into the inner chamber. Unless . . . I glanced up at the break in the cavern roof
again. Maybe I could still manage to climb the shaft? I was
hurt, but I had motivation—the pain would be a lot worse if
I waited around for Dredge's cronies to catch up to me.

Slowly, fumbling for a handhold here, a toehold there, I
started climbing the rock again. I tried to control my breathing as each lungful of air brought with it a dizzying muscle
spasm.

As I inched up the wall, a million thoughts ran through
my mind, most of them centering on how I was going to tender my resignation the minute I got back to Y'Elestrial. *If* I
made it back to Y'Elestrial. Why the hell had the OIA assigned me to this task? There were other scouts, other acro-
bats in the agency who were better than me. Had this been a
punishment? Or had the powers that be decided that the case
really wasn't *that* serious? The idiots had their heads up
their butts and now I was about to become another statistic
because of their stupidity. I glanced around, surprised to see
that I was nearing the top. Maybe anger was the ticket—it

kept my mind off of the pain. I visualized our supervisor and mentally took aim with a crossbow as I forced myself toward the crevasse. Just a few more feet . . . a few more inches and I'd be out.

And there it was—blessed starlight splashing on my face. I clawed at the edges of the chasm, slowly pulling my aching body up and out to roll over on the fragrant grass that carpeted the top of the hill. I'd made it. I actually escaped. Now I just had to get to the forest where I could hide out until morning. Relief pouring through me like sweet cool water, I struggled to stand up.

"Need some help?"

A hand fell on my shoulder and I froze. His voice was dark and low and the sound of his words made me dizzy. Shivering, suddenly all too aware of the sound of the crickets and frogs, of the gentle caress of wind on my skin, I turned slowly, praying that I was wrong. *Please, please let me be wrong.*

But there he stood, the tall swarthy man in leather with the dazzling smile. Dredge leaned down to gaze at me and I let out a faint whimper. His eyes were as black as the night sky etched with glittering hoarfrost, and when he smiled, the tips of his fangs glistened in the starlight. I tried to move, tried to run but I couldn't look away. He trailed one hand down my cheek, gently caressing me with fingers as cold as the grave.

"Have you lost your way, little girl? The OIA is out of its mind if they think you're any match for the Elwing Blood Clan. I'll take you home with me and we'll have a nice long talk," he said, gathering me up in his arms.

"By the way, in case you don't know, my name's Dredge. And you, my sweet, are going to tell me *everything*. Then we're going to play a few games."

I let out a little moan as my fractured ribs shifted, sending another wave of pain to lance through me.

"Poor baby. You're hurting?" His face took on a twisted grin and he leaned his head down to whisper in my ear. "Don't worry, you won't be thinking about your broken ribs much longer. First, I'm going to bleed you, cut by cut by cut until the pain drives you mad. And then I'm going to fuck you so long and so hard that every nerve in your body screams for release and you beg me to kill you. Oh, yes, my pet, you're going to find out just how much pain a body can take and still live."

He paused, then a light flickered in those dead eyes. "You know, I just thought of a little gift for your precious OIA. I'm in a whimsical mood. I don't think I'll kill you—well, not for good. No, I think I'll make you one of us and then send you home to feed on your friends and family. How does that sound? Eternal life? Eternal beauty? An eternity of knowing you killed those you loved the best? I shall grant it to you, and you don't even have to ask for it."

Terrified, I tried to beat my hands against him, but my arms were as still as dark water. I managed to force my words to the surface, to breathe out hard enough so I could speak. "No, I won't let you—I won't become one of you!"

"Hush," he said, and my voice disappeared again. "There's nothing you can do to stop me. Come girl, you're in for the longest night you've ever had."

Mutely, I thought of home. We'd just taken in two more stray animals—Trevor and Harlis, stray rabbits. Would Delilah remember to tend to them? She was always bringing home stray animals, and sometimes she forgot to feed them. Camille was busy with running the house, so I took over when Kitten fell down on the job.

And the Harvest Home celebration was approaching. I'd been planning on wearing my new dress and going with our neighbor, Keris. We'd been dating for several months now. His lips were sweet and tender on mine, and when I lay in his arms it was as if I'd discovered a safe haven in which to nestle. Now, like a match to paper, all my plans for the future crumbled into ashes.

How would my family handle my death? Camille seemed so strong but under that veneer of self-assuredness there was a tear-filled well so deep that it would never end. She'd pushed her grief aside when Mother died in order to pick up the pieces for the rest of us. Would she do the same when they found out what happened to me? And Delilah . . .

Kitten relied on me a lot. She needed me. And Father . . . he hated vampires. Would he hate me, too? Would he blame me?

When they found out what happened, would they search me out and stake me? Would they mourn for a long time? Or would I be forgotten, a painful memory they'd want to bury with the remains of my soul statue? If I could only give in and let go *now,* lose consciousness, die, and be done with it . . . but my mind was too strong and I couldn't will myself to faint. One look at Dredge told me he wasn't about to let me miss a moment of his delight.

Wishing I'd never been born, I gazed up at the stars as he lightly jumped into the shaft and floated back down into the caverns, holding me in his arms. It was my last view of true beauty through clear, untainted eyes.

"Menolly. Menolly? It's time to wake up."

The delicate voice filtered through my dream, yanking me out of the abyss just in time. All memories of the dream shattering, I shot up in bed, a gnawing ache in my stomach urging me to leap up, to grab whoever had disturbed me and make a meal out of them.

I glanced around, taking in my surroundings. I was safe in my bedroom, and the lovely green toile of the bedspread was gently illuminated in the soft glow of the knockoff Tiffany lamp that sat on the desk. Iris was in the rocking chair, far enough away to avoid my grasp during those first seconds of waking when I had the most chance of reacting without thinking. Camille had learned the lesson the hard way—and so had I.

"It's sunset. Time for you to wake." She stood up and smoothed her apron, giving me a gentle smile. No matter how many times Iris had seen me with fangs extended and eyes bloodred, she seemed perfectly at ease. "Anna-Linda's been up since late morning. I've had a long talk with her. She knows what you are, by the way. Apparently you're not the first vampire she's met."

"You're kidding. When did she meet another vampire?" I

opened my closet, trying to decide what to wear. Almost all of my clothes had long sleeves and covered my arms and legs. The scars had long faded, but they latticed my body and it was easier to hide them than to explain their presence. I rummaged through the hangers and finally pulled out a pair of low-rise jeans, a hunter green turtleneck, and a brown suede vest. Add in my spiked heel boots and I'd clean up pretty good.

Iris grinned. "When was the last time you wore panties or a bra?"

"Try never," I said, shimmying into my jeans and fastening the buttons. They were tight, but since I didn't have to breathe, I just had to make sure that I could sit down without splitting them. "At least, not Earthside. When I was alive, I wore undergarments, but why bother now? My breasts will never sag."

Repressing a smile, she shook her head. "Whatever you say. Anyway, Anna-Linda told me during breakfast this morning that there's a vampire clan down in Portland, Oregon, where she comes from. Her brother was a wannabe and hung around a group of messed up kids who kept daring the local vamps to take them on. He finally got his wish, except the vampires didn't change them, they just sucked the kids dry. It made the news as a series of ritual killings, but Anna-Linda was hiding in the woods, spying on her brother when it happened. Shortly after that, her mother brought home a boyfriend who started molesting the girl. That's when Anna-Linda hit the streets."

I dropped on the bed to pull on my boots and zip them up. As I gently caressed the suede, I thought over what Iris had told me. The girl was clearly messed up, and if she was telling the truth, we obviously couldn't send her home again. On the other hand, we weren't equipped to take in a human child.

"You think she's playing straight on this?" I stared at Iris. She was an excellent judge of character. She'd know if the girl was lying.

Iris raised her eyebrows. "Interesting you should ask. Yes, I do. However, I did ask Chase to double check her story. He called the Oregon cops and sure enough, there was a mass-murder down there that matches the description of her brother's death. Ritual killings, according to the cops, five victims, drained dry of blood. But the vamps slit all of their victims' wrists and let enough blood flow out to make it look like a murder rather than a suckfest. One of the victims was named Bobby Thomas—Anna-Linda's brother."

I stood up and made my bed as Iris fluffed the pillows for me. She was an expert housekeeper, that was for sure. Until she moved in, we'd never had crisp sheets or pillows that whispered when we nestled our heads on them. In fact, we hadn't bothered with an iron or ironing board, but now one was set up in the laundry room and it got its weekly workout. That was one chore Iris chose to handle the old fashioned way rather than via magic. I tugged at the corner of the fitted sheet, pulling it taut to smooth out the wrinkles, then slid the clastic under the mattress.

"Stupid . . . just so stupid. I don't know whether I feel sorry for those poor kids or just wish somebody would have slapped some sense into them. I guess it's too late for either," I said, pulling the comforter into place.

Iris added the pillows. "Most of them don't know any better. They're all angsty and full of hormones. Some of them come from broken homes. You vampires, you're predators. Maybe you aren't really immortal, but you're invulnerable to a majority of woes. You wield power, something so many of these kids crave—power and control over their lives. You can't blame them, really. I think we're done here," she added, glancing around my room. "Everything seems in order. I'll come down tomorrow while you sleep and dust."

"Thanks," I said, following her up the stairs. "You're probably right. A lot of them get so hung up on the glamour, they don't see the reality. And a lot of my kind start out with the best intentions. Drink only enough to keep alive. Don't take an innocent life. But the truth is, those resolutions get harder to keep the longer you go on unless you have some tangible reminder of why they're important."

"Whatever the case with her brother, Anna-Linda knows you're a vampire and she didn't seem fazed. In fact, oddly enough, I think she was pleased," Iris said as we entered the kitchen.

Voices were coming from the living room. I assumed one was Anna-Linda—it sounded like a young woman, but the other, I didn't recognize. "Who's here?" I asked.

"Chase is here. So is Zachary Lyonnesse and one of the women from his Pride," Iris said, an odd tone filtering into her words. "I like her. Her name's Nerissa and she specializes in helping troubled youngsters. She works with DSHS, though they have no idea she's a Were."

"DSHS?" I asked.

"Yes. The Department of Social and Health Services. Nerissa suggested we find a foster home with a Supe family for Anna-Linda because that way, anything the girl says to the foster parents won't be suspect. Delilah thought of Siobhan and called her. She said she'd be happy to keep the girl for a while."

Siobhan Morgan was a friend of ours. A selkie originally from Ireland, she was a wereseal who passed in society for a full-blood human. She was gentle, kind, and loved children in a way that I didn't fully understand. She was also diplomatic, smart, and able to keep control of a situation.

"Really? I know we can't keep Anna-Linda but . . . it just seems wrong to farm her out again. Although letting her stay with Siobhan would be far more satisfactory than pawning the girl off on strangers."

Iris shook her head. "This morning, Anna refused to go to a shelter. The girl was threatening to run away the first chance she got if she had to leave here. Chase doesn't like the situation, but he won't interfere. I think it helps that Nerissa has a background working with troubled youth—she convinced him a Supe home would be perfect." Iris motioned me on while she stopped in the kitchen. "Now you go on while I make some tea."

As I entered the living room, I could sense that tensions were running high. Delilah was sitting between Chase and Zach, a tight look on her face. Ever since Chase found out Delilah had slept with the werepuma, the two men had kept a careful distance from one another. Chase and Delilah had been through a couple of rows about it, but they seemed fairly stable at this point.

I had a feeling the only reason Chase wasn't rocking the boat was because he feared an ultimatum that would result in her choosing Zach. Though I wasn't fond of Chase, I did feel sorry for him. I had serious doubts that Delilah could weather a relationship with an FBH, but it was her business.

The last bit of light slipped away and dusk proper hit as I nodded to our guests. I walked over to the window, peering out at the blanket of white that covered the yard. The temperature was still hovering around the thirty-degree mark and hadn't budged in days.

Anna-Linda flashed me a tentative smile. "Thanks," she said. "I forgot to say it last night because I was so tired, but thank you, for saving me." She scooted over on the sofa and patted the cushion next to her. "Here, you can sit here next to me."

As I debated the wisdom of sitting next to the young girl, I saw a glimmer in her eyes and suddenly understood. I was her heroine, her savior. Vampire or not, she wanted to make a connection with me.

I glanced over at Nerissa, who was curled in the recliner. Definitely one of the Rainier Pumas, all right. She had the same feral topaz eyes and golden hair the rest of the clan did, but she was dressed in a skirt suit and pumps, and her hair was caught back in a neat chignon. She looked like she'd come directly from work.

"You must be Nerissa. I'm Menolly D'Artigo. Iris and I found Anna-Linda last night in an alley." I held out my hand and Nerissa stood and smoothly took it, giving no indication that she noticed my skin was far cooler than her own.

"You mean you rescued me," Anna-Linda broke in.

Nerissa gave her a smile. "Anna-Linda, maybe you should let Menolly and me have a little chat. I think Ms. Kusi said she's going to be making some tea. She could probably use some help."

Nerissa had a nice voice. Smooth skin . . . she looked sweet and firm. And I wasn't just talking her demeanor. The appealing glow of her tanned neck entranced me for a moment and I felt my fangs begin to extend. Startled by the direction my thoughts were taking me, I nodded abruptly. "She's right, Iris could use some help. Why don't you go see how she's doing?"

Anna-Linda looked disappointed but she unfolded herself and headed toward the kitchen. As she disappeared into the hallway, I motioned for Nerissa to join me in the parlor. "We'll be back in a moment," I told Delilah. Glancing darkly at the two men, I added, "Meanwhile, you all keep your claws in. Promise?"

Delilah blushed and Zach ducked his head. Chase just rolled his eyes, but they all nodded. I led Nerissa into the parlor and closed the door, just in case Anna-Linda returned before we were done with our conversation.

"I gather Iris told you what we found out, and Chase filled in the blanks?" I asked.

She sat on the arm of the Morris chair, balancing herself lightly with one hand. It was all I could do to tear myself away from the sight of her legs as she crossed them, left over right. Unnerved by the intensity of my attention, I forced my gaze up to her face.

"Yes, they did. Poor girl's been through a lot, but I really don't recommend you keep her here. Trust me, a lot of street kids come through my office. While they may idolize you if you rescue them, they're not always trustworthy. Anna-Linda's a victim, and she would have been far worse off if you hadn't gotten her away from those pimps, but she's still in survival mode. And people in survival mode . . ."

"Are capable of a lot of things they normally wouldn't do," I finished for her. "She's still running scared and who knows what she might think of."

Nerissa let out a long sigh. "Exactly. I hate to say it, but you can't let your sympathy blind you. She's been traumatized to the point of where she's acting on impulse. Right now she's enamored because you saved her from the pimps, but give her a day or two to calm down and she might start thinking about her brother and how he was killed by vampires. Staying with Ms. Morgan would be best for her at the moment."

Nerissa was right. Anna-Linda was a walking time bomb. We had too much riding on our shoulders to take care of an FBH child. And if her mother found out we had her, there could be hell to pay. But Nerissa passed in society and she worked within the system, so she knew how to play it for all it was worth. She'd be able to hide the fact that Siobhan was a Supe, because Siobhan kept it under wraps so well.

"Makes a lot of sense; but how are we going to convince her to stay with Siobhan? She's already threatened to run away, I gather." My nose twitched.

Nerissa smelled of rose soap and a wisp of talc. As I watched her, the glow in her cheeks brightened as her breasts rose and fell, lifting with each breath. I found myself wanting to reach out, to run my fingers over the smooth skin I imagined was hiding beneath her silk blouse. Quickly I beat a hasty retreat to the other side of the room where I ostensibly stared out the window.

The air in the room felt close, thickening as the silence between us grew. About to jump out of my skin, wondering why she hadn't answered, I turned too quickly, only to bump into her. Nerissa had silently crossed to stand at my back.

"Maybe you can help us," she said, her voice soft.

Startled, my fangs came out and I grabbed her wrist. I was so thirsty, all I could think about was kissing the delicate skin of her neck and sinking my teeth deep with luxurious abandon.

Nerissa's eyes widened but she stood her ground. "Menolly. You're hurting my wrist," she said, her voice firm. I could sense fear there, but it was well controlled.

Forcing myself to let go, I rose to the ceiling until I could gather my composure. As my fangs retracted, I tried to figure out what the hell had just happened. I usually kept better control of myself than that, although I'd warned Delilah over and over not to startle me. She walked so softly that I couldn't detect her, and Nerissa had done the same.

"Are you okay?" Nerissa asked.

Hornier than I'd been since before my death, I lowered myself to the ground but kept a careful distance between us.

"You damned Weres. One piece of advice you might want to pass on to the Pride: Never sneak up on vampires. Weres, especially werecats, have the ability to skulk. Trust me, you do not want to surprise a vamp who might not be willing to pull her fangs back in." Angry that I'd been caught unawares, I folded my arms and stared at her.

She blushed a delicate shade of rose and her hand fluttered to her neck. "I'm sorry. I guess I have a lot to learn about your kind. I apologize."

"Yeah, yeah . . . just remember next time. Now, how can I help convince Anna-Linda to go with you?"

I needed time to process my confusion. I'd always been attracted to both men and women, so that wasn't what scared me. No, what bothered me was that Nerissa hadn't backtracked when I'd put the moves on her. That had been a good thing, actually. If she'd broke and run, I might have attacked without thinking. But there was something else—a look in her eye that told me that she wasn't blushing just out of embarrassment.

"I was thinking you could charm her. It might be the easiest way. Or your sisters could. Don't you all have some sort of ability to enchant humans?"

The idea hadn't even occurred to me. "Well, yes. It's part of our father's bloodline—the Fae can charm with a kiss or a touch or sometimes just a look. And the fact that I'm a vampire doesn't hurt matters any. I suppose you might be right. If she thinks she's going along with the idea of her own accord, she won't feel we've abandoned her."

"Exactly," Nerissa said. "So will you do it?"

With a shrug, I nodded. "I don't see why not."

"Good, then it's settled." As she headed for the door, she stopped and turned. "By the way, just so you know, I felt it, too," she said, her lips curling into a suggestive smile. "The heat, that is. I'm not seeing anybody right now. Give me a call if you want. I'm not afraid of a good challenge, you know, and Venus the Moon Child trained me."

As she headed out the door, I followed more slowly, wondering what the hell to make of her invitation. Just what had

Venus the Moon Child trained her for? He was a wild old shaman. Nerissa wasn't a vamp wannabe. But she had a kinky side hidden under that chignon and Ann Taylor suit, that much was clear. The question was, did I want to find out just how kinky?

CHAPTER 5

It was a simple matter, really. I sat down with Anna-Linda in the kitchen and took her hands in mine. As she looked at me, I let down my shields that kept both vampire and Fae glamours in check.

Anna-Linda blinked a couple of times, but it didn't take long before I felt her will capitulate. She was still young and easy to control. A flicker of guilt raced through me. I was about to mess with her mind, to fill her head with my own thoughts and make her believe they were her own.

I paused, trying to convince myself that I was doing the right thing. After all, if she did snap and decide to avenge her brother's death, I'd be a handy target. *Unacceptable risk.* Kids had a knack for ferreting out secrets. It wouldn't take her long to discover my hiding place. So I pushed aside my doubts and turned on the charm.

"Anna-Linda, listen to me."

My voice echoed slightly, and she blinked, then looked at me as if I were the only person who existed in her universe.

"You want to stay with Siobhan. She's going to take good care of you and you won't give her any trouble. You'll think this was all your idea, and you won't run away unless your life is in danger. If something bad happens, you'll come tell us about it. Do you understand?" My voice slid over her like warm honey, and a peaceful look spread across the girl's face.

She nodded, her face blank. "I want to stay with Siobhan."

"That's right. And you won't cause any trouble. You'll help her out and listen to her." As she repeated my instructions, I slowly withdrew my energy, like a wave rolling back out to sea, leaving behind only the aftermath of the storm surge. After that, it was a simple matter to send her off with Nerissa, who promised to call the next morning. As I shut the door behind them, Camille put her hand on my shoulder.

"Anna-Linda will be better off at Siobhan's house," she said. "We aren't set up to take care of a child and you know it."

I stared at the silent door. "It's been a long time since that girl's been a child, Camille. She's seen things and done things no child ever should be forced to do." Images of Dredge flashed through my mind. I wasn't his only victim. No doubt, there had been plenty of Anna-Lindas to suit his twisted desires. I'd been lucky, I was older, more capable of coping with the aftermath than a child.

Camille swallowed. Her blood was running hot today, I could feel the warmth from where I stood. And her emotions flared in her aura. She was angry, wanting to run with the Hunt, to track down and destroy. But all she said was, "I know, Menolly. That's why we do what we do."

"I'm heading to the Wayfarer early unless Chase has any news on our missing vampires. Maybe I can catch a few faces who don't make it to the late shift when I'm working. I might be able to find out something." As I pulled on a leather jacket—not against the cold, but because it looked good on me and made me look tough at the bar—Camille stopped me.

"You did the right thing, Menolly. Don't feel guilty."

I let out a little huff and, once again, told her the lie that I kept repeating to myself and everyone else. "I don't feel guilt anymore. Not really."

As I headed out the door, she whispered just loud enough for me to hear, "Right. But just in case you do, remember—guilt is a luxury that we can no longer afford. We have to use whatever comes our way to battle the coming darkness."

I gave her a sharp nod, thinking that my oldest sister was turning into a clone of me, and that had me a little worried. Then, as silently as shadows dancing, I darted down the steps toward my Jag. Camille was right, of course. I'd saved Anna-Linda. So why did I feel like I'd let her down?

A blast of noise hit me as I strode through the doors of the Wayfarer, the conversation shoring up the music to create a cacophony of reverberation that thundered off the walls. Business had picked up over the past few weeks and now all shifts were swamped. A good thing, considering the OIA no longer paid us a salary, and whatever money we made, we had to earn through our cover jobs.

Every table and booth was jammed. The Wayfarer had gone from being a quiet respite for OW visitors to a down-and-dirty hangout joint for everybody from Fae to the Earth-side Supe community to FBHs.

I slipped behind the counter and Luke—a werewolf I'd recently hired—shot me a grateful look.

"Am I ever glad to see you. Every night we're getting busier. Any chance we could hire another bartender?" He brushed back a lock of unruly hair from his forehead. In his midthirties, he was a cutie.

Short—barely five-eight—Luke's muscles glistened in all the right places. His wheat-colored ponytail trailed down to his waist. A long scar decorated his face, jagged and faded, obviously an old injury. I wasn't sure how he'd gotten it and I wasn't going to ask. Luke would tell me if he wanted to. All I cared about was the fact that he could whip out a round of drinks in record time and they were never returned with complaints.

I tied on my apron and started working on the next order. Two Long Island Iced Teas, a shot of Cryptozoid ale, and a Fire-Snorter, an OW drink that involved way too much alcohol and a match. As I picked up the Anadite brandy, I scanned the room, then abruptly put down the shot glass I'd been about to fill.

"Luke, has anything out of the ordinary happened to-night?" There was a sense of dread in the air, something out of kilter, and I didn't like the way it felt.

He shook his head. "Nope. Had to break up a brawl about an hour ago, though." With a nod, he directed my attention to one of the booths. "See that guy in the booth there?"

The man Luke pointed out looked like an OW Fae, but there was something odd about him. Something other-worldly that took him out of the Fae realm entirely.

"Yeah, what about him?" I kept my voice low. Odds were nobody could hear me over this din, but I wasn't taking chances. Almost all Supes had superior hearing and I never knew just who might be in the bar.

"I suddenly see this dude standing by the booth. Another guy shows up and they get into it. Loud and obnoxious. I'm not sure what the argument was over, but I tell you, this guy is scary. I pulled out the shotgun and was headed over to break it up, when all of a sudden, the other guy just vanishes. Poof."

Shit. Teleportation?

"So this guy takes a seat. I go over there to take his order and get a feel for what's going down. Damn, Menolly, I got the creeps so bad that I made Chrysandra take his order over. She came back smiling like she'd had a shot of joy-juice. Guy gave her a twenty-dollar tip."

Luke had a high fear threshold, so the fact that he'd been spooked by the stranger was as good as a warning.

"A twenty-dollar tip? What did he order?"

"Nothing odd. A glass of cognac, that's all." Luke paused, looking confused.

"What? What aren't you telling me?"

"It sounds a little nuts, though considering the crowd we get in here, I guess it shouldn't." He blinked and stared at me, unafraid. I liked that he didn't fear me. But then again, he'd never seen me with fangs out.

"Oh for cripes' sake . . . just tell me what happened. You

know who you're talking to. I won't think you're nuts." I folded my arms and waited.

"Okay, here's the deal. When I took his order, I . . . Menolly, you know I'm straight. You know I'm real straight, but damn, I wanted to crawl into the booth and make out with the guy. And then he looked right at me and said, *'Tell the pretty lady who owns the bar I need to talk to her.'* "

I frowned. No wonder Luke had been spooked. When he said he was straight as an arrow, he wasn't kidding. The guy was almost homophobic, which led me to wonder if he wasn't latent.

"So the strange Fae wants to talk to me?" That alone set off my warning bells. "Was there anything else you noticed? Anything at all?"

Luke frowned. "Let's see . . . yeah . . . I never saw him come in."

"Well, that's not so strange. You're busy, the room's full."

"Yeah, but here's the thing—I was keeping an eye on the door because Tavah was due to come in and I needed her help to get something off the top shelves in the storeroom. I didn't want to miss her." He paused, wiping the counter with his rag. "Next thing I know, the dude's having it out with the other guy. Neither one was in the room before that. I guarantee it."

I trusted Luke and his powers of observation. And the more I stared at the man in the booth, the more I realized he was no more Fae than Luke was.

"I'll be damned," I said, as a faint flicker of recognition tickled the back of my mind.

"Something wrong?"

"With my luck? Probably. Let me go talk to the guy." I handed Luke the drink order I'd just started to prepare and wove my way through the room, heading for the booth. Most of the customers recognized me and quickly moved out of the way. My reputation was set in granite and it was common knowledge that I was a vampire. Nobody gave me grief and when I was on shift, we didn't need a bouncer because everybody was too afraid of me to rock the boat.

As I approached the booth, I glanced at the man. He

wasn't Fae, not entirely, and definitely not one of the Sidhe, but he had a wild look to him and probably came from a feral branch of the family tree. His eyes narrowed as he looked me up and down, but he merely inclined his head and said nothing.

"I hear you're looking for me," I said, pulling up a chair. I turned it around and straddled it at the end of the booth. "Hear you had some trouble earlier. Luke was about ready to get out the shotgun. I don't like it when Luke has to get out the gun so maybe you'd better tell me what went down." I flashed him a hint of a smile and let my fangs down, just enough for the tips to show. "And introduce yourself."

The man blinked twice and then straightened his shoulders. Wearing a long black leather duster, a pair of indigo jeans, and a gray turtleneck, his brunette hair fell to his shoulders, and his eyes were green and glimmering with magic. "The name's Roz."

It was my turn to stare. "You're from Otherworld, I assume? What alliance do you claim?"

He gave me a faint grin. "None. I'm a mercenary. I work for the highest bidder, and currently I'm employed."

I leaned in, wary of the smug look that flickered in his eyes. "Maybe you'd better tell me who hired you before I decide to kick you out of the bar. There are certain groups from OW that aren't welcome in the Wayfarer."

Roz let out a snort. "Don't try your tricks on me. I know who you are, I know what you are, and none of that matters. I'm not in the Opium-Eater's hire. She's the least of our worries . . . but then, you know that."

He swung out of his seat and swaggered over to the jukebox, where he plugged a quarter into the slot and chose a song. Turning back to me, he held out his hand as he nodded to the dance floor.

Feeling like I was walking in a fog, I joined him as the industrial wailings of Yoko Kanno's "Lithium Flower" started. Roz took my hand and led me to the floor, pulling me close as the beat enveloped us in a frenzy of electronic thunder. He wrapped his arms around my waist and leaned his head down to burrow close to my neck. The smell of his cognac-soaked breath, the feel of his pulse as it raced through his fingers, intoxicated me as he swayed to the music, pulling me along with him, grinding his hips against mine.

"Why are you here?" I whispered, knowing he could pick up my words even though they were buried by the music.

"Queen Asteria hired me to come here and help you. I'm a bounty hunter. I specialize in vampires and greater demons."

There was something off about him, though, and I tuned in, trying to pick up on his energy. And then, I knew. "Not Fae. You're a minor demon."

He cocked his head. "Do tell?"

Studying his face, I could sense the charm oozing through every pore in his aura. Very few demons could pull off a glamour like this dude. As I ran through the categories in my mind, it hit me. "You've got to be kidding. Queen Asteria hired an incubus to help us?"

He snorted. "You have a problem with that?"

I pushed him to arm's length. You don't tempt the devil when you're trying to retain some control. As a vampire, I was immune to a lot of charm, but an incubus—and this one in particular—well, I didn't want to count on my self-control. I hated to think what he could do with Camille, and I was determined to squash that possibility in the bud before it had a chance to flower.

"Other than the fact that you're a demon—"

"So are you." He was quick on the ball, all right.

I raised my hand to stop him before he could continue. "Other than the fact that you're a demon? Well, you've already instigated a disturbance in my bar and you haven't been here twenty-four hours, yet. Have you?"

He shook his head. "Nope. How'd you know?"

"You still smell like Otherworld." And he did. I could smell the scent of starberry flowers and usha trees on him. He must have come in from a portal near the southern regions. "Well, this is just dandy. So is Roz really your name, or is it a ruse?" I motioned him to follow me back to the bar.

He obeyed but I caught the edge of his lips curling in smug satisfaction. Incubi weren't always evil; therefore, if

Queen Asteria thought he had some redeeming qualities, he probably did. But they *always* managed to encourage havoc wherever they went. They could charm the pants off just about anybody, straight or gay. Including a number of husbands who let them get away with murder, or at least with screwing their wives. Incubi were hardwired for giving and taking pleasure.

The incubus stared at me for a moment, then shrugged. "My name's Roz, short for Rozurial."

"Why do you hunt your own kind?" I was suspicious of a demon who hunted other demons, although I suppose I could technically be accused of the same thing.

"I'm out to protect myself, and I like money," he said. "Besides, I don't hunt down my own kind. I only tend to track greater demons and vampires. I've been in the business seven hundred years, crossing between Otherworld and Earthside in search of one vampire in particular. I finally located him back in OW, but when I broke into his nest, he was gone. His trail led me to the Elfin Queen. She listened to me—under a truthseer's scrutiny, I might add—and then sent me to you." His somber expression made me feel like I was balancing precariously over the abyss.

I knew the answer to my next question before I even asked it. It was one of those moments where, against all better judgment, I had to find out for sure. "What vampire are you talking about?"

Roz leaned across the bar and in a voice as cold as my skin, said, "Do I have to spell it out for you? D-R-E-D-G-E . . . the scourge of the land."

I leaned against the bar, and for the first time in a long, long while, I felt faint. Queen Asteria had warned us that the Elwing Clan might be headed our way. Now it looked like she was right. Why else would she send this bounty hunter to us?

"Are you sure he's crossed over?"

"He and a few of his mangy crew, led by that nature freak you dumped on the Queen's doorstep." At my look of surprise, he held up his hand. "I know all about the situation. And I also know that Dredge captured you. I know what he does to his victims, Menolly. Except you, he turned. My sister, my mother, and my brother, he tossed aside when he was done with his fun. Seven hundred years ago, he sucked them dry, tore them from limb to limb, and then fed what was left to a pack of hellhounds. I was hiding in the attic, watching through the floorboards. I was seven years old. I saw everything."

He was telling the truth. I could see it in his face, I could hear it in his voice. Dredge had destroyed his family.

"You weren't an incubus then, were you?"

Roz shook his head. "No, but that's another story, for another time."

"Then we have something in common." I straightened my shoulders and glanced out the front windows into the dark, snow-filled night. "Do you know where he is?"

"Not yet," Roz said, "But I intend on finding out."

"Don't you dare kill him," I said. "Don't you dare dust him without letting me be the one to plunge that stake through his heart. Your family died, and I understand your pain. But they're with your ancestors now. I'm still here, and I know *exactly* what Dredge does to his playthings. I can *never* forget it." I thought for a moment. "Who was the dude you were mixing it up with earlier? Luke said he just vanished."

Roz grinned sheepishly. "Local vampire. His daughter's still alive and I slept with her, thinking I might be able to get a lead on where the sub-cult clubs are but all I got was a bad bruise when her father showed up in her bedroom. She doesn't know he's a vampire, turns out, and he was keeping watch over her. Kicked my butt and then followed me to kick it some more and warn me that if I ever touch his daughter again, he'll summon a Protector so fast that I'll be sucked into the Subterranean Realms and never be able to get free."

I blinked. Well, well, well . . . a vampire who could summon a Protector? The spiritual guard dogs were usually only accessible to high level mages or witches, and they were often used to catch and deport unwanted netherworld creatures. Did we have a vamp running around who had access to magic? It was something to talk over with Wade, that was for sure.

"So, do we have a deal? We work together to find Dredge. When we do, I'll let you have the honor of dispatching him, as long as I get to watch?" Roz's smile told me he was certain I'd say yes. I found myself smiling back. I didn't trust him, but the old saying wasn't a bad one. *The enemy of my enemy is my friend.*

"I'll think about it," I said. "But there's one condition. I want your oath, or you can just walk out that door and go back to hunting through bedrooms for clues to Dredge's whereabouts."

"What's that?" Roz leaned against the counter, folding his arms. He winked at me, but I ignored the come-on. It was second nature to an incubus to try and seduce any woman within arm's reach. I had no plans on giving him the opportunity of adding me to what was no doubt an incredibly long list of conquests.

"My sisters—they're beautiful. You leave them alone. I find you trying to seduce one of them and I will make sure you're off Earthside and headed forcibly to the Sub Realms. They have enough troubles without adding an incubus's wandering hands to the list."

He snorted. "But if they make the first move—"

"Then you very politely thank them, tell them you're flattered, but refuse. Get it?" Hands on my hips, I leaned toward him, and gently smiled to show him the tips of my fangs.

With a cough, he straightened his shoulders. "Got it. No problem. Now, when do I get to meet these delightful treats?"

"Just as soon as I'm off work," I muttered. "Go back to your drink." As he moved to return to the booth, I stopped him. "By the way, how did you get through the portal without us knowing?"

Roz laughed then, a full, rich, deep-throated chuckle. "I didn't use the Wayfarer's portal. Let's just say that we incubi have our own methods of transportation." With that, he saluted me and returned to the booth.

First chance I had, I called home to tell them about Roz and ask whether they wanted to meet me in town, or whether I

.should bring him out to the house. Both Camille and Delilah felt it safer to drive in to talk to him after hours rather than let him know where we lived, at least until we had a better idea of what he was up to. They showed up near two A.M., closing time for the Wayfarer, and settled into a booth to wait.

I could see Roz looking them over but when I glared at him, he went back to nursing his second snifter of cognac. As Chrysandra and I put away the last of the glasses and finished cleaning the counters and tabletops, there was a noise at the door. I hadn't bothered to lock it before cleaning up, just flipped the OPEN sign to CLOSED. The door slammed open and as I turned to tell whoever it was that we were closed, I saw Chase and Sharah standing there.

"What's wrong?" I hurried over to them. Both looked woozy, and Chase, especially, looked like he was about to puke. I led him to a chair as Delilah rushed over and knelt beside him. Camille hurried behind the counter to get a little sparkling water and ice for him to sip.

As he tried to gather his composure, tasting the water with tiny sips, Sharah looked up at us, her expression pained. "The vampires have struck again . . ."

"Damn it, I was afraid of that. Wait," I said, "are you talking about the original ones or—"

"Or the four newbies?" She flinched. "We don't know; it could be either. For all we know, the newborns could have joined up with their sires. Whatever the case, we've got three new bodies in the morgue and I'm afraid they're going to rise. How long do we have?"

I glanced at the clock. "Depends on when they were killed. Depends on how they were killed, and how much blood from their sires they drank. Come on," I tossed the rag on the counter. "Chrysandra, finish cleaning up. Lock the door after we leave and call Togo to come walk you to your car. If he bitches, tell him I'll rip out his throat if he doesn't haul his lazy ass over here. I'm not kidding." Unlike Tavah, Chrysandra was no vampire and she was all too vulnerable. She nodded, keeping her eyes on the counter.

Camille, Delilah, Roz, and I followed Chase and Sharah out to the street. Chase had brought an SUV.

"Get in, we don't have time for everybody to find their respective cars." The fact that he didn't even ask who Roz was told me how upset he must be. Chase was all about caution.

We packed into the back seats and Sharah rode shotgun. As we headed toward the hospital, I prayed that they were wrong, that it was just some everyday nut job who'd decided to go Freddy Krueger on his victims. The last thing we needed was a growing nest of bloodthirsty vampires in the city. News like that couldn't be kept quiet for long.

As Chase flipped a switch and the siren began to scream, I looked over at Roz. He stared back at me, a look so deadly on his face that I only prayed I'd find Dredge first. Because from his expression, it was clear that Roz wasn't about to take prisoners. And I wanted first crack at my sire.

CHAPTER 6

A cold wind was moaning in off the harbor, rattling the windows of the car as the lights of the city passed in a blur on our way to the FH-CSI morgue. The skyscrapers lined the horizon like a string of diamonds. I-5 was empty at this time of night, and I glanced at an overpass as we sped by. We were in a race against time, but how much we had, I didn't know. I'd never sired another vampire, nor did I plan on doing so. But now I wished I'd talked to the older vamps around town about the process. Knowledge, even dark knowledge, is better than ignorance.

"Chase, were the bodies found together like the other four? That might indicate they were killed by the same vampire—or group of vamps—who killed our missing newbies. The last thing we need is a bunch of bloodsuckers scattered around the city, randomly attacking people."

He let out a sigh. "Yeah, but they weren't anywhere near the Delmonico Cinema. We found this trio over in the Green Lake district. In Green Lake park, actually."

Delilah gasped and I elbowed her quickly but gently, giving her a warning shake of the head. Sassy Branson lived in the Green Lake area. Could she be involved in this? We'd attended her Christmas party the month before.

Sassy was a socialite whose friends still thought she was alive. She pulled off the reclusive eccentric with elegant panache, and had done her best to keep her death secret. She lived in fear of being outed. With impeccable manners, she was the last vampire in the world I'd expect to take a savage turn. But the predatory instinct eventually took over most vamps. Was it possible that we weren't facing down Dredge after all? Had something shifted in Sassy's nature? No, I refused to believe it. But she *might* know something about the murders.

I kept my mouth shut as we burst through the doors and hurried down the stairs, past the magical sensors to the morgue. The OIA techs were standing sentinel, guarding the bodies. The reek of formaldehyde and disinfectant permeated the corridor, and both Camille and Delilah looked ready to puke, but the smell just floated on by me as I turned my attention to the room.

We could have been in a bus station, for all the lockers that covered the walls. Or a school. But behind the doors of those gray metal compartments lay the remains of carnage and time. Tables lined with instruments filled the room. Scalpels. Scissors. Saws. Bright lights hung from the ceiling, tools to destroy illusions, to invade and explore and discover. Jars filled with odd shapes floating in them rested in rows on a shelf.

Look close, look away. At the end of the day, I thought, *this is all that remains.* I tried to wrench my gaze away, but the circus of colors and shapes fascinated me.

In the center of the room stood six long tables, and on three of those tables were bodies covered with sheets so pristine, so white they were spun sugar on snow. Brilliant, unnatural. Where were the stains? No laundry in the world could erase the scars of blood that tattoo the dead.

Chase motioned me over. "It might be better if the others stand back, just in case something happens."

"Just in case the victims rise, you mean."

He nodded and leaned close to me. "If that happens, do

you think you can handle them? I've never fought a vampire and I'm not sure how to go about it. And neither have the techs here." With a glance at the others, he added, "I don't want to see Camille or Delilah get hurt . . . or anybody else."

He made a good point. And the truth was, I wasn't sure I could take on all three before they got past me to the others. When they rose—if they did—they'd be ravenous, looking for the nearest jugulars to satisfy their thirst. And they'd drain their victims dry, and the next, and the next. On the way home, after I rose, I'd left a trail of carnage that I could still see if I closed my eyes and let myself remember. By the time I reached our house, I'd managed to quench my thirst enough to lock myself in my room and yell for Camille to get help. And then, it was all black, for months. A black abyss, a void in my memory that I'd never, ever remember. Memories I didn't want to reclaim.

I thought for a moment, then turned to the others. "Get out. Roz, you stay. You're an incubus, you'll be able to help me. But the rest of you—Chase, that includes you—get out and bar the door until I tell you it's okay. And peek through the windows to make sure it's me giving you the A-OK and not somebody trying to mimic my voice."

Camille and Delilah started to protest but when I shook my head, they herded everybody else out of the room. I turned to Roz. "You ready? If they rise, chances are their sires are from the Elwing Clan, as much as I don't want to believe it. I expect you to follow my instructions if you're working with me. You aren't in this game alone. Got it?"

He gave me a lazy smile. "Got stakes?"

I blinked, realizing that I didn't exactly walk around carrying wooden pointy things. "Uh . . ."

"No? I thought so." He stood back and unbuttoned his duster.

I had a sudden giggle fit when he grabbed the lapels and opened the coat, reminding me of some two-bit sleazy flasher from the wrong side of the tracks, but my giggles were cut short when I saw the arsenal attached to the inner lining. Wooden stakes, daggers, a nasty looking semiautomatic, a blowgun, shooting stars, a pair of nunchakus, and

I'm not sure what else dangled from their respective loops. This bounty hunter meant business all right, and it was obviously he'd spent considerable time Earthside.

He smiled at my reaction. "Catch." He pulled out a couple of stakes and tossed them to me, square end first. I caught them, cautiously giving them the once over. A simple stake, and yet it could dust me for good. Of course, it could kill a human, too, if properly aimed with enough force, but to my eyes, the toothpick on steroids had that whole mystique thing going on and I couldn't help but feel like I was holding a time bomb.

"Thanks, I think." I glanced up as he pulled out a pair for himself. "I guess we'd better see what we're up against." I edged forward to the first body and yanked the sheet off, jumping back out of reach.

The man on the slab was a big one. Tall, with bushy gray hair, his chest a barrel. His abs covered with a layer of fat but definitely steel belted—it would be hard to take him down in a fight. And from a peek under the covers, it was obvious that he'd probably made some woman very happy. He could have been a mountain man, an old hippy, a retired football player gone ZZ Top. But whatever he'd been, he would never again walk in the daylight. His face was frozen in horrified terror, caught by the folds of his wrinkles.

"What's that around his mouth?" Roz pointed to something that had dried to the skin, maroon and splattered.

I leaned close, sniffing. "Blood." I pried open the man's lips. Blood had dried on his teeth, too, and as I watched, thin, needle-sharp teeth were descending out of his gums to cover his incisors. I let go and jumped back. "He's turning. I don't know when he'll wake, but it won't be long."

Roz and I quickly examined the other two—a young Japanese woman who could have been a model, she was so pretty, and a nondescript young man probably in his late twenties. Both were on their way to signing up for my side of the street. I looked at Roz, hesitating. I'd never staked one of my own. While I didn't have any qualms about it, somehow it seemed unfair to kill them because of what they were, before they'd had a chance to do anything.

"You know when they rise, they'll go on a rampage without their sires here to guide them through the transformation." He tapped the stainless steel slab. "We have to do it."

He was right, but it still seemed one more step toward a life from which my sisters and I would never be able to return. We were quickly sliding into territory in which lived only the most hardened agents from the OIA. The shadows were unrelenting when asked to give up those who walked their paths.

A thought struck me. "What if they head back to their sire? Shouldn't we follow one? They might lead us to Dredge and the Elwing Clan."

Roz frowned. "That means letting one of them go free to wreak havoc. Are you willing to sacrifice innocent lives to these monsters? If you are, then by all means, I'll stand back and let one of them go, but it's on your head."

Damn it, I didn't want the choice. I weighed the benefits. If the vamp made its way back to Dredge, we'd be able to track it and bingo, have one up on the Elwing Blood Clan. But what if it didn't go back to Dredge? What if, instead, the new vamp just went on a murderous drinking spree and left a trail of bodies in its wake? Could I sacrifice innocents on hope alone?

I didn't have to ask Camille and Delilah, I already knew what their answers would be. I sucked in a deep breath and walked over to the mountain man. "I guess we'd better stake them before they wake up."

As I stared at the naked man, I knew precisely what he'd be thinking. Images of his death would run through his mind, along with the realization that he was forever trapped inside his all-too-dead body. And then, the thirst would hit, and the rage. And when those took over, everything else went out the window.

The burly corpse suddenly sat up, his gaze darting around the room.

"Holy crap!" I jumped back as he took a swipe at me, thanking my reflexes. A newborn's hunger pangs hurt so badly that they empowered the fresh vamp with phenomenal strength.

Within a fraction of a second, he was off the table, eyes burning bloody crimson, and he was headed right for me. As I crouched in position, the sheet on the second table fluttered and the young Japanese woman sat up. Roz raised one of the stakes and cautiously moved in, the hem of his duster fluttering against his long legs.

"Be careful, Roz! She's small but deadly." My shout startled Mr. Meaty. The big man jerked his head around, staring at Roz, as confusion rippled across his face.

And then, it was all about the fight.

I hoisted one of the stakes in my left hand while sliding the other through my belt, point to the side so I wouldn't suffer a nasty accident if I fell. Then I waggled my fingers, beckoning him in. "Bring it on, boy. Come and get me."

With his massive head of frizzy hair cascading around his shoulders, the naked behemoth lurched toward me, eyes aflame. He sniffed the air and paused.

"That's right, you can't smell a pulse. It's because I'm one of your own kind." As I muttered an oath, he lunged. I swiped with the stake, missing by inches, and suddenly we were entwined in a grappling match. He clapped his hands against the sides of my shoulders and shoved, slamming me to the floor. I arched my back and vaulted to my feet, landing with ease. Thanks to my training, my acrobatic skills had blossomed after death. I was twice as quick as most vamps. My adversary glanced at the doors leading out of the morgue. If he could get to them before me, he could escape to hunt.

"You want to feed? You have to get through me first," I said, jumping between the newborn and the doors.

As I waited for him to bring it on, a glance showed me Roz was in the midst of a life or death struggle. The young woman—strike that, newborn vamp—was straining to reach his neck. She could kill him, but Roz's demonic nature was a big plus. It would give him an edge that might just keep him alive.

The third vamp hadn't risen yet, but we didn't have much time. I turned my attention back to the burly man, who was angling, trying to get past me. I feinted to the left, letting him think I'd taken too wide of a step. As he charged the door, I whirled, stake in hand, to meet him chest level. The wooden point plunged deep, impaling him with muscle-rending impact.

He turned to me, holding out his arms, a pleading look on his face. He was an animal at this moment, a frightened and hungry creature. The pain and confusion in his eyes made my gut ache. Been there, done that. Didn't like being reminded of it. And then, he was dust, bursting into a cloud of smoke and powder. The stake fell to the ground.

I snatched it up and raced over to the still-covered third body, shoving a lab cart out of the way. The tray tipped, instruments spilling everywhere, the sound of metal and breaking glass shattering the air like an alarm. I leapt over the mess, raising my stake above the third body.

Twitch. The vamp was about to rise. Oh shit. I brought the stake up and plunged it through his heart before he could open his eyes. He let out a long whispering sigh, sounding like a breeze filtering through a hollow husk, and then vanished in a puff of dust and ashes.

Two down. I turned my attention to Roz. He was just bringing his stake down into the girl's chest and she let out a screech as she, too, disappeared into the abyss.

The immediate danger gone, I felt my legs ripple and I slid down onto the floor, staring at the stakes. Roz joined me.

"You okay?" he asked.

I shrugged. "There but for the grace of the gods, go I . . ."

"Nope. It won't happen. I watched you take down those two vamps. You're a survivor, Menolly. That's how you managed to break away from Dredge when he'd stripped everything he could from you. That's how you managed to fight your way back from the madness that he inflicted on you."

At my look of surprise, he pushed a lock of unruly hair off his forehead. "I know more than you think I do. Anyway, we still don't know where the Elwing Blood Clan is, but we'll find them. Don't worry."

"Right." He might know a lot about me, but I still didn't know him well enough to trust him. And yet . . . Roz seemed to be determined to help. And if it *was* Dredge and the Elwing Blood Clan, we needed everybody we could scare up

for the hunt. I pushed myself up and dusted off my jeans,
then held out my hand, yanking him to his feet.

"Come on, we need to let the others know we're okay. We
have to figure out what the fuck is going on before it gets any
worse."

On the way back to the bar, I asked Chase, "So what are you
going to tell their families? And what did you tell the families of the first four?"

He paled. "Officially, we haven't found any of the missing. Since we run everything, including the bodies, through
the FH-CSI office, we can fudge documents, as much as I
hate doing it. All the techs from the investigation at the theater were our men, and we told the management there that a
police informant had gotten beat up. Hush hush stuff. If any
of their staff was found discussing it, they could go to jail."

"That's using your badge," Camille muttered, grinning.
"You know somebody's going to leak something to the
tabloids."

"Probably, but we can't control everything." He rolled his
eyes. "You know, as well as I do, that everything had to be
done in secret because they were vamp murders. There
isn't—nor will there ever be—a record of those bodies. I
hate doing this to the families, leaving them to wonder why
their loved ones vanished, but at the moment, that's all we
can do if we don't want full-scale panic to break out."

"Any missing person reports filed yet?" Delilah asked.

He shook his head. "Not yet, but my guess is by tomorrow. We'll officially 'look into the situation' but we can't
keep up this charade. Seven people in two nights? Camille's
right—this kind of story doesn't stay under wraps for long
and pretty soon some savvy reporter's going to put things together. At the least, the department's going to take shit for
not having a clue as to what happened to those going AWOL."

Delilah's cell let out an obnoxious series of beeps and she
flipped it open and spoke in low tones. After a minute, she
folded it closed and smiled. "Well, one bit of good news. I put

out the call for a community Supe meeting. Seems like Zach, Siobhan, and Wade have been broadcasting like crazy because it's on for tomorrow night. We'll meet at the V.A. hall."

At least one thing was going right, I thought. But something nagged at me. I looked over at Roz. "Have you ever been to Aladril?"

He blinked. "No, actually, I haven't. Their city is highly warded against astral demons such as myself. I tried to get in once and couldn't set foot through the city gates. They don't need much of a military with their magical abilities, I'll tell you that much."

No wonder they weren't worried about the war between Lethesanar and Tanaquar. Any city that had the ability to magically deny entry to demons was far more powerful than Y'Elestrial's queen, or the sister battling for the crown.

Camille looked at me. "You really think we should go, don't you?"

I gave her a curt nod. "As in, yesterday. Queen Asteria told us to find the seer named Jareth. She seems convinced that the Elwing Blood Clan is behind this; she sent Roz to help us out because of that. Maybe this Jareth can give us some insight. After all, we aren't making much progress on our own, are we?"

"We don't even know what we're up against," she said, glancing at Delilah. "Not really. I think Menolly's right. But we'll have to leave at dusk and return before dawn. Tomorrow night's no good, with the Supe meeting. What about the night after—Sunday night?"

Delilah shrugged. "Fine with me. What do you think?" she asked, glancing in my direction.

I frowned. "If we have to wait until Sunday, then Sunday night it is. But don't be surprised if we see more dead bodies and more vamps rising."

"Why is the Elwing Blood Clan doing this?" Chase asked. "I thought Wisteria would try to help them head for the Sub Realms."

I stared out the window. "Maybe that's not their primary focus. Maybe they're out to raise some other sort of havoc."

Camille blinked. "Scary thought."

Chase dropped us off at the bar. While he and Delilah said good night with a little make-out fest, I leaned against the building, talking to Roz.

"I'll contact you tomorrow night," he said. "I'll be at your meeting. Until then, keep watch, and be wary." His eyes flashed a dangerous shade of desire as he gazed at Camille. She was heading toward her car.

"Remember what I told you," I whispered. "One slip and I'll make sure it's your last."

He snorted, but inclined his head. "Perhaps you'd care to take my mind off her?"

If I hadn't been a vampire, he would have had me right there. I could feel his focus, the sensual thrust of his words. Incubi were sex incarnate, and there was a reason they never wanted for partners.

"Be careful what you wish for," I told him. "Trust me, there are some paths not safe for even demons like you to tread. I take no lovers, and with good reason."

As Roz headed down the street, Delilah broke away from Chase. "Drive safe, babe," she said.

"I'm heading back to the lab to give Sharah a ride home," he said.

Delilah blew him a kiss and headed over to Camille's Lexus.

As Chase pulled out of his parking spot, I watched him drive away. He looked weary. As had Sharah. I wondered what it must be like, working with the dead and injured day after day.

It was one thing to walk among the undead. We were trapped in our bodies, living in limbo but still in existence. But the healers and medics who worked in silence at the sides of those who'd crossed over, who tended wounds and held the hands of those in pain . . . they were a special breed.

And for someone like Sharah, niece to Queen Asteria, to stand her ground even when a horde of demons was headed our way . . . Well, in my book, she had more balls than most men I'd ever met. This wasn't even her world. But OW was one step away from Earth, and would be next in line when Earth fell. Without our help, both worlds were doomed.

There was no question of "if it happened" . . . only when.

Iris was waiting up for us as we trekked into the house. She waved a video camera. She beamed as we came in. "I've got wonderful news!"

Camille dropped into the rocker and leaned her head back. "We could use some, believe me," she said.

Delilah slumped on the sofa and began to pull off her boots. "Man, am I beat. I got contracted for a possible case, by the way, so I should be bringing in some more money in a few weeks. Some sort of cheating spouse thing again, I think. Boring, but it pays the bills."

Now that we were responsible for our own expenses, we all were working harder. It had been kind of fun when the OIA paid our freight and our day jobs were covers, but now that we were fending for ourselves we had to make sure we brought in enough to cover expenses. Luckily, both buildings—the Wayfarer and the Indigo Crescent—had been bought outright by the OIA, who seemed to have dropped all interest in them when Lethesanar stirred the cauldron with her dirty little war.

Iris eyed Camille and Delilah, a frown playing across her face. "I notice neither one of you touched your suppers. They're still in the refrigerator. Something wrong with my cooking?"

"Of course not." Camille yawned. "We had to go meet Menolly down at the bar, so we didn't get a chance to eat. I could sure go for a plate of lasagna right about now, though."

"Me too!" Delilah flashed the house sprite a bright grin and looked ever so hopeful.

"Yeah, yeah." Iris snorted. "You both eat like farmers. I'll heat your plates in a moment, but before another—" Here she stopped and looked at me. "I know you have bad news, it's written all over your face. But hold it for a moment."

I held up my hands, shaking my head. "Not a word. Not a word."

"Good." She held up her video camera and motioned for us to gather round. Camille and Delilah groaned, but Iris wouldn't take no for an answer. "Get your butts over here. You're a long sight younger than I am and I'm not complaining, so hurry it up."

We gathered around her and she set the camera to playback. There, in living color, was our Maggie, taking her very first steps by herself. The little gargoyle clutched at the coffee table as she came to the end, holding herself upright, and then, one finger at a time, she let go, balancing precariously as she toddled toward the camera, arms outstretched.

We could hear Iris murmuring in the background and then Maggie took two steps, let out a particularly loud *mooph* and fell back on her butt, her tail splaying out to the side. She started to wail and the camera went dark, but there it was, in full glory. Maggie's first steps on her own.

Delilah clapped her hands and Camille immediately headed toward the kitchen while I grabbed Iris and spun her around, proud as punch of our little girl.

"Put me down this instant!" Iris said and I complied. When Iris chose to be stern, her voice took on that do-not-disobey-me tone and nobody, not even me, ignored it. "And just where do you think you're going?" she added, pointing at Camille.

Camille stopped in midstep. "Nowhere," she said, turning with a grin on her face. Uh huh, score one for Iris.

"You're going to wake up Maggie, aren't you? Well, I won't have it. That poor baby's sleep schedule is scattered to the winds thanks to the three of you. You have to start coordinating your play time with her or she's going to be all out of sorts. I just got her down to sleep an hour ago and she's going to *stay* asleep, so keep out of my room. You can give her a kiss tomorrow. Menolly, you can peek in on her before you go down for the day, but don't you dare wake her if she's still snoring."

Her hands on her hips, Iris looked ready to take on the world.

Even I had to admit that I wouldn't want to face her when she was in fighting form. For one thing, none of us were quite sure just how strong a Talon-haltija's powers were. But we'd seen some fairly impressive displays and we knew they weren't the sum of her talents.

"Iris is right," I said, glancing at Delilah and Camille. "We should work up some sort of a play schedule. We all like to tote Maggie around, and it's not fair to her if we can't get our act together."

Delilah grabbed her laptop off the coffee table. "Let's just do it, then, while Iris is making our dinner."

Iris nodded her head. "Smart girls. And I thought you'd like that news. You can tell me what happened tonight after you get your schedule together. Post a copy on the bulletin board in the kitchen so I know who's planning what."

As she left the room, Delilah pulled up Word, and created a new file using a calendar template. "We'll start with one week. When does Maggie need her naps? Does anybody know?"

Pushing thoughts of rogue vampires and grisly murders to the side for the moment, I settled in on her right as Camille curled up on her left. We glanced at each other and though it went unspoken, I knew they, too, were grateful for something to think about that wasn't covered in blood, reeking of demon scent.

CHAPTER 7

We finished the schedule and posted it on the bulletin board while Iris served up Delilah and Camille's dinners. As they ate, we told her about Roz and the three new victims.

"So you've no idea why they were chosen?" Iris dished out second helpings to my sisters. I wasn't fond of watching people eat—it brought up too many memories of being alive and how much I'd loved a good meal—but I put aside my discomfort for the sake of discussion.

I shook my head. "No. We really don't know any more than we did before, except that these murders took place up in the Green Lake area."

"That's where Sassy lives," Delilah said, stabbing a noodle with her fork.

"Which is why I'm going to pay her a visit tonight." I leaned back in my chair and crossed my legs.

Iris frowned. "Do you think she had anything to do with it?"

Camille and Delilah both jerked their heads up. Apparently the thought hadn't occurred to them, though it had lurked in the depths of my brain.

I shook my head. "Sassy doesn't strike me as the type to play renegade, but then again, when . . . if . . . the predatory nature takes over, she might lose the ethics she's tried to cultivate since her transformation."

Camille glanced at me. "What do your instincts tell you?"

I stared at the table a moment, trying to explain. "My instincts aren't like yours. And vampires are adept at hiding themselves, at cloaking their true natures. I honestly don't know, though I doubt she's behind any of this. I'm pretty sure we're dealing with Dredge." After a moment, I looked up to find Camille watching me, a strange expression on her face. "You're wondering about me, aren't you?"

She sputtered. "No, not at all—I didn't mean anything—"

Delilah paled and dropped her napkin on the floor. I sighed, leaning my head back to study the ceiling. "It's okay. Really. I know you're still wary of me. And you should be. I will never hurt you . . . not so long as I know what I'm doing. But we have to face facts. I'm a demon now. Sometimes things happen." I raised my head, feeling the tears well up in my eyes. Damned emotions—even though they'd been altered, they were still there.

Camille leaned forward, pushing her plate back, her expression somber. "What do you want us to do if you ever . . ."

"If I ever lose control? If the predator within fully takes over?" I stared at her, unblinking. "Stake me. Kill me any way you can. I refuse to let Dredge win. I refuse to become a carbon copy of that deranged sadist. I'd rather return to our ancestors than stay alive as a monster."

Delilah's lip trembled and she began to shiver. I motioned to Camille, who hurried around the table. "Delilah," she said, "honey, it's okay. Everything's okay—"

"We're just speaking hypothetically, Kitten. Don't worry—"

The words barely left my mouth when a shower of golden light surrounded Delilah and she began to transform. Shit. Both Camille and I should have known better than to bring up such a sensitive subject without warning her. Even though Delilah was marked as a Death Maiden serving the

Autumn Lord now, even though she was able to shift into a black panther when he ordered her to, at heart, she was still that fragile golden tabby cat.

Camille reached her first. Delilah looked up from the floor and mewed, and Camille held out her arms. With a single leap, Delilah hurtled into her arms and buried her head in Camille's substantial boobs.

"I didn't think," she said. "Or I would have asked you privately, then broached the subject to Delilah slowly." She sat down in Delilah's chair and stroked her long fur gently, kissing the top of the cat's forehead. "Oh baby, for all your bravado, you're still too gentle hearted." Camille gave me a bleak look. "I worry about her in the coming war. Shadow Wing's only thrown his minor minions at us. What happens when the hordes break through?"

I shook my head. "We deal with that when it happens. Delilah will survive. That mark on her forehead guarantees her an ally stronger than demons. Nobody can best Death . . . or his henchmen. And like it or not, our sister's now married to the Lord of the Harvest. It will take her some time, but want to make a bet she ends up tougher than either one of us?"

Iris had remained silent during our exchange. Now, she pushed herself off of her stool and skirted the table to take Delilah from Camille, resting Kitten over her shoulder. Delilah complied without protest, her wide round eyes staring at the wall with that cat like single-minded gaze.

"You girls are *all* stronger than you think," Iris said. "You have to be. And I'll be there by your side, no matter what happens. And I'm pretty sure that at the Supe meeting tomorrow night, you'll realize just how many allies you're gathering. Word's gotten around."

"What do you mean?" I stared at Iris.

She tilted her head to one side and a sly smile crept to her lips. "Think about it for a moment. The Hunters Moon Clan—one of the more feared Were clans in the area— wiped out." She snapped her fingers. "Decimated in one night. Everybody knows who's to thank for that. People know you have a dragon on your side. Why, even Delilah's transformation into a Death Maiden has hit the grapevine. You don't realize just how famous you're becoming. When the Sub-Cult network figures out what's really going down with Shadow Wing, they'll want to survive. They'll follow you, when push comes to shove."

Camille dusted off her dress and returned to her meal.

I closed my eyes. "Weary is he who wears the crown of a king," I said.

"Don't set yourself up on a throne yet," Iris warned me. "Wearier yet are those who seek to knock it off his head, and more desperate. The battle lines are being drawn." She sat back and closed her eyes. The energy in the room grew thick and Delilah settled down on her chest, purring. "Over the coming months, the Supe community will be coming out of the closet and banding together. There are going to be rough times ahead. I'm afraid humans will think the Supes are rising against them. If so . . ."

"Gang warfare." Camille slid off her chair and knelt beside Iris. "Iris, are you a seer?"

A slow smile spread across the Talon-haltija's face and she let out a whispered, "When the need arises. There are many things I've done in my past that you know nothing about. Trust me, I'm here for a reason." And then, without opening her eyes, she turned toward me. "You *must* go to Aladril. *He* is waiting for you. Do you understand?"

A shiver ran through me, chilling me far colder than the death pall of my skin. Magic was in the air, the magic of Sight, the magic of prognostication, the magic of wind and ice, which Iris wielded with skill.

"We're going Sunday night."

Camille placed one hand on Iris's knee. "Is there anything you need? Anything you require?"

Iris let out a soft breath. "Bring me a crystal. You may have to buy it from one of the shops. Aqualine—a clear blue stone that only comes from the depths of the Wyvern Ocean. Sirens mine it and sell it to the seers. It will cost more than you can afford, but tell them that a priestess of Undutar needs it. That should do the trick."

"Undutar?" As I spoke, Iris shook out of her trance and

blinked. I was about to ask again when Delilah let out a loud purp and leapt down from Iris's shoulder, racing toward the curtains. She only made it halfway before the golden mist surrounded her and her body began to transform, contorting in on itself as she twisted in the most painful-looking convulsions, a blur of fur and flesh caught in the throes of our family's magic. As she landed on her knees, letting out a loud "oof," Camille rushed over to her side.

I looked at Iris, who gazed silently back. When I opened my mouth to speak, she shook her head. "Don't ask. Not yet. It's not the time, Menolly. I couldn't tell you about my relationship to Undutar even if you threatened me. There are events in my past about which I cannot speak . . ." Her words drifted off as her eyes sparkled with a shining vortex of light. The silver of the moon, the indigo of twilight, white clouds racing past on the wind.

Iris let out a long sigh, and then her eyes once more returned to the color of morning sky. As much as she'd piqued my curiosity, I knew better than to press. Iris would tell us when—and if—she could. I nodded silently, then hurried over to help Camille with Delilah, who was looking dazed, but no worse for the wear.

"You okay, Kitten?" I asked as she slid into her chair.

Camille picked up the teapot and began refilling their cups.

Delilah nodded, blushing. "Sorry. I thought I was gaining more control over my shifting but apparently I'm not. Either that or it's just as sporadic as Camille's magic."

"Hey!" Camille stopped in midpour. "I'll have you know, I'm doing much better on certain spells now."

"Yeah, if you count death magic. But I'm talking about moon magic—your *innate* skills." Delilah gave her a toothy grin. "I'm not being snide, Camille. You seem to have a knack for the dark magic that Morio's teaching you, but can you honestly say you're any better with the spells you learned from childhood?"

Camille let out a loud sigh. "I don't know. And I don't understand why I take to death magic so well. It's rather unnerving, but I know I have to learn what he's teaching me. It feels important, but I don't know why." She glanced at the clock. "We all need sleep. As it is, Delilah and I will only manage a few hours. Menolly, we'll wake you up before the meeting and all head out together."

I nodded as the two of them gave me a peck on the cheek, waved to Iris, then headed upstairs. They walked in the world of the day. I lived during the nighttime. Two very different worlds, separated by the sun.

"I guess I'll head out to Sassy's." I pushed myself out of the chair and glanced at the clock. Still four hours till sunrise. Plenty of time to drive over to the Green Lake area and see if anything was going down that I should know about. "Iris, keep watch over the place," I said.

She patted my hand. "I always do, my dear. You be careful, you hear?"

"Loud and clear," I said, snatching up my keys and purse as I headed out the door for my Jag.

The drive to Sassy's took about twenty minutes this time of night. Seattle's streets were clear, with only the occasional car slinking through the dimly lit streets. The ice still frozen on the pavement shimmered under the street lights and the world felt muffled, hushed by the cushion of snow that had frozen solid over the past few days. Once again, I made a note to ask Camille about the winter. She and Iris could look into it and see if there was anything magical going on behind the sudden Arctic freeze that still held Seattle in its grip.

Sassy's house was actually a mansion, set back on two acres of well-kept grounds with a spiked fence that circled the property. The actual gate worked on an intercom system and so I punched the button, grateful that I wouldn't need to get out of the car and open the thing myself. Not that the cold would bother me or the work, or even the iron—much—if I hurried, but the night had already been stressful. I wanted this visit to go nice and easy.

"Yes?" Janet's voice echoed out of the intercom. Sassy's assistant, Janet, had been with her for forty years, since Sassy's sweet sixteen.

"It's Menolly. I need to talk to Sassy. Is she home?" Janet

knew who I was. Janet was also the only nonvamp besides my sisters who were privy to the fact that Sassy now carried a prime-card membership to the bloodsuckers club. Apparently the older woman had accepted the change as placidly as she might accept a notice that the garbage route had been shifted to a different day or that her neighborhood market was having a fifty-cent-off sale.

Janet was a woman of few words. She didn't answer, but the gate clicked and slowly opened. I waited until I could drive through without scratching my car, then wound up the narrow driveway at five miles per hour to avoid hitting any stray animals that might be passing by. The Branson estate was overgrown with weeping willow trees and oak, fir and lilacs. Sassy had married well, despite her natural inclinations, and when Johan had died, he left her with enough money so she'd never have to worry again. Of course, he hadn't counted on providing for her for an eternity, but Sassy would cross that bridge when she came to it.

I parked outside the four-story manor that resembled a plantation house, complete with wrap-around porch. As I dashed up the steps, I wondered what the hell Sassy was going to do with this joint over the years. In thirty years or so, people would be expecting her to die. Then what would she do? Fake her own death?

The door was adorned with a Marley knocker. Sassy had a wicked sense of humor. As the large brass knocker hit the striker button, a resounding *thud* echoed from within and the theme from *The Munsters* chimed through the hall.

A moment later, Janet opened the door.

"Good evening," I said, giving her a quick smile. Janet had a strong influence on Sassy. Stay on her good side and treat her with respect and she'd go out of her way to help you if she could. Sassy was rather scatterbrained, and Janet watched over her like a mother hen.

"Evening, Miss Menolly," the older woman said. Tall, with snow white hair and skin barely beyond the albino white of my own complexion, Janet carried herself with a Julia Child hump. She never gave any indications of being tired or in pain, and was always impeccably dressed in a linen skirt suit.

"Miss Sassy's waiting in the parlor for you." She gestured to the first door on the right.

"Thank you." As I opened the door, the stark whiteness of the room blinded me, contrasting with the brick red of the stuccoed hallway.

Sassy's parlor was as classy as her entire life had been. Not a speck of dust dared to linger on the highly polished tables, every plant was lush and green. Each morning, Janet opened the heavy velvet drapes and windows, allowing the room to air out so it always smelled fresh and clean.

Sassy, wearing a pale blue Ann Taylor pantsuit, was sitting in a wingback chair upholstered in a neutral jacquard. Her hair, as usual, was perfectly coiffed. She'd been agonizing whether or not to dye it for weeks now.

"If it's horrid, then I'll have to bleach it back," she'd say.

"So don't do it," I'd answered back.

"But I miss having gorgeous red hair—I want hair the color of yours."

And I'd shake my head and remind her that, vampire or not, abuse the hair often enough and she'd end up sporting an eternal bald spot.

I knew it wasn't exactly PC, but at the core, I was relieved that—if I had to be turned into a vampire—at least I'd been young and in good health when it happened. Barring the little *gifts* Dredge left on my skin, that is.

"Menolly!" Sassy jumped up, a brilliant smile spreading across her face. She held out her arms and I reluctantly let her embrace me. She kissed me on both cheeks. Air kisses, yeah, but I didn't really like being touched by anyone other than my sisters or Iris. "What brings you to visit?"

"May I?" I pointed to a rocking chair. Single seat, so Sassy couldn't sit too close.

"Of course. Make yourself comfortable."

I glanced around the room, taking in the fine art and sculptures and baby grand piano, all of which reminded visitors they were in the presence of old money. "I wondered if you'd heard about anything odd going on in the vampire community during the last few days?"

She narrowed her eyes. "What do you mean? What's happened?"

"There have been seven murders this week that we know of. Three last night in the Green Lake area. They were all killed by vampires, and all of them rose." I watched her closely, looking for some sign of recognition in her face, but she only looked shocked.

"No," she said, her hand fluttering to her throat. "*Seven?* Are you sure? How horrible."

I believed her. Sassy was good, but not good enough to hide guilt. Unlike a lot of vamps, she still had a conscience.

"All too sure. I had to kill three of them tonight. Staked them with the help of an incubus bounty hunter." I paused, then plunged ahead. "I've only told you a little about my own transformation. Thing is, we think that the vamps who tortured and turned me have made their way Earthside. For what ends, I'm not sure, but whatever it is, trust me, it's not good. Their leader—Dredge, my sire—is a sadist. His greatest joy is inflicting pain on others."

Sassy's look of disbelief shifted into dumbfoundedness. "Oh my God. Menolly, do you think they're after you?"

I stopped short. That particular thought hadn't really occurred to me. We'd assumed they were searching for a way into the Subterranean Realms, but maybe we were wrong. Wisteria also had a grudge against me—against all of us, actually. If she had paired up specifically with the Elwing Blood Clan, there might be a personal motive behind the attacks, rather than some grand plan involving Shadow Wing.

"Holy shit, I hadn't thought of that," I said.

Sassy shook her head. "I'm not sure what else you think they might be up to, but that would be my first line of thought. Does your sire have a grudge against you?"

I blinked. "That's like asking if Hannibal Lecter has a grudge against his victims. It's simply . . . my sire enjoyed playing with toys."

"But you escaped. You aren't with the clan, are you?" She

stared right through me and I got the feeling she was reading more than I wanted her to. "Just what did he do to you?"

I debated. Could she handle it? She was a vampire, true, but she still had that gentle side to her that had won her a whole passel of friends during life.

"You know," she said, leaning back on the divan where she was sitting as she dangled one diamond-studded wrist over the back. "I have my own secrets. If they'd have gotten out while I was alive, they could have destroyed my place in society. Especially when I was a teenager in the late sixties."

Not sure where she was going with this, I cocked my head. "Really?"

She nodded. "Oh my, yes. For me, the sixties were an era of parties and sororities and finishing schools. The unrest of the youth culture passed me by, much to my parents' relief. They bundled me off to a finishing school in France, sure that I'd come home the perfect, proper young socialite ready to take her place in society."

"And did you?"

She gave me a slow smile and I realized just how stunning she must have been when she was young. She was still a beauty, but the bloom of youth must have added a striking flourish to her looks.

"What my parents didn't realize is that during those last two years in France, I discovered that I prefer . . . the company of women. Thanks to a wonderful girl named Claudine. I realized that I'm a *lesbienne*, as Claudine put it. We had a torrid affair for ten months, and then fought over something—I don't remember what. I was devastated. Claudine left me and I finished up school and returned home." Sassy motioned to the walls and the ceiling. "And this, this is where I ended up."

Delilah had mentioned something about Sassy making a pass at her but I thought that had started after she'd been turned, not before. "But you were married for years and years . . ."

"Oh yes," Sassy said. "I was married, and Johan was a lovely man. He took care of me and I looked good on his arm at parties and dinner functions. I stood behind him, put my money and family name behind him. He rose in the world of medicine and made sure that I never wanted for anything. He had a few affairs, but then, so did I. We were both discreet. And then, he retired, and three months later, he died." Her eyes clouded over with tears, bloodred, and she blinked them away.

"Did you love him?" I asked, caught up in her story.

She thought about it for a moment. "Yes, I believe I did. But not in the way one has passion for a lover. I loved him because he was a good man, he respected me, and he never embarrassed me. When he died I thought, *Perhaps now I can come out of the closet—reveal myself for who I really am.* But then I looked around at my friends. They're wonderful people, but set in their ways, and I knew . . . I knew that if I told them the truth, they'd leave me."

"I see." And I did. If her friends deserted her, she'd have no one to turn to. She'd had one daughter, who died young from a drowning accident. Most of Sassy's own family was probably dead by now.

"Well, it didn't matter so much at first. I had finally made the decision to disrupt my life, shake things up a little. I thought about moving to Soho or San Francisco. But then one night I met Takiya at a party. He was handsome, and suave. I thought he just wanted a friend, and when he called, he sounded lonely so I invited him over for dinner. I had no idea I was on the menu."

She raised her head, a rueful smile on her lips. "He'd fallen for me and turned me into a vampire to keep me with him. I was horrified. The irony, though, is that two nights after I rose, someone staked Takiya. He vanished in a puff of ash, and now I have to face eternity alone."

"Who staked him?" I had a sneaking suspicion of the answer.

With a toothy grin, she said, "I did. I had just started figuring out how to spend the rest of my life in the open, to be who I really am, and he went and screwed it up." She cocked her head. "Do you know why I'm telling you all of this?"

At my bewildered shake of the head, she laughed. "I

thought not. I told you my story for two reasons. One: If I tell you my secrets, you'll know that you can tell me yours. Sharing builds trust, Menolly. And the second reason . . . I don't approve of siring others. Not unless they beg for it, not unless they're dying and they ask you for help and you know—you absolutely know—they won't regret it. Whoever's attacking these poor people has to be stopped. It's bad enough to bleed them dry, but to raise them into the life against their will? That's unconscionable."

As she spoke, I began to sense her strength, the will behind her words. I gazed into her eyes and thought, *Here's a woman who understands what it means to stand up for a cause you believe in.* She'd staked her own sire—an invitation to disaster if any of his other children of blood were in the area.

"Wade and the V.A. group are the only reasons I haven't walked out into the daylight," she added. "He gives me hope. Maybe we can't stop vampirism from spreading, but maybe we can put a dent in the violence and bloody mess it causes. We can't deny our natures, but we can control them."

I leaned back, positive that she had nothing to do with the murders. "I take it that you haven't heard anything that would lead you to suspect any local vamps who might be doing this?"

"The sun is due to rise in an hour or so. You'd better get along home." She rose and rang the bell to summon Janet. "It's well known that I staked Takiya. I sincerely doubt if I'll ever be privy to any secrets from other vampires. I'll keep my ears open, though. And do a little snooping. I still have a few contacts in the right places."

I took the hint and rose, heading toward the foyer. "Thanks, Sassy."

At the door, I paused, my hand on the knob. Without looking back, I said, "Dredge tortured me until I went mad. First, he used his fingernails and a small dull knife to lacerate every inch of my body except my hands, feet, and face. He worked slowly, millimeter by millimeter. Then he raped me until I thought I was going to die from the bitter chill of his flesh. After that, Dredge slit his wrist and forced me to drink. When I rose, he sent me home to feed on my family."

Behind me, Sassy gasped.

"Some secrets are better left secrets," I said. "But you asked. I want you to understand just what kind of monsters we're up against. Are you game? Will you help us if we need you?"

"You can count on me," she murmured.

I nodded before closing the door behind me. First light wasn't far off, and it was time to sleep.

CHAPTER 8

My dreams were silent on Saturday, a welcome relief. When Camille woke me near sundown, she and Delilah had already eaten. Iris was busy burping Maggie. I dressed quickly, throwing on a pair of black jeans and a brick red turtleneck, then a black denim jacket to match. As I slid on my stiletto ankle boots, Camille sat on the bed decked out in a gauzy skirt and skintight bustier, a preoccupied look on her face.

"Something wrong?" I slipped into my bathroom and quickly lined my lips with peach gloss, addeding a dusting of emerald shadow and a thin line of black around my eyes before finishing up with a sweep of mascara.

I'd never felt the need for makeup until my skin color decided to move beyond the pale. Even then, it took coming Earthside to jog me into action. After a few disasters thanks to the twenty-four-hour drugstore cosmetics counter, Camille had gotten into the act. She went shopping for me during the day, when the department stores were open, and came home carrying bag after bag of cosmetics until we'd found the perfect look using cosmetics that didn't react with my skin's chemistry. Now, five minutes in front of the mirror made me go from death warmed over to glamour chic. I was still terribly pale, but at least I looked good.

She sighed as I returned to the bedroom. "I spent the afternoon with Morio. Trillian walked in on us."

I let out a loud guffaw. "Oh boy, I wish I'd been a fly on the wall for that one! What happened?" Unlike Delilah, I dove right in with questions unless the topic was off-limits. Blunt was my middle name. Okay, it wasn't. My middle name was Rosabelle, but I wasn't reticent about poking about when the door was left ajar.

Camille leaned back, her arms folded behind her head. She stared at the ceiling. "Morio had partially transformed and we were getting pretty damned hot. His fangs were out in full force and his claws had emerged. Not only that, but his eyes were glowing and he looked like he'd jumped right out of the bowels of hell. Gorgeous, but scary."

"You really don't like vanilla, do you?" I stared at her, grinning. So she liked fucking Morio when he was in his demonic form? And apparently this hadn't been the first time. "Go on, what happened?"

"The thing is, Trillian's never asked much about what I do with Morio. As long as we all keep our calendars straight." She sat up, the corners of her eyes crinkling. "Oh Menolly, I had such a hard time keeping from laughing. Trillian looked like he was going to have a fit."

"Pissed, huh?"

"No, that's the thing. He wasn't mad, he was just . . . well . . . he looked almost shocked. I guess he didn't know just how far on the fringe I'm willing to play. But you see, when Morio transforms, he takes me to a whole different place—it's like we enter a different world. I can't reach there with anybody else."

"Did Trillian threaten to Cuisinart Morio?" Her oath-lover routinely threatened to slice up the fox demon but we all knew it was just talk. At least, it was just talk as long as Morio acknowledged that Trillian held alpha male status in Camille's life.

With a visible swallow, Camille shook her head. "Not exactly."

"Then what's the problem?" I asked, getting a little impatient.

"I don't know if there is one. You see, Trillian demanded to stay and watch. Before I knew what was happening, he was right in there with us. Trillian isn't bi, he isn't into men, and neither is Morio. And I ended up having the best sex of my life. Now Trillian's decided that a real triad isn't such a bad idea. He likes to see me . . . happy."

Well, *this* wasn't what I'd expected to hear. I scrunched up beside her, folding my legs into the lotus position. "So how does Morio feel about this?" I asked, suddenly grinning. It felt so good to dish like normal sisters about something other than Shadow Wing and war and bloodshed.

Camille let out a low laugh. "He's hard to read. He's not possessive, though if I were in danger he'd kill for me without a second thought. But he . . . he just welcomed Trillian onto the bed." She gave me a soft smile.

"As long as you're happy," I said, gazing at her.

"I am," she said. "I guess I take after our father's people a lot more than Mother's, but I know I'll never fit into either world."

I shook my head. "You fit fine in both. You just stand out. Delilah's the one who has trouble fitting in, back home in OW. Regardless of the mercy fuck she gave to Zachary, you know her heart belongs to Chase."

Camille made a face. "Yeah, and only the gods know how she ended up with him. But that's her business." Abruptly she stood and shook out her skirt. "Ready to go? We'd better get to the meeting before too many people show up. Trillian and Morio are going to join us at the community center. Smoky said he's busy and won't be there. I have no idea what he's doing, nor did I ask."

I raised an eyebrow. "Smoky's a big complication in your life. And there isn't much you can do about it." Dragons made their own rules. Learn that and you were halfway home to avoid being eaten by one.

"Tell me something I don't know," she said. "Think we'll ever know his real name?"

I snorted. "Oh sure, any day now. Hey, if he decides to kill us, he might just spill it." At her look, I said, "Honestly, ask a stupid question, get a stupid answer. You know very well that dragons guard their names like they horde gold. They're all a bunch of mercenaries." I expected her to argue but she just laughed.

"You got me there," she said as she headed up the stairs. "But sometimes they're too damned gorgeous for their own good—or ours." I followed silently behind her. At least we couldn't complain that our lives were boring.

Chase was waiting for us when we entered the living room. Delilah had volunteered him to watch Maggie, and he'd reluctantly agreed.

"I still think I should go to the meeting with you," he said.

Delilah laughed. "Oh come on, Chase. No way. For one thing, we promised everybody that at the first meeting, we wouldn't allow any FBHs around. If we break that promise, there will never be another meeting, I'll guarantee you that. I'll fill you in on everything when we get home. Be good, sweetie." She leaned down to cadge a kiss from him. He broke into a boyish grin and pulled her onto his lap.

"All right, you two, break it up," I said, bringing Maggie in from the kitchen. Her face, oddly cherubic, lit up when she saw Chase. For some reason, the gargoyle liked him. "Here, lover boy, take care of her while we're gone."

"Okay, okay," he said as Delilah climbed off his lap and he cuddled Maggie in the nook of his arm. "Just make sure that you don't leave me here all night. I'm not cut out for babysitting."

"Tell me another one," I said. "You look every bit the part of a proud papa."

Chase planted Maggie on one knee as Delilah handed him the remote. Iris brought him a tray with a bowl of chips and a couple cans of Sprite. She set it on the table next to him. Maggie busied herself playing with a plush bear that he'd bought her for Yuletide, and together, they looked entirely comfortable.

"Okay, okay . . . get out of here. Be safe. Hurry back," he said, shooing us out.

Iris rode with me as we headed out to the Supe meeting. Delilah took her Jeep and Camille, her Lexus. We might have to split up afterward and we'd learned the value in taking multiple vehicles. It cut down on scrambling for a ride. The motor of my Jag purred in the dark crystalline night as we sped along toward the V.A. building.

Iris had donned her blue dress and white cloak for the meeting. Her ankle-length golden hair was braided into an intricate design on her head. After a moment she said, "Bruce called me today."

"Bruce?" For a moment I drew a blank, then I remembered. "The sprite in the bar the other night?"

"Actually, he's a leprechaun. He asked me out on a date next week. I can't believe it—after thirty years, I'm finally wading back into the dating pool!"

"It's not like you haven't had other offers," I said. "Henry Jeffries adores you."

She made a face. "Henry Jeffries is a very nice man, but I'm not looking for a human companion, and he's too old for me. I may be older than he is in terms of years, but I'm still young enough to want a family and he's . . . well . . . it's just out of the question."

I repressed a smile. When Camille's devoted customer, Henry Jeffries, had finally steeled up his nerve to ask Iris out, she'd pleaded a stomachache. The second time, she feigned a headache. The third time, she couldn't come up with an excuse and had half-heartedly gone to the movies with him. He'd been a perfect, old-school gentleman and she'd been bored out of her mind. Since then, she'd made sure to stay out of the Indigo Crescent on the days she thought he was likely to come in. One of these days, she was going to deal with his infatuation.

"You're underestimating your influence on men, my dear."

"Oh, sure," she said in a snarky tone. "You do realize that being around the three of you all day is enough to squash anybody's ego. You're all so damned gorgeous."

I flipped on my left blinker before making a turn onto Baltimore Drive. "Iris, you don't get it. True, a lot of men immediately react to us, but most of them end up either scared shitless or get turned off by the fact that we don't fit *their* fantasies once they get to know us. But men love your openness, your smile, and your ability to stand up for yourself without making them feel like you could eat them alive. Even though you could," I added, thinking about her ability to swing a good heavy skillet, not to mention her way with magic. "We're here," I said, pulling into the parking lot. "Will Bruce be at the meeting tonight?"

She shook her head. "No, he's got something going on with some Irish historical society. He's a charter member and has to be there."

The Belles-Faire Community Hall had once been an elementary school. As we entered the large basement meeting room Wade was there, along with Sassy, but none of the other Supes had shown up yet. They were busy sprucing up the hall. Sassy had hired a caterer, and an incredible buffet of finger foods covered one long table. Just about everybody should find something to eat here, I thought. Wade motioned me over. I allowed him to press a quick kiss on the top of my hand.

"Menolly, good to see you. You too, girls," he added, nodding at the others who straggled into the room behind me. "Could you help set up chairs? I'd appreciate it."

"We'll do that," said a gruff voice from the door. We turned to see Zachary Lyonnesse and Venus the Moon Child enter the room, followed by several other members of the Rainier Puma Pride.

"Girls . . ." Zach said, nodding as his gaze came to rest on Delilah's face. His longing was transparent. Chase wasn't the only one smitten with our Kitten. Come to think of it, doubly good that we'd left the detective at home. The promise of testosterone feuds was already too great, given the caste structures of the different clans and nests. The last thing we needed was a rutting contest over my sister.

As I looked beyond him to the rest of his retinue, I spotted a face that sparked a sudden flame in my heart. Shaken, I froze. Nerissa was staring at me as hard as I was staring at her.

She detached herself from the group and crossed to my side. "Menolly, I'm glad you're here. I specifically asked to be included as one of the emissaries from the Puma Pride tonight in hopes that we'd have another chance to talk."

Taller than me by a good head, she was also strong. Lean muscles rippled under the smooth skin of her arms as she slipped out of her coat and draped it over a chair. Of course, I had her beat because of the vampire *thang*, but she was more than capable of taking down a good-sized man.

She reached out, paused a moment, and then as I watched, she lightly placed her fingers on my arm. Something uncoiled at the base of my spine and I shivered. As I stared into those brilliant topaz eyes that mirrored a pool of limpid sunlight, she wavered and I took a step closer.

Everything began to phase out as the scent of her perfume, the scent of her skin, the beat of her heart overwhelmed my senses. Inhaling deeply to fix her fragrance in my lungs and memory, I felt the thirst begin to grow as my fangs unfurled. Her neck was shimmering under the glow of the light, beckoning me in as she licked her lips and quivered under my gaze.

"Menolly? Menolly? Come back," an urgent voice whispered from behind me.

I whirled as my eyes shifted for the hunt. Wade let loose a low growl and gave me one shake of the head. He glanced at Nerissa, then back at me. Suddenly aware of where we were, and that one wrong move could set off a panic among the Puma crowd who might misinterpret what was going on, I closed my eyes and fought for control as I edged my way back from the abyss. *Damn it.* It would be so easy to push Wade aside, to sweep Nerissa under my spell, into my arms, to taste her blood, to leave a trail of kisses down her body . . .

"Menolly. Stop. Now."

The words echoed through my passion-addled brain and I

opened my eyes to find myself staring at an old hag, a woman cloaked in forest gray with steel teeth. She had more lines on her face than a tree had rings.

Oh shit. Grandmother Coyote! I'd never met her, but Camille had, and her description was enough for me to know whom I was facing. My fangs retracted and I swallowed the lump that appeared in my throat. One of the Hags of Fate, Grandmother Coyote could wipe me off the map without so much as a whisper, and she'd do it without remorse if the need arose.

"I'm sorry," I said. "I . . ."

"It isn't her fault," Nerissa said. "I started it." She glanced over at Zach, who was staring at her, his face a crinkled mask of confusion.

"I don't care who started it," Grandmother Coyote said. "Remember where you are. Remember *why* you are here. Much hinges on this evening. Do not disappoint me." She turned away then, and made her way over to Camille, who smiled uneasily. "So, are those demon fingers proving handy, my dear?" she asked, as I slowly relaxed and turned back to the werepumas.

Zach stared at Nerissa. "What the hell is going on? Nerissa?"

She shrugged. "I think I'll be staying in town after the meeting, cousin," she said, shooting a questioning look at me.

I hesitated. I hadn't given myself to anyone since Dredge. He was the last man—living or dead—to touch me in my most private of places. Was I ready for another relationship? The thought of a man's hands on me scared me shitless—the memory of Dredge still way too fresh. But a woman . . . not just any woman but there was something about Nerissa . . . Could I take her into my world and keep her safe? I gazed at her as she blew me a gentle kiss. I had to find out, one way or another.

"She's staying at our house for the night, Zach. Nerissa, you can ride back with me." Without another word, I turned and headed back to the front of the room where my sisters were in a whispered conference with Wade, Sassy, Grandmother Coyote, Morio, and Trillian. Iris had taken over hostess duties and was greeting folks at the door, putting them at ease.

Camille cleared her throat. "Good of you to join us," she said dryly. "People are starting to trickle in. We've lined up several guards from the major clans to keep order and planted them around the room. Let's hope nobody gets his muzzle bent out of shape."

I glanced around the rapidly filling hall. Most of the groups who agreed to participate had sent a handful of emissaries, the number depending on the size and position of the clan within the Supe community.

The Rainier Puma members stood out, of course, with their height and their Scandinavian good looks. But the wolf clans were just as striking. Lean and muscled, the majority of their members looked Mongolian by nature and they walked with a refined arrogance that was hard to ignore. There were members in from the Olympic Wolf Pack, the primary pack in the state, but also a few from the Loco Lobo and Cascadia Packs.

The werepumas were limited to two groups—the Rainier Pumas and the Icicle Falls Pride, who were leaner and shorter than Zach's group. They rivaled Trillian for the obsidian glow of their skin, but Trillian had that OW look in his eyes and his hair was brilliant platinum, while the Icicle Falls Pride looked more like earthborn humans than Fae. They were black panthers, hiding out in the wilds of the forests, and their hair was as dark as their skin.

Camille hedged in beside me, Trillian right behind her. She nodded at the door. "Looks like some of the real closet cases have decided to show."

She was right. I wasn't sure just what kind of Supes they were, but a group of three disparate looking characters entered the room. And characters they were, with a fashion sense that looked about two hundred years out-of-date. I nodded at her and said, "Let's go greet our new friends."

We headed over in their direction and Camille gasped. "They're old Fae, Menolly. Very old Fae. I can feel it from here."

A woman and two men, they turned as we approached.

Their eyes glowed with an inner light impossible to miss. I wasn't sure whether they belonged to the Sidhe, or whether they were from a line far older than that, but whoever they were, the pall of dark magic hung heavy in their auras.

The men were average height, on the short side even, but they were sturdy with shoulder-length hair caught back in braids, and they wore golden cloaks around their shoulders. The woman was shorter than me, four-eleven at best, with long dark hair and a silver crescent branded on her forehead.

She inclined her head ever so slightly toward Camille. "Good meet, my Sister of the Moon."

Camille seemed transfixed, her face flushed with excitement. She returned the bow and held out her hands. "Welcome. We sure didn't expect to see the likes of you come through these doors."

Still in the dark as to who they were, I cleared my throat. "Camille, do you know this woman?"

Camille glanced at me, a wary look on her face. "Mind your manners," she whispered, then turned back to the trio. "Thank you for coming. We need all the help we can get."

"We'll reserve our decision on whether to get involved until we know more," the younger of the men said. He glanced at me. "Creature of the night, and yet one of us . . . though not quite. You and your sisters are from the Otherworld, correct?"

I inclined my head slightly, still wary. "I'm Menolly D'Artigo, this is my sister Camille, and the blonde over there is Delilah. We're from Otherworld, yes, though our mother was Earthside human. And you are?" Camille might be willing to pussyfoot around them but until I knew who they were, I wasn't about to drop to my knees for anybody.

The woman smiled then, faint but with a twinkle in her eye. "You may call me Morgaine. I'm a Daughter of the Moon, like your sister here."

Morgaine? My jaw went slack and I hastily backed up a step. "Not *the* Morgaine?"

She let out a low chuckle. "The one and only."

One of the greatest sorceresses to ever live, Morgaine was half-human, half-Fae like we were, although it seemed she'd managed to avoid the short circuits in her wiring that afflicted most half-breeds. Morgaine had chosen to stay behind during the Great Divide and it was thought she'd faded into history. From her appearance, it was obvious that the rumor mill had been working overtime. She was as alive as any of us. Well, as alive as Camille and Delilah.

I glanced at the men. "Then these must be . . ."

"Mordred, my nephew, though many make the mistake of thinking he's my son. And this," she motioned to the older man, "is Arturo, my mate from the Golden Wood."

Her eyes flashed with the same violet as Camille's. Maybe a connection because of the moon magic, maybe something else. I glanced at Arturo. He looked FBH, but there was something about him that didn't quite track. Mordred, on the other hand, was obviously part Fae.

Camille gazed at Morgaine, totally playing the fan girl. "My teacher taught us about you. You were the greatest sorceress that ever lived. We are honored by your presence."

Morgaine reached up to caress Camille's face, lingering on her cheek gently. "So you have returned to our world. Why, might I ask?"

Her question seemed innocent but something tripped an alarm. "We have our reasons," I said before Camille or anyone else could respond. "We're here to find out about our mother's heritage. We wanted to know more about her." A blatant lie, but I had an uneasy feeling that wouldn't leave me alone. "So what brings you to our meeting tonight?"

Mordred stared at me, impassive, but I had the feeling he didn't buy my story. "It's time to wake the great powers. Time to reclaim what is ours."

Wake the great powers . . . reclaim what is ours . . . That didn't sound friendly. I turned to Morgaine. "And by great powers, you mean . . . ?"

Camille gasped. "*The Merlin?* Are you searching for the Merlin? Is he even alive?"

Morgaine shrugged, and her glamour fell away. She suddenly looked tired and wrung out. "Yes, we're looking for the Merlin. We hoped you might have heard something about him. I don't know if he still lives or not, but Mordred,

Arturo, and I are doing our best to find him. If the crystal caverns still exist, then we'll do whatever it takes to wake him up. And the Lady of the Lake, too."

"You are attempting to bring Avalon back from the mists and shadows?" I wondered, Just how powerful were these three? Or how powerful did they think they were?

"No." Morgaine shook her head with a wry grin. "Avalon is long drifted from this realm. And Arthur, my darling Arthur, if he woke, he wouldn't be able to adapt to the modern age. But we can still reach through the veil and call our allies from ages past."

"Don't count on Titania. We've met her," Camille grumbled.

Morgaine raised her head. "Don't be so quick to judge. It's not easy to be overthrown and cast out of queenship." She glanced around. So far it seemed that nobody else had noticed her and I began to see that she'd woven a glamour around her that she'd only lowered for a few of us to see.

I shrugged. "What's your purpose? You say you want to reclaim what's rightfully yours, but what are you talking about?"

Camille gave me a nasty look. I knew I was bordering on outright rude, but I didn't care. I didn't like glib platitudes from humans, and I didn't like it when the Fae offered them either.

The sorceress tapped her nose. "You'll know in good time. Meanwhile, if you hear word of the Merlin, let us know."

"And how are we supposed to do that? You settling in around here?" I asked, wary now. If they were going to become permanent fixtures in the area, we'd have to keep an eye on them.

"I apologize for my sister," Camille broke in, her voice edging on pissed. "You'll have to excuse her; she's forgotten a lot of her manners since she died."

"No matter," Morgaine said. "We'll be in touch. Trust me." She glanced around. "Your meeting's about to start, so we'll be off. You may not hear from me for some time. Don't bother hunting us out. Look to ravens and crows for word from me." She paused, then patted Camille's cheek again.

"Don't let anyone," she added, glancing at me with a baleful stare, "make you jump to conclusions."

Then, with a brief nod and before Camille or I could say another word, they turned as one and swept out the door.

I cleared my throat when they vanished up the stairs. "What do you make of that?"

Camille snorted. "I don't know, but you sure were Miss Pissy. Although, I have to say, they really didn't tell us much, did they? I wonder where she's been keeping herself all these years. She certainly seems in better shape than Titania, I'll give her that much."

"Something about the encounter doesn't ring square to me. Are you sure she's actually who she says she is? That she's on the up and up?"

Camille let out a long, shuddering sigh. "As starstruck as I am, to be honest, I'm not entirely sure. Let's ask Grandmother Coyote," she added, and before I could protest, grabbed me by the arm and dragged me across the room.

I managed to catch a glimpse of several members of the Blue Road Tribe—werebears—entering the room before, once again, I found myself face to face with Grandmother Coyote. She'd ensconced herself in a chair in the corner and was observing the room as it filled up.

Camille brought her up-to-date on Morgaine's appearance. "So, we want to know, is it really her and what does she want?"

Grandmother Coyote motioned for us to sit down. At her feet. Camille dropped to the floor and I wasn't far behind. When one of the Hags of Fate told you to sit at her feet, you sat.

She looked around to make sure we weren't being overheard. "Morgaine she was, indeed. Remember: Not all help can be trusted, even if it does not run in evil paths. There are few who can rival the sorceress, but she carries a great thirst for power. That thirst has been her undoing in the past. I doubt if she's learned much over the years."

At least Grandmother Coyote wasn't being cryptic this time. I frowned, wondering just what this little jewel of information was going to cost us. With the Hags of Fate, there was always a price.

"Then we shouldn't trust her?" I glanced at Camille, who stared at the floor, crestfallen.

Grandmother Coyote held my gaze. "There are few you can trust in this world. Even those who mean well can crumble under pressure. The more people who know your secrets, the more the chance for betrayal. That's why I'm here tonight. A warning: Think twice before you spill secrets about the Demonkin, because once you push Humpty off the wall, you're left with a mess of scrambled eggs." With that, she stood and made her way over to the buffet.

Camille and I sat, staring at one another.

"I'm sorry," I said. "I know you wanted to hear something different."

"My teacher regarded Morgaine as a heroine. I feel like one of my role models just fell off the pedestal. I wonder what all that talk about reclaiming what's rightfully hers is about. If she's going around mucking with ancient powers, then we'd better keep our ears open until we figure out just what the hell she's trying to do." She smacked her hand against the ground, then pushed herself to her feet. "Damn it, I hate this. There are so many variables, so many unknown factors at play in the balance now."

"Maybe she won't find the Merlin. Or maybe she'll go somewhere else. The Merlin can't be around here," I said, a nasty thought creeping in. "You don't think she knows about the spirit seals, do you? That she's looking for them in hopes of using them herself?" Surely someone like Morgaine would refuse to play second fiddle to a demon. If she were after them, she'd want them all for herself.

Camille flashed me a stricken look. "I hadn't thought about that. Well, hell in a handbasket, as if we didn't already have enough to worry about."

"Well, push it to the side. We'd better grab Delilah and the boys and have a quick discussion about the rest of what Grandmother Coyote said. I'm not so sure this meeting's a good idea after all," I muttered.

Camille nodded. "Me either."

Just then, the Hag of Fate returned, an incongruous Harry Potter paper plate filled with cookies in her hand. "One last thing, girls."

If she had one more discouraging word to say, I was going to bag it and take off for home. But she just gave us one of her steely grins that would have sent shivers down even Dredge's back.

"My payment for advice . . ."

Camille cringed. The last time she'd owed an I.O.U. to Grandmother Coyote, she'd had to play chop-chop with a demon's fingers to pay her debt.

"What do you want, old witch?" I asked, deciding that I'd had enough bullshit for the night. Camille gasped, but Grandmother Coyote just laughed.

"I like you, girl, but *mind your manners*." The cautionary tone was unmistakable and I swallowed, acknowledging her warning with a nod. "I'm giving you a particularly delicate assignment."

"Just me or Camille, too?" It didn't seem fair. Camille had been the one to ask the question. But fairness wasn't par for the course in the world of the Immortals. Any which way it worked out, I wasn't going to whine about it. No sense in ticking her off any more than I already had. Walking a thin line in the playground of the gods required both balance and timing, and I wasn't at all sure I mastered either when it came to diplomacy.

"Both, though the lion's share will fall to you. It will be up to Camille to convince you to go through with it."

Uh oh. Camille and I looked at each other.

"This can't be good," I said. What the hell was going to happen now?

Grandmother Coyote let out a long, low breath. She squinted, laugh lines creasing the corners of her eyes. "Menolly, you're going to have to do something you have vowed never to do. When the time comes, you'll know what it is, and you'll balk. But do it you must, regardless of your aversion to the idea. A long thread of destiny hinges upon your action . . . or inaction. Don't fail me. If you shy away, you'll upset a critical balance."

Before I could ask her to elaborate, she turned and vanished like a wisp of cloud under the glimmering sun.

I blinked. "Things are spinning out of control."

Camille shook her head. "I hate to tell you this, but things spun out of control the day we decided to accept this assignment from the OIA." She glanced at the front of the room. "Come on, we've got to put the skids on our original plans for this meeting. And we have to come up with something to replace it with in less than ten minutes."

As she hurried to the podium where Wade was conversing in quiet tones with Sassy and Delilah, I couldn't help but think that we'd already set in motion the wheels to a very big, very dangerous machine.

CHAPTER 9

Trillian and Wade stared at us like we were crazy.

"You want us to cancel the meeting?" Delilah said. "Listen, we have a room filled with Weres, vamps, and other assorted Supes here, many of whom don't like each other. Do you really want to tell them they came all this way for tea and cookies?"

"What's going on?" Trillian asked as he closed in behind Camille and wrapped his arm around her waist.

"I didn't say to cancel the meeting, but we have a problem." I nodded toward the crowd. "Grandmother Coyote warned us to keep our mouths shut about Shadow Wing. I'm not keen on going against her advice, especially when I've apparently got some whopper of a job coming at me in order to pay for it."

"Not only that," Camille said, "but we have another problem. Morgaine and Mordred showed up here—"

"Wait a minute," Trillian broke in. "You mean to tell me that Morgaine was in this room? As in Morgan Le Fay?" He glanced around, looking all too interested. Camille elbowed him a good one in the stomach.

"She was," she said. "Don't get too interested. She's not your speed. Apparently she and her little retinue are out to find and awaken the Merlin. We don't know why, but according to Mordred, it involves some plan to 'reclaim what is ours.'"

"Whatever that means," I said, interrupting. "Problem is, Grandmother Coyote warned us not to trust them— Morgaine is up to something and we better be cautious in any future dealings with her." I let out a little hiss of irritation. This was turning into a nightmare before it even began.

Wade, who had remained silent until now, cleared his throat. "You trust this coyote woman?"

"She's not a woman, she's one of the Hags of Fate. The Hags of Fate watch over the threads of destiny. Occasionally—when it suits their purposes—they intervene to right the balance." Camille rubbed her chin. "Believe me, if she gives advice, pay attention. She doesn't offer her help to everybody, and her advice doesn't come cheap."

Morio, who had been listening quietly, spoke up. "Camille's right. Ignore Grandmother Coyote at your peril. She's on our side, even if it doesn't seem like it at times. I have an idea on how to bail out of this mess. May I?" He gestured to the podium.

Wade cleared his throat. "Go ahead," he said. "I'm drawing a blank."

With a glance to see if the rest of us objected—and no one did—Morio moved to the podium as we took our places in the chairs on either side of the lectern. I could feel Camille holding her breath, and I knew she was wondering what the youkai was going to pull out of his bag of tricks this time.

Morio held up his hand. "Please take your seats. We're ready to start the meeting." Everyone slowly milled to his chair and in a moment, the room was silent, a pensive apprehension in the air.

"Thank you for coming out to the meeting and supporting our attempts to reach a broad section of the local Supe community. We appreciate your time and attention." He waited for the perfunctory clapping to subside. "I'm Morio, a youkai-kitsune, and as you know, these are Camille, Menolly, and

Delilah, from Otherworld. And this is your host tonight, Wade Stevens, the leader of Vampires Anonymous. Together we're hoping to forge important bridges in the Supe community, especially given the serious nature of several events that occurred over the past few days."

That caught their attention. The crowd quieted down, waiting.

Morio motioned me up to the lectern. "Now would be a good time to mention the vampire slayings," he whispered.

Not entirely positive he was on track but willing to give it a try, I took my place in front of the microphone. "My name is Menolly D'Artigo, and I'm the owner of the Way-farer Bar and Grill. The issue that set this meeting in motion is one that the Supe community must address. We need your help with an immediate crisis. Over the past few days, several rogue vampires have taken to murdering humans. They not only murdered them, but they've been raising them. This is not just a problem for the human community. These vamps could just as easily target Weres and other nonvam-piric Supes."

A low murmur raced through the room. I'd caught their attention, all right. I cleared my throat and continued. "Obviously, we can't tell the general public about the slayings. We feel that, at this point, no other humans should know about this problem other than those affiliated with the Faerie-Human Crime Scene Investigation team. But we thought if we appealed to you, to the Supe community at large, we might be able to form a Sub-Cult network in order to better police ourselves."

The buzz that ran through the meeting hall sounded like a hive of bees. Back in OW, this would be a given. Earthside Supes had a ways to catch up, but that wasn't surprising given how most of them had stayed in the closet until the past couple of years.

Camille joined me at the podium. "My sister is correct. We must stop turning a blind eye to those who insist on breaking the codes of conduct, whether vampire, Were, or any other form of Supe. If we can create a network, we can prevent the innocent, be they human or Supe, from being targets of any—and I mean *any*—hate group or psychotic killer."

As the silence grew thicker, I realized just how touchy this issue was. But if we could manage to stir up a united front, then when the time came to truly inform them about the demons, they'd be ready and able to fight.

After a moment, Brett, a vampire who'd wholeheartedly thrown himself in with the V.A. group, stood. "I understand that nobody wants to be a snitch, but if somebody's hurting the community, they're hurting all of us. We owe it to ourselves to root out the troublemakers."

He appealed to the crowd. "We *all* lose if we let rogue Supes break our code of ethics. The leaders of all the clans and nests forged treaties and agreements long ago, in secret. They agreed to stand by those canons. What good are oaths and pledges if we ignore those who break the rules?"

Venus the Moon Child stood. All eyes turned. Everybody knew who the shaman was, and everybody—regardless of what clan they were from or what kind of Were or Supe they were—acknowledged his strength and wisdom.

Delilah, who was out in the audience, microphone in hand, made her way over to him.

"I'm authorized to make oath-pledges for the Rainier Puma Pride," the shaman said. "The D'Artigo sisters and their friends have made an excellent point. I need no more encouragement. Tonight I pledge the Rainier Pumas to help out in building a true Supe community, in whatever way we can. You have us as allies." The sturdy shaman spit in his hand and held it out to Delilah. She spit in hers before clasping it tightly.

As soon as Venus the Moon Child sealed his pact, the marshal of the Olympic Wolf Pack followed suit. The Sellshyr Nest, a group of vamps who ran the Sub-Cult club BloodVain, also pledged their support. Two emissaries from an Earthside Fae family, the Vineyard Nymphs, also pledged their family's aid. The Blue Road Tribe and the Loco Lobo Pack agreed to discuss the matter with their elders and get back to us by midweek.

"How do we do this?" one of the Loco Lobo members asked. "Who's going to be in charge?"

Morio took the podium again. "We haven't decided on details yet. We're hoping to form a unified council from all tribes involved. Ideally we'd like to forge a network so that when one clan or nest or pride has a problem, everyone knows within a couple of hours. Only through unity can we ensure that we don't lose our rights as laws are enacted that affect our lives. Humans are well aware of our existence now, and you can be sure that soon there will be groups trying to both protect our rights, and—like the Freedom's Angels seek to do—to strip them away."

A murmur ran through the room. Smart boy, I thought. Appeal to their sense of security and they'd pay attention. Morio had a good head on his shoulders. The fox demon was far more brilliant than any of us had realized.

A member of the Blue Road Tribe raised her hand. Delilah recognized her. "Please state your name and then your comment or question."

The woman, who was tall and stately, took the microphone. "I'm Orinya, with the Blue Road Tribe. You make a valid point. Our half-brothers are the native peoples of this land, and they were slaughtered like cattle. Even when they were given their rights, the damage was too severe to repair. We should act now to prevent this from happening to us."

Another man raised his hand. He was sturdy, with a gruff voice and wore torn jeans and a leather jacket. Delilah hurried over to him.

"My name is Trey, from the Olympic Wolf Pack. I agree, this is an important issue, but how can we do this without causing panic? Humans are skittish enough as it is. Look at the Guardian Watchdogs and Freedom's Angels. They're getting more and more outrageous in their claims. It won't be long before somebody's killed in a human-Supe confrontation, and gangland war won't be far behind."

I tapped Morio on the shoulder. "May I field this one?" He stepped aside and I took the mike.

"With regards to that issue, we've been thinking that if

we create an organization *now* and set up committees, we can then approach the lawmakers who might be receptive to our cause. Hell, we can make our first task to discover whether any of our representatives or senators might be closet members of the Supe community. If we could ferret them out and gain their support, we'd have a real head start."

Just as I hoped, my remark about the possibility of closeted Supes in government hit the mark. A dozen hands shot up. I turned to Wade. "Would you start a sign-up sheet for people interested in volunteering with us?" He immediately sprang into action and within two minutes, a clipboard was being passed around the room and people were actually signing up.

Since nobody was forthcoming with any info on the vampire problem, we allowed the meeting to break into a question-and-answer period, and by the time we were done, we had enough volunteers to start several committees, including one to encourage the Supe groups to register with the volunteer database we were building. Wade had also agreed to host another meeting in a month to take stock of what we'd accomplished during that time. The one thing we didn't have were any leads as to what the hell was going on with the rogue vamps.

As I was wending my way through the crowd, I saw Roz leaning against one of the walls and made my way over to him. "I'm surprised to see you here."

He ignored my comment and gave me a lazy wink. "You didn't get what you hoped for, did you?"

I shook my head. "Nope."

"Don't be too disappointed. Nobody here is going to be able to track the Elwing Blood Clan. Dredge is too smart for that. You know that only too well, my dear." Leaning down, he brushed against my ear and whispered, "Don't ever try to forget about Dredge and what he did to you. If you get cocky, or if you ignore history, Dredge will find you and kill you. I don't claim to understand why he's tracking you, but he is. That much is obvious, whether you see it or not. And what Dredge wants, he gets."

"Don't be so sure about that." I shivered. Roz's energy

oozed around me like a sensual cloak and I was surprised to feel myself respond. I leaned in, smelling the pulse of his blood, feeling the heat radiate off of him in waves. "Dredge already had me. He'll never touch me again. If I have to stake myself before letting that happen, I'll willingly do it."

"What say we stake Dredge instead?" Roz said, letting out a low laugh. He reached out to tip my chin up, his fingers barely grazing my skin and lowered his head so that his breath tickled my ear. "You're a survivor, not a victim, Menolly. Don't ever blame yourself for what happened, and don't let him win. You're worth far more than that."

I licked my lips, hungry for him and yet terrified of my own reactions. As we were interrupted, I quickly pulled away.

"Excuse me. I don't mean to interrupt but . . ." Brett was standing there, staring nervously at the incubus.

"What is it?" I said, composing myself as quickly as possible.

"What you were saying earlier? About the newborn vampires?" He looked decidedly uncomfortable, but I could tell that he knew something.

All business again, I cleared my throat and led him over to an unoccupied pair of chairs. Roz followed us, even though I frowned a "no" at him. I sat down and motioned for Brett to join me. "If you have something to tell me, please do. They're dangerous and they're preying on innocent people."

Deflating like a loose balloon, Brett sank into the chair beside me. "Last night while I was out patrolling the rooftops, I heard something. It was a woman. She was crying. I followed her voice, thinking somebody might be in trouble."

"What did you find?" I knew the routine by now. Brett was shy, but he loved to talk about his adventures, so I would draw him out without hurrying him, little by little, until he dished.

"I was over on Phinney Avenue North, in my Vamp-Bat gear—"

Giving him a long look, Roz said, "Vamp-Bat?"

Breaking in quickly, I said, "Brett was a comic book fan when he was alive. Once he realized he'd been turned into a vampire, he decided to take on a superhero persona. He's Vamp-Bat. Every night he patrols the city, looking for people who need help."

I carefully kept my expression neutral. The whole situation might sound ridiculous, but to Brett, it was deadly serious. He had been a caring person during life, and in a way, death had given him what he could never have before and what he'd wanted so desperately—the chance to shine through as a hero. And if it took a cheesy name and a black cape to accomplish, so what? He was out there, making a difference.

Roz took a cue from the expression I shot him. "Really? You've saved people then, from trouble?"

Brett nodded. "Not to toot my own horn because that's just not cool, but I've rescued three women from being raped. And last week I helped a man who was in a nasty car crash. I stayed with him and kept him alive until the medics arrived. I disappeared before they could catch me."

"Brett feeds on the perverts and lowlifes like I do. He's a staunch supporter of Vampires Anonymous and the mission that Wade has put forth for the group." I turned back to Brett. "Anyway, tell us what you saw."

"I was near the Woodland Park Zoo. I followed the crying until I came to a woman in the parking lot. By the looks of her clothing, she was an employee of the zoo. She was near her car, probably headed home for the night. A vamp had hold of her, and he was trying to pin her down."

"Shit. What did you do?"

"Grabbed him off her. He looked really confused, too. I managed to hold him at bay while I yelled for her to run. The dude took off and I followed him, but he slipped into one of the exhibits and got away." He shifted from one foot to the other. "Something didn't track right, Menolly. I wasn't sure what it was until I saw this." He held up a photocopied picture of one of the first four victims. "The vamp—it was this dude. I'm sure of it."

"David Barns. Are you sure?" Until the first time they rose, vamp victims still showed up under the camera's scrutiny. I'd made a bunch of photocopies of the morgue pictures I'd managed to persuade Chase to give me, and we'd passed them out during the Q&A to anybody who seemed willing to take a look.

"Yeah. And I'm positive that he wasn't just going to take a few sips and then walk away. He looked out for a kill." Brett frowned.

Roz cleared his throat. "You think she might have filed a police report by any chance?"

I shrugged. "I don't know. She wouldn't necessarily know it was a vampire attack. For all we know, she thought he was a rapist and that some Good Samaritan happened by to put a stop to the assault. I'll ask Chase to check it out when I get home."

"I can't remember anything else that might help," Brett said. "I hope that this gives you something to go on."

"You did great," I said. "Meanwhile, anything out of the ordinary and you call me. Okay?"

Brett looked ready to burst. "Glad to be of help! And I'm glad I said something. If you need anybody on patrol, I'm your man."

I lightly touched his shoulder, very gently. Most vamps didn't like being touched and among ourselves a shoulder tap was the equivalent of a full-blown hug. "Brett, you just keep up what you're doing. But be careful. There is evil in the world far greater than you dream of. Sometimes it's hard to scare it away."

Pausing, I debated on whether to warn him about Dredge. We hadn't gotten that specific in our talk to the audience. But what good would it do? If Brett ran into my sire, Dredge would just mop up the floor with him. "Just keep alert, and don't play hero unless there isn't any other choice. I'll be in contact."

As he walked away, I looked over at Roz. "The Woodland Park Zoo is right up near the Green Lake district. Ten to one, Dredge or the newborns have a hideout up there."

"I'll scout around tonight," Roz said. "And you don't have to warn me what I'm up against. I know." He blew me a kiss and then took off out the door. As I watched him go, Camille came over and stared at his departing back.

"What do you know about him, Menolly?"

I shook my head. "Not enough. Too much. He's a merce-nary, but he's out to get Dredge. I recognize the hatred."

She gave me a questioning look, but I shook it off. "Come on, we'd better start cleaning up. People are leaving and I want to stop at the bar after we're done."

As we began folding chairs, Camille's cell phone jangled the Gorillaz song "Dare." She glanced at the caller ID and raised an eyebrow. "Hmm, it's Tim—Cleo. Let me take this. He never calls this late."

She moved aside and we went on cleaning up. Tim Winthrop, or Cleo Blanco as he was known in his alter ego, was a flamboyant friend of ours. Computer student by day, female impersonator by night, he was brilliant, smart, and funny. Tim's gorgeous boyfriend, Jason, had put a hunk of ice on his left finger. They were engaged and the wedding was set for summer. Tim also did the programming for the Supe database he and Delilah were building, and he was working for our newly revised OIA on a contingency basis, strictly need-to-know only.

All of a sudden, Camille let out a loud, "Son of a *bitch!*"

Delilah whirled around. "What is it?" she said, but Camille waved her silent, listening with a strained expres-sion on her face, looking like she was going to throw up.

"We'll be right there. Get your butt into a safe place and don't come out until we get there and give you a safe word. I'll shout out . . . oh . . . *babe in the woods.* Got it? . . . That's right, don't come out till you hear me yell *babe in the woods.* We'll be there as soon as we can, Tim. Just hang on. Everything will be okay. I promise." She flipped her phone shut. "Leave the mess. We'll clean it later."

"What happened?" I dropped the chair I was holding. Whatever it was, it was bad enough to make Camille scared. That made it *bad-ass* bad.

She'd already hit the door and we scrambled to catch up to her.

On the way to our cars, she told us what happened. "After one of his shows, Tim and Erin stopped in at the Wayfarer for a drink. Then they walked by Erin's shop before going to a movie. Tim was in the back, changing out of drag when he heard Erin scream. He ran to the door leading into the front of the shop but managed to stop short. A group of vamps were dragging Erin out the door. They didn't see him before he had a chance to duck into the utility closet. That's where he is now."

Shit! Erin Mathews was owner of the Scarlet Harlot lingerie shop and president of the local Faerie Watchers Club, a human-based fan club focused on the Fae from OW. Erin was also one of Tim's staunchest supporters and one of Camille's close friends.

Camille was halfway to her car by the time she finished telling us. I looked around to see who had come with us. Wade, Iris, and Nerissa broke off in my direction. Zachary headed toward Delilah's Jeep. Trillian and Morio were hot on Camille's heels. As we pulled away from the curb, Camille was streaking down the road, her Lexus silent in the frost-shrouded night.

"Do you think there's any chance Erin will be alive?" Iris asked.

"First we have to find out who took her. If it was Dredge . . ." A thought had sprung to mind. One that I didn't want to entertain. Dredge was out there, hiding in the shadows. If Roz was right and my sire was out to make my life hell, what better way to start than by hurting my friends? Tim and Erin had been in the bar before they hiked the few blocks over to the Scarlet Harlot and everybody there knew they were close friends of ours. If Dredge was watching the joint, then it would have been an easy matter to follow the pair to Erin's shop.

Wade let out a low whistle. "You think it's your sire?"

I growled. "Don't call him that! I refuse to acknowledge any link to that murderous bastard."

"But you have to face the facts, Menolly," Wade said. "Denying that the link is there won't help you. In fact, it's going to hinder you."

"What the fuck do you mean?" I hated exposing this side of myself to Nerissa, who sat silently beside Iris in the back seat.

"Think about it. I'll bet you that he can follow you through the bond of his blood. Don't you realize that you'll always be tied to Dredge as long as that bond exists?" Wade stared at me. "What the hell did the OIA teach you?"

I bit my lip as I pressed on the gas. How could I have been such a fucking idiot? *Of course* Dredge could find me merely by the fact that he was my sire.

Wade cleared his throat. "You okay?"

"No, I'm *not* okay. That fucking sadist may have one of our friends. An FBH no less. I *know* just how far Dredge can twist the mind and body. He almost destroyed me. There's no way Erin can survive if he decides to torture her. And if he turns her afterward, we'll have to destroy her because she'll go stark-raving mad. How do you think I feel, knowing I may have to stake a friend who should never, ever have gotten mixed up in something like this?"

Nerissa leaned forward. "I don't mean to interrupt, but if he's this bad, why did the OIA let him live? Why didn't they deport him to the Subterranean Realms?"

"I see you've been talking to Zachary. That boy needs to keep his mouth shut before he says something to the wrong person." I deliberately took a shaky breath. "I'm sorry. I shouldn't yell at you. Here's the deal. Dredge was on the list for deportation. We were ready to go in to verify what we knew and I was assigned to the case." I paused, trying to push back the tears that I felt sting my eyes. Blood was saltier than water. It hurt to cry.

"You don't have to go on," she said, but I stopped her.

"No. You deserve to know what you're headed into. If you want, I'll drop you off at a safe place and you can go home. Dredge wasn't deported because I failed at my job. He caught me. He tortured me. He raped me. He killed me and when I rose as a vampire, I went over the edge. By the time the OIA figured out what happened, he and the nest had moved on."

"How long did it take for you to . . . to return to sanity?"

I flashed her a cold grin. "Any day now, babe. I keep hoping."

She laughed, but her laughter was tinged with sorrow. "Oh, Menolly . . ."

"Seriously . . . it's okay now. I've adapted. But I went nuts for over a year. I couldn't tell the OIA a thing for a long, long time. You can't hold a trial when nobody's there. You can't deport someone you don't have locked away. Dredge and the Elwing Clan stayed on the move for a long time and the OIA didn't want to risk another operative going in. And I refused to go back. The rest, as they say, is history."

"Don't stop," she said quickly. "We have to get to your friend's shop as soon as possible. I want to be there with you."

I glanced in the rearview mirror. Nerissa couldn't see me, since I left no reflection, but I could see her, and her gaze was fastened on the back of my head. The look of desire was naked on her face and I could smell the perfume of her heat fill the car.

I caught Wade glancing at me, then back at Nerissa. A slow smile spread across his lips, making him look geeky-sexy. He gave me a wink and I saw the tips of his fangs extend.

"Don't say it," I said so quietly that even the werepuma shouldn't be able to pick it up. It was like whispering words made of mist that vanished the moment I spoke.

Wade winked at me. "You hooked a hot one," he whispered back. "Want to make it a threesome?"

"In your dreams, psych-boy." But I grinned back. I wasn't the only one repressing feelings. Wade was true to his ethics, but sometimes I thought he sublimated the predator within to the point where, one of these days, he was going to slip. When he did, I hoped it would be his mother he'd take out, for the peace and quiet of everybody in the vamp community.

"I'll just keep dreaming," he whispered back.

I ignored him this time. We had to focus on Dredge, who never slipped because he'd jumped into the shadows feet first and sucked them into himself until now his entire being reeked of the abyss.

Flipping on my left turn signal, I silently took the light and caught up to Camille. Delilah was right on our tail. And then we were there—the Scarlet Harlot. Parking was plentiful during the dark of the night, and I smoothly guided the Jag into an open space and flipped off the ignition.

Iris leaned forward. "Menolly, could this have something to do with what Grandmother Coyote asked you to do?"

Again the ton of bricks. Shit. Was I clueless tonight?

"Fuck, fuck, fuck, fuck," I said, jumping out of the car. Was I going to have to stake Erin? And would Camille be put through the wringer, forcing me to obliterate her friend? "The gods are walking on our graves tonight," I muttered as I headed toward the door. "By the time we face Shadow Wing in battle we'll be demons ourselves."

And then the irony hit me and I laughed, my voice hoarse and scratchy. I *was* a demon. I was already on the wrong side, according to logic, holding on only by making the conscious choice to avoid diving into the hellfire. I ignored Iris's questioning glance as we ran to the door, steps behind Camille and her boys.

We blew through the door like a tornado, Camille and Morio with magic at the ready. Trillian had his serrated blade out. We immediately went into search mode, and Morio cast a *Reveal Illusion* spell. Nothing. After a few minutes, we were sure the shop was clean, and Camille called out the safe word that brought Tim out of hiding.

Dressed in Dockers and a thick sweater, he looked nothing like Marilyn Monroe, the current fave in his retinue. His short brown hair had grown out into a curly mop, and he had faint traces of stage makeup still dappling his face, but what struck me was the fear that lingered in his eyes.

"She's gone . . . They took her. I couldn't stop them. I knew that if I tried they'd—"

"Shush," Camille said as Delilah enfolded him in her arms and gave him a gentle kiss on the forehead. He leaned against her shoulder, looking war scarred and weary.

"Did you hear anything, Tim? Did they say where they were taking her? How many were there? What did they look like? I know you're upset, but you need to tell us everything you can remember." I hated to press him, he looked so bewildered, but the sooner we could go after them, the better.

Nerissa noticed a microwave on the side counter, along with a box of tea and a bag of Oreos. She hurried over and popped a mug of water in the microwave and in less than two minutes, pressed a steaming cup of peppermint tea and a few cookies into Tim's hands. "You're in shock. Eat, drink . . . the sugar and mint will help."

Wade started sniffing around the shop, trying to catch a scent, while Camille and Morio moved off to the corner and crossed hands. I caught his whispered comments to her.

"Breathe deep. Focus, now focus . . . the vamps live in the realm of death and we can reach there through the *Summoning Dark Ones* spell that I taught you last week. If we leave out the last stanza, we won't risk calling them to us. If we're lucky, this just might point the way to them. Add the Moon Mother's energy to the spell if you can."

"I'll try," Camille said. "I can bring down a *silver arrow* and we might be able to turn it into a compass."

I glanced at Delilah, who had caught the exchange. By now, we all knew Morio had been teaching Camille death magic, but I wondered just how deeply entangled she was becoming with the fox demon. Truth was, none of us knew all too much about him, nor did we know how far in the shadows he walked. He was on our side, Grandmother Coyote had made that clear, but I was beginning to think there was a lot more to him than he let on. Sex magic, death magic . . . just what kind of youkai was he?

Delilah shook her head and I let it drop. Now was neither the time nor place to enquire. We had too much to do. I turned back to Tim, who clutched the mug in his hands like a shield. He looked over at me and shuddered.

"You asked me some questions?" Haggard, he'd lost any fight he might have had. I could tell that we'd have to direct his every move to get anything useful out of him. It wasn't that he didn't want to help. He was just too exhausted to do anything on his own.

"Let's start with what you saw. Tell us every detail that you can remember." I motioned to Iris, who pulled out a notebook and pen. She had a photographic memory but I didn't want to take any chances.

Taking a deep breath, he let it out sharply. "I was changing in the back when I heard Erin scream. I pulled on my pants—I was naked—and by the time I got to the doorway leading into the main store, I could see three men. They had hold of Erin, and she was putting up a fight, but then one waved his hand in front of her face and she stopped, like she'd forgotten what was happening."

"You said they're vampires. How do you know? What did they look like?" I was clinging to a nebulous hope that Erin had been dragged off by a bunch of FBHs who maybe wanted to rob her. It was a ludicrous hope, but one that would make it much easier to save her.

Tim dashed my hopes though. "They were standing in front of the big mirror, over there." He pointed to a three-way mirror Erin had set up in the main room of the lingerie shop. "The only one I could see was Erin. None of the men showed a reflection. Are there any other creatures that don't show their reflections?"

I closed my eyes, trying to come up with something that would give us hope. "Maybe . . . a few spirits but . . . no, Tim. Chances are good that you're right and vampires kidnapped her. Tell me what they looked like. You said three men? Are you sure there wasn't a woman with them?" The four newborns from the theater—the only ones we knew about who were still out there running around—had been two men, two women. Unless the guys had ditched the girls and taken up with a third male vamp, it didn't seem likely it was them. Newborns nesting together tended to be cliquish.

Tim frowned and I could tell he was trying to remember every detail. Erin was his closest friend, and he was hurting like hell. The pain oozed off him like motor oil, burnt and thick. I also suspected Tim was feeling a little bit guilty over hiding out rather than trying to stop them. Sometimes doing the *smart* thing didn't track as doing the right thing.

"The one who was holding her was stocky, short . . . He had a buzz cut. The second man was . . . I don't know . . . ordinary. Those two looked like they belonged here, today, in this world. But the third . . . he scared the hell out of me."

I looked up into his eyes. Raw fear. Primal terror. And I

knew, right then. "He was tall, with long curly dark hair, wasn't he? And he had a five o'clock shadow and wore black studded leather, didn't he? And you knew, just *by looking at him,* that you were looking into the face of hell."

Tim nodded, eyes widening. "Yeah, how did you know?"

"Did he say anything?" My stomach felt ready to leap into my throat.

"Just two words. He said, *Take her.* He's evil, Menolly. I swear to you, I was so scared just watching him that I almost pissed my pants. I wanted to help Erin, but . . . he looked like he'd eat me up and spit out the bones. I lost my nerve. I hid, damn it. I hid and didn't do a damned thing!"

As I stood back, letting Delilah move in to comfort Tim, I knew then that Dredge had Erin. At least for now. It had to be Dredge. He fed off of fear, and when you looked in his eyes, you knew your life was over, that you'd lost the battle and the punishment was about to begin . . .

"What's your name, girl?" His voice cut me to the quick. Ice cold, and I knew no tears would work on him, no amount of begging would get me out of what he had planned. "Tell me your name."

Even though I knew better than to give my name to a vampire, I couldn't resist the command. "Menolly," I whispered. "Menolly D'Artigo."

Dredge leaned over me, the crooked smile on his face filled with dark delight. He slid one sharpened nail along my cheek, stopping just before he drew blood. "Well, Menolly D'Artigo, I'm about to carry you up to the highest mountain. There, I'll drop you into the abyss and watch you *fall, and fall, and fall.*"

He ripped open my tunic and my nipples hardened in the cold dampness of the caverns. I heard whispered laughter from around the room and realized we had an audience. Murmurs reached my ears, catcalls and suggestions, but Dredge waved them away. "Patience. We have all the time in the world."

Leaning down, he slowly licked me from breast to navel.

I shuddered, not wanting to respond, angry that my body was betraying me. A quiver in my stomach made me catch my breath, and again he laughed.

"You like? Good. What about this?"

He interlaced his hands, cracking his knuckles. The next thing I knew, a line of razor-thin blades ripped across my stomach, slashing a trail of shallow lines that burned along my flesh. Unprepared for the pain, I shrieked and Dredge shuddered, drinking it in. "Scream as loud as you want. There's no one to hear you. No one to save you."

Another line of cuts and the sudden sting of salt water over the wounded flesh. I bit back my cries for the next few minutes as he laboriously began etching thin patterns along every inch of my body, drizzling salt water over each cut, each scar-in-the-making. After the tenth cut, a spiral right between my breasts, I started screaming. After the thirtieth, I was beyond words. And after a hundred, the torture began in earnest.

"Menolly? Menolly? Are you okay?" Delilah touched my shoulder, startling me. She quickly danced away when I hissed.

I shook my head, trying to clear my thoughts. No time for me to get lost in memories. Dredge had Erin and that meant she was doomed unless we got to her before he had a chance to.

"Sorry . . . just thinking." I saw Delilah glance at Camille, who was holding a silver arrow made of moonlight. "Did your spell work?" I asked, ignoring the glance that passed between them.

She paled and shook her head. "No. Not a single clue."

"We have five hours till sunrise. We'll have to just start searching the city—" I stopped as Delilah's cell phone rang.

"Chase," she whispered, flipping it open. Please, please let everything at home be okay, I prayed, hoping that for once the gods would be listening. She hung up. "We have to go home. Chase just got a call from Sharah. Four more vamp victims—the FH-CSI team got to them before the regular force heard. They haven't risen yet, but you know they will."

I glanced at Tim. "Tim, we have to go. We have to take care of them before they rise and hurt somebody else. We don't have any choice."

"Can't Chase take care of it? Erin's out there with that monster . . ."

"I know, and if there was any way I could go get her right now, I would. But we don't have a clue to where they took her. I promise you though, we'll do everything we can. Morio and Camille will drive you." I glanced at them. "Along the way, try to figure out if there's something you can do to locate Erin." I begged them silently to play along, even if they didn't think they could help. Tim needed to hold onto hope for a little while. And I had to go to the morgue and stake some bloodsuckers.

Camille jumped on board. "There are still spells we haven't tried that we can cast at home. Come on, Tim. Menolly, are you going alone?"

I glanced at Wade and Nerissa. "No. Take Nerissa, Iris, and Trillian with you. Trillian, once there, head out to the morgue with Chase. Delilah, Wade, and I will meet you there." I hated putting Delilah in danger, but we had no choice and she was better in a physical fight than Camille.

Things were bad now, but I had a feeling they were going to get much worse over the next few months and here on the front lines, we didn't have the luxury of retreat. As we headed out into the night, my thoughts flashed to Erin and I felt queasy all over again. Whatever happened to her, I prayed it was quick. But in my heart, I knew Dredge would never offer anyone that much mercy.

CHAPTER 10

"Morio, take Nerissa and Iris in your SUV. I'll ride with Camille and Tim," Trillian said.

Camille bundled her arm around Tim and led him toward the door. She glanced back at Delilah and me. "You guys be careful, okay?"

Nerissa held open the door as they hurried out into the glittering night. I turned to Delilah. "You and Wade go on ahead to the morgue. I'll meet you there. Don't play hero—wait for me before going in. Wade, we need stakes. Got any handy?"

He snorted. "Yeah, like I keep those around."

"He may not, but I do." The voice from the door made me jump. I spun around. Roz entered the shop.

"Have you been spying on us?"

"Not exactly. I checked out the zoo like I told you I was going to, then followed your . . . trace . . . here." He tugged at the belt of his duster, looking almost bemused.

"My trace? I've got a trace?" Traces were like a magical GPS and usually meant you'd been tagged by some wizard or witch. If I had one, then somebody had slapped a spell on me to monitor my position and I damned well wanted to know who'd done it.

His eyes flickered and he looked surprised. "You didn't know about it?"

I frowned. "If I'd known, I'd have put an end to both the trace and the person who triggered it."

Wade feather-touched my arm. "There's no time to debate whether or not you're being spied on. We have to take care of those newborns before they rise."

"He's right," Delilah said. "We can ask Camille and Morio to find out who's behind it later. For now, let's get moving. Chase will be on his way to the morgue pretty soon and I don't want him there alone. And it's not safe to leave Sharah holding the bag, either. If those vamps rise before we get there, she's dead meat. Or maybe undead elf."

They were both right. I motioned to Roz. "Come with us."

Wade jumped in Delilah's Jeep, while Roz climbed in my Jag. "After we're done," I said, "we need to have a little talk. Dredge captured one of our friends—a human. We can use your help rescuing her."

"What do I get in return?" Roz turned his head out the window and stared as the blur of dark buildings and incandescent lights flew by.

I didn't answer. As I pushed the gas pedal to the floor, I thought about the trace. Could Dredge have somehow whammied me? But that wouldn't make sense. He didn't need a trace to find me.

"Did you put the trace on me? You'd better give me the truth because Camille and Morio will ferret it out."

Roz didn't even turn at the question. "I had no need. The trace was already there. I just picked up on it."

"Do you know who did? Was it Dredge?" I had the feeling he knew more about it than he wanted to admit.

"Your guess is as good as mine but if I had to come up with an answer, I'd say no. Your sire wouldn't need to do that. My guess is that Queen Asteria had it fixed to you and your sisters. That way she can find out where you are, should something happen."

Queen Asteria! I'd never have thought it, but it made

sense. "You might be right. She's protective, and she knows we're in danger. And dropping in on her with a few dead demons hasn't exactly put her mind at ease." I glanced at Roz. "No doubt she told you all about it, so don't even ask. I don't want to think about Bad Ass Luke and his cronies."

Roz laughed, throaty and deep and I suddenly was all too aware that I was in the presence of another demon who, like me, walked between shadow and flame. "I wasn't going to. All I care about is hunting down Dredge and destroying him."

I shifted and headed up the hill toward the morgue, Delilah's Jeep keeping pace right behind me. "What will you do after he's dead?"

"Go back to doing what I do best, I suppose," he said. "Seducing women in the night. What else is there?"

"You ever think about putting some of your talents to use for the greater good?" Roz was helpful. We needed to know more about him, but I could see him becoming a strong ally in our fight against Shadow Wing.

"No, but I might be open to suggestions," he said, looking through his bag. "I've got seven stakes. That should be enough. I hope."

"Three more victims. Three more chalk marks on the board. I wonder if the female contingent of our four new-borns are the culprits. After all, Dredge and the men were busy kidnapping Erin." I found it odd that nobody had noticed any of Dredge's cronies wandering the area. They would look just as out of place as he did, but the two vamps who helped him kidnap Erin had been our newborns. What was going on?

"You think he's trying to build a master nest here?" Roz frowned. "If he can form a big enough one, then he can hive them off. Maybe he's looking to take control of the area." He paused for me to answer but before I could speak, he waved toward the park. "Something's going down over there. I can feel it."

He was right—something nasty was going down. The scent of blood hung so heavy in the air that it seeped through the closed windows of the car. I skidded to the curb and thrust open my door, hitting the bricks before I had time to say a word. Roz was close behind me. I heard a screech as Delilah's Jeep skidded to a halt near ours, but I was already on my way into the park on the corner lot intended to beautify the area.

As I lightly skimmed the ground, my heels making the barest clicking sound, my fangs extended. The smell of vamps filled the air—that unmistakable fragrance of blood and death and hunger.

The park was half a block square, and filled with fir and maple and weeping willow. I dashed into the dark, following my nose. At this point, I could hear the last gasps of someone dying.

Strike *someone,* and make it a mob, I thought as I broke through into a small clearing shrouded from the view of the street. Our gang from the theater was there, having a heyday. Two women lay on the ground, each with her very own hunka-vamp leaning over her. The two females were holding a struggling young man between them. He looked around fifteen and he'd already been bitten. As I watched, he went limp in their arms.

"The master said take them with us this time!" one of the women yelled as they spotted me racing toward them. "Let's go."

"What about this bitch?" asked one of the men. His name was Bob. I recognized him from the morgue photos.

The other shook his head. "Leave her. Dredge said she's all his."

I poured on the speed as they tossed their victims over their shoulders and took off running. "Follow them!" I yelled back to Roz as I dodged trees and leapt over rocks trying to keep them in sight. They were fast, but I was faster, and I managed to get within arm's reach of good old Bob, who was struggling to keep hold of the plump matron hanging over his shoulder.

He spun, hissing, and I let loose with a swipe that ripped his shirt, leaving a trail of deep scratches down his back. As he tossed the woman's body to the side, a *crack* fractured the night air as something inside her snapped. There was no time now to let myself worry about her. She was already dead.

As Bob spread his arms, ready to meet me, fangs out and eyes glowing, I leapt at him, growling as I body-slammed him to the ground. I was older, I had more experience, and I was far more ruthless. As he keeled over backward, I swiped at his throat, gashing a long slice from ear to ear.

"Here!" Roz tossed a stake to me and I caught it firmly in midair. As I held it over my victim, though, I paused. "What are you waiting for?" Roz said. "Stake him now—stake him while he's down."

"No. He's alive and he knows Dredge. Maybe he can tell us where that cocksucker is!"

Roz knelt beside me, keeping a wary eye on the retreating backs of the others. They'd managed to elude his attempts to catch them. "They sure learn fast, don't they? Give loyalty to Dredge, and to Dredge only. Anybody else falls, leave them behind."

"You got it. That's how he works," I said. "Hey, have any silver twine on you?"

"I've got better than that," Roz said with a grin. "I put this little goody together today." He pulled out a rope and I recoiled immediately. It had been drenched with garlic oil. "Yeah, I thought that would do the trick," he added, smiling at my reaction.

"Keep that shit away from me," I said. "Tie him up with it. You think it's strong enough to hold him?"

"You want me to tie you up and see if you can get loose?"

I flashed him the evil eye. "Yeah, and I want to go dance in the sunlight, too. Hurry up. We've got to get out of here in case they return with reinforcements."

Just then, Delilah and Wade caught up with us. "What's going on?"

"Check that woman over there. Is she still alive?" I motioned to Wade. "You do it. Delilah, I need you to help Roz tie up our friend here with this delightfully stinky rope."

As Roz held the dude down, Delilah wrapped the rope around his arms, and another length around his feet. The minute the rope hit the vamp's skin, he screamed.

I kicked him in the side. Hard. He'd been in on the kidnapping and I had zero sympathy for him. "Shut up or I'll give you a good reason to scream. My sister's learning death magic. I'm sure she and her partner have something to corral a vampire." I was bluffing, but he didn't have to know.

Wade motioned me over. "She's dead, and she drank. Look at her chin."

The woman's face was splattered with blood. Bob had forced her to drink before she died. It wouldn't be long before she started to rise. I blankly turned back to Roz. "Give me that stake."

Wade blanched as I leaned over her. "I'm sorry," I said. "I hate doing this but . . ." Grimacing, I plunged the stake into her heart and shuddered as a low wail filled the air and her body exploded into dust. She'd been turning fast. The newborns were gaining power at a rapid rate. Dredge's blood was strong. All of his children—including me—were exceptional in strength.

"Menolly, the morgue," Delilah said. "We don't have much time."

Shit. The morgue! In my excitement over catching one of the newborns, I'd almost forgotten. "What are we going to do with him until then? We don't dare leave him alone or he might call his grave-mates and he has information we need."

"You go on ahead. Wade and I'll take him home. You'll just have to take care of the vamps in the morgue yourself." Delilah dusted off her jeans as Wade yanked our prisoner to his feet. Lucky for us he was in obvious agony from the sting of the garlic-infused ropes and paying little attention to what we were saying.

"Are you nuts? We can't allowing that creature in our house! Let me think for a minute." I mulled over our options and then snapped my fingers. "Got it. Come here, the two of you. Roz, can you watch over our buddy here for a moment?" Roz traded places with Wade as I motioned for Delilah and Wade to follow me over to where I hoped we couldn't be heard.

"I want you to take him to the Wayfarer. It's closed now, so there won't be any customers there to question you.

Downstairs, near the room with the portal in it, you'll find a metal door. Tavah knows you, so she won't attack. Here's the key for that room." I removed a heavy key from my key ring and pressed it into Delilah's hand. She curled her fingers around it and let out a little mew. The key had some iron in it. A tiny puff of smoke rose from her hand. "Yeah, I know it hurts, but it's not enough to damage you."

"What's behind the door?" Wade asked.

"A magic-proof chamber, built to house rogue OW visitors the Wayfarer might need to deport. The OIA built it, and Jocko kept it top secret. I don't think he ever told Wisteria, and none of my bartenders know about it. When I took over, Headquarters let me in on the secret. That room will hold a minor demon, so it should hold a vamp. He shouldn't be able to send any messages out on the astral, either. Lock him in and head for the morgue. And don't dawdle."

Delilah let out a rough laugh. "That's going to come in handy, probably more than we think. Okay, get moving and don't worry. Wade and I can handle it. But . . . give us one of those stakes. Just in case?" Her eyes took on a feral gleam and I had a dark sense that someone was watching through her eyes. The scent of bonfires filled the air and then, with a gust of wind, was gone.

"I think you have company on your shoulder," I said softly, handing her my stake.

"I know," she whispered. "I can feel *him* here. The Autumn Lord has been around since the first bodies were found."

"Well, we don't have time to ask why. Go. Keep your cell phone on." I pushed her and Wade back over to Bob's side, where they yanked him to his feet and headed toward the Jeep, dragging him between them. Roz and I followed, keeping an eye on them till they sped off in the night.

"I hope they'll be okay." I couldn't bear it if something happened to Kitten because of me.

"They're strong, they're experienced." Roz shrugged and handed me the purse the woman I'd staked had been carrying. "Here, you might want this . . . to identify her with. Come on, let's get to the morgue. I hope we're not too late."

I carried the purse gingerly. Within it were the last things she'd touched. Dredge had purged her of her life. I'd purged her of her death. I could only hope she was walking with her ancestors.

We were only a few blocks from the Faerie-Human Crime Scene Investigations building where Sharah had ordered the new bodies brought. As we screeched into the parking lot, we saw Trillian and Chase climbing out of the car.

"What the hell took you so long?" Trillian asked. "Stop for a drink or something?"

"Shut up, *Svartan*. We came across the first four newborns in the park, harvesting more victims. Three of them got away. The other vamp is on his way to a holding pen for now."

"And their victims?" Chase asked, paling.

I stared at him, daring him to comment. "They carried two of them off with them—one a teenaged boy. The third we dusted. She was already starting to turn."

He paled, then rushed to the building with me hot on his heels. Roz and Trillian brought up the rear. Roz was readying stakes and tossed one to Trillian, who grunted, catching it lightly.

I paused at the door. "Here we go again. Take two on Stake-That-Vamp. Let's go see what we have. If they already rose, Sharah's in a heap of trouble." I pushed open the doors and once again, we hustled down the stairs to the morgue.

During our trip the other day, I hadn't noticed the surveillance cameras but now they stood out, near the magical detection that allowed the guards upstairs to track OW guests and prisoners. As we raced by one of the sensors, it started to howl.

Chase pulled out his gun, turned, and shot it point-blank. As the ward exploded in a fiery shower of sparks, he let out a low laugh. I stared at him. "What the hell are you on, Johnson?"

"Just blowing off steam," he said.

Trillian grunted something to him that I couldn't hear.

The morgue was in the basement and as we approached the doors to the second examination room, I could sense that something was terribly wrong. We were too late. I knew it in the center of my core. I pushed ahead and slammed the doors open, flipping on the lights. Three steel slabs lay empty, sterile sheets draped on the floor, no longer pristine.

"Oh, hell! They've risen. Watch your backs." I immediately slid into reconnoiter mode, circling the room, stake at the ready.

"Sharah!" Chase let out a harsh bark as Trillian moved to cover him. I traced the scent of the freshest batch of newborns. Three more vamps on the loose. With the three that we'd lost in the park and their two new victims, that meant at least eight under Dredge's control.

They could be anywhere—in the building or out of it. I just prayed Sharah had gotten out of the way.

"Chase, stay with Trillian and keep an eye on each other. I'm going to explore the back. Roz, cover me." I headed toward the backroom off the morgue, where they performed tests and disposed of the remains.

Roz swung in behind me as I raised my booted foot and slammed it against the door. The sound of ripping metal shrieked as the hinges twisted and the heavy metal door fell, toppling into the other room. I leapt over it, Roz right behind me.

I'd only seen this backroom one time before, when Sharah gave us a tour during the post-Christmas party Chase had thrown for the FH-CSI team. The walls were lined with cupboards and sinks, counters filled with serrated knives and bone saws and dental hooks, and instruments that I didn't even want to fathom the uses for. The room was lit by a dim florescent light, and the scent of decay undermined the sterile odors coming from the antiseptic soap and bleaches used to clear away the traces of the dead. The last stop on the train. No more journeys, no more travels in the current body. That is, unless they'd been given their tickets by Dredge.

"Every cupboard—open and check." I slammed open door after door, looking for any sign of Sharah or the newborns. There were bottles of liquid with hearts and eyes and livers floating in seas of formaldehyde, bottles of blood, and bottles containing items better left unidentified. But no vamps.

Roz took the other side and we worked in silence until we came to the end, facing the other door. Without a word, I took the front and he covered my back. As I shoulder butted it, the wood shook, then splintered as the lock gave way.

The hall was dimly lit—again the low shimmer of fluorescent lighting—and it led to bathrooms and a fire exit. The fire exit was open, the wires to the alarm cut. I stuck my head outside, staring at the greenbelt that lay beyond the back of the building. They were gone. I could smell their essence, but they'd passed through and left.

I turned back to see Roz pointing at the women's bathroom.

"Someone in there?" I said, barely whispering. He nodded.

I slipped over to his side and cautiously cracked the door. The bath held a shower and two toilet stalls, and I could hear a faint whimper coming from one of them. I recognized the voice.

"Sharah! Sharah, is that you? It's me, Menolly. Come out." I carefully made my way over to the stall. What if they'd attacked her, turned her, and she'd already risen? Vampiric elves could be freakier than regular vamps. Like vampiric Fae, their powers were usually stronger and darker. And with elves, the change went against their basic natures and usually sent them over the edge into madness. Very few found their way back.

The door to the toilet stall swung open. Sharah staggered out. She was hurt, that much was obvious, with blood dripping down her shoulder and from her wrists. But her mouth was clean and I caught no sense that she was one of the undead. She was still alive.

"Quick, did they make you drink from them?" I asked, tossing my stake to Roz, who caught it and kept watch on the door to the hall.

She shook her head. "No, no . . . smell if you want."

I motioned for her to stay her distance. "You know better than that. You're covered with blood and I'm in hunting mode. Don't come near me." I paused. She needed attention, and fast, but we'd have to get her back to the others. I couldn't chance staying with her while Roz went to get help, and I didn't want to chance leaving him here with her unprotected, just in case the newborns took it into their heads to return.

"Roz, you carry her back into the main morgue."

"Do you think we should move her?" He handed the stakes to me and caught her up in his arms.

At the flicker in his eyes when she pressed against him, I shook my head. "Don't get any ideas, wise guy. She's hurt bad."

With a sly grin, he shrugged. "A demon can fantasize, can't he?"

Sharah gasped. "Demon?"

"Hold still or I might accidentally drop you," he said gruffly. "I'm an incubus. Get over it. We're facing far greater dangers than I will ever pose to you, my elfin lady."

She glanced into his face, then nodded and leaned against his shoulder as he swung out of the room and I followed. I stopped to close the fire exit. There wasn't much I could do to brace it shut, but we didn't need to leave an open invitation to anybody who might be passing by, be they vamp or human or Fae.

We rejoined the others in the main morgue, where we found Delilah and Wade had made it back. Delilah was looking pissed out of her mind.

"That didn't take you long. Have any trouble with Bob?" I asked.

Delilah nodded. "Yeah. Halfway there he managed to get loose from his ropes. We had to stake him or we would have been toast."

"Damn it—" I started to say, but Wade raised his hand.

"There was no other choice. Chalk it up to bad luck, or whatever you like, but he's gone. Let's focus on the here and now."

I grumbled but knew he was right. There was nothing we could do now, and Delilah was a good fighter. She wouldn't stake our potential informant unless the danger had been all too real.

Delilah took one look at Sharah as Roz carried her into

the room before she raced over to help him, Chase right on her heels.

"Upstairs," he said. "We have a medic station. Follow me."

"Be careful. We don't know if they rampaged the joint before they escaped. They might have circled round and come in topside." I wouldn't put anything past Dredge and his children, especially if it was sneaky, underhanded, or designed to inflict as much pain as possible.

Wade and Trillian guarded the rear while Roz and I led the way. We stopped by the elevator doors, which were next to the stairwell.

"I don't want to chance the elevators," I said. "If there are a bunch of vamps up there, we don't want to be trapped in a little metal box."

Chase eyed the stairs. "That means we have to carry Sharah up three flights and she's pretty badly hurt."

I stepped back. "I could carry her with no problem, except . . ." I paused, and Delilah immediately understood.

"She's bleeding. Let me do it." Delilah was stronger than Chase.

Not one to get in a snit about it, he immediately acquiesced. "Take her. You can carry her easier and quicker than I can."

Delilah swept Sharah into her arms and, with Roz and me at the helm, began the climb. Chase kept pace right beside her, helping to steady or balance her when she needed it.

At the top of the stairs, I peered through the windows gracing the double doors that led into the main room. While Chase worked out of an office at police headquarters, he also had an office here and divided his time between the two stations.

"Chase, do you know that guy at the desk?" I asked, motioning for him to edge up the steps and peek through the window.

Chase nodded. "Yeah. That's Yugi. He's an empath from Sweden."

"Human?" I asked.

"An FBH just like me," he said. "Do you sense something wrong?"

"No, but—" I stopped as Yugi spotted me. He jumped up and called something over his shoulder. Three men came racing around the corner and headed our way. "Why the fuck didn't they hear the magic sensor go off and come to check on what was going down? Or hear your bullet hitting it?"

"I don't know—" Chase said, pulling out his badge. He stood back as the men burst through the doors. They skidded to a halt when they saw him.

"Sharah!" Yugi said, his face draining of color. "Detective, is she okay?"

"No. We need to get her to Medical right away. Be careful. There are vamps on the loose and they aren't the friendly kind," Chase said, pushing through them and motioning for us to follow him.

"Should we head down there?" Yugi asked, motioning to the stairs.

I interrupted before Chase could say a word. "Do and you put your lives in danger. Seal off this door for now and call in your reserves. This building's going to need a thorough search. You have to be prepared in case the newborns return. The fire exit downstairs is broken and the wires cut. And why the hell didn't you hear the magic detector go off? Chase shot the damned thing and nobody even bothered to come check what was happening. What are you guys running? A Burger Bonzo's or a high-tech crime unit?"

I didn't wait for an answer, but swept past them, following Chase and Delilah, who was cradling the still-bleeding Sharah in her arms. The scent of her blood was driving me crazy, but I'd managed to keep myself under control. I glanced over at Wade. He caught my stare and nodded, almost imperceptibly, and I knew that he, too, was fighting his basic nature.

At the door of the medic lab, Roz and Trillian went in and scoped it out. Trillian popped his head out. "Get her in here."

"Menolly, Wade, why don't you two wait outside the doors? Keep an eye on things?" Roz said.

A shiver ran down my back. He knew. He knew that this was torture, to hunt and chase, then smell the blood and not be able to touch.

"Thank you," I said softly, and he stepped to the side as everyone else entered the room. He took my hands in his.

"I know. I know . . . for me it's a different thirst, but I understand," he murmured. He suddenly caught me in his arms and pressed his lips against mine. I let out a short gasp as the fire of his kiss ricocheted through my body. Floundering in the waves of sensuality that rolled off of him, I felt like I wanted to drown, to dive into his depths and never surface.

Roz lightly cupped my chin. "If you need me, for *anything,* you have only to ask. I understand the nature of the chase. I can relieve your stress in ways you can only fantasize." And then, without a word to Wade, he turned and returned to the medic lab.

I leaned against the wall, trying to calm the quivering flames that had flared to life in my stomach. Wade silently crossed to my side. He didn't touch me, but merely stood near, a comforting anchor in the sea of desire that was screaming through every fiber of my being.

"So much . . . too much," I said, feeling like I might break into brittle shards if one more thing happened before daylight.

"Take a breath. Focus on releasing your hunger," he said.

So I breathed. My lungs didn't need the air, but I needed the ritual, the pattern, the drill. I breathed through my mouth so I wouldn't smell the blood, or Roz's heat that still radiated on my face. I breathed to calm the hunger, to calm the thirst, to subdue the fire that rose darkly within me. I breathed to remind myself that even though I'd left life behind, I was still a sentient creature who had options, who could choose to follow a strict path in which the blood and passion only came through consent, not through the ravaging of the innocent.

And when I'd lost count of the breaths, I stopped and raised my head. "I am Menolly D'Artigo," I said. "I am the daughter of a Guardsman. I am half Fae, half-human. And I am a vampire who chooses to walk the tightrope, who walks in shadows even while I remember what it was to dance under the light. I am in control. Not my nature and not the predator within. I make the choices."

The litany that the OIA had taught me still served me well. I looked over at Wade, who gave me a thin smile.

"I'm back," I said. But somewhere, deep inside, I could hear a dark laughter as the words *for now* echoed in my mind. And for once, I longed for the hint of first light to pull me into my dreams where I had the chance to escape, to forget, to erase the constant battle that raged in my heart.

CHAPTER 11

On the way home, we knew two things: Sharah would live, and the alarms on the magic detection system didn't reach the guys topside because somebody had thrown a dampening spell on them. In the hallway, on the steps, they sounded. Behind the doors to the main room, they didn't make a sound.

Everybody was exhausted, except me, and even I was emotionally drained. We were missing a friend captured by Dredge and his crew, and we faced at least eight rogue vamps running through the streets, one of them a cute teenage boy who would probably start right in feeding off the high school girls. A gruesome thought, but all too real.

Roz had declined to join us. "I'll see if I can track anything down," he said. "I don't have to sleep much. I can scout around while you get some rest."

Still not sure what to think about him, I accepted his help gratefully. He'd proven himself so far, and while that didn't necessarily mean shit in a cow barn, it did give me hope that maybe he was on the up and up.

Wade had taken off for his nest and Delilah said she'd

drive Chase to his apartment before heading for home. Trillian rode back with me. He scowled the entire way.

"What's eating you?" I said as we sped along the highway.

"Camille's totally freaked out about Erin. She was telling me that it's all her fault. That she should never have befriended a human because the potential for collateral damage is too great, considering Shadow Wing and his posse." He glared out the window. "I don't like it when she's unhappy."

"I don't like it either. Pretty soon the 'collateral damage' is going to skyrocket if those demons break through. But if Dredge wasn't out to get me, then there would be somebody else threatening us. Camille should be proud she's here, helping out. If we hadn't stopped Bad Ass Luke, he might have opened the way for Shadow Wing. She's the one who figured out what his weakness was." I skirted a slow moving car and turned up the music.

Trillian grunted. "You and I know that, but I think Camille's just worn out. For all her bravado, she's devastated over the events of the past few months. And she's worried about your father and aunt."

A little exasperated, I said, "Well, so is Delilah. Probably more than Camille. And so am I, for that matter. I just keep my worries hidden better." I stared at the road as my wheels ate up the pavement, grinding it beneath the Jag. "We're in this together. There's no way out and we have to just get used to it."

"You have no friends," Trillian said with a snort. "How can you understand what Camille's feeling? If that sadist kills Erin, Camille will never forgive herself."

"She'd better learn," I said gruffly. "I have to forgive myself for my actions every day. The longer we're at war with Shadow Wing, the more the casualty rate will skyrocket. The demons will become more aggressive and we'll have to do the same. We aren't playing hopscotch here. Yeah, it sucks, but we're talking reality."

Even as the acerbic words left my mouth, I regretted them. I wasn't hardhearted, not really, but I sounded like a total bitch. No wonder Trillian looked down his nose at me. I expected him to make some cutting reply, but he simply turned his face to the window.

After a moment, he said, "You're right, of course. I understand that. I've seen the face of battle all too frequently. And I see it every time I travel home to OW. But Camille and Delilah . . . They aren't used to all this death and carnage."

"I am," I said softly. "I wish I wasn't, but I am."

"You live with the taste of blood in your mouth. I live with the stain of blood on my hands. We accept it as part of our lives. But those two . . . they're just starting to find their places in the shadow realm. Delilah's been drafted as a Death Maiden. Camille's taking lessons in death magic from that wolf boy yakuza."

"Knock it off. I'm not impressed. Morio's a youkai, not a member of the yakuza," I said, automatically stepping into Camille's role. But even as I spoke, it struck me that, as hedonistic and self-centered of a manipulator as he was, Trillian really did care.

"Don't flatter yourself, O Fanged One. Impressing you is a low priority on my list." Trillian shook his head. "Aren't you hearing anything I'm saying?"

I rolled my eyes. "You made your point. Is there anything I can do to help them out that I haven't thought of?"

He shook his head. "Unfortunately, no. All we can do is offer support and help them adjust. All of the realms are beautiful, but true to nature, there's more terror in the world than joy. And sometimes the two are enmeshed." He looked straight at me. "Like you. You with your bloody bites and your passionate kisses. You can charm the life out of a man and leave him happy to die. You're no less a demon than the creatures we're fighting, but you've chosen to remain true to your ethics."

And with that backhanded compliment, we pulled into the driveway. I didn't bother to answer. He was right, as much as it pained me to admit it. Everything he said was spot on, and I couldn't deny it.

Camille and Morio were sitting in the middle of the living room when we walked through the door. Camille was crosslegged on the floor, a blindfold around her eyes, her wrists bound with silver chains. Morio was kneeling behind her, his hands resting on her shoulders. His hair, silky smooth and flowing to his shoulder blades, reflected the light in its blue-black brilliance. He wore a loose blue and white kimono over simple muslin pants. Camille was dressed in an indigo robe that barely covered her breasts. One of Erin's flannel shirts lay draped across her lap. The music was loud, a throbbing world beat, and Morio was whispering in her ear.

I took one look at the mists that swirled around them and headed for the kitchen. Considering Camille's faulty wiring, and the fact that they'd been delving into death magic, I didn't think it wise to stay in the same room while they were in the middle of conjuring.

Trillian followed me after a grudging glance their way. Delilah sat at the table with Tim and Nerissa, drinking hot cocoa. Iris was making a late-night snack, and Maggie was playing in her playpen. Everything seemed so peaceful, that I longed to believe the illusion that it was a normal night with nothing amiss.

I slid into the chair beside Nerissa, who flashed me a troubled smile. "Delilah told us what happened," she said.

Iris shook her head. "There are too many variables to this situation. You need help. You must to go to Aladril tomorrow night and seek out that seer."

"I agree," I said. "But we're going to pay hell getting Camille to leave now that Erin's missing."

Tim whirled on me. "Iris told me about Dredge. Erin's as good as dead, isn't she?"

Damn it. I flashed her an irritated look, and she shrugged in return. No doubt Tim had pressed her into telling him what she knew. But what he was thinking couldn't be as bad as the reality.

"I don't know for sure, but if we don't find her soon, then yes. Dredge will kill her." I didn't mention torture. Why bother?

"First light is coming, Menolly," Iris said.

"I know, I can feel it." And I could. The slow gentle draw into unconsciousness was tapping at my shoulder. Not long before I'd have to withdraw to sleep. And, if I was lucky, I wouldn't dream. I glanced at the clock. An hour left, at most. "Nerissa, come with me?"

We headed into the parlor from the back way so as not to disturb Camille and Morio. As I closed the door behind me, I said, "Do you want Delilah to drive you home?"

"Now?" she asked, sounding surprised.

Thoughts of Camille's fears echoed through my mind. "Nerissa, our enemies are far more dangerous than you know. You could get hurt if you stick around here. If you get involved with . . . us . . . me."

She slowly closed the gap between us and gently raised her hands to cup my face. "I know that. I knew that before I made up my mind that I wanted to be with you. I'm not asking for a lifetime. I'm not asking for any commitments. I just want to be here, right now, tonight."

I searched her eyes, looking up at her. Roz's kiss had burned like fire, almost frightening me, but Nerissa's lips looked warm and inviting, lush and filled with unspoken promises. I thought of what we had to lose if I said no, and slowly reached up on tiptoe to press my lips against hers.

She slid her arms around me, pulling me close, her tongue parting my lips as she explored, searching. I let out a shudder as her hand slid under my shirt, and then jumped away.

"What is it? Did I do something wrong?" A look of disappointment washed over her face.

"I have to tell you something first." Every scar on my body tingled. "My body is covered with scars. And I mean *covered*." I looked away. "No one has touched me in . . . that way . . . since Dredge finished with me and turned me into a vampire. My sisters think I slept with Wade but the truth is we never reached that point. I've never slept with a human or an Earthside Supe. I don't know what to expect."

"Do you want to be with me?" she asked. "Be honest; it's all right if you say no. I'll be disappointed, but I'm a big girl. I can take rejection."

I shook my head. "It's not that. Just . . . see, I don't know if I can control myself once you take your clothes off. I had a bad experience at a strip club last summer when

Camille got the bright idea we should soak up some of the culture here. There's so much I don't know about that part of myself . . ." I stopped as she brushed one finger against my mouth.

"Shush," she said. "You don't have to worry about me. I'll be okay. I partnered with Venus the Moon Child. He trained me well."

I blinked, staring at her. "What does that have to do with it?"

Her lip quivered into a smile that lurked between a grin and a leer. "Venus taught me how to master my fear and give in to passion. He taught me how to heal old wounds of the heart and psyche with sex."

Nerissa gave me a gamine smile, but behind that winsome face and proper reserve, I sensed a wild and free spirit. I swallowed my worry and slowly removed my shirt, waiting to see myself reflected in her eyes.

"This is who I am. If you want me, take me. It's all up to you," I said, feeling stripped bare before her.

Her gaze landed on my stomach and trailed up my chest, lingering on my breasts, then up my throat, finally locking with my eyes. She didn't flinch, didn't turn away from the hundreds of white lacerations that signified Dredge's psychotic attentions.

"He did this to you? This Dredge?" she asked after a moment, her voice almost a growl.

I slipped out of my boots and jeans in answer, to show her that the scars continued down my body. My hands, feet, and face were the only places he'd left pristine, untouched by those dagger sharp nails of his. I had no pubic hair; he'd shaved that, and written his name in a coiling scar on the curve of my mound. "I own you," he'd said as he slashed into my flesh. "Body and soul, I claim you and sire you."

Nerissa undressed and tossed her jeans and shirt to the side. She was glorious, with swelling breasts and a golden thatch of hair that nestled around her sacred sex. A Viking warrior, when she shook her hair loose of the chignon and it fell to her shoulders she radiated an energy that I couldn't define.

I wanted to reach out but I was still afraid. Would I hurt her? Would I snap, go into an uncontrollable frenzy when I smelled her perfume, felt her heart beating under my fingers? I was about to turn away when she suddenly covered the distance between us and pulled me into her arms, pressing her mouth against mine. Her lips tasted like sweet honey wine, and I stopped resisting, wanting the kiss to go on and on and on.

"You're beautiful," she whispered, coming up for air, staring into my eyes. And the look in her eyes told me she meant it. She dipped her head again and I let her lead me to the sofa and pull me down on the thick plush rug in front of it. Her lips worked their way down my neck and a small cry ripped from my throat as their sweet touch trailed over my shoulder and to my breasts.

Kissing my scars, she murmured something that sounded like, "We'll kill him, honey. Don't worry, we'll kill him," and then she caught one of my nipples between her teeth and tugged ever so slightly.

Waves of thirst grew in my belly and my fangs began to extend but I forced them to retreat as I reveled in Nerissa's attention. She sucked gently, then harder, and I closed my eyes, letting myself float on the sensations that worked their way up my body. A cloud rising in the brilliant sky, golden sunbeams glistening down on my hair, my face, that was my Nerissa.

Her kisses warmed me for the first time in years and as the lazy pull of first light began to drag me down into lethargic slumber, she parted my legs, gazing down at my sex. The thought of Dredge's name there made me try to pull my legs together, to hide what he'd done to me, but Nerissa gently pried them open again and leaned down to kiss the taint he'd left behind.

"He may have left his name, but he'll never touch you again," she whispered, brushing one finger over the ridged skin as tears welled up in her eyes. She let them fall, then carefully scooped up the sparkling diamonds with one finger and bathed me in them. "With my tears, I reclaim you for yourself. With the salt, I purge him from your body."

A ripple ran through me, whether it was her words or her touch or some strange magic she'd learned from Venus the Moon Child, I didn't know, but as she rested her lips on me, I tumbled into flame and fire. A wracking thirst welled up, a thundering desire to drink deep from the well of her life. I reared up, eyes blazing, fangs extended, unable to stop myself.

Nerissa didn't jump or jerk away. Instead she rested one hand on my shoulder and shook her head. "No, Menolly. Just let yourself drift."

Her lack of fear echoed through my ruby-drenched sight, and I fought for focus, fought my inclination to sink my teeth deep into her neck in a blissful communion. Nerissa pushed me back to the rug, leaning over me. Her lips moved lower on my stomach, leaving a cascade of kisses in their wake.

And then she was there, pressed against me, her tongue swirling a pattern of passion that drove all thoughts out of my mind, leaving only the wave on which I was riding. I stubbornly tried to cling to my fear—if I let go, would I lash out and overpower her? Would I tear her throat open? But the steady lapping of her sandpaper tongue broke through my barriers. I fell, tumbling into a different abyss, this one filled with a lush garden, a rain forest of delight instead of the ever-present bloodlust that ruled my life. With a sharp cry, I gave myself up to her and let the release swallow me whole.

Silence. Peace. And then Nerissa sat up and stretched, lazily glancing at the clock. "It's almost first light. You'd better go to bed before morning hits."

I blinked. "What about you, though? Aren't you . . ."

She grinned, daintily wiping her mouth. "Don't worry about me. I have my ways. Now go. I'll be a phone call away. I have to go back to the compound. I know you have plans tonight, but call me later, when things calm down. If you'd like." Her smile was infectious and I found myself grinning back, giddy for the first time that I could remember in a long, long while.

"I'll call, Nerissa," I said, hesitating. Then, heedless of

what it might mean, I plunged on. "You're incredible. You're beautiful and you're fearless. I never knew . . ."

She shrugged into her clothes and gave me a quick kiss. "Menolly, I'm not fearless. I'm just aware of what world you live in. Venus the Moon Child walks under the shadow of death. He taught me to look it in the face and find the beauty within all of its aspects. And he taught me how to return from the abyss." And with that, she scurried out of the room.

I watched her retreating back, thinking I should say something, but then she was gone. Anyway, no matter what I said now, it would be anticlimatic. Whatever this thing between us was meant to be, it would grow at its own pace.

With a last glance at the curtained windows, which were starting to show the overcast glimmer of morning, I slid into my jeans and top and hurried into the living room. Everyone was getting ready to crash. Trillian, Morio, and Camille were about to head upstairs, and Tim had fallen asleep in the rocking chair.

Iris wandered in. "The kitchen's clear," she said as Camille said good night. "Delilah's driving Nerissa home." She gave me an expectant look and I just smiled. As I passed her to head down to my lair, she whispered. "Good for you, Menolly. But be careful. There are so many complications."

"I know," I said softly. "I know." And I did. But I wasn't willing to walk away. What I'd told Trillian was the truth: collateral damage was going to happen, like it or not. And it seemed a crime to walk away from friendship and love, the things that make life worth living—even for those of us long past life. Wondering if I'd regret my choice, I stopped to give Maggie a gentle kiss on the forehead, then headed downstairs for the night.

Camille woke me just past dusk. "Menolly, we have to go if we're heading to Aladril."

I sat up, blinking. My dreams had been filled with passion and the vision of a golden goddess, a fiery mane of sun-kissed hair trailing down my skin. A nice change from the usual.

Surprised to hear her so eager to leave, I said, "You still want to go, with what's happened to Erin?"

"Now more than ever. Morio and I did our best last night but we couldn't track them. Dredge is too good at hiding. We have to do something and soon." She paused, then burst out, "It's bad. The local tabloids have gotten wind that at least a half-dozen people are missing and they're screaming at the cops to find them. The one saving grace is that while *we* know they're dead and that some of them have gone vamp on us, nobody else knows yet. Think of the panic that's going to erupt if this continues."

"What do you mean *if*? Dredge won't quit until he's stopped." I slipped into a pair of skin-tight jeans and a long-sleeved tunic made of spider silk, cinching it with a black-studded leather belt. Pulling on a pair of leather gloves and my spiked heel ankle boots, I was ready in five minutes. I nixed the makeup—it took me too long to apply without being able to see my reflection, and why bother when we were headed back to OW anyway?

"It gets worse," Camille said, staring at the floor. She was wearing a flowing skirt from Otherworld, and a custom corset made from a plum-colored jacquard. Unlike me, she was in full makeup. Her hair flowed over her shoulders in a cascade of curls.

"You look like you're made up to pay a visit to Court and Crown," I said. "And what do you mean, 'it gets worse'?"

"Hey, we don't know who we're going to meet over there," she said. "I want to look my best. To answer your question, Chase got a report in from the red light district on the strip near SeaTac. Last night four of the regulars—all girls—disappeared with a couple of rowdy guys and never came back. Their roommate, also a hooker, reported them missing. Chase picked up on it and showed her the photos of the two guys killed at the theater."

"And?" I didn't even have to ask. I knew the answer already.

"She ID'd them all right. Our vamps have struck again, and who knows if those were their only victims. The girl's already on the run—apparently she's afraid it's another

Green River Killer thing. Chase couldn't convince her to stay." Camille shook her head. "I want to find Erin, but we can't do that if we can't find Dredge. Maybe this dude in Aladril can help us because we sure aren't having any luck on our own. Queen Asteria seems convinced he can help. We have to go."

"Delilah ready?" I looked around the room, wondering if I should take anything else with me. Deciding that my claws and fangs were better than any weapon I could carry, I motioned to the stairs. "Let's go."

"Delilah's not coming. She's staying here to help Tim on the database. The sooner we can field more info out through the Supe groups, the better. And somebody should stay with Iris and Maggie. It's just you and me. And Trillian."

I let out a low grumble. "Why is he coming along?"

"Because he knows the territory and Tanaquar has called him back for a mission. Which means we'll be shorthanded over here."

"Morio going? I'd like to have the fox demon with us." Morio was good in a fight, and I trusted him to help Camille from going totally haywire on magic.

She sighed. "I'm a little worried taking him into Aladril—he sure doesn't know the customs, but yes, he's willing to come with us."

"So Delilah and Iris are staying here alone? I'm not sure how I feel about that. Dredge is on our tail. If we're gone . . ."

"Don't sweat it. Zachary and Nerissa are staying here with them. Speaking of which . . . you two make a cute couple."

I rolled my eyes. Of course she knew. When it had anything to do with love or sex, Camille was always on the inside track. "About that . . ."

"Don't say it. Don't say anything. I know there's nothing solid there, but the fact that you let her into your life . . . Just let it be what it is," she said. Then as we reached the kitchen, she added, "I'm happy for you, Menolly. I think this will be good for you."

Trillian might think Camille was afraid of getting involved with locals, but she certainly seemed to have my back on the subject. As we entered the living room, Trillian was there in his OW garb, and Morio was standing beside him in what looked like a ninja costume.

I repressed a snort, but couldn't resist saying, "Halloween come early?"

He gave me a measured look, but all he said was, "If you like."

Trillian shot me a nasty glare. "That was rude."

I bounced it right back. "Since when are you standing up for bachelor number two?"

"You and Delilah watch too much TV," Camille said.

"Not lately." It had been a week or two since one of our late night trash-TV fests. I wasn't about to admit it, but I kind of missed them—they gave us time to just hang out and chill. "Tell you what, though. I'd rather be doing that than chasing down rogue vamps."

Delilah let out a sigh. "Jerry Springer's kind of yummy, don't you think?"

Camille and I shouted her down and she waved us off. "Get out of here. Tim and I are going to start building the database for the Supe community roster. And I might just do a little spying tonight with Roz."

"What? You can't go with him—he's an incubus!" Oh yeah. That's just what we needed. My sister the Death Maiden all wrapped up with an incubus.

"Uh, I *know* what he is. And he knows better than to play touchy-feely with me. But he's helping us out. I don't like the idea of him out there alone. And remember—the Autumn Lord was standing on my shoulder the other night. We know I'm being watched."

"Just be careful, you idiot," I muttered, giving her a peck on the cheek.

Delilah shivered. "I'm not the one who's in danger. If Lethesanar should catch you—" She let her words drift, but we both knew the ending. If the queen of Y'Elestrial caught us, we might as well roll over into the roasting pit.

"That's not going to happen," Trillian said. "Grand-mother Coyote's portal leads to Elqaneve, and it's easy transport down to Aladril via one of the private elfin portals."

Queen Asteria had informed us—on the q.t.—that Elqaneve had several secret portals they didn't tell outsiders about. One led to Aladril and one led to Darkynwyrd. There were probably more, but those were the only two she mentioned. We were offered use of them, should we need. And it looked like now we needed. Of course, Trillian knew about them. He seemed to have his fingers in just about all the pies.

"Once we reach the gates of Aladril, we should be safe, at least from Lethesanar and her cronies. She wouldn't dare attack them or the seers would level Y'Elestrial." Camille glanced at the clock. "Time to go."

"Let's get moving." I headed toward the door. "Who's car are we taking?"

Morio held up his keys. "My SUV. Come on, let's get on the road."

Ten minutes later, we pulled into the turnout and piled out of the vehicle. After locking the doors, we began the trek through the woods. Camille had come this way before, alone and in the dark, which impressed the hell out of me since the snowbound stillness of the woods was enough to spook even me. I preferred the dark glare of the city streets at night to the wilds here Earthside. There was more control, more ability to predict what was going down. Rooftops were easy to scale, and I never felt like the buildings were watching me.

Camille led the way. We moved silently, any sound we made muffled by the thick cloak of snow. The moon shone through the parted clouds, the edge of her full, round beauty slowly being eaten by the dark gods. During the black of the moon was the time in which the dead preferred to prowl. The Moon Mother owned the Hunt and witches like my sister, but the Dark Mother watched over those of us who had passed; the icicles of the Crone mirrored in the reflection of Grandmother Coyote's steel teeth.

We came to the portal, and Grandmother Coyote, who was there, silently stood aside to let us pass. As we stepped through the shimmering web of magic that stretched across the standing stones, I wondered what we'd discover in Aladril. And would it be enough to help us find and destroy Dredge, before he created a panic that would sweep the human community and stir up a violent hatred against all things supernatural?

CHAPTER 12

I'd forgotten that the lack of neon and electricity made for darker nights in Otherworld, with a clearer view of the stars. The world seemed far larger and bigger than over Earthside, and it shocked me to realize just how used to my adopted home I was becoming.

Earlier in the day, Camille had sent a message through the Whispering Mirror that we were on our way, and Trenyth was waiting for us. He brushed aside pleasantries.

"Her Majesty sends her regrets—she won't be able to meet with you tonight. Do not go to Y'Elestrial, no matter the temptation." He bustled us toward a road near the barrow in which the first portal rested. "Follow me. I don't have a lot of time, so I won't be able to go all the way to Aladril with you, but you may return this way to go home again."

Everything about Otherworld was different—from the feel of the air to the energy coiled within the ground. As we stepped out of the portal, it was as if the entire world had come to life and was aware of our presence.

Earthside, I'd gotten used to the muted sense of awareness and actually had developed a taste for it. When my senses were hyped to every noise, every smell, every pulse that walked by, it was nice for a change not to be inundated by the natural energies of the elements, too. But here that *aliveness* was still a glowing, living entity that permeated the essence of our homeland.

A look of bliss spread across Camille's face. "Oh, it's so good to be home. I've missed this."

Morio gawked at the panorama of stars. "I've never seen the stars so clearly—not even on the slopes of Mount Fuji." He took a step closer to Camille and she dropped her head back and sucked in a deep breath.

"It's quite the sight, isn't it?" she said. "I wish we could show you Y'Elestrial. Our home is incredibly beautiful."

"We need to hurry," Trenyth said, motioning to us. "I wish we had time to tarry, but we don't."

I touched Camille on the arm.

She let out a long, tremorous sigh and her shoulders drooped. "I'm coming, I'm coming."

I swung in behind her and Trillian, next to Morio, and we continued on another quarter mile until we came to an ancient oak that must have been a good six hundred or seven hundred years old. The tree rose into the night, a dark silhouette framed by a faint glow. The branches spread over the path, draped with oak moss and ivy. Spiderwebs stretched between limbs, and the spiders within watched us with careful precision, their jointed legs crooking in the air when we got too close.

Camille let out a low gasp. "This oak must be ancient."

"I've never felt this much power from a tree before," Morio said. "Or maybe I have, but not this much . . . connection."

"The woodlands here are more connected to those of us who walk the magical path," Camille said. "Earthside, the forests are wild and unpredictable. They keep to themselves and harbor their secrets, darkly. Here the power of the forests is stronger, and allows us an easier communion. Though the forests don't like everyone, of course. There are those who enter the woodlands, never to emerge."

Morio nodded, staring up at the ancient behemoth, a rapt expression on his face. "I think I understand."

"We grew the oak around the portal," Trenyth said. "I remember when we planted the acorn. The moment you walk through the door, you'll enter the portal. May the gods be with you." He motioned to the guard on duty, who opened the door and stood back.

Trillian stepped to one side. "Here's where I must leave you. I'll return Earthside as soon as possible. Be safe." He turned to Camille and held out his arms. She silently walked into his embrace and their lips met. They looked perfectly matched. He loved her, and she loved him. In their own ways, they were as good as married, though I knew they would never wed. When she stepped away, Camille's eyes shimmered with tears.

"Every time you head out, I worry that you won't return. You make sure you keep your butt alive, you hear me?"

He held her hands in his. "These are dark times. I can't make any guarantee, but I'll always come back if there's a way."

"Walk under the Moon Mother's protection." She reached up and brushed his long silver mane back from his face. "You are mine. You belong to me."

Frost-colored eyes flashing, he merely inclined his head, then turned and disappeared into the night. Camille watched after him for a moment as Morio rested his hand on her shoulder. She motioned toward the tree.

"Let's go for it," she said and stepped through the portal, the energy sizzling as it sucked her in. Morio followed suit, and then it was my turn. Walking through the portal was like walking into a magnet factory in full metal armor. It was as if every cell was being yanked apart and then smashed together again before you realized just what was happening. There were no sights or sounds save blinding flashes of color and a perpetual buzz that rattled the skull. And then, as quickly as it had begun, the journey was over.

As we emerged into Aladril, I hoped that the man we were seeking in Aladril would be as anxious to meet us as we were to meet him.

* * *

The portal from Elqaneve to Aladril opened up into a small shrine about a quarter mile outside of the City of Seers. The guards had been alerted that we were coming through and were waiting for us. Though they looked full-blood human, there was an aura of magic about them. They positively reeked with it, smelling of ozone and burning metal.

Two men and one woman waited for us. All extremely tall, over six five, their expressions were forbidding. Long capes masked their bodies, the woman in orange, the men in indigo, but not a weapon was to be seen. I had the distinct feeling they didn't need them.

"Trenyth vouched for you," one of the men said. His hair was swept back, almost a buzz cut, and his skin was the color of coffee. He gave us the briefest of nods. "We usually don't allow demons of any kind within our city gates but your circumstances demand an exception. Don't disappoint us."

I bit my tongue. Not the time to come back with a witty retort.

He held out three necklaces. "Wear these at all times. Before you put them on, place the necklace and your hand onto this plate." He held out what looked like a square piece of silver and he must have noticed me shudder. "The metal isn't silver, so don't fret. It won't hurt you. What this alloy *does* is to key your identification necklace to your body chemistry so no one can steal your identity."

Now that was an interesting fact to tuck away. Sneaking into Aladril would be difficult at best, but identifying yourself to the guards would be useless without the magical GPS system they had going. Better than a trace, even.

"If you *don't* wear your identification, you will be considered a threat to the city and members of the guard are free to do as they see fit." Apparently that was the end of his spiel because he placed the necklaces on the table and stepped back.

I swallowed my pride and placed my hand and one of the necklaces onto the scanner. A few seconds later, a bright burst of light flared and the seer motioned for me to drape the beaded circlet around my neck. Nothing happened—no burns, no stings, no sense that I was hampered in any way. Camille and Morio followed suit.

"Thank you," I said. "We appreciate your help."

Camille grumbled something under her breath and I elbowed her. "Shut up," I whispered as low as I could. She quieted down.

"You are free to walk in our city. Obey the rules. If you don't know whether something is allowed, ask first. You have three days before you must return here and apply for an extension." The woman wasn't any warmer than the men. She motioned toward the path waiting just outside the door. "This trail will lead you to Aladril. Don't delay, and don't stray off of the path or you run the risk of death."

She didn't bother explaining exactly how we'd die, but I, for one, decided to take her word for it. Once outside, we found ourselves on a well-defined stone path leading toward the gleaming spires of Aladril. The path was clearly marked by globes of floating light lining the sides. We had no excuse for making a mistake and taking a wrong turn, that much was clear. As soon as she stepped aside, we hightailed it down the road.

I'd sat up late one night watching *The Wizard of Oz* with Delilah and Camille. Trust me, Dorothy's yellow brick road had nothing on this trail. The slate stones might not be yellow and uniform, and the surrounding forest wasn't exactly neon Technicolor, and Aladril wasn't the Emerald City, but we sure as hell weren't in Seattle anymore, Toto.

The walking was simple, though the lights illuminating the path gave off a creepy "we're watching you" vibe.

"They're eye-catchers," Camille said.

"Eye-catchers?"

"Magical orbs designed to catch the attention. Not exactly charm magic, because they're usually used as warning signals, but . . . like the bright yellow yield signs back over Earthside." She glanced at Morio. "Do you know the enchantment that makes them? They seem right up your alley."

He shook his head, drawing near her. "No, I don't think that's in my repertoire. Other youkai might know it, though I can't say for sure. I haven't dealt much with most other nature-demons back Earthside. But I can see someone like Titania using these. At least back when she was holding her own instead of holding the bottle."

"I learned very few higher spells when I was training," Camille said. "My teacher didn't bother trying to teach me anything he thought I'd screw up too badly, except for the energy bolts. By the time I moved on to the more advanced stages of training, word had spread that I was a klutz. I'm beginning to think that maybe I wouldn't have so many problems if I'd had teachers who cared more and didn't turn their backs on me because I'm a half-breed."

I recognized the sting in her voice.

Morio just patted her on the arm. "You're doing fine with the death magic," he said. "Maybe we can help you relearn some of what you missed out on." His voice was so tender that I jerked my head up and stared at the two of them. Camille might be Trillian's, but it was apparent that Morio had been slowly, silently staking his claim. Was he trying to undermine the Svartan or just complement him? I shook off the thought. The only thing that mattered right now was what sort of man this seer we were searching for turned out to be.

As we rounded a bend in the trail, the curving spires of Aladril rose up from behind the city gates. Minarets rose from the domes, marble and alabaster gleaming with a finish so highly polished that they reflected the starlight. Aladril's architecture was much like that of Terial, the port city at the edge of the Mirami Ocean, but there the resemblance between the two cities ceased. Terial thrived, a noisy city of vendors and merchants. Aladril was a quiet city of scholars, seers, and magic.

When we approached the gates, a guard, wearing a turquoise and white uniform with golden epaulets on the shoulders, motioned for us to stop. "Proper identification, please."

We held out our necklaces. Using what looked a lot like the crystal bug detector Queen Asteria had given us, the guard touched the crystal to the platelet on the cord and a soft beep sounded. Giving me an odd look, he stepped back and motioned to the gate. "Enter Aladril, the City of Seers, and be welcome."

I paused. "Do you know where we might find a seer named Jareth? Queen Asteria directed me to seek him out."

The guard gave me another strange look. "Are you sure she said Jareth?"

"Yes," I said. "I'm positive."

He resumed his unreadable stance. "You'll find Master Jareth in the Temple of Reckoning. Follow Arabel Avenue to the central park, then cross through the gardens to the Hall of Temples. You'll find him there." As I turned to go, I heard him whisper under his breath, "And may the gods smooth your way, little demoness."

I glanced back, about to ask what the hell he meant, but he ignored me. No matter. We'd find out soon enough.

As we passed through the thirty-foot tall gates, a hush descended around us, as if the world were muffled by a magical blanket. Even though it was night, the streets were bustling with activity, people in long cloaks coming and going, all looking intent on their journeys.

The streets were made of cobbled brick. The buildings varied from stucco to marble to what appeared to be bronze facades. Rounded domes dappled the skyline with spires and minarets raising into the air, complete with flags of blue, white, and gold fluttering from their pinnacles. We saw no farm or transportation animals in Aladril, at least no horses or cows, but dogs and cats and rabbits dashed through the streets and I had the feeling they were familiars.

"There," Camille said, pointing to a street sign. "Arabel Avenue."

We stood at the edge of the avenue. A major thoroughfare, it was filled with a throng of people, silently bustling toward their destinations. The moon was on her way toward dark, but the same globes of light that had guided us along the path to Aladril also decorated the city streets.

As we joined the mass of pedestrians, I found it difficult to tell male from female. Most of the inhabitants seemed to be cloaked in voluminous robes with hoods, and their scent was far less disparate than that of human male and female.

Or Fae, for that matter. I'd found that most races had distinct scents—perhaps pheromones—for the differing genders but here that didn't seem to play true.

Even in the midst of winter, the fragrance of night bloom-ing wyreweed filled the air with a luxurious scent and I thought I could hear music coming from somewhere until I tried to focus on it. Then it slipped away and I wasn't sure if I'd heard anything or not. I'd been to Aladril once before, and Camille had been here several times, but it was as if my memory of the city had faded the moment I left the gates, leaving only a vague impression of what I'd seen or done.

"The energy here is so thick that it's giving me a headache," Morio said, wincing. "How many seers live here? The cerebral pulse of the city is throbbing like a stac-cato drumbeat."

Camille shrugged. "Nobody knows much about the makeup of Aladril, or even who or *what* the original inhabi-tants are. Very few are ever given permission to relocate here and those who do seem to disappear and are seldom heard from after that. Remember cousin Kerii?"

I nodded. "I remember. Her teacher thought she had so much talent as a divination witch that he recommended she seek further training in Aladril." Turning to Morio, I added, "We heard from her once or twice after she moved, then nothing. We know she's still alive, her soul statue is still in-tact, or was the last time we checked our ancestral shrine, but we haven't had any contact with her since those early days."

"Soul statue? What's that?" Morio pinched the bridge of his nose, and squinted. "I feel like I do when I've been around high-speed Internet too much. Starbucks is hell for me due to all the wireless activity."

Camille glanced around. "The magic here is so heavy that it's even wearing on my shoulders. As to soul statues— when we're born, the shamans forge soul statues for each of us. These are placed in the family shrines and when we die, they shatter." She glanced at me. "Menolly's shattered when she died. When she was raised, the pieces reforged them-selves, but the statue came out . . ."

"Misshapen. You can say it," I said. "I've seen it and I

know what it looks like. When I die the final death, it will shatter for good."

Morio blinked. "That's interesting. So you can tell if your father and aunt are alive—"

"Exactly," Camille broke in. "Every time he returns, Trillian takes a moment to have someone check on our shrine and sure enough, both Father and Aunt Rythwar's soul statues are still intact. They're alive, just missing."

"There's the park," I said, pointing ahead. We'd been walking a good hour and now faced a large, enclosed wild space. Though wild might be a misnomer considering the fact that this was Aladril. Nothing seemed wild or untamed in the city of seers.

We came to the edge of the gardens, which were enclosed by a six-foot marble wall that stretched to either side as far as we could see. The central entrance was unlocked and the gate open but even so, as we passed the borders, I could sense the separation between the main city and the sunken gardens. For one thing, the temperature rose a good thirty degrees once we passed the main gate.

Marble steps led down through terrace after terrace of roses, jasmine, and lilies. Flowers and foliage entwined in an exotic embrace, while walkways guided pedestrians through the blossoms. The gardens were fifteen tiers deep, and both ramps and stairs led to the bottom terrace. Benches along the way, wrought in brass and stone, offered the footsore a place to rest and meditate. At the bottom, a railing enclosed a large fountain, where an amber water, lit by some form of magic, sprayed out from a large series of geometric cubes.

"It's so warm here," Morio said, glancing around.

"Think of it like an outdoor greenhouse with an invisible ceiling, heated by magical energy. There are public baths here, if I remember right." Camille glanced around as we began to descend the stairs. She looked totally blissed out.

"Enjoying the contact high?" I asked, grinning.

"Oh yeah," she said, closing her eyes for a moment as she soaked up the energy. "Magic runs like wine and I'm getting tipsy. I could enjoy living here, I think."

"Not likely," I said. "I doubt you'd mesh in well. You're

too full of life to be comfortable around such sedate energy, no matter how magical, and you know it." I flashed her a smile as we wended our way along the path. Occasionally we passed someone sitting on a bench or on the grass, but no one looked up or gave any sign they noticed us.

A sudden screech startled me. An owl, perched on the limb of a willow tree, watched us. I could feel its stare burrowing through the night.

"We're being examined," I muttered in a low voice. "Owl at two o'clock in the willow."

Camille's gaze flickered up to examine our voyeur. "That's no owl," she said. "Possibly a familiar, but no ordinary owl."

Morio concurred. "Not a Were either. It might be some other form of shapeshifter, or perhaps a shadow-scout—an illusion set to spy on us."

"I think we should ignore it for now." Camille let out a low breath. "If we interfere with it, we'll alert whoever's watching. We have no idea who sent it, and if they're not one of the bad guys, we might hurt our alliances by being obnoxious about it."

"What alliances?" I snorted. "We're just hoping that something will come out of the meeting with Jareth. We don't know for sure that this trip is going to be anything except a big waste of time."

"Queen Asteria seems to think otherwise. And there's no sense in breaking an alliance that's barely begun." Camille frowned, thinking. "For now, let's just keep our eyes open. If somebody's following us, they'll slip up eventually."

As we crossed through the gardens the owl followed us, silently gliding from tree to tree. I tried not to focus on it. Most likely the three guards who'd given us our identification decided that we weren't to be trusted and had sent the owl to follow us. Whatever the case, we were almost to the other side.

The climb up fifteen tiers of steps took a little longer than going down, but Morio was in excellent shape and neither Camille nor I were tired. Living Earthside had done little to diminish our endurance. At the gate, I saw the owl veer off.

Interesting. Perhaps our sentinel merely wanted to make sure we were going where we actually said we were.

As we exited the gardens, I hesitated. The thought of just finding a soft space in which to rest and relax was so tempting that I was reluctant to leave. When we had time and energy, maybe my sisters and I could come here and enjoy the lulling hush.

The park opened out onto the Hall of Temples, which was actually another avenue, this one filled with one great marble structure after another. The name was spot on. I could see at least fifteen different temples stretching in either direction. I wondered how the priests managed all that disparate energy swirling around in such close proximity but no doubt the founders of Aladril had thought of a solution for that, too.

"What are we looking for, again?" Camille asked.

"The Temple of Reckoning," Morio said with a grin. "And may I add that the name doesn't inspire feelings of confidence?" He stared at the massive row of temples. "I've never seen anything quite like this, not in all my journeys. I wonder if this is what ancient Greece or Egypt looked like?"

"I dunno, but I agree with you on the name thing. I wonder what gods this Jareth follows?" Camille looked at me, but I shook my head.

"I have no idea. Religion has never been my strong suit. It's not something to which I aspire," I added. The gods had ignored me in my time of need and I'd pretty much made up my mind that they only meddled in mortal affairs when it suited their private agendas. If you relied on them, you'd be left holding the bag of tricks at precisely the wrong moment.

The streets were sparsely populated, unlike the main thoroughfare, but there was enough activity to ensure we should be able to ask someone for directions. The temples ranged in style from Grecian architecture to Egyptian design, providing a surreal, avant-garde feel to the area. Aesthetically the Hall of Temples jarred the eye. Energywise, it whirled like a vortex.

"The magic here is incredibly thick," Camille said in a raspy voice. "I can barely speak—it's clouding my senses."

"Maybe I should go alone," I said, glancing at her. "You look out of it." And she did. Both Morio and Camille had glazed looks on their faces, almost bewildered, as they stared at the row of buildings.

Camille tugged at the hem of her top. "I don't know. I don't like the idea of you wandering around by yourself."

"I'm in Aladril. Who's going to bother me here as long as I behave myself? Roz couldn't get in through the gates. The energy repelled him. I doubt if Lethesanar's welcome here, and Dredge's crew . . . well, if they hesitated letting me in, I scarcely think he'd be given free reign." I gave her a little shove. "Go back and wait in the gardens where it's warm. I'll find the Temple of Reckoning and talk to this Jareth dude."

She hesitated, but Morio took her hand.

"Menolly's right," he said. "I can barely focus on walking, let alone on our mission. We have to shield properly before we can handle the energy up here. We can do that while we're in the gardens."

Camille frowned, then nodded and let him lead her back toward the gate.

I stopped them. "Hold on. What did Iris ask us to bring home? Some kind of crystal?"

"An Aqualine crystal from the Wyvern Ocean," Camille said in a faint voice. "And be sure and tell them that Iris is a priestess of—"

"Of Undutar. I remember that much. Go work on your shields. I'll be back in an hour or so. If I'm not back in two, come find me." I glanced at my watch. Camille couldn't wear one, but I liked them. "Do these even work here?"

Morio held up his wrist. He had a gold watch—it looked like a Rolex—tucked under his sleeve. "Yep, I checked first thing. Let's see, it's eight-thirty now, Earthside time. If you're not back by eleven, we'll come looking for you."

I gave them a quick wave. "Stay out of trouble. And if you see that owl, try to find out what it wants."

As they returned to the garden, I headed into the street, wondering which way to go first. Arbitrarily making up my mind, I turned left. I had a fifty percent chance of being right, so why not go with the path that seemed to mirror my destiny?

As I strolled down the street, trying to act like I belonged, it occurred to me that *not* having magical abilities was—at times—a handy thing. Neither Morio nor Camille could handle the excess energy here until they shielded. I, on the other hand, could barely feel the massive waves of magic riding through the streets.

I looked around. Most everyone wore robes, and it was hard to gauge their natures or temperament within those darkened hoods. Finally I played the eeny-meeny game and my finger came to rest pointing toward one man in a golden kimono who leaned against a wall, smoking something that suspiciously looked like a cigarette. As I drew closer the pungent smell of wormwood and mugwort drifted to my nose and I grimaced. Mugwort was just plain nasty, and wormwood wasn't all that good for the brain cells.

"Hello," I said, approaching him. "I was wondering if you can answer a question for me—"

"Shush," he said, cutting me off. "Hold on. Hear that?" He cocked his head as if he were straining to catch a whisper.

I listened, deciding that direct and forceful just wasn't going to cut it in this city. After a moment, I began to catch a faint rhythm beating on the breeze; it sounded like a slow drum, trance-work music like Camille often used to deepen her trances and sweep her into an altered state.

"What is it?" I whispered after a moment.

"The Temple of Hycondis is having their ritual tonight. They're making a sacrifice."

Swallowing a hasty retort, I forced myself to keep my first impressions to myself. Back in Y'Elestrial, temples were restricted in what they could—and couldn't—do. Though most rituals were approved, any involving deliberate sacrifice were banned, though fanatical sects often went underground to perform their darker rites.

"Hycondis?" I asked, desperately hoping that whoever the god was, he wasn't part of the Temple of Reckoning.

"The lord of disease. His followers sacrifice dead bodies to him to cleanse and purify them to return to the Mother's womb." He sounded bored, like he was reciting from a text-book.

"You mean they're already dead by the time they're sacrificed?"

With a disgusted look, he rolled his eyes. "Of course they are. Unlike the sacrifices you make to your stomach, vampire. Now what do you want?" He tossed his herbal ciggie away and it disappeared in a flash of light, leaving no litter to clutter the streets. Handy, very handy.

"I'm looking for the Temple of Reckoning," I said.

"No doubt. I'm sure you have a great deal to atone for," he said, letting out a little snort. Oh, yeah, he thought he was clever. "You'll find the temple two blocks down, turn right, and walk another block and there you go."

I started to thank him but he turned away, ignoring me as if I didn't exist. I let the matter drop—no use picking a fight with someone just because he was rude, especially since I was a visitor here.

The streets began to empty as I headed down the road. I glanced at my watch. Eight-forty-five. Dinner time? If there was a curfew, the guards hadn't mentioned it. Whatever the reason, by the time it was nine P.M. our time, the streets were clear of all foot traffic. Now and then I heard something pass that sounded like a carriage, though I couldn't see a thing. The hairs on the back of my neck had been standing at attention since I entered Temple Row.

And then I was in front of the Temple of Reckoning. A set of huge scales, as big as the shed in our backyard, stood in front of the temple, carved in stone. I paused, staring up at the megalithic building. The doors were lit by a purple flame that encircled the archway, and as I stepped toward it, the flame flared, crackling brightly. The inscription over the arch read, "Enter within, those who seek atonement and justice."

Hoping sincerely that I wouldn't burst into flames, I pushed open one of the heavy doors and stepped through.

CHAPTER 13

As I passed through the fire, the distinct scent of charred soul hit me. Was this the end? The next moment my foot hit the floor and I was through the door, standing in the temple foyer, relatively unscathed. Hell, I felt like I'd been turned inside out and wrung out to dry, but when I gave myself the once over, everything seemed in place.

The temple resembled an ancient Egyptian ruin, without the rubble. Huge statues of a woman rose on either side of the tiled walkway, guarding the entrance to what appeared to be an enormous hall. The statues' arms stretched out to form an arch through which all supplicants had to pass.

At first I thought the statues were representations of Ma'at, the goddess of truth and justice, but when I looked closer, I realized that it wasn't her. So who was she?

The foyer was wide, incredibly wide, but the opening between the statues very narrow. There seemed to be no other way into the hall than to walk through the small space. I stepped forward, half-expecting the statues to move. Nothing happened, so I took another step, and then another, and then dashed between the towering stone figurines.

Once I'd passed through the arch, I turned around to see if the statues had moved but no, they were still standing silent, watching the door. Relieved, I turned back to the chamber. Unusual. No chimes had sounded when I entered, and nobody was around to ask who the hell I was and what I was doing. Rather lackluster in the security department, I thought.

The hall was larger than any I'd ever seen, and back in Y'Elestrial, we had some ostentatious halls. Dumbstruck, I could only gaze around me at the beauty of the temple.

White marble tiled both walls and the floor, and the chamber shimmered under the glow of a thousand orbs of light that danced along the ceiling. The walls were adorned with polished brass sculptures, depictions of the gods and mortals wandering the halls of the dead. Tapestries, woven of golden and black threads embroidered on ivory linen, hung across one wall. Panel after panel of the linen pictographs told the story of the dead as they formed a line to enter the kingdom of the afterlife.

If this wasn't an Egyptian temple, then what culture was it? Very few of the Fae that I knew followed the Egyptian gods. Delilah was an exception, with her worship of Bast. Usually the Fae paid more attention to the Celtic and European deities and, to a lesser extent, Greek and Roman. Then again, nowhere was it written that the seers of Aladril were Fae. While they looked human, it was obvious they weren't the regular run-of-the-mill-type FBHs.

I looked around for some sign of life. Nothing.

A series of doors lined the great hall. I'd have to take my chances. I finally decided to start with the one directly opposite the entrance. As I strode to the door, I planned out just what I might say to prevent them from killing me before I'd had a chance to explain who I was and what I wanted.

The door was unlocked and I cautiously pushed it open. The sound of wind whistled through the darkened corridor beyond. Shrugging, I decided to take a chance.

The corridor stretched beyond my line of sight. I caught the whiff of blood on the wind, but no fear attached to it. Deciding to follow my nose, I turned left into one of the branching halls and continued almost to the end, where the scent was emanating from behind a door to my left.

Maybe they were preparing meat for a meal, I thought, my hand on the knob. Or maybe a woman had given birth recently? Finally I gave up with the guessing game and opened the door.

As I entered the room, the first thing I noticed was a naked man sitting on a raised dais. His legs were folded into the lotus position, his back was straight. A half-circle frame forged from bronze spread like a rainbow from the center of his back. His arms were stretched out to his sides, parallel to the floor, supporting the thin strip of metal that formed the base of the arc.

Needle-sharp rods were spaced evenly around the semi-circle, like spokes in a bicycle wheel. At the bottom, they angled in toward his back, piercing not the metal frame, but threading into his flesh. There was no blood, though I could smell it coming from somewhere. And by his expression, I'd have to guess that he was both very much alive and feeling very little pain. He had to be taking some good drugs. Either that or he was in a deep trance.

He opened his eyes and stared directly at me, but made no motion to move. I slowly walked toward him, more curious than worried for my safety. Even though the scent of blood was clear and pure, it wasn't affecting me. Fascinated, when I reached three feet from the dais, I stopped and cocked my head to the side.

The man rested on a turquoise pillow with golden tassels. Even though he was sitting with legs folded, I could tell he was taller than any man I'd ever known. With dark brown hair and eyes so black I could lose myself in them, he wasn't classically handsome. But there was something compelling about him and I stood silently, watching him, unable to look away.

Five minutes passed, maybe ten . . . maybe twenty. Finally the door to the back of the otherwise empty room opened and another man entered. Shorter than the living statue, this man bore the same exotic look, but he was dressed in a pair of loose linen trousers and a light jacket belted by a golden sash.

"You've come to question the Dayinye Oracle?" he said.

He was so calm. Didn't he know I was a vampire?

"I don't know," I said slowly. "I'm looking for a man named Jareth. I was told I could find him here in the Temple of Reckoning. Will you take me to him, please?"

The man returned my stare until I felt suddenly faint and had to look away. Who was he? Almost no one could withstand my smile when I turned on the old vamp charm, but it hadn't fazed him in the least.

"Why don't you ask the oracle?" he said after a moment.

Tired of games, but acknowledging that I was in somebody else's playground and that I'd have to play by their rules, I sighed and turned to the man on the dais. "What should I ask him?"

"That is entirely up to you."

I centered myself. This could be a trick—like wishes gone bad from some of the djinns who thrived on chaos and twisting meanings. Cautiously I said, "I'm looking for Jareth. Is he here in this temple, and will he help me?" There, that seemed clear enough.

The oracle blinked and then closed his eyes. I could no longer sense either of the men breathing, nor were their hearts beating the rhythm I was so used to hearing. *This doesn't make sense,* I thought. They were both alive—but it was as if all my sensory equipment went on the fritz.

After a moment, a thundering voice filled the room, departing the moment I caught the words, as if it had never been.

"The man you seek is here, and he will help you. But the question is: What help do you really need? The path is long and tortuous, leading within. Demons are only demons when they choose to live in the fire." And then, he fell silent, sagging for a moment before his eyes snapped open and he straightened, once again staring forward. Silent, like an image caught in freeze-frame.

I turned to the other man. "Now will you take me to Jareth?"

He inclined his head and motioned toward a door against the back of the room. I followed him, skirting the dais.

"Is he . . . does he always sit there with that thing on his back?" I asked, trying to keep my tone respectful.

My guide didn't look back at me, but said, "Yes, day and night, year after year. He is the Dayinye Oracle. He will answer questions until the day he dies, and then his soul will join Great Mother Dayinye's paradise in the after-life."

We passed through the door into another hall that led farther back into the temple. Here I could sense more movement, though snores reached my ears from behind a few of the doors. Obviously a number of the temple's residents were sleeping.

"How long has he been the Oracle?"

"Two hundred and fifty-seven years. Each oracle serves but a short time—five hundred years—and then they die. A new one is selected in the four hundredth year of the old. They are trained for one hundred years to take over the position, before ascending to the oracular throne." He seemed quite amiable and willing to answer my questions. I decided to try for a couple more.

"And who is Mother Dayinye? I'm sorry, I'm not familiar with your path nor this city." I glanced around as we entered a dining hall. My guide motioned for me to sit at one of the tables and I took my place on a bench.

"Wait," he said before disappearing through an archway. A moment later, he returned with a goblet of wine and—whoa!—a goblet of blood. He knew what I was, all right.

I accepted the crystal flute, sniffing it carefully. Human—more or less, tinged with magic. Not wanting to seem rude, I took a tiny sip and almost swooned. The blood was like nectar on my tongue. In fact, for a moment, I could have sworn I was drinking a fine merlot or burgundy or a glass of Elfin elixir. Another sip and I tasted apple juice and honey and cinnamon.

"Great gods, what is this? It's wonderful." I gazed at the goblet, thinking that if I could have a glass of this a couple times a week, I wouldn't be nearly so scritchy.

"The blood of our oracle. We bleed him twice a week and save it for special occasions and rituals. And for special guests." He gave me an indulgent smile and took a swallow of his wine.

I wasn't sure what to say. Apparently it wasn't doing the dude any harm, and if he'd been sitting there for a couple hundred years, then who was I to mention that it seemed like a raw deal? Considering the fact that I bled a lot of people myself, I decided to keep my mouth shut.

"I'm Jareth," my guide said, holding out his hand.

I stared at him. Why the hell hadn't he said so in the first place? Or had the oracle been some sort of a test? Once again, I bit back a retort and took his hand. "How do you do. Queen Asteria sent me to find you."

"The Elfin Queen sent you? Strange days, these are, when elves and Svartans combine forces, and when Asteria sends a vampire to me for help. Tell me what you *think* you require." He didn't even blink.

I ran my finger over the cut crystal goblet and stared into the magical blood before taking another sip. Finally I set the glass down and delicately wiped my mouth.

"I didn't choose to become a vampire. I was turned by the Elwing Blood Clan. Currently I'm living Earthside on assignment, and it's come to my attention that the Elwing Clan has crossed over the divide. Dredge, their leader and my sire, is after me. He may be in cahoots with a floraed who's joined forces with Demonkin from the Subterranean Realms. I need to know how to find Dredge, and how to kill him."

Jareth leaned forward, propping his elbows on the table. "And you think I know how?"

"Queen Asteria seems to think so," I said, contemplating his expression. He was hard to read, this monk.

"You don't believe you have the power to defeat him right now?"

I looked into his eyes and saw something there I hadn't seen in a long, long time. Understanding. Pure, crystal clear, understanding. It made me want to weep as I slowly shook my head. "No, I know I don't."

"You can find your sire. *All* vampires can find their sires, if their sire still walks the world." As he continued to stare at me, I had the weirdest feeling that he was looking into my soul, looking past the anger and memories, deep into the me that once had been.

"You know a lot about vampires, do you?" I tried to gauge his expression. Something about him fascinated me. He obviously possessed great power, but he kept it behind a mask.

"Enough for what you require," he said. "I've helped a number of vampires gain control over their impulses. And I've lost a few, too."

A chill ran down my back, colder than my skin, colder than death. "Lost a few?"

"There have been a handful who sought me out. I couldn't help them. Either they didn't want to face their inner demons, or they embraced them too readily. They sought no balance and turned into monsters." As he caught my gaze and held it, I knew. I knew why Queen Asteria had instructed me to seek him out.

"You tried to help Dredge, didn't you?"

Jareth lowered his gaze to the table. "Sometimes, no matter how hard you try, you lose the game. Dredge was my first—and greatest—failure."

I considered the possibilities. If Jareth had known Dredge way back at the beginning, he must be incredibly old. *And he knew what made Dredge tick.* Which meant invaluable information on how to take down my nightmare.

"Will you work with me?" I drained my goblet and set it down. "Dredge captured one of our friends. I don't hold out much hope but maybe . . . maybe we can get her back. He's out to hurt me. I don't think he'll kill her right away."

Jareth leaned across the table. "If you ask for my help, I'll force you to walk down some dark paths, Menolly. You must come to terms with your memories before I can lead you to Dredge. He's your sire. If you face him now without my help, I guarantee he'll end up controlling you. Dredge isn't like most vampires. Do you know what he was before he was turned? Did he tell you his story?"

I shook my head. "He didn't tell me anything, except exactly what he was going to do with me. He kept every promise he made that night." I pressed my eyes shut, trying to shove aside the images that flashed through my mind.

"As long as you fear your memories, you'll be at his mercy. I have to take you back into that pain, to that night, in order to free you of the chains that bind you to Dredge." He stood up. "Are you strong enough to withstand the journey? Can you give yourself to me and let me break you down so we can put the pieces back together?"

"I thought that's what the OIA did when I managed to get home," I said, wanting to find some way out. "They spent a year working to bring me back to sanity. Can't you just tell me what I need to know about Dredge?"

Jareth motioned for me to walk with him. We made our way through a winding corridor back into the great hall. "The OIA merely slapped a bandage on your wounds. They taught you how to cope with the memories but not to overcome them. I'm a shaman. I can teach you how to rise above all of this, to take control over what happened. Only then can you face Dredge and hope to win."

He paused. "What do you think will happen if you and your sisters go up against him, and you suddenly turn to his side? As much as you hate him, he can make you his puppet."

I stopped cold. "You're telling me that he can control me, even if I don't want him to?"

"For all of your ability to mesmerize others, you don't think his is far greater? Dredge is eight hundred years old, Menolly. He's a greater vampire, and before that, while he lived, he was a high priest of Jakaris even though he's not Svartan. He should have been cast into the Subterranean Realms centuries ago, but he always managed to outwit those seeking him."

A high priest of Jakaris. A priest of the Svartan god of vice and torture. No wonder he enjoyed inflicting pain so much. It had been his path in life, and he'd kept up the practice in death. I pressed my hand against my stomach, queasy. "Kind of makes Dracula look like a boy toy, I guess."

"You could put it that way," Jareth said. "But Vlad has *some* ethics, regardless of how ruthless he seems on the outside. Dredge is devoid of conscience. If he's truly after you, he'll systematically destroy every single person you care about in the most horrible way possible before coming for you. He doesn't want to kill, he wants to rain fear and pain down on his enemies."

Shit. I didn't have a choice. "Do you know an incubus named Rozurial? He's after Dredge, too."

Jareth nodded. "He wanted to study with me, but I don't work with incubi and he was denied access to the city. He went Earthside, then, to find Dredge?"

I nodded. "He's been helping me."

"Very good, then. You can trust him, as far as this matter goes. Like many others, he has a longstanding grudge against the Elwing Blood Clan. Now there's no time to waste. Will you put yourself in my hands? Queen Asteria sent you. I can help you, but you have to surrender yourself to me."

The thought of handing over control was terrifying. My *trust no one* instincts were screaming like I'd set them on fire. "Can I have an hour or so to think it over? I want to talk to my sister first."

"Of course. I'll be here. But mind you, if you refuse, then don't bother returning to the temple. *Ever.* This is the only time I will make this offer." He guided me through the larger-than-life statues toward the door.

"May I ask . . . who is she? You mentioned Mother Dayinye earlier. Are those statues of her?" I nodded to the stone figures.

"She is our goddess. Great Mother Dayinye is the guardian of souls, the keeper of conscience. We pursue truth through her. She divines the path of our destiny. If we stray, she reminds us gently the first time. The second, a sharper reprimand. The third and she destroys us with the violet fire of reckoning."

He turned away as I opened the door, but over his shoulder he called out, "I won't hurt you, Menolly. No more than I have to in order to make you an opponent capable of meeting—and destroying—your enemy."

I found Camille and Morio in the park, holding hands under the Moon Mother as she slowly progressed into the darkness of her cycle. They were working magic of some sort, probably shielding themselves. I silently glided up behind them.

Without a beat, Camille said, "I know you're there. Come out of the shadows, Menolly."

She was getting better, I thought. Delilah and I could sense when people snuck up on us. Camille wasn't quite as good, but she'd been practicing. I sat down beside her.

"We need to talk. Can we find an inn?" I knew better than to touch her right after she'd been working a spell—sometimes the exchange of energies sparked off more than we bargained for.

She shivered. "Sounds good. I'd like to get off the ground and onto something soft. Any luck finding Jareth? Who is he? What is he like?"

I glanced over at Morio. "I don't want to talk out here in the open, even in this city. Protected or not, I'd feel safer indoors."

He held out his hand to Camille and helped her up. When he proffered me his hand, I snorted. "You know I don't need the help . . . but thanks anyway. I appreciate the offer."

We headed out of the park the way we'd come. Inns and rooming houses were in the main part of the city. We'd only walked for about ten minutes before we came to the Mussels and Ale Pub.

"Looks promising enough," Camille said, opening the door. And she was right. Except for the difference in décor and lighting, it could have been any good hotel back Earthside. The walls were bathed in a rich teal and rose color scheme. The registration desk was manned by an elf. I blinked. We hadn't seen many races here besides whatever race the seers hearkened from.

"May I help you?" the clerk asked us. Polite, but as with every other person in this place, reserved.

"We need a room," Camille said, pulling out a purse from between her boobs. I grinned. Leave it to my sister to find a handy hiding place for her money.

"How many beds?" the clerk asked.

"Two. We're just here for a bit of a rest and a meal. We'll

need food, for two, sent up to our room. Something with protein in it." Camille placed three coins in his hand.

Elqaneve coins, I thought. Accepted almost everywhere in OW. We'd made sure to keep a nice little stash of money from various city-states tucked away in a wall safe at home, just in case we had to return here quickly. And Trillian never seemed to want for money, at least that he could spend here. He was perpetually broke over Earthside.

After showing our passes to the clerk, we headed upstairs. The stairwell was carpeted with hand-woven rugs. Our room was the first door to the right on the third floor. Camille opened the door and ushered us in.

Twelve by twelve, the room contained two beds, a small table and two chairs, and a bathtub. Baths were problematic in hotels, at least in most cities. Maids had to fill them by hand unless there was some magical—or rough mechanical—system in place. They cost a good deal extra to compensate for the work and the wood used to heat the water. Camille dropped on one of the beds and pulled the blanket around her shoulders. The room wasn't cold, but it was chillier than the gardens had been.

Morio straddled one chair and set his bag down on the floor. "So tell us, how did it go?"

I frowned. "I'm not sure, to be honest. I met Jareth. He's a powerful seer, all right. Or shaman. I'm not sure which."

"A shaman, huh? What can he do to help?" Camille pulled off her boots and Morio slid over to the bed, taking her feet in his hands and rubbing them gently. "Thank you, babe," she said, leaning over to kiss him lightly on the lips.

"He can help me find and destroy Dredge," I said. "But there's a catch." I told them everything.

"Are you sure—" Morio started to say, but Camille hushed him.

"He wants to train you to withstand the pain. I've talked to Venus the Moon Child about this sort of thing. You learn how to relive the pain, cleanse it, and then you can finally let it go. A good enough shaman can use the pain inflicted on himself to cause a backlash strike against his enemy."

She caught my gaze and held it. "What are you going to do?"

I shrugged. "I don't think I have much of a choice. Dredge will work his way through everything and everyone I care about till he comes to me." I looked at Camille. "You know he's going to torture Erin, if he hasn't already. He'll keep her alive for a while, because he'll want me to see his handiwork. But he'll tear her apart. She'll never be able to heal from what he does to her. I may not be able to stop him from destroying her, but I can stop him from destroying anybody else."

"He's gathering an army," Morio said, interrupting.

"What?" Both Camille and I stared at him.

"He's building himself a nice little army. I think he means to create himself a troop of vampires so he can go on a killing fest through the city." Morio shifted position and took Camille's other foot in his hand.

"Think about it," he continued. "The dude is crazy, that much we know. But he's also power hungry. You're who he's after, yes, but think what being Earthside means for him. He has an untouched canvas on which to paint. A lot of people still don't know much about vampires. By the time the word hits the streets, he'll already have a toehold in ruling the underworld of Seattle."

The image he painted spread out for me in so many horrific ways. The Elwing Blood Clan, only far larger. With potentially hundreds of newly born vamps under Dredge's control. They'd hunt, and they'd take down anyone who got in their way. Wade and Sassy and I couldn't hope to make a dent against that—no way in hell. And soon, all Supes would be targeted for destruction because of Dredge's minions.

"Holy shit." I stood up. "You're right. Dredge is forging an army in a world that can't protect itself from him. I *have* to accept Jareth's offer. I can go up against Dredge if I'm prepared. Otherwise . . . I don't have a chance."

Camille slid off the bed and crossed to my side, draping one arm around my shoulders. "Menolly, you can do this. You survived Dredge, you came out of the abyss . . . you can survive anything Jareth throws at you."

"But that's just it," I said, feeling faint. "I'll have to go back to that night, to the darkness when he tried to destroy my soul." My voice ripped out of my chest like a bean-sidhe, and I dropped to my knees. "I don't want to relive it! I remember too much in my dreams."

My sister knelt by my side. She took my hand. "It's not fair, and it never will be. But, Menolly, you have to do this. You know it, and I know it. And when it's over, you can find Dredge and obliterate his soul. The gods will smile on you."

"The gods can go to hell," I said, roughly grasping her hand. "I'm so grateful you're here. Will you help me and stand watch? Will you come with me if Jareth says it's okay? I need you."

She nodded. "You can count on me. You can forever and always count on me."

And then it was okay. Camille would be there. My big sister, who had taken over when Mother died, who had become our rock, who had kept her head when I tore into the house in a manic bloodlust to kill, who had led us against Bad Ass Luke and the first Degath Squad . . . She would be there, watching over me as always. All of a sudden I realized that, torture or not, I still needed my family. I still needed their love. I needed to belong.

CHAPTER 14

We waited until Camille and Morio ate before heading out to the Hall of Temples again. I perched on one of the beds, watching as they sat at the table. As I tuned out my thoughts, which were raging with fear, I noticed an odd light emanating from their auras. It was a silverish-green cord, linking the two of them. What the hell had they been up to? Camille was linked to Morio in much the same way she was to Trillian, but it seemed more than sexual.

"Menolly," Morio said, tearing a piece of bread in two and handing half of it to Camille, "I've been meaning to ask you something. You don't eat food anymore, right?"

I nodded. "I can't. I can't drink anything but blood, either. I get violently nauseated when I ingest anything else. Food won't kill me, but the aftereffects sure aren't pretty. Why?"

"I've been thinking. My skills with illusions are extremely good. I thought maybe we could play around a bit. I can try to cast an illusion on the blood you drink while you're at home. Maybe I can make it smell and taste like something different ... something you miss eating, perhaps?"

I stared at him, mouth agape. Nobody had ever thought to suggest anything of the sort before. "That has to be the sweetest thing I've heard in a long time. But wouldn't that be a waste of your energy?"

"What waste? I don't go around casting major spells every day, and that sort of thing wouldn't require much effort, I think. It's worth a try, if you're interested." He shrugged. Camille wrinkled her nose and smiled.

Not sure exactly what to say, I stammered out a "thank you" and then thought, *Why not?* What could it hurt?

"I'd like to give it a try," I said. "Maybe after we get this mess with the Elwing Clan cleared up. I miss ... there are so many things I miss."

"Like Mother's buttercream biscuits?" Camille said.

I laughed then. Of all the things to discuss on the night before I handed myself over to a shaman prepared to tear my soul apart. "I haven't thought about those in a long time, but yes, her buttercream biscuits. Do you have the recipe?"

She nodded. "I kept all of her recipes. I can't make them nearly as good as she did, but maybe Iris can. I never thought of asking her to try."

And then we were off, talking about the wonderful meals Mother had fixed when we were young, and how she'd done her best to recreate Earthside food enough times to give us a taste for things like hamburgers and fries when we were still very young. I avoided watching the clock that sat on the shelf, but finally, by the time Camille and Morio finished their dinner, I knew we couldn't delay any longer. At least the small talk had kept me distracted from what I was about to do.

"I guess we'd better go. You two going to be shielded enough to come over to Temple Row?"

Morio nodded. "I think we'll be okay. We cast a pretty strong protection barrier to guard against excess magical energy, so we should be fine. You're ready?"

I took in a deep breath, holding it for a long time before

slowly letting it out. "No, but there's no time like the present. Let's go find out where Jareth wants to take me."

The trip back to Temple Row took us all of thirty minutes now that we knew where we were going. Morio and Camille looked decidedly uncomfortable once we hit the other side of the park, but their spell held and by the time we came to the doors of the Temple of Reckoning, they seemed to be doing fine.

Jareth was waiting in the great hall. "I knew you'd return," he said. He nodded at Camille and Morio. "You are welcome, of course, but this isn't going to be pleasant. Are you sure you want to watch? You may find out more than you ever wanted to know about what happened to your sister, Camille."

Camille looked at me. "I said I'll stand by you, and I will, if you want me there. You shouldn't have to carry this alone. We're family, and whatever happened to you, happened to all of us."

I rubbed the bridge of my nose. "I've worked so hard to hide what Dredge did to me, to protect you and Delilah and Father. I guess . . . it's time to let go of my secrets."

Jareth nodded. "Come with me then. All of you. We'll be working outside of time. You'll make it home shortly before first light." He led us through a different door than I'd taken when I first arrived at the temple. We scurried down hall after hall until we came to a darkened room so large I couldn't see the other side. The ceiling and walls were black, and the only furniture was in the center—a long narrow dais draped in an indigo cloth, with pillows on the floor surrounding the platform.

He motioned for me to stand in front of the dais. Camille and Morio stood off to one side. "We don't have time for the usual rituals and rites that happen before an awakening, but I must ask you this. Do you come here of your own free will, to learn to control your own power and sever the chains that bind you to your sire's bidding?"

I swallowed the fear that rose. "I do so affirm."

"Will you surrender yourself to my hands, knowing that I will lead you into the darkness?"

The words hung heavy on my tongue. I didn't want to say them, but found them slipping between my lips of their own accord. "I surrender to you."

"Then take your place on the dais, Menolly." Jareth indicated for me to lay down on my back. When I'd done so, he pulled out silver cuffs that were lined with velvet. "These won't touch your skin, so they won't hurt, but you won't be able to break them."

I stared at the cuffs in horror. Silver, a blessing to the Fae, was bane to a vampire. Wincing, I held out my arms and he fastened them around my wrists. Nothing. They were well cushioned, like he'd said. He produced a second pair and fastened them around my ankles, then helped me lay back so that my head was on a small pillow. After I was in place, Jareth held up a blindfold and slowly covered my eyes.

I could hear Camille and Morio talking to him in low tones.

"Are you sure she'll be okay?" Morio was saying.

"I make no guarantees, but I believe Menolly is strong enough to make it through the rite. If she's to have any hope of confronting her sire, she must master her fear. She must rid herself of the chains he forged between them. Do you understand?"

Camille's voice broke in. "It makes perfect sense, but listen to me, Monk. If you hurt her in any way that isn't part of the ritual, if you try to fuck her up, I'll rip out your heart and feed it to a Corpse Talker. Do *you* understand *me*?"

There was a brief pause, then, "You make yourself perfectly clear, Daughter of the Moon." Jareth busied himself at something. The sound of blood trickling into a goblet reached my ears. The fragrance filled the room, metallic and brilliant and beautiful. Then a bell chimed three times and I sensed him circling around the table, widdershins, going against the sun.

"Once I begin, we must finish. You understand this? There's no stopping, or the energy could backfire." Jareth was standing near my head.

I let out a shudder. "This whole trip isn't going quite the way I expected. Get on with it."

> *Angel of glory, angel of blood,*
> > *rise to meet your maker.*
> *Angel of glory, angel of blood,*
> > *rise to confront your sire.*
> *Angel of glory, angel of blood,*
> > *rise to reclaim what is yours.*
> *Angel of glory, angel of blood,*
> > *return to the time you were newly born.*

He was circling the table, his voice drifting on a stiff breeze that had suddenly sprung up to sweep through the room. The energy shifted and I felt myself drifting lower, my consciousness lulled by the cadence of his speech, by the rhythm of his heartbeat.

> *Surrender your expectations. Surrender your doubts.*
> *Surrender your fears. Surrender your strengths.*
> *Surrender your anger. Surrender your control.*

Three drops of blood splashed on my forehead, their scent enticing me. Even though I'd drank just a few hours earlier, the thirst rose and I found myself ravenous. I jerked against the cuffs, wanting to be free to go and hunt. *I can't,* I thought, *I can't leave. I can't just go traipsing off in search of fresh blood on the city streets.*

> *Creature of the night, demon of the blood,*
> *Turn back the clock, turn back the minutes*
> > *and hours and years.*
> *Return to the night you were born anew.*
> *Return to the night of your siring.*

Three more drops, but this time he placed them against my lips, pressing gently with his fingers. I forced myself to keep from biting the warm flesh as he withdrew his hand.

My tongue snaked out and before I could stop myself, I licked the blood off my lips.

"Holy crap!" A searing flame ran through me and I convulsed against the chains. For a moment, I thought I'd been staked, but as the pain subsided I realized it was magic, carried within the blood I'd just tasted. I had barely digested this thought when I began to tumble, spiraling away from my body, away from the room, away from the table and Jareth and my sister and Morio.

"What the—?"

I stopped as I landed on a hard surface. As I opened my eyes, I realized I was back in the cavern where Dredge had taken me after he caught me. And he was there, standing over me, a dreadful expression on his face as he latticed my body with his nails.

The pain rolled over me in waves. It seemed like hours since I'd lost my ability to scream. I was lying naked on a stone slab deep in the cavern complex.

If I could only faint, pass out until it was all over and I walked among my ancestors. I tried to will myself into unconsciousness, tried to coax the fog of forgetfulness out of hiding. But my mind was too strong, my grasp on the present too firm. If I closed my eyes, I could almost grasp the edge of oblivion, but each time I started to slide into that blessed abyss, Dredge dug in a little harder, twisted my flesh a little sharper to bring me back.

"Don't give up on me yet, love," he said. His voice was like a gentle balm, soothing me for a fraction of a second until I relaxed and then he ripped at me again. "Don't think of it as punishment," he whispered. "You really have nothing to do with this—I'm sending a message. And you just happen to be my canvas."

As I bled, drop by drop, I could hear tongues rasping against the floor, lapping up the tears shed by my body. My stomach lurched. Dredge noticed, stopped, and tipped me on my side as my breakfast came pouring out.

"Can't have you dying in your own vomit, can we?" he said.

"Fuck you, you bastard," I said, spitting out the vile phlegm that remained in my mouth. "If you're going to kill me, just do it. I'm not afraid to die." Until the moment he'd caught me, that would have been a lie, but the pain I'd gone through in the last few hours made dying seem like a slow cruise into the underworld, where it would all be over and I'd be free.

"I know you're not. That's why we're taking it nice and easy," he said, then stood back. "And now that you're decorated, it's time for the real fun to begin."

I blinked. What more could he do to me? And then he started to disrobe.

"No—no . . . You're not fit to wipe my boots, you motherfucker—" The pain and fear of what was to come spurred on my anger and I struggled against the heavy cuffs securing me to the stone slab.

He laughed. "Spirit yet. I like it." Leaning over me, his curly hair trailed down to tickle my face and shoulders, hurting as it stuck to the bloody lines crisscrossing my body in a latticed design. Dredge's eyes were steel and ice, diamonds in the rough, and his lips were so full and inviting that his face almost made me weep. How could someone so beautiful be so savage? I shuddered as he climbed on the slab, erect and throbbing in the night.

"You want me, don't you? You want this so bad that you're dripping wet. Well, baby, I'm all yours," he said, driving deep inside me, his shaft of ice-frozen flesh grinding against my hips. The slashes across my body sent stinging jolts of agony through my nervous system as he moved against my skin, tearing the cuts further. I felt like a piece of meat under a mallet.

Count to one hundred. Think of nothing but the numbers. If I can count to one hundred, it will be over.

And so I focused, counting under my breath, making every single number the sole sum of my existence. I counted to one hundred, five hundred, two thousand. Finally the world blissfully began to fade. Still deep within me, Dredge leaned back, shaking me out of my stupor. As I stared at him, glassy eyed, he lifted his hand and smacked me across my face.

"Don't you die on me yet," he said, growling as he slashed his left wrist with one of his dagger-sharp nails. I stared at the glistening blood as it dribbled down his arm. Without warning, he brought his wrist to my lips and forced the cut against my mouth. I gasped, trying to twist my head away, but the blood flowed into my mouth and I felt like I was drowning. There was nothing I could do but swallow.

"Good girl," he said. "Good girl. Drink deep. Satisfy your thirst."

And suddenly, I realized that my mouth and throat were parched from screaming. Without thinking, I sucked against his wrist, taking the precious liquid within, soothing the wracking pain.

"That's it, suck hard. Drink it down, little girl. Drink it down." Dredge cradled my head. He moved gently within me, his eyes triumphant. As the pain lifted, I struggled, soaring higher and higher. *No.* I didn't want to enjoy this. *Don't let him make me come,* I prayed, but then, before I could stop myself, I teetered on the edge and tumbled into an orgasm that shattered the stars.

As the whirl of energy fell away, I realized that I wasn't hurting anymore. I looked around and saw my body on the slab, Dredge standing next to me, looking victorious. *What do you know,* I thought. *I'm dead, and I'm free. No matter what he does to my body now, he can't hurt me any longer.*

I began to walk and found myself in a cavern of ice, the color of glacier water, glistening and pure and clean. It was time to meet my ancestors. A light beckoned at the end of the tunnel and I began to run toward it, feeling free and joyous and ready to enter the Land of the Silver Falls where my father's people went after they died. As I hurried forward, a figure began to form from mist and shadow. My mother, waiting for me on the other side.

"Mother!" I raced toward her. So she *had* been allowed to join my father's ancestors, even though she was human. Now we'd walk together in death.

"Menolly, come to me, baby!" The look on her face was so beautiful, so welcoming that tears began to course down my cheeks. She would protect me, cleanse me, soothe my soul.

But just then, I felt a tug at the back of my neck. I glanced over my shoulder and saw a silver cord connecting me to my body. *Damn, what the hell? But I'm dead.* What would it take to get away from this monster?

The cord slowly began to change color. It was turning bloodred, and the color was seeping from my body toward me. What the hell? Whatever it was, the energy felt tainted and I wanted no part of it. I tried to reach the end of the passage but the cord began to drag me back. As the trail of red hit my spirit, I felt myself being sucked back into my body.

No! "I don't want to go back!" To enter that scarred and pain-wracked body again? To face Dredge again? Never!

I tried to fight. As I struggled against the pull, Mother watched, frozen, a horrified look on her face. "Menolly! My baby . . . Let her go, damn you!" Tears ran down her face and she fell to her knees, holding out her arms. A warm and embracing cloud of sparkling light filtered toward me.

"Mother!" I screamed for real now, struggling. If I could just reach the safety of her light . . . but the force of the cord was growing stronger. "I won't go back. Mother—save me, *please save me.*"

And then, the light began to fade. I heard her scream my name again, but she vanished into the darkness as I went tumbling out of the ice cavern, back into my stone-cold body. I fell through layer after layer of skin, feeling the lack of a pulse, the lack of breath as I stretched out in the still shell that had been my home all these years.

As I searched frantically for the beating of my heart, I began to panic. I was going to suffocate. I struggled, rocking right and left. Dredge's laughter filtered into my ears and I opened my eyes and reared up into a sitting position, ripping the chains out of the slab.

"She's a strong one, Master," one of the shadows from the corner of the room said.

"Yes," Dredge said. "She is. We'll be able to make good use of her." As he spoke, he held out his hand and I saw that a miniature figure stood in the palm of his hand. It was a shadow of me. He squeezed and my ribs constricted. I yelped. And then he let go and I could relax again.

"Dance, puppet," he said.

My legs swung over the edge of the slab and I couldn't stop myself. I stood and began to dance. "No—you can't control me. *I won't let you.*"

Once again, he laughed. "Are you thirsty, newborn? Go home. Drink deep. Go home to your family and rip out their hearts, and then become a scourge on the world. Destroy all in your path."

With his words, the thirst hit me like a ton of bricks. Blood. I needed blood. I needed to drink. All I could see was a red haze of pain and desire, and I yanked the chains off my wrists and ankles. Dredge stood back, his laughter echoing against the ceiling of the cave as I raced into the wee hours of the night. I had to get home to feed. And then the world went black . . .

"Menolly, can you hear me?"

The man's voice penetrated the haze of pain buttressing the periphery of my thoughts. Where was I? Was I still in the cavern? And then I remembered—I was safe, in a temple, tied down but under the watchful eyes of someone who was helping me.

I licked my lips, expecting my voice to sound raspy from screaming, but it came out clear and calm. "Yes . . . yes, I can hear you."

"We witnessed what happened to you. Now that we know, we can work on breaking the cord that binds you to Dredge. Do you understand what I'm saying?"

The words drifted through my thoughts and I flashed back to dancing when Dredge said dance. *A puppet.* He'd called me a puppet. "What do I need to do?"

"You must return to that moment and find the thread of energy that connects the two of you. It's not just his blood that makes him your sire."

Go back? Did he say *go back*? The last thing I wanted to do was dive back into that mire of pain and anger. But then the thought of being free dangled, the carrot in front of the horse.

"What do I have to do? How do I do this?"

"It's simple. You go back and I'll be here, shoring you up. Focus on finding the cord that binds you to him. We need to know precisely where it connects in your aura so we can pinpoint and sever it. But before we make the break, we need to find out where he is. For that, you'll have to reach out from the present through the binding cord and touch his soul."

Jareth brushed a stray hair out of my forehead and that simple kindness made me sniffle. Reliving the past was exhausting, painful. *But if reliving it is this bad, think what it's doing to you every day, every hour, every minute you carry the burden.* The words echoed in my mind and I blinked behind the blindfold. All of my anger and sorrow couldn't be wiped away as if it had never happened, but perhaps I could lay it down? Quit carrying it and let it go?

"All right," I said. "Let's do it. How can I keep from being sucked under by the memories?"

"I'll be by your side, now that I know what you're facing," he said. "Lean on me. Call on my strength."

As the smell of blood came close once again, I said, "Dredge tried to do this, didn't he? You took him back to his time of turning?"

Jareth let out a long sigh. "I did. I had no idea he'd been a priest of Jakaris in life—the years of perversion that twisted his soul. And so the ritual went terribly wrong. Instead of being willing to let go of the anger, he was looking for a way to absorb his sire's power into himself. And it worked."

I thought about that for a moment. Dredge had sought to embrace the power, and to that end, tricked Jareth. He'd given in to the very soul of evil. I wouldn't follow in the footsteps of my sire, no matter what the cost. "I'm ready."

A pause, and then Jareth began the incantation again, sprinkling three more drops on my forehead.

Surrender your expectations. Surrender your doubts.
Surrender your fears. Surrender your strengths.
Surrender your anger. Surrender your control.

And then three drops on my lips and I reached out and sucked them in as I held on for the ride to come.

> *Creature of the night, demon of the blood,*
> *Turn back the clock, turn back the minutes*
> *   and hours and years.*
> *Return to the night you were born anew.*
> *Return to the night of your siring.*

Once again, I was back in the cavern, back in my now-dead body. But this time, I felt a golden glow cradling my head as I frantically tried to place myself. I was dead—I was dead and Dredge had turned me into a vampire. *But wait,* this was a dream, a vision I was walking through.

That's right, I thought, breaking through the fear. *My name is Menolly and I've been a vampire for twelve Earthside years, and I'm really lying on a platform in the Temple of Reckoning. These are merely shades of the past.*

I tried to focus, to find Jareth. Then, I realized he *was* the golden glow that was cushioning my head. He was here, watching over me. I instinctively tried to take a deep breath, but my lungs didn't want to work right.

Wait, I'm dead.

My thoughts began to sort themselves out, as memory kicked in. That's right, I thought. It had taken me over a year to learn how to take a breath. Meanwhile, I'd spent far too many days dreaming that I was suffocating.

Jareth's hands ran down my shoulders, reminding me that I wasn't trapped here with Dredge. I wouldn't have to go through the year of madness again, locked like an animal in a silver cage while the OIA tried to retrieve my soul from the shattered state Dredge left it in.

Now . . . time to find that cord. I forced myself to relax and sought out the tendrils of energy racing through my body. The blood and the rape and torture had created implings—parasitical creatures created from intense emotions. For the first time, I could see that they'd attached themselves to my aura and they were probably still with me after all these years. Shuddering, I tried to push them aside but Jareth patted me on the shoulder and I let it go for now.

I examined my body, searching for the cord that chained me to Dredge, seeking the ties that bind. My body was torn and scarred. When I'd died, the wounds were still fresh. As I woke to my new state, they would be faded, no longer raw, but the scars would be there forever, neck to ankle, branding me as one of his disciples.

Suddenly I stopped. There it was—emerging from the back of my neck. I blinked. Why hadn't I ever seen this before? *Probably because I never bothered looking.* But there it was, connecting me to Dredge, locked into his lowest chakra, the vortex of survival.

Resisting the urge to try something stupid like removing it myself, I did my best to let Jareth know I'd found what we were looking for.

The next moment, I found myself shooting out of the cavern, back into the present, and when I opened my eyes the blindfold was gone and the shackles had been removed from my wrists and ankles. Jareth helped me sit up and gave me a soft smile.

"It's connected from the back of my neck to the lowest chakra on Dredge," I said.

"Menolly!" Camille rushed over to my side, her face so wet it looked raw. Good thing she wore waterproof mascara, I thought. Morio stood back.

I looked at Jareth. "How much do they know?"

Camille spoke. "We saw it all. It was like watching a movie. We heard everything." She sank to her knees, her hands clutching the hem of her skirt as tears trickled down her face. "I didn't know it was that bad. I'm so sorry—I didn't know. I didn't know . . . forgive me, please . . ."

Sliding off the dais I discovered that I was a little seasick, but otherwise I felt normal. I knelt by her side and pulled her into my arms. "I didn't want you to know. Delilah, either. I still don't want her to know. She's not strong enough to handle it."

Camille pressed her lips against my face, kissing my

cheeks, my eyes, my forehead. "My precious Menolly. Mother tried . . . she tried to help you."

"I know," I said, staring at the ground. "And I've always blamed her. I thought she wasn't strong enough and I blamed the fact that she was human for that. Now I understand. She wanted to help me but she couldn't fight Dredge's hold."

"You'd been turned into a vampire. Menolly, no mortal spirit can sever that transformation, not in the physical realm, not on the astral. But she tried—she loves you."

I wondered just how much Mother could love what I'd become but pushed the thought out of my head. "The important thing is that we have the location of my bondage to Dredge."

"And I know what you went through," Camille said. "Now . . . I can understand you a little better."

"That too," I said, softly. Maybe it was better this way. Maybe Camille would be able to help me when the rage and hunger threatened. I looked up at Morio, who was staring at me, a solemn expression on his face.

"Menolly, don't underestimate Delilah," he said. "Someday she may need to know, for her own safety. Don't write her off as a weakling."

I blinked. Trillian had said the same thing. Maybe I should pay attention. "I'll remember that." I allowed Jareth to help me up. "What do we do now? How much time before first light?"

He sucked in a deep breath. "I told you, we're working outside of time this night. You'll be home before sunrise. Follow me." He led us into a room to the left of the chamber we'd been in. There was a pentacle inscribed on the marble floor, carved into a deep trench and inlaid with hematite. Even I could feel the grounding pull of the polished metal as it settled the magic into the floor.

The rest of the room was empty, except for four podiums, one at each quarter of the circle, where pronged stands held gemstones as big as my fist. Camille's eyes went wide as she stared at the jewels. To the north was an emerald. To the east, a diamond. To the south—a ruby. And to the west, a sapphire.

I tapped her on the shoulder. "Your jewelry fetish is showing."

She flashed me a smile. "Amazing, aren't they? I didn't know some of those gem crystals could grow so big."

"They must be worth a fortune." I turned to Jareth. "How do you protect them from being stolen?"

Jareth stared at me, clearly amused. "Do you really think anybody could manage to not only infiltrate the City of Seers, but then get through our temple with all the wards and bindings? For one thing, we're outside of normal time. Within this space, we've entered a parallel realm and there's only one way in or out. The door through which you entered is only visible when we deem it so."

Morio and Camille wandered around the edges of the pentacle. Morio sniffed. "Magic is thick here."

"Yes, and this is where we will pinpoint Dredge's location, and sever his connection to Menolly." Jareth motioned to Morio. "Take the element of air, if you will." Morio looked surprised but obeyed, and Jareth turned to Camille. "If you will guard the west." She walked over to stand beside the sapphire.

"Where do you want me?" I asked, ready to get the show on the road.

"In the center, but don't move yet." He clapped his hands and the door opened again. Two robed figures glided in. I couldn't even begin to see their faces behind their hoods. One silently stood by the ruby, the other beside the emerald. "Once they activate the stones, you'll walk into the center and I'll follow, then they'll close the circle."

The globes of light dimmed. Jareth motioned to the figure standing by the emerald. "Just follow suit," he told Camille and Morio.

The cloaked woman—in this space, I could smell her delicate scent—reached up and grasped the emerald tightly in both hands. The stone began to glow, a glimmer in the center at first that radiated out. A beam shot from the crystal to land directly in the center of the diamond.

"By soil and branch, sanctify and protect this space," the woman's whisper echoed in the chamber.

Morio glanced at Jareth, who gestured the go-ahead. Morio grasped the diamond with both hands and inhaled sharply. Once again, the crystal began to glow with a shimmer so white it almost burnt my eyes. The beam shot out to kiss the ruby.

"By wind and gale, sanctify and protect this space," Morio said, his voice trembling ever so slightly.

Jareth nodded to the robed man standing near the ruby. There was something familiar about him but I couldn't pinpoint what. He reached up and once again, a light shot forth, this one crimson as blood.

"By flame and sun, sanctify and protect this space."

"A moment," Jareth said, holding his hand up to stop Camille. "Come, Menolly." He led me through the opening between the west and north gates to the center of the pentagram, then turned back to Camille. "Close the wards," he said.

Camille took hold of the sapphire and the beam shot forth, touching the emerald. "By water and ice, sanctify and protect this space." As she spoke, a rumbling from the floor sounded, from the very center point of the pentacle, and a platform rose from the tile, upon which sat a huge crystal ball.

"And now," Jareth said, looking at me. "It's time for us to find out where Dredge is. And to sever your ties."

I knelt by the dais and took hold of the crystal ball. This was it. And I sincerely hoped that Dredge wouldn't notice and go on a killing spree before we could make it home.

CHAPTER 15

The crystal ball began to glow as a ripple tickled my fingers.

"Look into the ball. Think of Dredge, remember that night." Jareth stood behind me, hands on my shoulders, letting me source his energy.

"Dredge, where the fuck are you?" I whispered. A swirl began to form within the crystal. Jareth steadied me, and I managed to keep my hands on the orb. We were still connected. If Dredge realized I was spying on him, he'd have the advantage. Which meant I had to slide into his mind, then out again before he knew I was there.

The mist in the crystal swirled, a phantasmagoria of red and bronze threads. I found myself sucked deep into the scintillating colors. They dipped and circled like snakes coiled in a mating dance.

The room darkened and I found myself spiraling through the ether, headed toward a brilliant crimson figure up ahead. As I drew near, the presence of my sire loomed large and deadly and then he was there, Dredge, in the center of the brilliant bloody light. Seen from this perspective, I understood why he commanded so much authority. Dredge was pure power trapped in an undying body by the greed and lust that had grown within him over the years. The chaos around him took aim like a hundred wanton arrows, firing at anyone or anything that drew near.

Nearby a deep laughter startled me and I twisted, trying to see who was there. A giant wolf rose above Dredge's shoulder, but this was no Were, no lycanthrope or native spirit. No, I knew who this was. Loki, lord of tricksters, lord of the giants, lord of mischief. And Loki held Dredge's soul firmly in his palm. So he'd traded a god of vice for the hand of chaos and madness.

I could see the cord of fire and frost that connected Dredge to the demigod. No wonder the vampire had grown so powerful over the years. Loki owned his soul, and Dredge was feeding the havoc monger. Which meant . . . oh great gods! *Loki* was Dredge's sire. No wonder Jareth hadn't been able to free Dredge. And Dredge had absorbed some of Loki's power.

Shaking my head, I focused on the task at hand. So far, the demigod hadn't noticed me and I wanted to keep it that way. I might be able to handle Dredge, but Loki? No mortal challenged the gods and lived. No vampire either, which was why Dredge was still bound to him.

I slipped around front to stare at him. Dredge didn't even blink. Jareth had promised me that he wouldn't be able to detect me unless he was deliberately focusing on the astral, and it appeared that his attention was wandering elsewhere. Even if I draped my arm around his shoulders, he wouldn't sense me, since he was my sire and we shared blood.

Now comes the hard part . . .

Jareth's thoughts merged with mine and I realized that he was hanging out in my head. Somehow he'd managed to tap into my mind. Normally that would piss the hell out of me but right now I was grateful that I wasn't alone.

What next? I focused the question toward Jareth, apparently doing too good of a job because I felt him jump.

Try to turn down the volume, would you?

I blinked. *Oops. I'm sorry,* I thought, but he shook it off. *Listen to me carefully. You need to walk into him. Look*

*out from his eyes and see what he's seeing. Try to figure out
where he is, from what he's looking at. You don't have much
time, though. As soon as you find something to gauge a location, then get out and we'll sever your cord to him. I can see
where it is now. Don't play hero—you can't stay inside of
him long before he notices you're there. Got it?*

Yep. I didn't want it, but I got it.

My stomach knotting, I made my way over to his side.
Even here on the astral, I could smell him and that smell
took me back. I spiraled back to his touch, to his laughter, to
him filling me deep with his sex that froze me to the core of
my heart. And then his wrist pressed against my lips, forcing
me to drink and I understood what it meant to die alone, in
pain, in anger . . .

Get moving. Don't get bogged down in memories. Jareth's
thoughts were urgent. I licked my lips, still tasting Dredge's
blood in my mouth.

Sorry. I'm going. I shook my head. The past was the past.
It was time to move forward. And moving forward meant
killing the motherfucker who'd dragged me down into this
nightmare.

I jumped. Playing walk-in didn't thrill me, but if I had to
infiltrate the devil, then infiltrate I would. As I entered his
body, a surge of power ran through me. The thought of
killing off his soul and taking over his form raced through
my thoughts. Kyoka had done it, and with Dredge, I'd have
power beyond my wildest dreams. But then I remembered
the cord tying Dredge to Loki and quickly disposed of that
idea. Trade a degenerate sire for a master who was ten times
worse? No thanks.

I quickly sorted out my bearings and, after a moment,
managed to get myself turned around so that I was staring
out of Dredge's eyes.

The room in which he was standing was actually quite
spacious and well furnished. I wanted to look around, to see
if I could find Erin, but Dredge was focused on the view out
the window, so I couldn't.

As I stared into the Seattle night I caught a glimpse of
two important landmarks: one was a statue over on the

docks that had recently been unveiled. Called *The Deck-hand,* it was a tribute to all the dock workers who'd labored away on the ships that pulled into port. And the other land-mark was the Sushirama, a restaurant Camille had been talk-ing about that had recently opened down on the Pier. That meant Dredge was in one of the old warehouses on the other side of Alaskan Way, and if I didn't miss my guess, he was probably staying at the Halcyon, a hotel and nightclub combo owned by an Earthside Supe. I got the vague sense that, although the hotel catered to Supes, the owner didn't realize Dredge was a vampire from OW.

With one last look out the window to try and gauge the height from the street—probably third or fourth floor—I slipped out of his body.

I'm ready.

Jareth led me away. As soon as we'd retreated from Dredge's astral form, in a whoosh, we were back in the cir-cle and I opened my eyes.

"I know where he is. Let's get this done so Camille and I can get home and take him out." I glanced over at her. I knew what she was thinking. "I didn't see Erin. I don't know where he's keeping her, but I do know where he is and it won't be hard to pinpoint the exact location." She nodded.

"To sever your connections with him, I need only one tool, along with your desire to be free." Jareth withdrew a crystal dagger from the folds of his robe.

I stared at the blade. Made of elaborately carved quartz, it was polished to a high sheen, with a sapphire cabochon em-bedded in the handle.

"Are you from the Tygerian Mountains? The Order of the Crystal Dagger?" If he was from the brotherhood of monks that guarded the Tygerian Well, no wonder he was so power-ful.

Jareth inclined his head. "Several of the brotherhood have come to live in the City of Seers." His tone told me that we weren't going to get anything more out of him about that little fact. "I need you to remove your shirt." He paused, as if trying to figure out how to say something.

"Just tell me. Whatever it is, I can take it."

"Very well. The tip of my blade needs to enter your neck where the cord binds you to Dredge. The blade is sanctified. While it won't physically harm you because you're a vampire, it will negate cords that hold oath and bind."

"You carry a warlock blade?" Camille flinched. Warlocks—or oath breakers—were traitors . . . magicians of the worst kind. Over Earthside, they'd been bounty hunters who infiltrated villages during the dark ages, looking for midwives and witch-women, who they then turned over to the Inquisition. In Otherworld, warlocks were actual magicians who'd broken their pacts with the gods and had been cast out of their orders.

Jareth gave her a cold look. She shut up.

"*I am no warlock.* But I *am* authorized to break oaths forced upon others unwillingly, such as your sister, or oaths coerced through unfair means. And the ritual requires a warlock blade."

Camille hung her head. "I'm so sorry. I didn't realize the significance. Please accept my apologies." She looked so repentant that I almost laughed. My sister seldom apologized, and it was obvious she felt like a heel.

"It's all good," Jareth said. "Let it be. Menolly, as I said, I have to insert the tip of the blade into your neck. I give you my word that I won't do you any more harm than necessary, but it will be painful. The severing of a vampire from her sire is one of the most drastic bond-breakings that can take place. The only thing it's on par with is being cast out by the gods, or being exiled from a magical order. You've been carrying the link for twelve years. I guarantee you'll notice the difference. Are you prepared for the change?"

I stared into his eyes. "The truth is I don't know what to expect, but I'm ready. Just get it over with. If I'm going to destroy Dredge, I have to sever the link. And I can't stand being chained to him another minute." I removed my shirt.

Jareth stared at me as my scars came into view.

Camille flinched. She always did when she saw my body, but now she knew exactly how I'd received them. I could read the anguish in her eyes. I gave her a thumbs-up and she forced a smile to her lips.

"Kneel in front of me by the crystal ball, and move your hair away from your neck. Bow your head so I can get a clear view." He skirted to my left, muttering a few words over the dagger.

I shook my braids out of the way and knelt on the marble, hanging my head. Scared out of my wits, there was a little part of me that was afraid that when the cord was severed, I'd go up in flames or poof into a thousand ash flecks. Stupid, but fear doesn't run on logic.

As Jareth continued to incant, the energy built like a cyclone around us, catching us in the eye of the twister. Jareth's voice rose. "Menolly D'Artigo, do you renounce your sire?"

"I do." The energy shifted counterclockwise—widdershins.

"Do you choose to walk an isolated path, cut off from the lineage you bear with Dredge, and with his own sire?"

"I do." The winds began to swirl against the turn of the sun and with every rotation, they wiped away a layer of the bond forged over the days and weeks and years I'd spent linked to Dredge. One by one, the connections began to unravel, to unknot, to unwind.

"Menolly D'Artigo, do you choose to walk the realms of the worlds, bound only to yourself and the gods to whom you have made oath, forsaking the path laid out to you by your sire?"

"I do." A shriek rose up and I suddenly felt Dredge starting to stir. "Hurry, he's noticing!"

"Stay where you are. He only senses a disturbance. Don't feed him with your fear." Jareth knelt behind me, his right hand on my shoulder, his left holding the dagger. "Menolly D'Artigo, do you refute Dredge's right to claim you? Do you renounce your sire?"

And this was the end. I could feel it. My answer to this question would turn me into a pariah among traditional vamps—they'd know I'd turned traitor. But then again, once I killed Dredge, I'd be doubly damned in their eyes.

"I renounce Dredge. I refute him. I banish him from my life. I forever revoke his right to connect with me or my path."

As I spoke, Jareth plunged the dagger into the back of my neck, directly into the center of the cord that bound me to the monster of my nightmares, to my maker and sire.

The blade entered clean, but the pain of the cord breaking was beyond anything I'd experienced since the night Dredge turned me. All of my anger and pain, all of his lust and greed, coiled up like a maddened serpent and turned on me. I could see it hovering, ready to strike, but then Jareth drew a runic symbol in the air between the snake and me. The creature let out a deafening shriek and exploded in a red cloud. I wavered, then as Jareth yanked the blade out of my neck, fell sideways, landing on the cold marble.

Jareth knelt down and gathered me in his arms. I grimaced. For the first time in years, my body ached. As he lifted me up and carried me out of the circle and over to a bench, I wondered if I'd be less powerful without Dredge shoring me up.

"Is first light coming?" I whispered, exhausted.

"No, you've still got a while before the sun rises, but you've been through what amounts to major surgery on your psyche. You need to regain strength. I'll make sure you all make it home safely, but before you go, you *must* drink."

"I can't hunt; I'm too tired," I said.

"You need fresh blood. Reserve won't do." Jareth pulled his robe away from his shoulders and knelt beside me. "Drink. You won't be able to hurt me. Take what you need. I've done this before."

I stared at him. "You want me to drink from you?" He'd saved my butt. In fact he may have saved all our lives. "I can't just treat you like a juice box after all you've done."

"Drink. I will shore you up until you regain your strength. You don't really have a choice. At this point, if you don't drink, you could die."

He hadn't mentioned that as one of the side effects. I blinked, looking over at Camille, who said, "For once in your life, just obey without asking questions. Jareth said to drink, so drink."

I cleared my throat. "Only if you and Morio leave. I don't want you to watch me feeding."

She nodded, silently assenting. Jareth motioned to the other two participants in the ritual who had guarded the elemental gates. "Take them into the preparation room. I'll call you when we're done."

As soon as they'd left the room, I said, "Jareth, I need you to sit by me. I'm too weak to stand."

He settled in beside me on the bench, the pale skin of his neck enticing and wan. "You don't get out in the sun much, do you?" I asked, attempting to break the tension. I gazed up at him. "You say you've played blood host to a vampire before?" Monk from the Order of the Crystal Dagger or not, I had to make sure he knew what he was getting into.

He let out a long sigh. "Many years ago, long before you were born, I was engaged to a woman named Cassandra. She was a vampire. The villagers near the monastery staked her. That's when I left the Tygerian Mountains and came here." There was no tremor in his voice, no change of expression, but I read the world into the little lines that appeared around his lips when he said her name.

Cassandra. I wondered what she'd looked like, who she'd been, why he'd loved her so much he'd take a chance on marrying her. But I asked none of those questions. His memories were none of my business. His pain wasn't mine to excavate and expose.

"Then you understand the beauty of blood." A statement, not a question.

Jareth nodded. "More than you think. Drink. Restore your strength. I can take care of myself, and I trust you to know when to stop."

His trust was a gift. I would not abuse it. I shifted over to straddle his lap and felt his erection as I gazed into his eyes. Could I? Dare I? He'd given me back my life, in a way. He'd given me freedom. The least I could do was give him a taste of bliss since he was saving my life. "Jareth, listen to me. I'm going to drink from you now. Let me kiss your throat, my dear." I put the full force of my charm into the words.

Jareth's eyes glazed over and it was obvious he'd let down his guard or I wouldn't have been able to mesmerize him. "Drink me," he whispered. "Drink me deep, Menolly."

And I did. My lips met the pale flesh that waited so patiently. I licked his neck with a slow, long stroke, and he moaned gently as my fangs extended, tickling him with their tips. I focused on passion, on bringing all the sensuality of the moment that I could to the surface.

"Feel no pain," I whispered. "Feel only joy."

He shuddered as I punctured his skin, my fangs sinking deep, stimulating the blood flow. As the drops welled up and began to trickle down his neck, I withdrew, then pressed my lips against him, sucking hard, drinking from the well of life that sprang up from his veins.

Jareth gasped as I sucked harder, the hot fluid pouring down my throat, sustaining me up, lifting me out of the stupor I'd fallen into. I pressed him back so that he lay on the bench. His robe fell away, leaving him exposed, hard and firm, pale and throbbing.

My lips never leaving his neck, I shimmied out of my jeans and climbed astride, sinking on the length of his desire. This was the first time since Dredge that a man had been inside me, the first time since Dredge I'd allowed myself to think I might be able to even *stand* a man's touch.

His body pulsated with magic. Jareth began to thrust against my hips as I continued to drink. Pure as life, pure as death, blood and sex met in a passionate embrace as we made love, and with every moment, my strength grew, the energy racing through my veins. Jareth clutched the sides of my hips, guiding me, begging me not to stop.

As images strove to flicker up—Dredge in me, Dredge staring down at me—I pushed them away, focusing on Jareth. Jareth, who was helping me reclaim my soul. Jareth, who walked into the fire with me. Jareth, who willingly offered me his blood so that I might live. And then, sensing that he was reaching his limit as a blood host, I pulled away, my braids clicking in the room that was silent save only for the sound of our desire.

"Menolly, Menolly, don't leave me hanging, don't leave me . . ." Jareth flipped me over onto my back and I didn't fight him. He spread my legs, hovering as he sought for my center, desperate to find something he'd lost long, long ago.

I let him lead me, but my mind was still trying to throw up barricades.

In an impassioned plea, he held my face between his hands, forcing me to look him in the eye. "Let go, let go of your reserve. Let go of it. *I'm not Dredge*. You don't have to put up walls with me. And you won't become a monster, I promise you that. Do you hear me? You can let go, Menolly," he whispered. "You can let go of all the fear."

For the second time in so many days, I lowered my shields, gave up control, and spiraled into the darkness of orgasm, and the peace that comes with release.

After dressing, I was almost ready to go. Camille and Morio politely avoided asking me how things had gone. I had to hand it to her, Camille knew when to be discreet.

Before leaving, I remembered to ask about the Aqualine Crystal for Iris. Jareth obligingly gave us one of the sky blue spikes, wrapped in a black velvet bag.

"How much do we owe you?" I asked.

He waved aside my question. "Forget it. You probably couldn't afford it anyway. If she's a priestess of Undutar, then she'll make good use of this. Now you should go. First light will soon arrive."

We didn't say anything about our interlude. Sometimes words are inadequate. As we headed toward the main temple hall, I wondered if I'd ever see him again. Perhaps . . . perhaps not. We'd been through such an intense few hours, why dilute the experience?

As we entered the great hall, Jareth stopped us. "I have someone to send home with you. I warn you, and I'm serious about this, don't ask any questions until you're back Earthside. There are spies everywhere, and the last thing you need is more trouble."

"Not a problem," I said. "I trust you." And then a rush of gratitude swept over me. Against my nature, I threw my arms around him, hugging him tightly. "How can I ever thank you? I'm free of Dredge. I can go up against him now."

"I'm glad I could help," Jareth said softly. "But don't ever underestimate him, Menolly. He's dangerous. And when he realizes you've broken the bond, he's going to be furious." He kissed my forehead. "If you ever come back this way, look me up. Trust me, we live a long, long time here in Aladril. I'll be here. Now because time is slipping by quickly, I'm going to transport you to the portal. I want you to close your eyes and hold hands."

A little uneasy, I obeyed. Camille was used to magic. Once she'd gotten used to the energy of the temple, she seemed right at home. But I still wasn't comfortable. The sound of a rushing wind gusted past and the world lurched under our feet. I squeezed Camille's hand so tightly she gasped.

Before I could loosen my grip, everything settled back into place and we opened our eyes. We were standing outside the portal in the woods, facing the same three guards who'd greeted us when we arrived.

They silently took our necklaces back and escorted us into the shrine.

"Master Jareth said for you to take this man with you. Don't ask questions. Don't even speak to him until you return home."

Waiting for us was the hooded monk who had wielded the ruby in the temple during the ritual. He kept silent. We didn't push it. Jareth was on our side and if there was a reason he wanted the priest to return Earthside with us, we'd have to trust him. In silence, we entered the portal, crossing back to Elqaneve where Trenyth met us. With first light not far away, he promised to take his report through the Whispering Mirror and sent us home.

As we emerged into Grandmother Coyote's forest, I glanced at the sky. Less than an hour before the sun rose. Even from behind the clouds and falling snow, the light would burn me to cinders. The pull of the dawn was hell, I could barely keep my eyes open as we hurried to Morio's SUV.

Camille glanced at our cloaked guest. "Who are you?"

"Never mind that for now," I said. "I need to get home."

"She's right," Morio said. "Don't worry, you'll find out his name soon enough."

Camille cocked her head, a curious look on her face. "You know?"

Morio shrugged. "Jareth and I had a long talk while you were helping Menolly." He fell silent again and no amount of cajoling could get him to open up as we climbed in the car. Our guest stared at the SUV for a moment before following suit. Whoever he was, I had a feeling he'd never been Earthside.

At the house, Delilah was waiting, along with Chase, Iris, and Nerissa. After I shut the door behind us, I whirled around to our new friend. "Okay, I don't have much time before I have to sleep and I'm not going to wait until tonight to find out just who you are. Cloak, *off*."

The man slowly reached up and pulled away his hood. Camille gasped as Delilah gave a loud shout.

"Well, who is he?" Chase asked impatiently.

"Shamas! It's our cousin Shamas!" Camille sputtered. "We thought you were gone for good!" She sprang forward and threw her arms around the tall, black-haired man who shared her pale skin, raven hair, and violet eyes.

Shamas, who had been fighting for Tanaquar against the Opium-Eater, had been captured by Lethesanar and sentenced to death a month ago. He'd managed to escape when a triad of monks were sent by Tanaquar to assassinate him before he hit the torture chamber. At least that way he'd die without too much pain. But somehow Shamas had managed to grab hold of their energy and use it for his own purposes—namely to get the hell out of Dodge. He'd vanished and nobody had heard from—or of—him since.

"Shamas! How did you . . . why . . . how did this happen?" I couldn't believe my eyes. "When you escaped from Queen Lethesanar, we all thought you might have imploded or something."

Our cousin laughed, but his voice was raw and strained. "Camille, Delilah, Menolly . . . it's so good to see your faces. I wasn't sure I'd ever see any of my family again until I crossed over to our ancestors." He shrugged off the robe, revealing a too thin body, with the pale sheen of healed scars lacing his arms. So Lethesanar *had* started on him before the triad of monks had intervened.

"Let the man sit down," I said. "Can't you see he's exhausted? Are you hungry, Shamas? Would you like something to eat?"

He rubbed his forehead, squinting. "I'm overwhelmed, that's all. So much has happened in the past few weeks." As we led him into the living room, he added, "I'd love a cup of tea or some broth."

Iris took the matter firmly in hand. "Soup it is, and tea, and some fresh, hot bread. You're far too thin. And you look so tired. Girls, get him a blanket and a pillow and settle him in the recliner. I assume your wounds have already healed and don't need treatment?" Iris didn't mince words.

Shamas nodded. "The monks of Dayinye saved my life. I was almost dead when I broke through their shields and landed in the temple."

"You broke through the shields of Aladril?" Morio stared at him. "You must be a powerful magician."

"I'll bet you ten to one Queen Asteria knew he'd be there," I told Camille. "I don't know how, but she's pulling some strings of fate herself."

Shamas motioned to Morio. "Apparently I'm more powerful than I realized, but only under pressure and even then, I can't control it yet. I'll tell you all about it once I've had a chance to get my bearings." He looked around, clearly bewildered. "I've never been Earthside. You'll have to fill me in on everything."

"Delilah and Camille can do that while I'm sleeping." I glanced at the clock. "I'd love to go nab Dredge right now, but if we do, I'll be toast before you can say crispy critter."

Camille nodded to the kitchen. "Go then, and sleep. Morio and I will catch everyone up to speed. Oh, Iris— here's your crystal." She handed the Talon-haltija the velvet bag and Iris's eyes sparkled.

"Oh, this will come in handy," she said. I wondered what exactly she wanted it for but decided not to ask.

After giving Maggie a hug, I headed toward my room. Would I be able to sleep without nightmares?

I wasn't disappointed. For the first time since I'd been turned, I passed the night without dreams, without worry, in the perfect peace of a quiet heart.

CHAPTER 16

When I woke, Camille was sitting in the rocking chair, a nervous look on her face. I shook my head to clear the cobwebs away. "What's going on? I can tell by the look on your face that it's not good, whatever it is."

She frowned. "You're right. Come upstairs—we need to have a meeting. Chase is here, and so are Wade and Siobhan."

Chase? Wade? Siobhan? Curious, I hurried into my clothes and followed her to the living room.

Sure enough, Wade and Siobhan were on the sofa, talking in low whispers. Iris and Maggie were snuggled in the low rocking chair we'd bought for the house sprite. Shamas was in the corner talking to Morio, while Delilah and Anna-Linda were playing a game of cards at the card table.

It struck me that Anna-Linda looked like a totally different girl—her face was freshly washed, she was wearing a new pair of jeans, not skintight, and a cute T-shirt. And she was smiling.

But it was Chase who caught my attention. He was holding his head in his hands and I couldn't see his face, but he looked thoroughly rumpled—unusual for his Armani-and-a-martini self. He looked up at me, wiping his sleeve across his face, and I was shocked to see that not only was he disheveled, his eyes were bloodshot and he looked about ready to puke.

Camille pulled up an ottoman and sat next to his side. "Let's get this show on the road."

"What happened? More murders?" I asked, landing on the first reasonable explanation.

Chase shook his head. "Not that I know of . . . not yet, at least. Worse, actually."

"What could be worse than another spate of murders?"

Unfortunately I was about to get my answer. Delilah tossed me the *Seattle Tattler,* one of those yellow rags she was so fond of. I wouldn't wipe my ass with it, that is if I still needed to, but she loved the tabloids.

I glanced at the headlines. There, screaming in huge black font, were the words: *Vampires Rule Underground Seattle.*

"What the fuck?" I flipped the maze of amazing-but-not-so-true stories until I came to the cover headline. As I began to read, I understood why everybody was so upset.

What well-known director of the Faerie-Human Crime Scene Investigation Team has been hiding the activity of a nest of nasty vampires? Rumor has it that several citizens of Seattle have gone missing, and that Seattle's star detective, Chase Johnson, has pulled the bamboozle of the century and simply ignored the whispers about these abductions.

We at the *Tattler* have leads pointing to the truth—that these AWOL innocents have been turned into bloodsucking leeches of the night. That's right, folks—you knew they existed, but did you realize that Seattle plays home to an estimated 45 of these undead menaces? And when the upstanding, tax-paying citizens of Seattle disappear, who can we look to in order to take care of the situation? The police? Think again.

Kylie Wilson, president of the Guardian Watchdogs, says the group has joined forces with Freedom's Angels and are planning mass protests over the next few months to combat the growing population of Supernaturals (commonly known as Supes). "If God had meant Supes, as they call themselves, to exist in any large numbers, we'd all be born degenerates and mutants."

Chief Richard Devins, when asked about the missing people, claims no conspiracy exists. "We've received no missing persons reports, and if we were in the business of covering up murders, we wouldn't be out there every day hunting down the bad guys," he said this morning. "But you can rest assured, we will look into these allegations and prove that they're false. Until then, we urge the citizens of Seattle to avoid panic."

"Great mother, if this isn't a shit storm waiting to happen." I put down the magazine and looked at Chase. "Why haven't our newborns been reported as missing? Anybody know anything about that?"

"Anna-Linda, why don't we go into the kitchen and get a snack?" Delilah said. "We can finish the game in there."

Anna-Linda snorted. "You guys just want to talk without me in the room." She looked over at me and broke into a run, racing over to throw her arms around my waist. "Thank you. Thank you for helping me!"

Mystified, I glanced at Siobhan, who gave me the thumbs-up. "Anna-Linda's going to live with her aunt in Boise," she said. "Nerissa and I found out she has relatives there. And surprise of surprises, her aunt's husband—"

"Let me tell her! Let me tell her!" Anna-Linda jumped up and down.

Siobhan laughed. "Okay, go ahead. Tell her your news."

Anna turned back to me. "My aunt's husband is a werewolf. They have twins who are four years old. Darrin, the boy, is an FBH, and his sister, Chrissie, is a werewolf. I can help them on their ranch, they have a small dairy farm, and I'll help Aunt Jean with the kids and learn to ride and get back in school."

Her eyes were shining and I felt an overwhelming urge to cry—not because of the shit she'd gone through, but because she'd lucked out. She was going to make it off the streets. Anna-Linda would be okay. She'd grow up and, if she was lucky, turn out to be a happy, healthy young woman.

"I'm so thrilled for you," I said. "I take it your mom and your aunt don't keep in touch much, huh?"

Anna-Linda's face drooped a little. She shook her head. "No, my mom said that Aunt Jean's a drag and doesn't understand her. But she said she doesn't care if I go live with her."

Ouch. I couldn't imagine not caring where my child lived.

Siobhan rested her hands on Anna-Linda's shoulders. "Why don't we go into the kitchen and get that snack? That way Delilah can stay here and talk to Menolly."

"Okay. Can I have peanut butter?" Anna-Linda danced a jig on her way to the kitchen.

Iris stood, resting Maggie on her hip. "Let me go with you. It's time to feed Maggie, anyway, and you can help. I think we can rustle up some peanut-butter cookies, along with a turkey sandwich and some milk. How's that sound?"

"Yay!" Anna-Linda disappeared into the kitchen, followed by Iris and Maggie.

Siobhan waited until they'd left the room, then turned back to me. "You saved Anna-Linda from hell on earth. Be happy . . . You've made it possible for her to spread her wings." She turned and followed them into the kitchen.

I swallowed a lump in my throat. For so long, I'd wondered if I ever really did any good in the world. Now I knew. As soon as they were out of the room, I turned back to Chase.

"About those nonexistent missing person reports . . ." He shook his head. "We have received a few, but I pulled some strings and now all missing persons reports are filtered through me. I went out, took reports from their families and friends, and have been stalling like crazy. I'm just praying none of the three families who've reported missing loved ones reads this rag and gets any ideas."

"I can't believe none of the other newborns have been reported as missing yet. That's just sad." Delilah looked decidedly unhappy.

"Sad, yes, but you'd better pray the trend continues for awhile," Chase said, a sour note in his voice.

"What did your boss say about the article?" I asked.

"Article? That's no article." Chase shook his head, a grim look crossing his face. "The sociopath who wrote that piece of crap hates all aliens equally, whether they're from Mexico, Mars, or Otherworld. Anyway Devins ripped me a new one for allowing a rumor to get started. He told me to clean up the mess before it gets out of hand or I'll be walking a beat on the street again."

"What are you going to do?" Morio asked.

"Well, I can force a retraction—I've got a buddy who holds the purse strings to major advertising for that rag and he can put the kibosh on . . . What's his name? The dude who wrote the article?"

"Andy Gambit," Delilah said, reading the byline.

"That's right. Gambit. He's a troublemaker from way back. Well, I can see that he's muzzled for a while, but Devins is going to be on my back about everything from now on."

"Does he think we're involved?" The last thing we needed was for Devins to take a closer look at the OIA—or what we were passing off for the OIA these days. But at least Chase put that fear to rest.

"No," he said. "This is just one more way for him to try to get under my skin. He can't stand it that my idea for the FH-CSI gained so much support. He tried to squash me like a bug when I first presented it, you know. When the OIA and Governor Tomas made it official and put me in charge . . . that's when Devins decided that he had it in for me."

Delilah crossed to him and leaned over his shoulder, resting her arms around his neck and kissing him gently on the cheek. "Is that why he's always been such a jerk to you?"

"Yeah," Chase said. "I guess he's jealous, when I really think about it. My friend will get the *Tattler* to back off and I'll come up with some reason those people went missing, but Devins won't be above using this mess to push me around."

Hell, the poor guy looked so forlorn that I almost gave

him a kiss, too, but that probably would have been more than he could handle.

Instead I just said, "We know where Dredge is—we'll take him out tonight. He's dangerous, but I think we can do it." I motioned to Delilah. "Of course, if the rest of his clan's there to back him up, it's going to be one hell of a fight, but we haven't heard anything about them. I dunno what's up with that. Can you bring up a map of downtown Seattle on your computer? Then I might be able to pinpoint where he's hiding out."

Delilah gave me a long look. "Sure." She opened her laptop and fired it up. "Camille filled us in on what happened in Aladril." Her words hung heavy in the air, filled with a thousand questions and comments. I had to do something before they spent every waking moment apologizing.

"Kitten, Camille, listen to me. What Dredge did to me . . . there's nothing that you can say or do to make it go away. But it's over and we work with what we have now." I had to alleviate the guilt I saw in their eyes. Survivor's guilt, misplaced if well intentioned. "I've accepted who I am, and thanks to Jareth, Dredge no longer has any control over me. Jareth gave me the greatest gift anybody ever could."

"Why didn't you tell us?" Delilah asked, tapping away on the keys. "We never knew you had to live with such horrendous memories."

"And if you had known? What could you have done? I thought it was better to just let it be." *Let it be* . . . The Beatles had it right, I thought, even if I didn't like their music.

Delilah opened her mouth, about to protest, but Camille interrupted. "She's right. We would have done the same thing if it had been us. Menolly's free now. Let's focus on the present, because you know damned well that Dredge isn't going to be waiting for us with open arms. Open *fangs*, maybe."

"Here it is," Delilah said, setting the laptop on the coffee table. "Here's a map of the downtown area. If you want to zoom in, just left click and use the scroll wheel, or you can use the mouse to drag the slider bar."

I knelt by the coffee table and looked at the screen. "There," I said, tracing Alaskan Way with my fingertip. I zoomed in a little. "Okay, here it is. See this warehouse here? That's where Dredge is staying, right across the street from the *Deckhand* memorial statue and the Sushirama. I'm guessing three to four stories up, but I'll be able to tell for sure when we get there."

Delilah peered over my shoulder. "That warehouse is now the Halcyon, a hotel and nightclub."

"I thought it might be. I've met the owner and he's one of those misguided types who believes that all Supes are inherently good, just misunderstood."

We all knew people like him, both at home in OW and here Earthside. People who believed that all members of their special group were inherently better than others. They usually ended up heartbroken when they found out that humans were just human, Fae were just Fae, Supes were just Supe, and that good and evil' weren't inherent qualities thanks to a label on a birth certificate.

"Let me see what I can find out about the place," Delilah said, pulling up a second browser. While she started her Web search, I wandered over to where Morio was sitting in the recliner with Camille now perched on his knee. Shamas leaned back in the opposite chair, a quixotic look on his face.

"How are you doing?" I sat down next to him. "Have my sisters filled you in on what life's like over here?"

"I spent all morning watching tee-vee," he said, elongating the *e*s. "I never quite realized how alien humans are. I had no idea how big of a schism has evolved over the millennia. I still thought they rode in buggies and fought with swords."

"Like we do at home?" I said, grinning. "Face it, we developed magic, they developed technology."

Shamas laughed. "Point taken. But how have you managed it? How did you adapt to the differences? I don't know if I can handle walking among the head blind all the time."

I stared at him, well aware that both Delilah and Camille had paused at his comment. It didn't bother me so much but I knew that any time one of the Fae—family or stranger— made a disparaging comment about FBHs it hit home for my sisters with a nasty smack.

Standing up, I leaned over and gave him a quick but sharp slap on the cheek. "Shamas, darling, you better remember one thing. Our mother was human. Full-blooded human. And that makes the three of us half-human. Walking among the head blind is no more difficult than walking among pompous asses who rely on their magic instead of their brains. Understand?" I gave him a little hiss to punctuate the veiled threat.

Blinking, he glanced at my sisters, then back at me. "I'm sorry." He ducked his head. "I had no idea how that was going to sound. I guess I'm a little frightened. I know my way around Otherworld, but I don't dare show my face back there anytime soon. But here . . . I don't know how to survive. I didn't mean anything by it."

"Well, plenty of our relatives stood behind their insults," Delilah muttered. "At least here we don't have to put up with it—this is our home." She squinted at him, and I could see the glimmer in her aura foretelling a change.

"Kitten, calm down. We don't have time for you to shift." I glared at Shamas. "Don't upset her like that. She's very sensitive to family criticism."

"It's all right, sweetie," Chase said, resting his hand on Delilah's knee.

Delilah glared at Shamas. "I'll be all right." But I heard her mutter something under her breath that suspiciously sounded like, "Fuck you, too."

"Can we get back to the matter at hand?" Impatient, I floated toward the ceiling. I always felt better off the ground. "Delilah, find anything yet?"

Delilah nodded. "Okay, here it is. Sixty years ago, the Halcyon was a lumber warehouse. The barges came in from the peninsula where there was extensive logging going on. Thirty years ago, as the lumber industry took a hit, the warehouse was converted to a storage facility. Four years ago Exo Reed bought it, lock, stock, and barrel, and converted it into the Halcyon Hotel and Nightclub, serving primarily Earthside Supes and some OW visitors. No connection with the OIA that I can see. Hmm . . . considered a four-star joint."

"And Exo Reed?" Morio asked.

"Lycanthrope. Activist on several fronts—Supe rights, NRA . . ."

"Kids? Wife?" Chase asked.

"Yeah, he's married. Three kids. It also says here that Exo's president of the Seattle Hunters League."

"Great, just what we need. A good ol' boy who carries a rifle and turns into a werewolf on the full moon," Chase muttered.

I tried to stifle a laugh but it broke through. Camille and Delilah looked at me quizzically.

"Hey, the man has a point," I said. "Lycanthropes can get trigger happy come the full moon. Anyway, so being such an upstanding businessman and a family guy, Exo wouldn't be likely to give Dredge a room if he knew what kind of a sick monster he really is, ya think?"

"Especially since he and his family live in the hotel." Delilah glanced at one last Web site. "Okay, well, that's about all I can find right on the surface."

"I think we'd better pay the Halcyon Hotel and Nightclub a little visit." I jumped up and grabbed my keys. "Who's riding with who?"

Delilah slammed the lid of her laptop. "I'll ride with Chase."

"Camille and I'll go together," Morio said as she slid off his lap and straightened her dress.

"Can I come?" Shamas asked.

"No, you stay here with Iris. You aren't ready for the kind of fight we're looking at. Damn, I wish Trillian was back from—" A knock on the door interrupted me. "I'll get it."

As I opened the door, a swirl of snow blew in on a cold gust of wind, followed by Roz, who was holding a bloody towel to his neck.

"Crap, get in here!" I hustled him into the living room. "He's been hurt. Get some water and bandages while I . . ." Stopping suddenly, I backed away. His blood smelled like ambrosia and a wave of hunger rolled through me. I couldn't take my eyes off that bloody towel. "Camille—"

She heard the tremor in my voice and immediately ran to

my side. "Go over in the corner and look out the window until you can steady yourself. Delilah, get Iris to help you—towels, water, and bandages. *Now*."

As Delilah hurried out of the room, I forced myself over to the window and stared out into the dark night, trying to ignore the fragrance that beckoned. After a moment, I was able to focus.

"What happened? Are you okay?" I asked, careful not to turn around.

"Yeah," came the rough reply. "I found them. I don't think I found Dredge's hangout, but I found the newborns. And that veg-head creature you call Wisteria."

"Wisteria? You found her? Where the hell is she?" I whirled around. The sight and smell of his blood didn't matter now—not when I knew that the little bitch was within our grasp.

Roz glanced up at my face and did a double take. "What the hell happened to you? You look so different," he said. "Calmer, if I had to guess."

"Never mind that. Just take my word for it. I can fight Dredge now, and I have a chance of winning. Tell us everything."

Delilah returned then, followed by Iris, bringing with them a basin of warm water, several towels, and a first-aid kit.

"I decided to scout around up by the zoo, since the attacks were taking place near there. By the way, did you see the headlines—"

"Yes, yes. Go on."

As Camille began to dab the wound with a warm washcloth, he winced. "Fine, just thought I'd ask. As I said, I went scouting. I decided to prowl around down by this one thicket of trees in the park, so I used a camouflage spell. Sure enough, about two hours ago, I heard what sounded like a struggle. I followed the noise and I saw one of the newborns that got away from us the other night. She was hanging around with a floraed."

"Floraed!"

"Yeah, by your description, I figure it's probably your babe. Anyway, that boy from the other night?"

"You mean the teenager?" Camille let out a long sigh.

"Yeah. He wandered into the thicket with a girl on his arm who couldn't have been more than sixteen. I don't think she knew what he was, but the minute she saw Wisteria and the other chick, she turned to run. Wisteria grabbed her and held her down so teen-boy could make a meal off of her right there."

"Did he succeed?" I gave him a hard look.

Roz cocked his head to the side. "You think I'm an amateur? I decided to break up their little party. The girl escaped with little more than a scare. The boy's toast, as is the other vamp. But Wisteria went crazy. That bitch caught me a good one with her nails." He jerked. "Ouch! What the hell are you doing?"

"Sit still," Camille said as she deftly slathered both an antibacterial ointment and a fungicide on his neck. "If you aren't careful, attacks from dryads can lead to a nasty fungal infection. Two more minutes and I'm done. One of these gashes is bad enough that I'm going to have to stitch it."

"Gross," Chase said, grimacing as he turned away. "You're going to sew the man's neck up? Here? I still can't believe the crap you girls expose me to. Next thing, you'll be introducing me to Frankenstein or . . . well, damn it, Dracula's real." He sighed so loudly that I snorted.

Shamas laughed. "They too much for you, man?"

"They're too much for any man," Chase said, flashing him a smile. "But I wouldn't change things. I guess."

Delilah wandered over to watch as Camille deftly wove the needle through the opposing sides of flesh, stitching up the worst of the gashes. "Boy, she got you worse than she got me," Delilah said, showing him the scar on her throat. "It seems Wisteria has a thing for throats. Maybe she wants to be a vampire?"

"I think it's more likely she's just lost every stitch of common sense she ever had. She's a scroo-loose, as bad as a rabid dog." Roz shivered as Camille leaned near his neck to bite through the thread. "Baby, you smell like sex," he whispered, wrapping one arm around her waist and speaking loud enough for the room to hear.

"What did I tell you—" I started to say, but Camille flicked him on the forehead with her thumb and index finger and sauntered away.

"And you smell like trouble." She grinned at him. "Hands off. I'm spoken for. Three times over."

"Touché." Roz looked around. "Okay, slap a bandage on this puppy and I'm ready to roll. I take it you were just heading out?"

"We know where Dredge is—"

"And I know where your friend is," Roz broke in. "That's the main reason I came—other than needing some TLC and a throat full of cat gut. No offense, Delilah."

"None taken," she said.

"You know where Erin is?" Camille leapt to her feet and shrugged on her capelet. "Why didn't you say so first thing?"

"Because I needed medical attention, wench. Anyway, yes, I smelled Erin. The newborns have her in their private little nest. I don't know where that is, exactly, but I'm pretty sure we'll find it in the general vicinity of Veggie-Girl."

"Then she's not with Dredge?" I didn't know whether to laugh or cry. If he didn't have her, she might not have been put through the wringer yet. On the other hand, that meant we still had to find her.

Camille broke in. "Dredge will keep for a few hours, but Erin might not. Especially if Wisteria's pissed. Look what she did to Delilah, to Roz . . . think what she could do to an FBH, Menolly. And you know how she feels about humans."

I stared at her. "You're right. Erin's in a nest of newborns, along with a wacked out floraed who has a bone to pick with humanity. Yeah, we have to go after her first. Roz, show us where you found them. Their nest has to be nearby."

He shrugged back into his duster. "Not a problem. Who's going besides you and me?"

"Delilah, Camille, Chase, and Morio." I glanced around. "Shamas, stay with Iris."

"I'll make sure he behaves," Iris said. "He can help Anna-Linda and me make cookies." And with that, she hustled our cousin out of the room before he had a chance to say a word.

I motioned to the door. "Let's roll." I wasn't sure how he'd gotten out to our house, but Roz hadn't come by car. "Roz, you come with me."

Delilah rode with Chase, of course, and Morio and Camille headed out in her Lexus. One thing for sure, I thought. We'd need a vacation by the time this was all over, because the playground we were headed for sure wasn't on the Travel Channel's top-ten list of destinations to see before we died.

CHAPTER 17

On the drive there, Roz unbuckled the belt of his duster and opened it, checking out his supplies. The clatter of metal was enough to tell me he was well armed. "Spikes, check. Nunchakus, check. Blow gun and darts, check. Micro Uzi, check. Daggers, check—"

"Slow down there, tiger. Did you say *Uzi*?" I glanced at him and sure enough, he was holding up what looked like a miniature machine gun. What the hell was an incubus doing with an automatic weapon? A *nasty* automatic weapon? "Where the hell did you get that?"

"I've got my sources," he said, grinning. "But this won't do us any good against vamps." He tucked it away in a shoulder holster and held up an assortment of spikes. "No, these, *these* babies are what we need tonight. By the way, I've also got silver chain and a few binding talismans . . . Let's see, what else . . ." He pulled his bag onto his lap and poked through it while I tried to keep my eyes on the road.

"You've got a regular arsenal there, cowboy. I'd still like to know why Queen Asteria sent you to us," I said.

"Yeah, well, I'd like to know a lot of things, too," he countered. "But she did, so just accept my help."

"Does she know you're packing all that crap?"

"Yeah, so don't sweat it." After zipping up the bag, he pulled his belt off, letting the duster hang open for easy access to his weapons.

I glanced at his skintight black leather pants, the mesh muscle shirt straining over finely honed pecs, and the glistening skin hiding beneath the clothing. His stomach glittered with a fine sheen through the mesh netting. Something flipped inside me, like a light switch, and I yanked my gaze back to the road. Enough of that.

He met my gaze with an insolent smirk. "Like what you see?"

"I'll ignore that. We're out to save Erin. Nothing else."

"Whatever you say." He shrugged obligingly. "But you do realize your friend might be . . ."

"Dead? Or worse? I know. Camille and Delilah do, too, but we can't just write her off. If there's any chance to rescue her, we have to try." I took a left on Aurora and headed south.

"Something's different about you," Roz said. He shot me a curious glance. "You've changed. Your fear's gone. Want to talk about it?"

"No," I said. "Not really. Just leave it at this: I can fight Dredge now, and I can win. I couldn't before, but now . . . I have a chance."

"Hmm . . ." was all he said, but I knew that wasn't going to be the end of it. "Turn up there. Left. Then left again in two blocks. We can park in the nearest lot once we're there. The newborn's nest isn't far."

As I took the lead, Camille and Delilah followed behind. We rolled through the dark city streets. The winter freeze still hadn't broken and a sudden flash hit me. Loki—Loki held Dredge's soul in his hands. *"Some say the world will end in fire, some say in ice . . ."*

"What?" Roz shot me a confused look.

"It's from a poem Camille read to me. Fire and ice . . . the unnatural winter . . . Loki and Dredge—don't you see,

Dredge is corded to Loki, the lord of chaos. And when he crossed over Earthside, he brought that energy with him, along with an unnatural winter. All the snow we've been getting. It's due to the incredible power Loki's given to Dredge!"

"What *are* you talking about? What about Loki and Dredge?" Roz sounded vaguely irritated.

I let out an exasperated sigh. "I found out that Dredge is corded directly to Loki. Somehow Loki sired him and Dredge has become a channel for the demigod, which is one of the reasons he's so damned powerful. Loki hangs with Fenris, that damned wolf-son of his, and the pair do their best to wreak havoc on the world. Which means Loki may be trying to use Dredge to usher in his own miniature scale Ragnarök. We've been having an unnaturally cold and icy winter here. Guess who came to town right around when it started?"

Roz straightened up. "Dredge and Loki are corded? Loki's a vampire?"

"Not in so many words, but yeah, in a way. Enough to turn Dredge into one." I didn't know how to explain it because I wasn't sure I fully understood myself. "It works out . . . just trust me."

"How did you find out? Holy shit, this makes him much more dangerous than I thought. No wonder he's gotten away with his mayhem all these years."

"Don't ask how I know, because right now I don't even want to go there." I paused, then added, "I've cut him off, Roz. I've performed the ceremony to refute my sire."

Simple words, but Roz sucked in a deep breath. "Menolly, do you realize the implications of what you did?"

"Fully. As I said, don't ask. I don't want to talk about what it cost me in order to free myself."

"Well, I'll be a son of a bitch. You've got guts, I'll give you that. You do realize that you broke the cardinal rule of your kind?"

With a shrug, I pulled into the parking lot and turned off the engine, patting the dashboard. "Do you think I really give a fuck?"

He let out a short laugh. "No, I can see that you don't." He glanced out the window. "Here come the others. Let's go stake us some bloodsuckers."

As he climbed out of the car, I caught a glimpse of his face: tall, dark, and shady but also looking scared shitless. Either the threat of Loki or my turning traitor against Dredge had thrown Roz into a tailspin. As we approached the sidewalk, the others swung in behind us. Roz handed everybody a couple stakes. I threaded mine through my belt.

We cut across the grass, off of the path toward a copse of fir and willow. I walked a little ways ahead, trying to pinpoint any undead who might be walking the area. As we neared the edge of the thicket, a tingle raced up my spine.

"We're near," I whispered. "Either their nest isn't hidden that well or somebody's out for an evening stroll."

Camille and Delilah separated, flanking Chase and Morio. Camille raised her hand toward the sky, while Delilah closed her eyes and began to sniff the air. Chase and Morio watched our backs, while Roz and I scanned the area in front of us.

After a moment Camille lowered her hand. "The Moon Mother's singing tonight. She says be very cautious in the trees. Something's got them up in arms tonight. They're acting sentinel for a creature who means us harm."

"I smell dryad on the wind. Want to make a bet Wisteria's lurking and she's stirred up some of her cronies?" Delilah pulled out her long silver knife with her right hand and flicked open the wrist blade fastened to her left. "I'm ready."

"Let's get in there and clear them out. We'll deal with Dredge after we clean up this mess. And remember—we take the offense. Wisteria's a handful, but if we go in with guns blazing, we can take her down." I strode forward, Roz by my side. The others followed, Chase and Delilah shifting positions to guard Camille and Morio, who were whipping up some sort of magic.

As we entered the thicket, a loud rustle signaled visitors. As a patch of overgrown ferns parted, out leapt three floraeds, Wisteria in their center.

"Well, well, if it isn't my pretty captors," she said. "Too

late, girls. You're on our turf now." She looked directly at me, smirking.

"Still a little too much swagger, I see." I motioned to Roz and we stepped aside as Camille and Morio moved forward.

Wisteria and her buddies joined hands. A low rush of brambles crept out from the undergrowth, their thorns looking way nastier than I wanted to tangle with. Camille stared at the runners and laughed.

"Is that all you've got?" She grasped Morio's hand and they let loose with an invocation that echoed through the trees. A flash of silver washed through the area and the brambles froze, then fractured like an ice sculpture hit by a hammer.

Wisteria shouted. While her friends lunged forward, ready for the fight, she held out her hands and runners spidered out of her fingertips. The vines enveloped Camille, entangling her arms and snaring her in a web of green.

Morio took a bead on Wisteria. "Foxfire!" He sent a globe of light zinging right at her eyes and as the orb hit, it exploded in a blinding flash.

As Wisteria screamed, Delilah ducked her way through the tangle of vines. Before the floraed could stumble out of the still glowing afterflash, Delilah brought her knife down hard against Wisteria's chest, sinking it deep into her flesh.

"Fuck you!" Wisteria gasped, stumbling in my direction.

I leapt and landed at her side. In a single motion, I caught hold of her hair and yanked her head back so hard and fast that I could hear the bones break. As I let go, she dropped to the ground. The sound of scuffling behind me stopped and as I turned, the other two floraeds were running like hell toward the parking lot.

"Should we follow them?" Delilah asked.

I glanced in their direction. They were headed across to the thicket beyond. "Leave them. Let's go after the newborns. But first, I want to make sure this bitch is toasted. Anybody got fire?"

Roz pulled a small, round ball out of his pocket. "Get back."

"That won't spread and hurt the animals, will it?" Delilah asked.

He shook his head. "Nope, it's magical. Lasts for only a few moments and it's localized. Now, move it."

We stepped back as he pulled off a seal and tossed it onto Wisteria's chest. There was a sudden flare and her body blazed with a light so bright it hurt my eyes. A few seconds later, the light faded. All that was left of our little trouble-maker was a pile of ashes.

"I want some of those firebombs!" Delilah said.

Roz snorted. "As if I'd give you any."

"What other surprises do you have under that coat?" Camille asked, scooting close to him and peeking in his coat.

"Any time you want to know, babe, I'll be glad to give you a taste of what else I've got hidden under here." Roz's voice was cushioned in silk and he batted his eyes at Camille. "Want to play *show-me-yours* now?"

"Enough. Let's get moving." I pushed ahead of them.

We headed into the thicket and Camille once again raised her hand. "The willows are quiet now. Wisteria was the one stirring them up. They're watching. Just watching."

The undergrowth surrendered to a path that had been hidden from the walkway. No doubt they'd gone to a lot of trouble to forge a trail out of sight to passersby. Snow-covered huckleberries and ferns shimmered in the dark of the wood, while scuttling noises announced the presence of squirrels and other night creatures who lived on the outskirts of the zoo.

"This way," I said. I could smell the faint whiff of vampire on the wind. All vamps had a scent. Not quite decay, not quite perfume, we smelled like graveyard dust and old bones and lilacs and yew trees and the faint promise of passion in the night. A vamp could always smell a vamp, which meant that if they were near enough, if they were paying attention, the newborns knew that I was on the way.

As we pushed on through the bushes, Camille tapped me on the shoulder. "Over there—see?"

I squinted, staring into the darkness. There it was: the entrance to an underground vault with stone steps leading down to the door. Probably a utility shed sunk into the ground for protection, or maybe an old foundation to a house long forgotten. Whatever it was, the newborns were using it. Which meant that the floraeds had probably scouted it out for them at Dredge's request.

"Let's go. Stakes at the ready. Watch your backs." I wiggled my finger at Roz. "Come on. We take the front. I'm the least likely to get hurt by this bunch, and you're next in line. Camille and Morio, you fall in behind Roz. Then Chase. Delilah, bring up the rear and keep a close watch on our backs."

The steps had cracked, with weeds growing through the fractures in the concrete. Patches of ice and snow dappled the dark cement, and I slowly began to descend the narrow stairwell, hand resting on one of the stakes in my belt. The door at the base of the stairs was dimly lit by a single touch light that hung at a lopsided angle on the side of the wall. Whatever this place was, it barely extended above the surface. We were almost fully underground.

I frowned at the door. Metal, it had a vaultlike wheel for a door handle, reminding me of the submarines we'd seen on late night World War II movies.

"A bunker," Chase said, his voice low.

"What?"

"Fallout shelter. I'll bet you this was built in the fifties during the Cold War." He let out a sigh. "Whoever owned this land must have sold it to the zoo at some point and forgot to tell them this was here."

Cold War. I vaguely knew the reference, but it wasn't important. What *was* important were the vamps waiting for us on the other side. I could smell them now, thickly. I couldn't tell how many might be inside, but my guess was that we'd be facing at least four.

"Be careful. I don't want any more company on my side of the fence," I said, raising my foot. With one well-placed kick, I smashed the door open, the metal shrieking as hinges twisted and the door crashed in against the wall.

As I rushed in, Roz followed me. A blur of motion greeted us.

We were in a short hall that opened into a larger room,

two more doors on the other side. A quick count told me we were facing three vamps. I took on one while Roz spun into the room, aiming at the second. The third rushed past in a blur, headed for Camille who was standing behind me. And the fight was on.

My opponent was a woman. She let out a long hiss and backhanded me before I could dodge to the right. *Shit,* I thought, flying back. A martial arts freak. She must have had an extensive background in it before she died. The moment I touched the ground, I rolled and flipped, coming to my feet again as I circled around to get a better angle while staying out of her reach. I learned fast. Once kicked, twice as quick.

"Why are you helping them?" She beckoned me to move closer. "Come over to our side, sister. You are one of us."

"I'm no more one of you than I am an ogre," I said, spitting at her feet. "I'd offer you the chance to live, to learn how to control the thirst, but something tells me you wouldn't be able to handle it."

"Why should I? Our sire's promised us a playground." And then she struck again, but this time I was watching every twitch and was ready for her. I turned to the side just as she lunged, grabbing her arm as it shot past me.

"So sorry to cut this short, but I don't have time to play," I said. She might be stronger than when she'd been alive, but I was a long sight more powerful and I yanked her to my side.

Fighting me, she lurched into my arms.

I thrust the stake up into her chest, watching her eyes as she realized what was happening. And then, like lava hitting the ocean, she burst into a thousand ash flakes. I snatched up the stake and turned to see how the others were faring.

Roz was tangled with one of the men. As I turned, he'd just managed to stake him. Two down, one to go.

The other vamp had hold of Camille's throat and was trying to bite her. As I moved in to help, Morio dropped his stake and before you could say *fox,* he started to shift.

I'd never seen him in full demon form before. Fully eight feet high with glowing golden eyes and fur the color of burnished copper, he'd changed into a fox-man, rearing up on two legs, long muzzle bristling. But no shy fox this—no, he was a demon fox. His nose was black and wet, and steam poured out of his nostrils. As he grimaced, a full row of razor sharp teeth gleamed in the dim light of the bunker.

Instead of paws, he still had hands and feet, but they were fully furred with long, curling claws. Without thinking, my gaze traveled down his length. Whoa! No wonder Camille appreciated him, I thought, staring at his nether regions. Morio might not be a tall man, nor muscle bound, but he sure made up for it in other ways.

He grabbed goth-boy by the scruff of the neck and jerked him off of Camille. The vamp gave a frightened cry. For a moment, I thought I saw a spark of humanity peering out from behind those dead eyes. Then the fear disappeared and the vampire swiped at Morio, catching him across the upper arm.

With a loud yip, Morio raked his claws down the man's chest, gutting him wide. Delilah, who'd been watching from where she was guarding Chase, leapt forward and thrust her stake into the exposed heart. The vamp twitched, then vanished, ashes like the rest.

Morio turned to Camille and in a voice that echoed through the chamber, asked, "Are you all right?"

"I'm fine. He didn't manage to hurt me," she said, gazing up at him. "But you're injured."

As he slowly shifted back into his human form, Morio shook his head and picked up his bag, slinging it back over his shoulder. "I'll be all right. It's barely a scratch." He glanced at the gashes showing through the ripped clothing. "Don't worry about me."

The fight over, I glanced around the room. The other two doors caught my eye. Two more chances for vamps to be lurking, waiting for us. The smell of blood hung heavy, but I was still so impressed by Morio's transformation that I barely noticed. However if there *were* other vamps here, it would draw them to us for sure.

"Be careful—your wound is as good as a beacon—" I started to say, but one of the side chamber doors slammed open and two more bloodsuckers came through. "Bingo!" I rushed forward, along with Roz and we spun into action.

This time the fight was pretty much one-sided. Camille cast a blinding light spell in the room, which backfired in a sense that instead of a globe in the center of the air, the light shot out from her eyes, effectively eliminating her ability to fight. But Roz and I managed to take down the two vamps before the others could move in. The illumination flared and sputtered out to dwindle back into darkness.

"Hell. I felt like a Roman candle," she said, blinking.

"You looked like one, too," I said. "Any damage?"

She swallowed, then coughed. "My throat feels like I just chugged a bottle of Johnnie Walker, but otherwise I think I'm okay."

Morio let out a snort, arching his eyebrows as she glared at him. "Don't blame me. You know that was funny," he said, but she held up a hand.

"Shut up. I hear something." She raced to the other door and swung it wide before I could stop her. "Erin! I found Erin!"

I darted into the room, glancing around to make sure we were alone. Delilah was right behind me, and the boys behind her.

Erin was bound on the floor, her flannel shirt nowhere to be seen. So butch in the outer world, here she looked terribly frail and terribly hurt. Blood splattered the room. It looked like the newborns had been feeding off of her. The scent of fear hung heavy in the air, and my fangs automatically extended, the hunger churning like an ocean wave.

Camille knelt by her and felt for her pulse. She looked up, ashen. "She's dying. She's not going to make it. Even if we manage to miraculously get an ambulance here in five minutes, they won't be able to give her blood fast enough." Her eyes flashed. "I want them dead. All of them!"

I slowly joined her, crouching to stare at Erin's lifeless form. She wasn't gone yet. There was still a flutter of breath in her struggling lungs, but Camille was right. She was going to die.

Camille turned to me. "You can save her," she said.

"What? How? Even I can't get her to a hospital fast enough." Confused, I glanced around at the others. Roz and

Morio had knowing looks on their faces, but Chase pulled a blank stare.

"You can," Delilah said, dropping by Erin's other side. "You can save her, Menolly. You have to—she didn't ask to die. She doesn't want to die."

And then, staring at my sisters, I knew what they were asking. "What? You can't mean it! You can't tell me you want me to turn her?" I leapt up and strode over to Roz's side. "I can't believe you'd ask me to do something I find so repulsive."

Camille gently laid Erin's head in Delilah's lap. She stood, eyes blazing, hands on hips. "What happened to you is totally different. You were tortured with every vile act Dredge could think of. Erin's been used as a feeding station, but she doesn't look scarred. And she didn't ask to be put in this position. Don't you get it? She's going to die if you don't do something *now*."

I stared at Erin's lifeless form. "People die, Camille. People live and they die. It's the way of the world."

"It doesn't have to happen," Delilah chimed in. "She doesn't have to be like those newborns. Look at Wade and Sassy—look at you! You're different. You choose to be different. You can help Erin from the beginning."

"Remember what Grandmother Coyote said?" Camille cocked her head. "Remember what she said at the meeting? You're going to have to do something you don't want to do. But *I'll* know it's right. And this is it. Turning Erin into a vampire is the right thing to do."

Frantic, I glanced at Morio for support. "Tell her she's wrong. This is just her desire to keep Erin alive talking."

Morio shook his head. "If Grandmother Coyote foretold this, then I have to back up Camille. Grandmother Coyote never says anything she doesn't mean."

Camille yanked me around, ignoring my hiss. "Trust me. Erin has a part to play in the future. *You* have to make sure she's around to do it. Turn her, damn it! You don't have to like it, you don't have to approve of it, but you *have* to do it."

She was so fierce that I almost feared her. I struggled with my conscience. What had Grandmother Coyote said?

"Menolly, you're going to have to do something you have vowed never to do. When the time comes, you'll know what it is, and you'll balk. But do it you must, regardless of your aversion to the idea. A long thread of destiny hinges upon your action . . . or inaction. Don't fail me. If you shy away, you'll upset a critical balance."

Was this it? Was raising Erin into the world of the undead what she'd meant?

I held very still, searching within, looking deep into my core, deep within my soul. The day I regained my sanity, I swore I'd never sire another vampire, never add to the host of demons raised from unwilling victims.

And yet . . . if Grandmother Coyote was right—if Camille and Delilah were right—had fate singled Erin out for transformation? And if someone was to sire her, who better than me? I could give her what few other sires would: guidance, a conscience, and care. I could usher her into her new life, cushioning the shock that usually accompanied the change. Was this the path to take?

"Hurry—she's almost dead," Delilah said.

Camille leapt toward me and grabbed me by the wrist. "Do this, do it now, or I swear I'll fucking sic the Moon Mother on you, Menolly. Trust me—it's more than just my friendship with her talking. I *know* Erin has to live, and this is the only way she can!"

Delilah let out a squeak and I saw her begin to shift. Both furious and frightened, I said, "Shit! Delilah, hang on, baby. Oh fuck. Camille, get hold of Delilah. Help her calm down so she can shift back. I'll do it, all right? I'll sire Erin. But don't you *ever* threaten me like that again."

Saying nothing, Camille rushed over to scoop up our golden tabby sister while I flew to Erin's side. Quickly, without thinking, I leaned down and drank from the bloody mess that was her neck. She'd have a scar all right, but it wouldn't be too bad. As soon as her blood went down my throat in that warm, luxurious flow, I held up my wrist and flicked a vein open with one nail. As the drops began to dribble out, I pressed them to Erin's lips.

"Erin, it's Menolly. You have to drink if you want to

survive. If you don't drink my blood, you're going to die." I held her in one arm like a baby, my wrist pressed to her mouth. She opened her eyes and blinked as she tried to focus on me. "Honey, listen to me. This is your choice. If you drink, I'll sire you and take care of you as you go through the change. I'll teach you how to control the thirst. You don't have to become a monster. But if you'd rather let go, then I won't force you. It's all up to you."

Camille caught Delilah and held her, watching us. Roz, Morio, and Chase stood guard by the door. Chase looked queasy, but he didn't say a word.

"Erin, please drink," Camille said. She shoved Delilah into Chase's arms and knelt on the other side of Erin. "We need you. The world needs you. Destiny has plans for you. If you don't do this, it could mess up the future. Grandmother Coyote warned us about this moment."

Erin's gaze fastened on mine. She opened her lips. They were so dry they cracked and bled. "Do you . . . do you promise to watch over me? Do you promise to kill me if I do anything horrible? I won't become like *them*." She spat out the word, and I knew she was talking about the newborns.

"I promise you with my heart and soul. If you drink, I'll guide you every step of the way. I won't let you turn into a nightmare." What the hell was I letting myself in for? I didn't know, but the moment I'd offered her the chance, every fiber of my heart told me this was the right decision.

With a flutter of breath—a very small flutter, she was on the edge of death—Erin opened her lips. "I'll drink."

I pressed my wrist to her mouth. "Suck as hard as you can. You only need a few drops to seal the pact, but drink as much as you can. It will make the transition easier."

As she began to lick up the blood flowing from my vein, I closed my eyes against the competing tides within me. Every shred of my ethics told me to stop, to let her go peacefully to her ancestors. And yet my intuition told me to let her drink, to sire her, raise her, and make sure she lived.

Surprisingly strong, Erin managed to drink about a quarter cup of my blood before she suddenly gasped, convulsed in my arms, and then went limp.

"Is she dead? I thought you were siring her!" Camille stared at me, her voice spiraling against the walls.

I looked at her. As much as I loved my sister, I wanted to smack her a good one, but I resisted, trying to remember that she was upset and didn't fully understand the process.

"Oh, she's going to change," I said. "It's simply a matter of time, now."

"What do we do until then?"

I glanced over at Chase, who was petting Delilah. She began to shimmer and I coughed. "Johnson, better put Kitten down, she's ready to shift back."

Standing, I dusted my hands on my pants and turned back to Camille. "It's simple. We wait. So cool your jets and pull up a chair. And, by the way, we need food for her—she's going to be ravenous. Unless one of you wants to play blood bank, we're going to need a donor."

Roz grinned. "I can find someone. I know the drill, even if I don't wade in the pool." Before I could speak, he slipped out of the door, leaving the rest of us sitting in silence.

CHAPTER 18

Having never sired a vampire, I wasn't entirely clear on the process myself, but I was damned certain it would go easier than my own rebirth.

The shock of opening my eyes, of believing I was still alive, had been bad enough. But the suffocating inability to catch my breath had been even more frightening. Then came the dawning realization that yes, I was dead, I just hadn't been allowed to cross over. And that's when the madness began to set in, as did the hunger. At least Erin had made her own choice. Hopefully she wouldn't regret her decision.

I glanced around the room. There were a few cushions, some heavy drapes that were being used as a floor cover. "Those curtains. Someone gather them and make a bed. Cover those blood-soaked cushions with them, and set the whole thing in the center of the room."

Morio and Chase set things up while Delilah and Camille rooted through the bunker in search of anything that might help us. "All of you, stay well out of Erin's reach. Especially you, Chase. She's going to wake up confused and ravenous.

The hunger will be so bad that she'll be ready to attack anybody nearby."

The jangle of my cell phone suddenly cut through the muffled hush of the nest and I yanked it out, wondering who the hell could be calling me. I'd warned Chrysandra that I'd be out of touch for a night or so, and not many other people besides my sisters had my number. I glanced at the caller ID. Iris. Oh shit, what was wrong?

I flipped it open. "Iris, what's up?"

The static was horrible. I hurried outside, onto the steps, where the signal strengthened. "Hurry it up. I'm in a dicey situation here. What's wrong?"

Iris took a deep breath. "I know you are. Roz is here and he wants to talk to you. And another thing—Trillian just returned from OW." Something in her voice made me wary.

"What's wrong?"

"He's been hurt. He was shot by one of Lethesanar's archers."

Holy crap. Had she called me so I could cushion the blow for Camille? Was Trillian dead? I suddenly found myself whispering a silent prayer that my sister's love-bunny was okay. "Tell me."

"He'll live, but he's lost a lot of blood. He's not going anywhere for a while. So don't count on him coming to help you tonight. His shoulder is pretty mangled. I've called Sharah to come out with a medic kit so she can work on him." Iris sounded rushed. "She'll be here any minute. Meanwhile, here's Roz."

"Put him on." I decided to wait on telling Camille about Trillian. If she wasn't worrying about him, she'd pay more attention to what we were doing. And since Iris said he'd live, there was no real urgency.

Roz took the phone. "I found a volunteer. I don't have that internal guidance system you do in picking out perverts—at least not the kind you're looking for. And I didn't want to risk somebody innocent, since Erin's going to wake up ravenous."

"Then who did you find? And how the hell did you get out to our house so fast? You don't drive, do you?"

"Never mind how I got here—I have my ways. Thing is, I have the feeling you aren't going to like who our donor is."

"Why?" A rumble in my stomach told me that he was right—I wasn't going to like his answer. "Just who did you find?"

He cleared his throat. "Your friend. Cleo—Tim Winthrop. I had the feeling he'd be here, and he seemed the best choice. I told them about Erin and he volunteered to be the donor."

Holy crap! *Of course* Tim would volunteer. Erin was like family to him. I let out a long hiss. This was a mess. Tim had a little girl to think about. What if something went horribly wrong?

"Hold on, let me talk to the others." I put him on mute and ran back into the bunker to tell Camille and Delilah. Chase and Morio listened, but they clearly understood that this was our call. "So what do you think? Should we tell Roz to bring Tim with him?"

"How long before she wakes?" Camille said, looking down at Erin's still form.

I shook my head. "I have no idea. Probably not long."

Delilah scuffed the toe of her boot on the floor. "The way I see it, we don't have a choice. Erin will need blood. We need a donor. We don't have time to be choosy, and Tim's volunteered. We just do our best to keep her from draining him."

"Delilah's right," Camille said. "Tim knows the risks. Tell Roz to get the hell back here with him."

By their expressions, I realized they both knew exactly what we were risking. I'd made the choice, accepted the challenge, now we all had to cope with the ramifications and not let Erin down. The last thing I wanted to do was to have to stake my own daughter.

I hurried back to the steps and punched the talk button. "Get back here with Tim. Hurry it up—we don't have long before she rises."

"We're on the way," he said, then hung up before I could ask him just how he planned on getting both of them over here in time. With a look around to make sure we were still alone, I returned to Erin's side.

"They're on the way. Let's hope that Roz can fly," I said as I knelt beside Erin. She was cold, colder than death. I held her hand and closed my eyes, remembering.

"What's it like?" Camille asked, squatting next to me. "What's it like where she's at right now?"

"After you realize you're still tied to your body, you're pulled back in. You saw my memories—the ice tunnel . . . then crimson veins spreading through the silver cord that connects the body to spirit—like arteries filled with fire. Everything smelled like blood and my stomach began to ache. I was so hungry, so thirsty."

"The bloodlust," Delilah said, sitting on my other side.

"Yeah . . . the bloodlust. It's like . . . everything vanishes except the thirst. An itch on an open wound. All I could think about was finding someone to rip into, to satiate my thirst." I hung my head. I seldom talked about my passions and the drive to drink. It wasn't a subject my sisters could easily understand. Or so I thought.

But Camille nodded. "Like me and the Hunt. During the full moon, I have to run with the magic or the Moon Mother will drive me mad. Unless I can make it into the woods, I'll lose my sanity. And when I'm caught up in the chase . . . there's no force on earth that can stop me except for death."

"Exactly," I said, startled that she hit it right on the nose.

"Or like when I have to shift on the full moon. There's nothing in the world that can prevent me from transforming. If something tried, I think I'd die," Delilah said. More softly, she said, "It's harder when my Death Maiden aspect emerges. The Autumn Lord controls my panther form, and if he wants her to come out and play, I have no warning."

I stared at Erin's body. They *did* understand, in their own ways. I hadn't ever thought to correlate the forces that drove my sisters' natures with the bloodlust, but it was true. We each answered to our true form, we each waged war for control with aspects of ourselves that were beyond our abilities to curb.

"Maybe I've been too hesitant to talk about things," I said. "I never stopped to think that you might both face your own inner demons, that you both answer to forces greater than yourselves. I knew, but not on that gut level that really rings home."

I glanced up. Chase and Morio were playing dumb, but it was obvious they'd been listening to us. "What about you? Chase, is there something you can't control, that you answer to besides your conscience?"

Looking startled at being included in the conversation, he frowned. "I'm not sure. Humans like to think we control our world, but truthfully, we can't direct even a fraction of it. I don't think I have anything that quite compares to what you're talking about, but there are some people who seem driven by forces beyond understanding—religious fanatics, criminal psychotics . . . a number of things."

Delilah looked at him curiously. "Do you believe in the gods?"

Chase shrugged. "I won't say there aren't higher forces at work, but do I pray to any of them? No. I learned the hard way that nobody looks out for me but myself. My father was a dope fiend who disappeared when I was a kid. My mother's a fruitcake. We lived on welfare most of my childhood because she couldn't hold a job." He glanced up at Delilah and their eyes locked. I had the feeling they'd been down this road before.

"Who took care of you?" I asked.

"Me. By the time I was a teenager, I was managing to stay in school while working at McDonald's in the afternoons, running a paper route before school in the mornings, and late night I delivered takeout for Hunan's Dragon Palace. Somehow I scraped up rent every month. My jobs at Mickey D's and Hunan's fed me."

"And your mother didn't do anything to help?" I could hear the resentment in his voice. No wonder he avoided talking to her as much as possible. Delilah had told me Chase was constantly getting hounded by his mother for not calling. This was probably the reason.

"She was too busy trying to find Mr. Right to care much about me. Her boyfriends bruised me up now and then because I'd mouth off to them. They gave her money for food—for her. She collected AFDC, but wasted the money on clothes and booze. I spent all my spare time working. It was either that or join a gang. And I'm not gang material."

"AFDC?" Camille asked.

"Aid to Families with Dependent Children," Chase said.

"Oh, did your father ever come back?" Camille frowned.

He shook his head. "No. Haven't seen him since I was a little kid. My mother finally got married, but by then I was in the police academy." He shrugged. "Water under the bridge, now."

A sudden noise put a stop to our conversation. Erin was starting to stir. We had, at best, five minutes. "Fuck. Oh fuck, where are Roz and Tim?"

"Right here," a voice said from the hall. Roz and Tim pushed their way into the room. Tim looked pale, as if he'd been yanked through a wringer. Or maybe Roz had dragged him here on a magic carpet. Either way, they were here and that's all that mattered.

"Tim, listen to me. There's no time to explain. Erin's going to wake up and she's going to be hungry. If you still want to go through with it, I'll be here for you. She'll need to drink enough to keep from passing into a coma, which means you're going to be giving her enough blood so that you'll feel woozy. You don't have any problems like anemia or anything that could compromise your health, do you? Viruses, infections won't affect her, but blood loss might hurt you."

He shook his head, eyes glazed over as he stared at Erin's wan form. "Will I become a vampire?"

"No, not as long as you don't drink from a vampire's vein. But listen—things could go wrong. I'm much stronger than she is. I can keep her from killing you. Or at least, I'm ninety-nine percent sure I can. I won't give you a blanket guarantee." I didn't add that she still had the chance to go rogue, that she could choose to turn toward the dark side of vampirism. If she did, I'd be forced to stake her and end her life forever.

Tim yanked off his shirt. "How much will she drink?"

I stared at his bare chest, which was hairless and ripped to a tight six-pack. "Man, you take care of yourself," I blurted out without thinking.

He smiled, ducking his head. "Jason likes me fit."

"Does he know that you're here?"

"Nah," he said. "He wouldn't . . . I don't think I'm going to tell him."

"Right." From the few times I'd met Jason, I could guarantee that Tim would be single if his fiancé ever found out what he was up to. "Here's the rundown. Your best bet is to offer her your wrist. That way she can't accidentally break your neck in her excitement and I'll have better access to control her. Don't be surprised if she doesn't recognize you. Don't let her scare you—when she first wakes up she'll be frightened and hungry. Eventually she'll remember who she is."

"Menolly!" Camille's voice held an urgency that immediately caught my attention.

I whirled. Erin had gone into convulsions "Everybody but Tim and me get out. Wait in the main room. Don't come in until I tell you to."

Chase and Morio obeyed immediately, but Delilah and Camille hesitated. "Now, damn it! Get out! Let me focus on helping her instead of having to worry about your butts." That got them moving. They shut the door behind them.

I turned to Tim. "Stay in the corner until I call for you. And you'd better decide now, for real, if you want to go through with this. Because if you chicken out, I'm going to have to stake her and it would be more merciful to just get it over with before she regains consciousness."

Tim blanched. "Erin took me in when my wife found out I was gay and kicked me out. She yanked me out of the closet and forced me to be honest with Patty and with myself. And she helped me rebuild my relationship with my little girl. It was hard as hell and I had to face the fact that I hurt a lot of people with my deception. But she was there to help me pick up the pieces and put them back together again. I owe her big time, Menolly."

With a nod, I crept over to Erin. Bloody foam was trickling from the side of her mouth. Transformation was ugly, that was a fact. It was messy, it was dirty, far from the delicate swoon portrayed in late night B-movies. Neither was it the sensual ride of a lifetime—at least not until after the change was over. Until the newborn drank and came to consciousness, it was a lot like a diabetic seizure.

"Erin, Erin, can you hear me?" I didn't try to hold her head. She'd lash out, and at this point a few bumps on her noggin weren't going to hurt her.

Erin opened her eyes and snapped up into a sitting position. She started to turn around, then I saw a familiar look cross her face. Not all newborns succumbed to panic when they realized they couldn't breathe, but apparently Erin was my daughter in more than just blood. She clawed at her throat, eyes wide with fear.

"Stop—Erin, stop! You'll be okay. Quit trying to breathe. You don't need to breathe. Relax, just relax."

Her shoulders shaking, she licked her lips as she quit struggling. Then she looked at me again, and flinched. I'd done the same with Dredge when I first awoke. Every vampire knew her sire. Every vampire was bound to her sire in a way that precluded all other oaths, even to the gods.

I could see the hunger in her eyes, the confusion and bewilderment as she groveled on the floor in front of me and, for a moment, I hated myself. Thoroughly, absolutely hated myself for what I'd done to her.

"Is it time?" Tim asked quietly, and the confidence in his voice shored me up. I glanced at him and saw, not revulsion, but relief as he watched Erin struggle. He caught my look of surprise. "She's my friend. She'd be dead without you. Let me help her, please?"

Not sure what to say, I nodded. "Come forward, slowly." I knelt in back of her and, with one hand, restrained her arms behind her. With the other, I stroked her hair. She'd be weak until she'd fed. She didn't struggle, merely glanced over her shoulder at me, looking for guidance. She was doing better than most newborns, that was for sure. I could tell that, hungry or not, there was already a spark of recognition beyond the fact that I was her sire.

Tim held his wrist out to her. "Erin, do you know me? It's Tim. I'm here to help. You can drink from me. It's okay." His voice was soothing, far from the bray that he used for his drag persona, Cleo Blanco. I could imagine him reading bedtime stories to his daughter with this voice.

Erin seemed to respond to it, too. She tilted her head, looking at him curiously. Her gaze never leaving his face, she leaned forward, eyeing his wrist, and her fangs extended.

Gently reassuring her as she placed the tips against his wrist, I guided her away from the main artery. She didn't need to drink from the main well. As the tips of her fangs sank into his flesh, Tim gasped and closed his eyes.

"Does it hurt?" I asked as Erin began to suck, licking it to stimulate the flow.

He let out a shuddering gasp. "No . . . no, it doesn't hurt. It feels like heaven. Oh God, I never expected this." His voice breathless, he looked about ready to come right there.

I felt a sudden surge of pride. Erin was so far beyond where I'd been at her stage. Dredge had turned me loose hungry, with barely enough blood to keep me going. I'd gone on a rampage all the way home.

After Erin started to settle down and I felt her energy stabilize, I gently disengaged her from Tim, who had dropped to the floor into a stupor, oblivious to his own danger. Erin struggled at first when I pulled her way, then glanced up at me and let go of his wrist.

"Tim. *Tim!*"

Startled, he blinked and looked up at me from his prone position. "Huh?"

"Get back. Slowly crawl away from her. Now. She's had enough for the moment." I waited until he rolled away, then gently turned Erin around to face me. "Erin, do you know who I am?"

She gazed at me for a moment, then nodded. "Menolly. But . . . what happened? Where am I?"

"Do you remember being kidnapped?" I spoke slowly, wanting to break it to her gently in case she didn't fully understand just what had happened. But she surprised me here, too.

"Yeah," she said, her gaze dropping to the ground. "The vampires captured me. They almost killed me."

"They did kill you," I said. "But before you died, we found you. Do you understand?"

As the blood raced through her, strengthening her, she glanced over at Tim. "I'm one of you now," she whispered, looking back at me. "I'm a vampire, and I just fed on my best friend and liked it. I want more. What's going to happen to me?"

I gathered her into my arms and held her tight. The older woman—who would be forever middle-aged with short hair and a little bit of a tummy—hugged me for all she was worth.

"You'll be okay. You don't have to follow a path of terror and destruction. You don't have to turn into a monster. We *are* predators, true. We feed on blood. Nothing can—or will—change this fact. But you can choose how you respond to the urges, and you can choose who you feed on, and whether you hurt them or give them pleasure. I'm here to help you, and my friends at Vampires Anonymous will help you."

After a moment, I pushed her back to arm's length, looking at her sternly. "But, Erin, know this. I'm your sire. If you do decide to head off into the sunset and go on a killing spree, I'll come for you and I'll stake you. I'll always be able to trace you. Do you understand me?"

Erin shivered. "Yes. I asked for this. I'll never blame you, Menolly."

I bit my tongue. If it hadn't been for me, this never would have happened. Dredge wouldn't be here causing havoc, preying on my friends. But what might have been was irrelevant. What mattered now was where we were.

If there was one thing I'd had to learn over the past twelve years, it was to let go of regret. Baggage, sure, it would always be there, but there was no turning back the clock. We could only change the present and future. And now, my cords to Dredge cleaved, I could focus on destroying him and ridding the world of a terror that should have been obliterated hundreds of years ago.

I looked up at Tim. "Go get Delilah, would you?"

He nodded, scurrying out the door.

Erin gasped suddenly. "I can't breathe!"

"No, remember? You can't, not like you used to. Don't try. Don't let it worry you. As I told you, you won't die, you won't suffocate. You see, we only breathe when we consciously make the effort. Your brain is trying to repeat the patterns that worked for your body in life, but as a vampire you don't need oxygen so your body won't know what to do with it."

"How am I going to learn all of this?" she cried, for the first time looking petrified.

I grabbed her shoulders. "Listen to me. *Listen*. First, stop struggling. Exhale. Don't inhale, just let go of the breath you tried to take."

She focused on my gaze, and I felt her deflate, the air whistling out of lungs that no longer needed to breathe.

"Good. Now I want you to close your eyes. Look inside of you and pay attention. Are you dizzy? Do you feel like you'll pass out if you don't breathe?"

She obeyed and after a moment of stillness, said, "No. No, I think I see—if I don't struggle for breath, I don't notice that I'm not breathing."

"That's absolutely correct. You'll only go into a panic when your brain tells you to breathe and your body isn't prepared for it. You can take a deep breath and let it out, but you have to prepare the lungs for movement or you'll disrupt your body. It's all part of the transformation." I kept hold of her hands as she focused on relaxing.

Delilah entered the room at that point, followed by Tim. "Is everything okay?" She knelt a few feet away, watching cautiously.

Erin looked over at her. "Hey, Delilah. I . . . I'm not sure . . . I mean, what do I *do*? I can't run my shop, can I? I can't just go home. Menolly, what happens to me next?"

I gave her a gentle smile. "You learn from the best. Delilah, take Roz and go over to Sassy Branson's house. Ask her to come back here. If she's not there, call Wade. In fact, call him first. He specializes in helping newborns adjust." I tossed her my cell phone. "He's in my contact list."

Delilah punched a few buttons. "Static. I'll have to go topside."

"Don't go alone. Take Roz with you. Come back and let me know if you get hold of Wade before you head out for Sassy's. We don't have time to waste so don't dawdle."

Tim cleared his throat. "Erin, I can call someone to take over your shop for a few days. Lindsey, from the Green Goddess Women's Shelter. She has clients who need a temp job." He bit his lip and I shook my head at him, motioning to the blood that welled up on the pale pink flesh. Wiping it away, he shrugged a smile at me.

Erin was still fighting for control. And doing a damned good job. Most vamps went a little crazy when they turned—the ramifications don't sink in until you realize that your entire life has just been turned upside down and you can never, ever go back to the way things were.

"Thanks," she said. "Please, don't tell her what happened. Not yet. I need to come to grips with this first. Just tell her I'm sick."

"No problem," Tim said.

"You'd better go into the other room," I broke in. "She needs to rest and to quit thinking about your heart, which is beating a staccato tremor so loud I can hear it all the way over here."

He nodded. "Okay. But, Erin, I still love you. I wouldn't have offered to be your donor if I didn't."

She managed a faint "thank you" as he left the room. We sat in silence until Delilah returned.

"Wade will be here in a few minutes. He said not to bother going to Sassy's, he's coming from her place, and she's already preparing a room for Erin." A few moments later the door opened and Wade strode in.

"Delilah told me all about it," he said. "You took out the newborns?"

"Most of them, though I think a few might have escaped. We'll have to all be on our guard. We'll talk about catching them after I destroy Dredge. But for now, can you escort Erin to Sassy's? And will you make sure Tim gets home safe? He's still in danger since he's my friend, and frankly, Erin drank a little too much from him, I think. He's pretty wiped out, even if he doesn't realize it."

Wade shook his head. "I think it would be safer if Tim went back to your house. Iris is more than capable of protecting him, isn't she?"

"You're probably right. Delilah, ask Roz to take Tim back to our house and then return as soon as possible. I'm not sure just how he travels so fast, but the important thing is that he does."

As she headed out the door, I turned to Erin. "Listen to me. Wade is a good friend of mine. He runs an organization that I belong to. You've heard me talk about it. Vampires Anonymous?"

She gave me a vigorous nod of the head. "Yeah, I know what you're talking about. Hi, Wade."

"Hey, Erin," he said softly. "Welcome to the underworld."

"Wade's going to take you to Sassy Branson's house. She helps out at the V.A. and she's a vampire, too. She and Wade will keep you there for a while and help you learn how to adjust. I've got a battle to fight tonight. If I win—and trust me, I'm planning on it—I'll come visit you. Probably tomorrow night once sunset hits. Meanwhile I want you to go with Wade and do what he says. You can trust him."

As I hoped, her intense desire to please me reared its head and she held out her hand to Wade. He helped her up.

Dredge had sent me home to destroy my family in the same way I was sending Erin to Sassy's. Luckily my anger and memories of the torture intervened. I'd managed to lock myself away before I could attack Camille. The OIA had taken it from there. At least Erin wouldn't have bad memories of me, and her transition was running far more smoothly than I'd hoped.

Wade led her away and I followed, watching as he guided her out under the night sky. Erin would never again look on the sun, never again bask under a warm summer afternoon. But it had been her choice—although not much of one. Die or live for an eternity. No vampire I knew of was over five thousand years old, so whatever happened to the ones turned before that . . . who knew?

Maybe there were none. Maybe whatever forces had started vampirism hadn't existed before then. Maybe . . . maybe all ancient vamps committed suicide after eons trapped in their bodies. I didn't plan on waiting that long to find out. Until my sisters left to meet our ancestors? Sure. A thousand years? Possibly. Most of the Fae lived that long. Forever? No chance.

After Wade led Erin away, I turned to the others. "She should be okay. I think she'll actually make it. But I wish it hadn't come to this."

Chase cleared his throat. "Yeah. And I'm going to have to come up with an excuse for her absence or the tabloids will have a field day rooting around for what happened to the owner of the Scarlet Harlot."

"We'll help," I said. "At least Erin can call a few friends, say she's taking a vacation. Something like that."

"Well, I guess we're done here," Camille said. "What next?"

I motioned for them to follow me topside. "What next? As soon as Roz returns, we go find Dredge, and obliterate the bastard." I checked the stakes in my belt. One way or another, he was going down. And I planned on staking the final blow.

CHAPTER 19

~◦◦◦~

Seattle was beautiful at night, dark and gritty in the back alleys with the brilliant lights of the skyscrapers and Space Needle glowing over the inlet. I'd grown to love the sights and sounds of the city as it slept. Oh, the usual derelicts and college kids and hookers and pushers wandered the sidewalks. And a few gang bangers and gangstas scattered the streets, low riding in their hopped up cars. But, overall, Seattle kept a hushed vigil through the dark hours.

The rippling currents of Elliott Bay glittered from the reflection of the lights that lined the pier as we swung into the parking lot near the hotel. Silent as the night, the six of us gathered in a shadowed recess between two buildings. To the west, we could see all the way across Alaskan Way to the inlet. To the east, a line of warehouses and buildings waited.

"There." I pointed to the Halcyon Hotel. "Supeville central. I hope Dredge is still there, the motherfucker."

We headed across the empty lot, which was really just a patch of gravel punctuated by lines of cement dividers indicating where drivers should park, illuminated by scattered lights here and there. Only a handful of cars besides our own were parked in the lot. One, a Hummer, had a personalized license plate that read, "SEXYSUCC."

I pointed it out. "Ten to one a succubus owns it."

Camille let out a short laugh. "Sometimes I think I'd have made a good succubus."

"Except that your first love is magic," Morio said.

I glanced at Delilah. Morio knew Camille better than I thought. "Okay, listen up, folks. You already know Dredge is terribly dangerous. Remember: He's a sadist. He enjoys inflicting pain. If he gets a hold of you, he'll do anything and everything he can to break you. Killing's too quick for his tastes."

"Do you really think we can take him?" Camille asked, suddenly sober. "What about the rest of the Elwing Clan?"

"They might present a problem. Odd thing is, we've heard reports about Dredge one after another, but nothing about his marshals. We'd better take him down, though, because if he gets away, we're going to be looking over our shoulders every fucking day of our lives. And we'll never again be able to have any friends or family nearby without putting them in danger."

Worst-case scenario, I could get away from Dredge. And Roz could probably escape. But the others—Chase was most at risk, but my sisters and Morio weren't invulnerable by any stretch of the imagination.

As we approached the building, I motioned for everybody to move to the side, out of the sight line of the windows overlooking the lot.

"I need to figure out what floor he's staying on. I doubt we'll be able to pry the info out of the registration desk. Dredge is charming, even without the vampire thang. You can bet they won't have a clue as to who we're asking about, or why, and he'll have them charmed into not handing out any pertinent information on our boy."

I scanned the windows, then turned back toward the pier. There—a statue of a figure carrying a large sack over his back as he stepped off a gangway. *The Deckhand*. That was the statue I'd seen when I'd looked through Dredge's eyes. And right behind it, the Sushirama. That meant . . . I glanced back at the hotel. "Fourth window from the left. I'm sure of it. Now let me figure out which floor he's on."

Slowly I began to hover, floating up. One story, nope. Two stories—no. Three—maybe, I thought. At the fourth, I snapped my fingers and immediately descended. "Four stories up, fourth window from the left. Come on, let's go." I led them into the lobby.

The Halcyon Hotel and Nightclub was just that—a hotel with a nightclub off the lobby. Like a number of the Supe clubs that had been springing up throughout the city, it catered to Earthside Supes more than Otherworld inhabitants, but welcomed just about anybody as long as they didn't cause trouble. The sounds of music and laughter came pouring from the lounge as we entered the lobby. The Doors were wailing away on the jukebox.

"It looks like an Ecstasy party here," Camille said in a low voice.

"As long as it's not Z-fen," I said, looking around. She was right. The décor was directly out of some psychedelic love-shack dream, right down to the glowing lava lamps and black light posters in the corner. I blinked, thinking that Exo Reed had some pretty kinky turn-ons.

"Do you think Exo's around?" Delilah asked.

"I don't know," I said. "But try to remember, he and his family live on the premises."

"Not exactly the best environment in which to raise kids." Chase glanced around. "If he weren't a Supe, I might think about calling in child welfare to check things out."

A little ticked, I shushed him. "That's not my point. This is their home, there are probably kids on the premises, so let's try to keep from wrecking the joint or putting anybody else in danger. Which is why I don't want to involve Exo in our fight. I don't even want him to know about it until we're done, because if Dredge charmed him, Exo might well give us away without meaning to. Get it?"

"There—the elevator. Or do you want the stairs?" Delilah pointed to the stairwell at the end of the hall.

Elevator would be faster, but his room was only on the fourth floor. "Stairs. That way we won't get a nasty surprise if the doors open and Dredge happens to be standing there. Or any of his cronies."

My thoughts raced ahead as we jogged up the steps. How would we do this? Dredge was terribly strong, and it would take everything we had to bring him down, especially since he was tied to Loki. My heart told me we could win, my head warned me that counting on victory was an invitation for disaster.

As if reading my mind, Delilah asked, "What's the plan? I assume you and Roz go in first."

I nodded. "Yeah, we have the best defenses against him."

"And we have the most payback to deliver," Roz said, his voice grim. "Don't forget, I lost my family to him. *Everyone* in my family."

"Are you just going to try to stake him?" Camille paused on the landing leading to the third floor. "Is he immune to magic?"

I leaned against the stairwell wall. "If we go in trying to stake him, he'll win for sure. No, it's going to take more of a battle than that. He is vulnerable to some forms of magic. You don't have the ability to resurrect, do you?" I was joking, but barely. Morio seemed extremely well versed in death magic, and I suspected he was far more than the youkai he let on to be. "That would probably kill him."

"You'd need a powerful necromancer for that," Morio said.

Chase glanced at him, apparently running along the same lines of thought I'd been. "You and Camille have been working some mighty powerful hoodoo. Got anything in that spell book for vampires?"

Morio glanced at Camille and shrugged. "Perhaps. We might be able to slow him down a little or to cast an illusion that might catch him off guard. Do you know what he's afraid of?"

I thought for a moment. "Yeah, or at least something that will make him hesitate. Can you create the illusion of Fenris standing behind us?"

"Fenris?" Roz asked, staring at me. "Ah . . . I think I see where you're going with this."

"Who in the hell is Fenris?" Chase asked.

Camille frowned. "A giant wolf. Son of Loki, the havoc monger."

Morio inclined his head. "I could probably keep up the illusion for a few moments, but he's going to figure out it's not the real thing before long."

"A few seconds will buy time. Time when he's not paying attention to us," I said. "When we go in, I want that wolf behind us. Change of plans. Camille, you and Delilah are in front with me. Roz, you're next with Morio. Camille, you shoot a bolt of lightning to fry his senses. Chase, stay back and be ready to grab anybody who gets severely wounded and drag them out of danger. Roz, what have you got?"

"I'm heading in with a stake, but I've got something else up my sleeve." He pulled out what looked like a cherry bomb. "This is a garlic smoke bomb. Ignites on contact with the undead. Yeah, this baby should throw him into a tailspin. If nothing else, it will jolt him into a world of pain while we fight. You won't be able to handle it, either, Menolly, so if I end up playing Emeril, then sweet cheeks, get your cute little ass out of the room *stat*."

I grimaced. "Ugh. Keep that thing away from me unless it's absolutely necessary and for the sake of the gods, warn me if you have to use it." I closed my eyes. There was no sense putting it off any longer. "Okay, let's go. Be careful, please. I don't want to have to sire anybody else tonight, and trust me, you do not want to fall into Dredge's hands."

Another minute and we emerged onto the fourth floor and headed down the empty hallway. I counted doors, stopping in front of the one that should contain Dredge. As we neared the door, the overpowering smell of vampire filled the air. He was here all right. Chances were he knew that his newborns—or most of them—were dead. If we were lucky, he wouldn't know who'd killed them. If not, then he'd be waiting for us.

I glanced back at everyone. "Let's rock this joint." I kicked open the door and rushed in. Camille and Delilah behind me. There was a sudden hush. At first I thought a lot of people had been talking and abruptly fell silent as I entered the room, but then I realized that I was only facing Dredge. There were no other vampires in sight.

"Menolly—" Delilah's voice quavered. I glanced over my shoulder for a fraction of a second, but it was long enough to realize that only my sisters had followed me into the room.

Dredge settled himself on the side of the writing desk that overlooked the window, a triumphant smirk on his face. He was as I'd remembered him, gorgeous and deadly, dressed in a pair of black leather pants and vest.

"Well, it took you long enough," he said. "What? Surprised that I'm ready for you?"

"Hell. He set up a magical barrier," Camille said glancing back at the door. "Menolly, the guys can't get through." She took two steps back and I could feel her energy flare as she let loose with a blinding light.

Dredge covered his eyes and I leapt forward, but the light fizzled and I barely sidestepped him as he almost grabbed my wrist.

Hell and hell again! Damn Camille's ever-present faulty wiring. I'd have to buy time, give the guys a chance to break through the barrier. "What's the matter? You're so afraid that you had to separate us?"

He let out a low whistle and shook his head. "On the contrary, pretty Menolly. I wanted to have a small, intimate party. You're going to find that no one without Otherworld Fae blood can enter that barrier. No humans, no demons . . . Oh yes, I know you're running around with that incubus spawn and the fox cur. But unfortunately, for you, the three of you are my guests here. You can't break back through the barrier, so, no girls, it's just us. You, me . . . and your sisters." He rubbed his hands together. "I'm going to enjoy tonight."

I glanced around. "Where are your cronies, Dredge?"

"Off doing other tasks I assigned to them. Trust me, I don't need them to clean up the mess that I'm going to make of you."

Hell, then they were still on the loose. "Bring it on, Dredge. I know all about you now. I know who you serve."

Dredge crossed his arms across his chest and waggled a finger at me. "Menolly, Menolly, Menolly, shame on you, girl. You've been running with the wrong crowd and now I'm going to have to tear you to bits. Then I'll take your sisters down, screw them till they beg me to die, and I'll turn them. Then I'll set them loose on your beloved city to terrorize the dreck that live over here."

"Leave them out of this. This is between you and me."

The smile disappeared and ruthless Dredge came out to play. "Shut the fuck up. I call the shots here, traitor."

Camille raised her arms and, with a feral look in her eyes that I'd only seen a couple times, began to chant.

By the light of the moon, by the brilliance of sun,
by the wrath of the Huntress, I command it begun.
By fuel born from anger, by the pain it can bring,
I call through my body, a shower of lightning.

A huge crash filled the room as a brilliant blue bolt shattered the window, splintering the desk behind Dredge into shards. A chunk of wood flew up, lodging in his arm. Close, but not close enough. Another fork of the blue fire wove through the metal frame on the bed. The bedclothes burst into flames.

Dredge narrowed his gaze. "You just earned yourself a special place in hell, girl," he said, and the next second, he was standing beside Camille.

"No!" Delilah slashed with her outstretched dagger. The silver clipped his arm and he jerked, giving Camille time enough to make tracks to the other side of the room. Smoke was starting to fill the air as the quilt burned brightly and she muttered something under her breath. A deluge of rain filled the room, soaking all of us and putting out the flames.

I took advantage of the chaos to leap forward, stake at the ready. Dredge whirled around and we collided midair, dropping to the floor in a desperate wrestling match. He was on top of me, clawing for my throat, but I managed to push hard enough against his shoulders to keep him from grabbing hold of me.

"Why? Why did you turn on me? You ungrateful bitch, you traitorous dog! You dare to defy me? You dare to sever the cord?" He leaned back and let loose with his fist, slamming the punch deep into my stomach. If I'd been alive, the blow would have killed me. As it was, it knocked me off guard.

"Leave her alone!" I heard Delilah scream. The next moment, Dredge groaned and launched himself off of me, Delilah's dagger lodged in his right shoulder. Still not enough to kill him, but the silver had to sting like hell.

I took advantage of the distraction to flip to my feet. Dredge started to turn when Camille let loose with another spell. Unfortunately as the bolt of energy headed toward him, Dredge grabbed Delilah and pushed her in the path of the oncoming spell.

Camille immediately broke off the attack and the energy went rogue, darting to the side, clipping Delilah in the shoulder as it ricocheted toward the open window and went streaking out into the night air.

Delilah shrieked in pain, then turned on Dredge, her eyes wild. "You fucking bloodsucker!"

At first I thought she was going to turn into a tabby cat, which would leave us seriously down on firepower, but then I began to smell the scent of bonfires. Uh oh. Apparently somebody didn't want his Death Maiden killed. She let out a low growl that rose to fill the room, and Dredge, for the first time, began to look nervous. The distraction was just what I needed, and I launched myself again, stake held high.

Dredge managed to dodge my attack, but he didn't see Camille sneaking up behind him. She had something in her hands—not a stake, but something small—and as she leapt on his back, her arms closing around his throat, she wrapped her thighs tightly to the sides of his waist. Before he could shake her off, she slammed one hand against his mouth and held it there, even as Dredge clawed at her legs.

There was a muffled noise and she let go and fell to the floor, rolling away, her calves bleeding profusely from where he'd raked long gashes in them.

I sniffed. Oh shit, I knew what she'd done! She'd swiped

one of Roz's garlic bombs and she'd just stuffed it into Dredge's mouth! The next second, Delilah shifted into her black panther form in a brilliant spray of light as the room echoed with her roar.

"What the—?" Dredge looked confused for a moment, staring at me, his eyes bloodred, before he suddenly started to choke. Clawing at his throat, he groaned, and I could see the pain etching its way across his face.

"Hurts, huh? But you *like* pain!" I strode over, ignoring the garlic, ignoring the disorientation the scent was causing me. I had one focus, one task: to eliminate the enemy. That was the only thing I had to do.

"Then maybe you'll like *this*!" I aimed for his stomach, kicking as hard as I could. The blow slammed him against the wall. Arms outstretched, he thundered against the stucco finish, cracking it with a long furrow. The room quaked again as he slid to the floor. He struggled to get up but Delilah landed at his feet, biting through one of the legs of his leather pants. She dug deep, I could see the bone as she ripped away a huge chunk of flesh.

"Delilah, get back. He's mine," I said. She gave me a questioning look, then padded away. Dredge was struggling to his feet as I raced in. I brought the stake down with all my force, driving it into Dredge's heart. "Die, just fucking die!"

He pulled away, staring at the wooden spike that was skewered partway through his chest. Why didn't he go poof? Was something wrong? And then I saw the shadow beside him. The form of a man, bathed in fire, holding a wolf leashed by a humongous chain. Both man and wolf stared at me, almost taunting me. But then, with a laugh, Loki turned to Dredge.

"Time to pay the piper," he said, his voice echoing through the room, a cacophony of drums and raging wind.

"No, no, not yet—not yet—" Dredge fumbled for the stake, trying to pull it out.

"No you don't!" I lunged forward, heedless of the scene that was playing out before my eyes. Grabbing the end of the stake, I fought with Dredge, fighting against his strength with all my might.

"This isn't the end," he whispered, staring up at me with those gorgeous, haunting eyes. "I'm not done with you yet."

"Haven't you ever heard of divorce, motherfucker?" I gave one last shove and fell against the stake, ramming it with my hands. The tip slowly slid the rest of the way through, piercing his heart, coming to rest against the floor beneath him. Loki let out a short bark of laughter, and Dredge gave one last scream before his body, born a thousand years before, burst into ashes that floated to the carpet. I tumbled to the side and came up in a crouch before the demigod.

Shaking my braids out of my face, I slowly rose to face Loki. He was holding an orb of energy in his hand. *Dredge's soul.* I swallowed, backing up a couple steps. What the hell was going to happen now? But Mr. L. merely ran his gaze over me, from head to toe, then winked. I could hear Dredge give one last scream as Loki, his wolf-child, and his vampire child vanished.

"Camille, can you stand up?" Delilah had returned to normal. She crawled over to where Camille lay on the floor, the calves of both legs bleeding at a good clip.

"Where is he?" Morio was first through the door. The barrier had disappeared. He took one look around the room, saw the bloody stake, and reached his own conclusions. "Is everybody okay—Camille? Camille!" He rushed over to where Delilah was trying to fashion bandages out of a sheet to stop the bleeding.

Roz and Chase were right behind him. Roz pushed both Delilah and Morio aside. "Let me. I brought a healing salve, just in case. It will at least stop the bleeding until we can get her medical aid." As he rubbed the ointment on her wounds, she grimaced.

"Oh Great Mother, that stings," she said.

"Payback for the stitches," he countered, smirking.

"So he's gone? Dead?" Chase glanced around and whistled. "You sure did a number on this room. Cracked the walls, burned down the bed, scorched the carpet, broke the windows . . . You're not ever staying at my place, that's for sure."

I snorted. "Thank you, Mr. Wise Ass. Camille invited a

lightning bolt to come and play, which started the fire, and then she put it out with a few buckets of rain. I'm the one responsible for the cracked wall."

Chase stared at us, then began to laugh. "Just another day in the life of the D'Artigo sisters, huh?"

I knelt by the stake, staring at the pile of ashes. The wind blowing through the window caught them up, set them spiraling, and then carried them away. Roz joined me as we gazed out into the chilly Seattle night.

"I don't know how we did it. I honestly don't know how we managed to kill him." I told him about the fight. "We're good . . . but are we that good?"

"Apparently so. But perhaps . . . perhaps you had a little help?" Roz picked up the stake and stared at the bloodied end.

"What do you mean?"

"Maybe Loki was ready to make Dredge pay his debt. Maybe not. Whatever the case, I'll bet you the winter dies down in a few days." Roz shook his head. "I can't believe it's over. I've followed his tracks ever since he killed my family. For seven hundred years I've traced him across plain and over mountain. And now, at the end, I didn't even get to look in his eyes as he died."

I hung my head. "I wish you could have been here with us. He's gone. But the rest of the Elwing Clan still lives." I glanced at the window. "They're out there, somewhere."

"And he was their leader. If he treated them like he did you, you'll be their savior." Roz wiped the stake on a blanket and stuck it in his jacket.

"And if they worshiped Dredge . . . they'll come after me. Eventually." I stood up and dusted my hands off on my butt. "I'll be ready for them."

"Now what?" Roz asked.

"We go home. We bind up Camille's wounds. We figure out what the next step is in our war against Shadow Wing." I turned to find Morio, but Roz reached out and caught my arm.

"I'm going with you. There's something you need to hear. About Shadow Wing. About the demons."

I started to ask what, but he moved too fast and before I knew it, he was gone, out of the room and down the hall. As we gathered up whatever we could find that had belonged to Dredge, I asked Morio to go explain what happened to Exo Reed and send us a bill for the damages.

Just what did Roz know about Shadow Wing, anyway? And what about Dredge? He was toast, but what was that grin and salute from the lord of chaos?

As I lifted Camille to carry her down to the car—it was easiest for me to carry her, and the blood seeping from her leg didn't even make my nose twitch for once—I realized that a little part of me would always be afraid that Dredge might find a way to return. Some wounds are forever, I thought. Even when you drop the baggage, the claim ticket's still burned into your soul.

CHAPTER 20

Iris was waiting in the kitchen. She looked up as we entered and burst into tears. "You're alive," she started to say, but then she saw Camille's legs and gasped. "Oh my stars, what happened? Let her rest on the sofa and I'll get the first-aid kit."

As she bustled out of the room, Tim looked up at me. "Is he dead?"

I nodded. "Yeah. Dust and shadows. All that's left of Dredge is a memory . . ." But as I spoke, I thought that there was one thing left of Dredge—his soul, locked forever in the grasp of someone even more sadistic than he had been. The karma police in action? Maybe. Or maybe just the universe, having one last laugh at his expense.

I glanced at the clock. Three-thirty. I'd visit Erin the next night. For now I was so exhausted, I just wanted to hide out in my lair, to shut out the world. But there were things to attend to first. I headed to the living room, where Iris was stitching up the gashes in Camille's calves.

"They'll heal better with a bit of thread," she said.

Chase watched, his face greenish. "Do all you women have a way with needle and thread?" he asked.

"I'm better at it than the girls. Comes from years of attending to the Kuusi family. No doctors near enough to fetch during times of emergency. And I could always heal wounds better than they could anyway." She bit through the thread and tucked the spool away. "Now, ointment, a bandage, and you should be just fine in a week or so. You'll have scars, but they'll be faint."

Camille shook her head, grinning. "They'll match the ones on my arms," she said, glancing up at me. "Irony, huh?"

"Irony like that, we can do without," I said, wondering when to tell her that Trillian was hurt, too. She wouldn't be too happy when she found out I'd kept that news from her, but it no longer mattered. "So, is Roz here?"

"He is now," Roz said from the doorway. He slipped out of his duster and carefully hung it over the back of a chair, then sat down, his pants tight around his legs in all the right places. His T-shirt was nice and form fitting, too, and I found my thoughts wandering in a direction I never thought they'd meander. Perhaps Roz *would* make a good playmate, at least for someone like me. I dallied with the thought, then pushed it aside. Perhaps . . . but not anytime soon.

"So what is it that you have to tell us?" I asked.

"I brought someone with me." He motioned to the door. I jumped to attention. Who the hell had he invited over now? But as a cloaked figure stepped through the arch, I recognized the energy. Elfin blood. Heavy, ancient Elfin blood. Not Trenyth this time.

Camille squinted, then gasped. "Your Majesty!" she said, struggling to stand up.

Iris pushed her back on the sofa. "I don't care if it's the Queen of Hearts, you just sit back down and don't move. You don't want to rip those stitches."

The figure pushed her hood back and I jumped, along with Delilah.

"Your Majesty! Great Mother, what are you doing over here?" I almost expected the world to implode. Asteria, the Elfin Queen, had made a trip to our home? What the hell was going on? "Is everything okay?"

"Father—has something happened to Father?" Delilah burst out, managing to drop into a curtsey and break into tears simultaneously. I hastily followed suit, sans tears, motioning for Morio and Chase to bow.

"Enough with the amenities," the ancient queen said, waving off our genuflections. "I don't want to be away from Elqaneve for long. But there are things we must discuss and better I come to you than wait for you to visit my city. Tell me first, though—what of Dredge?"

We filled her in on the fight, and the fact that he'd been aligned with Loki, not Shadow Wing. She took everything in stride, nodding quietly as we unraveled the chaotic mess he'd left in his wake.

"Dredge has always been steeped in mayhem and delighted in causing confusion. I had hoped that Jareth could help him, but no wonder it didn't work. With Loki behind him, it's a wonder Jareth survived the ordeal. None of us knew. He managed to fool us all until the end." She paused, looking over at Camille. "My girl, you've been wounded. Does Trillian know? I was so sorry to see him hurt—"

"What? Trillian's been hurt?" Camille managed to get to her feet. This time I shoved her back on the sofa.

Iris broke in. "He's going to be fine. He just won't be running to OW anytime soon, especially seeing that he's been outted as a spy." She stood, hands on her hips. "He's tucked away in your bedroom. You two can convalesce together, and may the gods take pity on you both. I certainly hope they do on me because I'm going to be the one stuck waiting on you." She rolled her eyes.

"That's why I'm here," the Queen said. "I wanted you to hear what I have to say directly from my own lips." She motioned to Roz and he moved to stand beside her.

"Rozurial is my new message runner. I didn't expect Trillian to be hurt, but since he's injured, Roz will take his place for now. And he will be my go-between for things I choose not to entrust to the Whispering Mirror. It's too dangerous to send Trenyth to you now—my aide is far too important to me to put in jeopardy."

"The war is truly so dangerous?" Delilah asked.

Queen Asteria shook her head. "War is always hazardous, but no . . . that's not the only reason. I've had my scholars busy studying the ancient texts. And I assigned several seers to the task."

She paused, then let out a long sigh. "Listen to me carefully. It appears most—perhaps all—of the spirit seals somehow found their way into the general area around Seattle and the vicinity. The area you refer to as the Pacific Northwest. But why the convergence? Are there forces here of great power that can amplify the seals' natures? And there are more portals—portals we didn't know existed—that have suddenly been opening up in Otherworld with no one to guard them. Do the demons know about these? Can they find a way to use them to infiltrate Earth and Otherworld? So many new questions, and no answers as of yet."

As I struggled to grasp the implications of what she was saying, Roz broke in. "There's something else. The third spirit seal—the third part of the ancient talisman—is hidden somewhere here in Seattle. Right now. The only thing I could discover is that there's some connection between it and a Rākṣasa."

Camille let out a low whistle and sat up straight. "They're dangerous."

"What are they?" asked Chase.

"Earthside demons. Persian," Morio said. "Very powerful."

"Is the Rākṣasa working for Shadow Wing, then?" Iris frowned at Camille, and once again, my sister dropped back on the pillow.

"I don't know." Roz rubbed his nose. "But it's up to you girls to find out and to retrieve the third seal. And there are several other things . . ."

"Which we don't want to hear, right?" I gazed out the window at the snow-filled night. The clouds were parting and it looked like the snowstorm was letting up. Maybe Loki *did* take the snow with him.

"Most likely, young woman," the Queen said, a faint smile on her face. "We managed to capture one of Shadow Wing's spies. The beast no longer lives, but before he died, he told us that there's a network of spies living in your area. We believe Shadow Wing knows that all the seals are to be found here. That's why he's sending his scouts through the local portals and not elsewhere."

Shit. "Then he knows what we know."

"For the most part, yes. So the race is on, and time and knowledge are no longer on your side. Dredge was a hideous monster. Shadow Wing makes him look like a schoolboy."

"What else?" Camille asked.

Roz snorted. "The Cryptos are up in arms back in OW . . . They have withdrawn from supporting anybody in Y'Elestrial's civil war and there are rumors that something's going on in the Windwillow Valley. Something to do with the Dahns unicorns. We have no idea what it could be at this point —"

"Not all of us are in the dark," Queen Asteria said, standing. "Be prepared for a messenger from the unicorns to arrive in a few months. It will take time for certain events to play out back in OW, though, so don't fret and don't ask questions." She arranged her cloak and turned to Roz. "And now I must return to Elqaneve. My guards await me. Rozurial, accompany me to the portal."

Rather unceremoniously, she turned and exited the room before we could say good-bye. Camille immediately began to demand Trillian's presence, as Chase, Morio, and Delilah spun into a frenzy of talk over the spirit seals. I headed toward the kitchen and to silence.

Maggie was playing in her pen, and I picked her up and snuggled her on my shoulder. So much had happened that I scarcely knew how to take it all in. In the blink of an eye, I was no longer aligned with my sire, I'd defeated the person I hated most in the world, and I'd been thrust into motherhood—of a sort—all within less than a week.

Iris joined me. "Are you all right?"

I shook my head. "More or less . . . no . . . yes . . . I don't know. I don't know what to think or do. I'm very confused right now."

She hopped up on her stool and leaned her elbows on the table. "About Nerissa?"

"About Nerissa and Jareth—I made love to him when I thought I could never stand a man's touch again. And then there's Erin. I'm a mother now, Iris. I swore I'd never sire another vampire and I did. And one of our friends, at that."

"You didn't kill her, Menolly. You saved her from death—at least the kind of death humans don't usually get up and walk away from."

"I just don't know what's happening to me." I stared at the little calico girl curled in my arms and chucked her under the chin, kissing her softly on the nose before I set her back in her playpen.

Iris frowned. "Sometimes people come into our lives for a reason, and when that reason is done—they leave. Rest your worries for now. Don't force yourself to make decisions you aren't ready to make."

I thought about Nerissa. Her skin had been tender, her touch healing. And Jareth—long ago, he'd loved a vampire. I'd given him a taste of that memory to cling to even as he gifted me his blood.

"Once Camille asked me if vampires dream. I gave her a simple answer to a complex question. Now I have a question. Can vampires love? Can I love? Have relationships like my sisters?" I waited, but no answer appeared, not even a whisper, to guide me.

"Menolly, you're not the same girl who stood in this kitchen last week." Iris pushed herself off the stool and started arranging cookies on a plate. "You've been through so much. How can you expect to know who you are or what you're capable of until the dust settles?"

"I guess I can't." I shook my head. "Dredge made me fear ever loving anybody again—from the beginning he tried to use me to destroy my family."

"And now he's gone. And you're still here," she said, her eyes glittering.

"Yes, he's gone. And I'm here. But what does that mean?" I asked softly.

Iris dusted her hands on her apron. "The world could end tonight, my girl. Deal with your fears one at a time, *if* and when they arise."

And then everything was okay again, and I laughed, feeling lighter than I had since the day of my death. "First light's coming, sweet friend. I'll see you tonight."

"Be at peace in your dreams." Iris waved as I slipped through the passage to my lair.

As I undressed for bed, I glanced down at the scars lacing my body. Dredge had marked me forever, but he was gone. Dust and ashes. My sisters and friends were safe. Like it or not, I had sired a daughter. And I'd received the greatest gift in the world—I was free, my nightmare shattered.

And now . . .
a special preview of the next book
in the Otherworld series
by Yasmine Galenorn . . .

DRAGON WYTCH

Coming soon from Berkley!

CHAPTER 1

There was pixie dust in the air. I could feel it seeping in from under the door of the Indigo Crescent, my bookshop, as it wafted up to tickle the back of my throat. There was no mistaking the stuff—it was different from just about every other manifestation of Fae magic. Sparkling, the dust shimmered on the astral, hovering in that in-between place, not quite physical, not quite ethereal. And yet pixie magic had more effect on humans and the human realm than it did on anybody else.

Curious, I thought. The fact that I could sense it all the way back in my office meant it came from a pixie with strong magic—Otherworld magic, if I didn't miss my guess. There weren't any Earthside pixies around my shop, or at least I didn't think there were. The creatures usually gave me a wide berth, partly because I was half-Fae and partly because I was a witch. Either way, they didn't trust me.

A number of Fae witches back in Otherworld made a habit of trapping pixies to harvest their dust. The pixies weren't hurt, but they took a severe blow to the ego during the process, especially when some of their captors sold the dust for profits that made even a leprechaun blink. Of course, the pixies didn't get one penny from the transaction and sometimes they banded together to raid a shop with some success, but for the most part they just tried to avoid us altogether.

Of course, *I* didn't trust *them*, either. Pixies were born troublemakers, and they enjoyed every minute of it. They weren't usually dangerous, not in the way your average pain-in-the-neck goblin was, but they were trouble all the same.

I finished counting the receipts and tucked the money from the cash register into a strong box, hiding it in the bottom drawer of my desk. So much for another slow day. The Indigo Crescent was having an off month. Either nobody was reading, or I wasn't moving enough new stock in.

I gathered my purse and keys. My sister Delilah was already gone for the day. She ran a casual PI business above my shop, but she'd been out on a case most of the day and hadn't bothered with more than a quick check-your-messages pit stop this morning.

Glancing around my office to make sure everything was in order, I slipped on a light capelet. My tastes ran toward bustiers and camisoles and chiffon skirts, not exactly weather appropriate wear, but I wasn't about to change my style because of a few storm clouds.

We were nearing the Vernal Equinox, and Seattle was still chilly and overcast. Roiling gray clouds seeded with fat, heavy raindrops had moved in from the ocean, opening up to splatter the sidewalks and roads.

Granted, the trees around the city were vibrant with budding leaves, and the moss gave off a rich, loamy scent, but spring in western Washington was a far cry from spring back in Otherworld. By now, the skies over OW would be stained with thin rivulets of gold from the setting sun, creating a watercolor wash as they blended into the indigo of the approaching twilight. The warm blush of the waxing year would be encouraging the night-martins to sing every evening, and the smell of Terebell's flowers would permeate the gardens around our house.

Sighing, and a little bit homesick—memories were all we

had of our home in OW right now—I set the alarm system and locked the door. Tired or not, I'd better find out where the pixie dust was coming from. If a group of them had moved into the neighborhood, all the shops would be in for trouble.

As I turned toward the sidewalk, a whinny caught my attention, crowding out any idea of tracking down the wayward pixie. I glanced up the street and froze. *What the hell?*

A unicorn was heading my way. He passed Baba Yaga's Deli that had moved in next to my bookstore, then stopped, close enough for me to feel his breath on my face.

With a nonchalant bob of the head, the unicorn said, "Good evening, my lady."

I blinked, wondering if I'd been working a little too hard. But no, he was still there. His coat shimmered with that silky, luminous white that only adorns magical creatures. Robin's egg–blue eyes glinted with intelligence, and his horn sparkled a lustrous gold. That's how I knew he was a male, other than the obvious anatomical signs, which were most definitely in attendance. Female unicorns have silver horns.

The more I looked at him, the more he reminded me of something out of one of those ethereal perfume commercials; the ones where I was never sure just what they were advertising until they splashed the bottle on the screen and the announcer said something lame like, "Magic—experience the thrill."

I blinked again.

He was still there. Clearing my throat, I was about to ask him what he was doing meandering through the streets of Seattle when a noise from up the street startled me. As I turned, a goblin, a Sawberry Fae, and a bugbear emerged from a nearby alley and started our way. They looked pissed.

I know, I know. A goblin, a Fae, and a bugbear wander into a bar where they meet this gorgeous wench with her boobs hanging out . . .

My train of thought stopped in mid-joke when, in a matter of seconds, the situation deteriorated from a whimsical *what-the-hell-is-going-on* to *oh-no-they-can't-really-be-meaning-to-do-that*. The goblin held up a blowgun and took aim at the unicorn.

"Hand over the pixie, Feddrah, or you're dead!" The bugbear's voice was guttural and he spoke in *Calouk*, the rough, common dialect familiar to most Otherworld citizens. The words were garbled. The threat was clear.

Cripes! Without a second thought—unicorns were dangerous and beautiful, but goblins were just dangerous and stupid—I closed my eyes and whispered a quick chant to the wind. My fingers tingled as a thick bolt of energy slammed through me, gathered from the gust of winds blowing steadily in an east-northeasterly direction. As the rippling force raced down my arms, I focused on forming it into a ball in my hands, then sent it tumbling toward the goblin.

Please don't let my magic fail me now, I silently begged. A lot of my magic went haywire because of my half-Fae, half-human blood. Call it faulty wiring or even just plain old bad luck, but I was never quite sure when a spell would take, or if it would take right, or if it would slam out of me racing ninety miles an hour like an express train out of control. I'd already ruined one hotel room this year playing around with lightning and rain. I wasn't keen on the idea of possibly tearing up the pavement and having a city street crew cussing me out.

This go-round, the Moon Mother smiled on me and the spell held true. The bolt hit the goblin square in the chest, knocking him off his feet before he could shoot his dart at the unicorn. The spell didn't stop there, though. After it KO'd the goblin, the magical gust of wind ricocheted off the side of my bookstore and bounced back, slamming into the bugbear and sending him rolling into the streets like a trash can on a windy day.

I stared at the chaos I'd managed to wreak in just a few seconds, caught between mild embarrassment and intense pride. I was getting pretty good! I usually didn't manage to pack that strong of a punch, especially with wind magic. Maybe a little of Iris's skill was rubbing off on me.

"Youch!" The tickle of a lash licked my arm, sending a white flame through my skin and jerking me out of my self-congratulatory mood. "That hurt, damn it!"

I turned to see that the Sawberry Fae was bearing down on me with a whip in his hand. Scrambling a few steps to the side, I said, "No thanks, I'm not interested in your kinky little games." Maybe I'd better focus on the here and now. There'd be time for patting myself on the back later.

He licked his lips, drawing back the whip once more. *Eww.* I had the feeling this dude was enjoying himself just a little too much. Apparently the unicorn had taken notice of the fight. The gorgeous stallion galloped past me, horn lowered, and skewered the Fae in the shoulder, tossing him three feet into the air and five feet back. The screaming man hit the sidewalk and laid there, bleeding like a stuck pig.

The carnage continued as a speeding car screeched around the corner and ran over the bugbear. Splat. Flat as a pancake. The Porsche—at least it looked like a Porsche— sped off before I could get the license plate.

I shrugged. I had my sincere doubts that the bugbear would have wished me any better luck, so I wasn't going to waste any tears on him. I turned back to the mayhem on the sidewalk.

"Well . . ." There wasn't much else to say. It wasn't everyday a bunch of Otherworld creatures got themselves mowed down in front of my bookstore.

The unicorn trotted over to my side. I glanced up into his face, mesmerized by the swirling vortex of colors in his eyes. Pretty. Very pretty. And, unless I was off the mark, he looked a little bit pissed, too.

"You might want to call a constable," the horned horse said, sounding mildly concerned. He nodded in the direction of the flattened bugbear. "Somebody could slip on that mess and hurt themselves."

He had a point. The sidewalk looked like a scene out of *Pulp Fiction* or *Kill Bill.* And I could hear Chase now. He was going to just *love* getting my call. He'd been swamped lately, trying to keep up the façade that we were still on the official up-and-up with the OIA—the Otherworld Intelligence Agency—and not running the whole show ourselves. Cleaning up after a trio of Otherworld thugs was probably the last thing he wanted dumped on his plate.

I let out a long sigh. "You're probably right. Would you like to come in while I make the call?" I motioned to the shop.

If unicorns could shrug, this one would have. "All right. You wouldn't happen to have anything to drink, would you? I'm thirsty and there don't seem to be any public watering holes around."

"Sure, I can get you some water. I'm Camille, by the way. Camille D'Artigo. I'm from Otherworld." I unlocked the door and punched in the security code to turn off the alarm system that I'd just armed.

"That's rather obvious." The unicorn's words rippled with a droll tone, and I realized we weren't speaking English. We'd automatically switched over to *Melosealfôr*, a rare dialect of Crypto that all witches who were pledged to the Moon Mother learned during their training. "You stand out in the crowd, my lady. How do you do? I'm Feddrah-Dahns."

"Feddrah-Dahns, eh? You're from the Windwillow Valley then." Something about the name rang a bell but I couldn't quite place it. Every unicorn coming out of the Windwillow Valley assumed Dahns as their surname. The area was teeming with Cryptos, and there were rumors that huge herds of the horned beasts roamed the plains, nomads who migrated across the vast valley during the summer months.

"You know your geography, Camille D'Artigo."

"Yes, well . . . What about the pixie? Where did he go? I noticed pixie dust a little while ago."

"I hope he'll be all right. He retrieved something from the bugbear that belonged to me. Technically, he was simply reclaiming stolen property, but the bugbear and his accomplices apparently didn't see it that way." Feddrah-Dahns blinked those beautiful big eyes of his.

I grinned. "Thieves rarely understand the concept of ownership, be they bugbear or human." I opened the door as wide as I could. As the unicorn cautiously stepped over the doorstop, he bobbed his head, a curious glint in his eye. Life in Seattle might be gloomy and wet, but nobody could ever convince me it was boring.